DIRE
AND
PUNY

ALSO BY MARTHA SKEWERMANN

Fifty Shades of Chump

SINGE – Chump on Fire

DIRE AND PUNY

OUTSIDE CHUMP'S BLACKENED HOUSE

MARTHA SKEWERMANN

DIRE AND PUNY

FIRST EDITION

First published in the United States in 2019 by Martha Skewermann
First published in Great Britain in 2019 by Martha Skewermann

A CIP catalogue record for the book
is available from the British Library.

eBook ISBN: 978-0-6484379-1-8
Trade paperback ISBN: 978-0-6484379-0-1
Audiobook ISBN: 978-0-6484379-2-5

www.marthaskewermann.com

For our kids
For a better world

Up is Down

East is West

Truth isn't Truth

Real is Fake

Arthur is Martha

CONTENTS

AUTHOR'S NOTE

There was, to begin with, no good reason to write this book. It had been obvious to all that the spectacularly talented R. S. Chump would prevail in the local council elections. There was no scoop to be had here.

Little did I know that researching this dead cert would lead me to uncover a tale of hot passions, drama, intrigue and collaborative teamwork, the likes of which had never been seen before in the history of mayoral reporting.

Ronnie Chump is well known as a man of integrity, decency, wisdom and humility, driven by the highest ethical principles. His magnanimity, particularly towards the disadvantaged, is humbling. His wit and sparkling intelligence are legendary. In our busy newsroom, I had often heard of his reputation as a charismatic humanitarian, but I had usually attributed this to mere hyperbole.

Yet perhaps, I thought, these reports warrant further investigation, and some effort to observe the great Chump in person.

So, when my editor sent out a note asking who would cover the mayoral inauguration, a lightbulb went off in the intrepid mind of your dear Martha Skewermann: Bazinga! This was my opportunity.

I applied then and there for the posting to cover the inauguration, and my editor was all too happy to send me off, yelling out the

advice "... and don't come back without a story!" This, dear reader
is that story.

Having arranged to attend the event at City Hall, the day arrived and
I was ushered through to the Press Gallery. A hush filled the
auditorium before Ronnie entered through an honor guard of
triumphant trumpets. As the mayoral swearing-in ceremony then
commenced, I first witnessed the formidable Chump only a few feet
away from me. There he stood, filled out in opulent ceremonial
ermine garb, like an emperor in splendid new clothes. He held the
brassy council mace aloft and looked heavenward with sparkling
eyes full of hope and passion, his orange skin glistening. I could
immediately recognize a man clearly devoted to serving the public
good. I saw before me the figure of a majestic and historic civil
servant who would inspire countless generations and whose legacy
warranted preserving, like a fine dill cucumber, or an excized
appendix.

At that moment my journalistic instincts were ignited and I resolved
to document objectively the coming days of his promising new
administration, albeit, as you will hear, from some distance.

You see, to bring you this account of the incendiary events behind
this municipal administration, I faced significant obstacles: no
security clearance, no direct contact with the mayor or his staff, and
no access to the corridors and couches of the mayoral offices. The
normal rigorous processes which would exclude a nosy journalist
such as your beloved Martha were carried out with the usual
professionalism of the administration, and I was banished beyond
the outer perimeter of the Town Hall precinct.

I must now disclose that it was an unfortunate and indelicate
incident in that first encounter with the incomparable Chump which
seems to have limited my ability to conduct my research at close
quarters. Although I am a seasoned political journalist, now in my
mid-sixties - and still a very handsome woman, despite just a little
facial hair - I do, like any cis-gendered, straight-identifying woman,
experience the occasional frisson of youthful excitement in the
presence of a virulent man. Until that moment, I had never met a

man with quite the aura of Chump, and confess to having been slightly awestruck on my initial meeting with the great man.

My pulse raced and the schoolgirl within me fluttered to the surface as he neared me. As a result, when I had leaned in to greet Councilor Chump with what was intended as a purely professional congratulatory kiss, I may have caused some accidental or inappropriate lip action. I have no recollection as to where my hands were in that moment, though I now dread to think.

Time seemed to stop for a while and when I came to my senses in a hot flash a few moments later, I found myself being torn off him by several security guards. I believe the usually cheery Chump may have felt himself somewhat embarrassed in that moment, as he then whispered something with a frown to his security chief, the dashing Keith Schifter. From that moment forth, I have had to conduct my research as an outsider looking in, as I was promptly escorted off the premises with the delightful young Keith on my arm and told to "stay on the other side of the wall lady".

Mayor Chump thereafter went to extraordinary lengths to inhibit my access to his staff, living quarters and bathrooms. Yet I believe that I have nonetheless succeeded in compiling a thorough and honest analysis of the first and last days of the Chump administration, as told by someone officially barred from City Hall and the mayoral residence, by virtue of an unnecessarily onerous restraining order.

Despite this harsh eviction, I continued my research undeterred.

Public records indicated to me that Chump had recently bought a beautiful new home in Ganacostya, on the outskirts of Washintown, a short walk from City Hall. Although I was also forbidden from the grounds of the mayoral residence, not long after he moved in on April 1, I took up a semipermanent seat on the grass outside the candidate's new house, near the east fence, by the lake, surviving mainly on takeouts and the kindness of strangers.

In hindsight, this would turn out to be an inspired decision, as the mayor habitually mixed his work and home life, holding regular council meetings in the sitting room of his own house. I was therefore well positioned to see the comings and goings of his staff from my sidewalk encampment.

On only my second day of research, I was present as Chump emerged from his residence on the way to council chambers in his mayoral limousine. At that very moment, a young boy fell from his scooter and landed, splayed on the sidewalk, his hands and knees badly grazed. Seeing the boy erupt in tears, Chump, moved by his natural compassion, signaled to his chauffeur to immediately stop the vehicle, alighted promptly then crouched down and, after a meditative 13-second delay, took the boy's hand to comfort him. In the next moment Chump had produced a lollipop from his pocket, and a beaming smile overtook the boy's tear-soaked face. Such is the magic of Chump - an almost divine capacity to consider the other ahead of himself, to empathize with those who are suffering or downtrodden. As Chump drove off, the lad excitedly raced back to his Mom; yet another heart gladdened.

Compiling this record of the Chump candidacy has taken months of painstaking journalistic effort, requiring hundreds of interviews with Chump's supporters, staff and Russian friends, and many months straining with strong binoculars through the thick hedge.

While the Chump administration fostered an intimate and fully cooperative relationship with the press, I remained marginalized throughout this project, like a journalistic version of James Dean in Times Square. I often cut a lonely figure out on the sidewalk, whether in the cold morning light, or under the beating midday sun, or out in the evening rain under my umbrella, waiting for leaks or for some passing dog-walker to give me a scoop. What was particularly galling was that my colleague from a rival publication, Michael Bearr - to me just 'Mikey' - was being allowed each day into the meeting rooms of City Hall alongside Chump. I had known Mikey since our days at journalism school and yes, it is true that we had been intimate back in the heady Summer of 1969. But now we were rivals, and the tension between us was of a rather different nature, though the heat just as intense.

I have been quite determined though, to match, and even to surpass, Michael's eloquent and cohesive reporting, which reads with the structure, drama and syntactic elegance of a company report.

Newsworthy events were rare as the administration ran with such precision, yet I persisted in my research, maintaining my outdoor vigil while disregarding all difficulties, and I believe my efforts have at last borne fruit in the pages of this book.

It is worth noting the incredible effectiveness and slick, flawless processes of the Chump administration due to a strict adherence to ethics, morality and the law, based on sound principles rooted in essential wisdom, humanity and compassion. As a result, I had no challenge whatsoever in giving context and meaning to the conversations, snippets of gossip and procedural material, council by-laws and amendments which were squirreled across to me.

Most of the events I recount here have been corroborated by hearsay, whispers, "shallow background" interviews, guesswork and, occasionally, innuendo. All are true. Some less so. Some documents blew past me in the street. Others were funneled to me by trusty staffers. Most of the time I have overridden the voices and stories of the players involved, since I am a highly experienced journalist, whereas they are mere elected officials or bureaucrats. I have quite inconsistently recorded some events, and made some up, because rushing to press at times necessitates artistic license; furthermore, I need to impress my editor.

I witnessed a loyal and disciplined staff, and in addition, a procession of high-caliber political candidates literally hammering at the doors to work for this administration, hammers at the ready.

I met a host of delightful and colorful characters: Joy Hickey, Mickey Crohney, Shawn Spinner, Gorby Ruineddogski, Paula Moneyport, Janey Kushynird and Stevie Bunyon, to name a few. They would pop out to buy ice-creams or cappuccinos and would leak for me by the fence before going back to be seated for their more productive council duties. Mayor Chump declined to be interviewed for this book.

In the end, the essence of this book is about a group of staffers and devoted minions who dearly love, and would never even contemplate leaving the service of, their principled figurehead and idol, Ronnie Chump, surely one of the greatest unelected public officials since Dinsdale Piranha.

These staffers owe me enormously, as they had me buy their coffees and often forgot to reimburse me when I returned from the coffee shop.

In documenting this team's joys and tribulations, I have striven to produce a work at least as professional, cohesive and well-structured as the Chump administration itself. Although that indeed constitutes a high bar, I believe that I have not only attained that bar, but have also flown over it, and flapped onwards and upwards, to attain, I hope, global notoriety and a lasting place in the great firmament of investigative journalists.

* * *

As I stand here now amid the ashes of Chump's blackened house, I cannot fail to recall the events which led to this moment, nor can I do any less than my utmost to relate these events to my readers with honesty and integrity, qualities exemplified unwaveringly by Mayor Chump himself.

* * *

PROLOGUE:
OGLES AND BUNYON

Bunyon arrived late after much trudging on foot with ill-fitting shoes. His unfortunate birth defect - having been born with two Right feet - did not help this situation as he had circled the previous block twice before finally being bumped in the right direction by a fellow pedestrian.

Bunyon had initially declined to come to the lunch gathering due to the unseasonal blistering heat which was enveloping the city. However the opportunity to see his old classmate Robbie Ogles, the former radio presenter at Moose FM, before Robbie departed on holiday to Kamilo Beach, had influenced him to brave the heat and hobble across town on his sore feet.

Back in their college days, Ogles and Bunyon - along with their drinking buddy Bart Kravenheart - had been members of the Hallux Vulgaris fraternity, and the boys had been as inseparable as Dan Aykroyd's webbed toes. During lunch breaks, Ogles would lead them down to the campus cafeteria, where Bunyon would charm the young female students with his slick hair, beginner French and insightful future prophecies.

Bart, a clean-living teetotaler who stuck to bottled water at all times, even at their frat parties, charmed the ladies with his impeccable manners, calm nature and honesty. While other college mates made fools of themselves with their drunken antics, Bart would remain sober, respectful and gentlemanly.

Initially studying ethics and feminism, Bart, inspired during these formative college years by his "lodestar", the Australian sanitation mogul Kenny Smyth, had run his own small business on the side, a popular PolyJohn franchise with the long-winded title "Sanitary Containers Rolled Out To Urgent Situations" (SCROTUS Inc.). In a deft career move, Bart had used this sanitary work experience to gain direct credit transfer into final year Law, carrying his business name through after graduating when establishing his own legal practice.

Bunyon, too, had flourished since college days like locker-room tinea and was now a successful blogger, policy wonk and digital media strategist with strong connections to Facehook, a little-known social media and dating site for those with mild genetic mutations, social disorders, podiatric handicaps and the like.

The trio, and their mutual acquaintances, were to gather that day to celebrate the recent win of their great friend Ronnie S. Chump in the Washintown City mayoral election, and to begin planning the social agenda which the new council, headed up by Ronnie, would be aiming to implement. An ambitious new era in social policy was about to begin, unlike anything experienced in the field of experimental governance since the days of King George III of England.

The sixty-seven-year-old Ogles, an ultra-fit marathon runner, a fine chiseled specimen of a man, champion of women's rights, philanthropist and well-known humanitarian, was sitting up at a window table surveying the passers-by. Seated on a high stool at the window, Ogles was initially not particularly keen to see Bunyon, as he had been enjoying watching the passing foot traffic, particularly the eye-catching young women who graced this part of town. Bunyon, despite his good-hearted nature, which would often see him accompanying elderly citizens on walks, could at times be rather annoying and somewhat insensitive, but there was no doubt he stood out from his peers in the digital realm. Ogles would often prod and poke Bunyon like Dan Aykroyd with a Phillips head screwdriver, but Bunyon had a thick skin and could handle Robbie's jibes.

If only the omens had been read. Wildfires were threatening, and the lunch had nearly been canceled. The wind had picked up, and papers - strangely, legal papers - blew through the streets, almost as though they sought out the touch of fire. The breeze resonated with a strange howl. Rickety Gates swung and creaked in the rising wind. Clouds hung low over the city, giving an oppressive air that made one wish they could be lifted, and a sense of Stormy foreboding encircled the city.

Despite his tardy arrival, Bunyon's dripping sweat belied his inner calmness. His hair, however, spoke of suavity and a certain *je ne sais quoi* which lent him an impressionable air as he wafted through the door, in spite of his soaked armpits and buttcrack.

He had a confident flair in the way he walked, which was, in a way, quite admirable given that the pungent odor of his sweat would have otherwise been his most noticeable attribute. His torn 1970s-style flared jeans were so retro as to be at the cutting edge of cool.

Ogles - who, though no 'spring chicken' was fitter than ever, having jogged in to town from their rundown rural house - was worried about ember strike back at home. Yet he had run through the flames of a grass fire on the town's outskirts, such was his determination to be here.

Both men, humble as they were, saw this as their moment to take their firm place in the annals of the city's history - Bunyon as a great social architect through his role as chief adviser to mayor-elect Ronnie Chump and Ogles following up as Ronnie's mellifluous voice on the airwaves of Moose FM. Both knew that this was the start of a period when their names could be seared into the fabric of the city, like a hot cinder on a nylon tablecloth, through their contributing roles in what was to be one of the most glorious city administrations ever stitched together.

Bunyon sat down, with an audible squelch. Bunyon's new secretary, Alexander Prostate, trained in administrative precision, took notes, recording even these noteworthy sound effects. Though generally soft and tender, Prostate could get a little gnarly when under pressure, and had been known to be a leaker when irritated. He had previously sought several government positions, both in the Department of Renewable Energy (DRE) and the Public Schools Association (PSA) but winning a role at the core of the Chump administration had fired him up, and he was so excited by his new appointment as an adjunct to Bunyon that he had promised not to leak.

The clean-shaven thirty-six-year-old Bunyon, wearing a neat pin-striped suit over the top of his previously-mentioned jeans, immediately grabbed a glass, roughly filled it with red wine and quaffed it then and there, in one shot. "There, that will help get the conversation rolling!"

He then launched into a systematic and measured discussion of possible hires for the new administration. Together with Robbie, they considered a series of names from diverse backgrounds, a veritable salvo of apt suggestions, including Vietnam veteran General Kitty Malaise, peace activist Jimmy 'Goddam' Mattress, top communicator Shawn Spinner, strategist Kris Krusty, pro paper-shuffler Dan Imgone and sweet do-gooder Paula Moneyport. They sought applicants of the highest ethics and educational levels, so discussed fine folk such as Harvard Law Graduate Gorby Ruineddogski, ex-boxer Rob Hurther and several other similarly talented people. Krusty had himself shot to prominence during the Gategate scandal, in which he had inadvertently left a farm gate open, resulting in numerous cows blocking traffic over the Washintown Canal, a waterway which Krusty - who now lived well outside the city limits - seemed to be fixated on in strategy meetings, as he kept shouting out the term 'far canal'.

"Ronnie's such a character", Bunyon quipped with a smile. "He's got this recurring joke he loves to play; he is such a wicked sport. No matter whom we hire, he'll ask them to get down on their hands and knees and beg for it. He can't help himself. Cracks him up every time. He gets them to crawl like a bug. But they do it, you know. When you're loved like Ronnie, they let you do it."

Bunyon himself felt that he was a shoe-in to one of the top jobs, hoping to dodge that witty indignity of Ronnie's, and was confident that he could achieve a couple of great outcomes for the administration in telling Chump where to go and how to do it. He also felt that Mattress, with his queen size personality, would act as a bolster for team morale.

Before anyone could get a word in, Bunyon added that he also liked peace activist Johnny Notlob as the potential hire for a planning position. Ogles wasn't so sure about Notlob, suggesting that he was a little backward, and suspecting that he also might smoke too much. Paula Moneyport was probably in fact an even greater risk in that regard, Ogles retorted, for she had a nasty cigar habit. Kris Krusty, a part-time assistant to Chump (and himself a heavy smoker) who worked on weekends as a clown at children's parties, chimed in too. Krusty didn't have a problem with candidates who smocked, but strongly recommended hiring Private Mickey Flout, a true patriot and wholeheartedly trustworthy guy, known to be a stickler for rules, who had also done incredible social work on behalf of women wrongly imprisoned.

The team even considered offering a cultural liaison position to the famous foreign dignitary Sir Les Patterson whom they felt was well-suited to the Chump team, however Sir Les had recently been appointed to a senior role with the UN. The disappointment on that point was palpable at the gathering, especially felt keenly by Prostate, as Sir Les would have perfectly embodied the Chump mission. Being a long-term smoker too, Sir Les would have made that practice seem less inappropriate in the workplace, so it was a real pity that he had made himself UN available.

So, the discussion moved on. One of the budding administration's most promising candidates was office legal secretary Dan Imgone, a talented office worker who had obtained a J.D. degree from the Wiener University School of Law and seemed to represent particularly good value in terms of payroll. Dan himself had suffered an accident in the college library when struck on the head by a falling Constitution, leaving him with significantly impaired memory. But he had indicated that, if offered one of the coveted spots on the Chump team, he would join the administration in a unique job-sharing arrangement with his long-time sidekick and personal scribe, Ernie Donoteson. Ernie, inseparable from Dan since childhood, was a talented cartoonist and scribbler, habitually seen with an artist's pencil between his teeth, a quilled pen behind his ear and a sketch-pad at the ready. Rarely was he not wielding these artist's implements with flair, putting them to good use producing witty quotes, pithy commentary or illuminating doodles. This "two-for-the-price-of-one" hiring arrangement would offset the additional salary cost of Paula Moneyport, who, being such an expert in her drainage field, was likely to demand, and certainly merit, a high salary. Ernie could also document the feats of the administration for posterity, particularly Bunyon's two feats.

Bunyon and Krusty felt that securing a position for Flout was so central to the success of the future administration that right there, on the spot, they arranged two in-person meetings and one phone call about Mr Flout. They were intent on securing Flout, or to phrase it another way, one could say they were acting with intent.

Krusty spoke up with passion in favor of Flout: "Flout is someone who will bring benefit to the Mayor, and to the administration, and I've made that very clear to candidate Chump and I'll make it very clear to Mayor-Elect Chump. That's my opinion, my view."

This would, in hindsight, turn out to be a prescient view, for Flout would indeed bring much to Chump in the months ahead. And he was certainly one candidate on whom they both agreed: "He's fabulous!" exclaimed Bunyon. "He's like Mattress and General Malaise at the same time, all rolled into one. A double-whammy of talent and ethics."

"Yes, and he'd defuse any difficult situation" added Ogles. "He is so incredibly honest. Ready to defend his city with truth and honor. A genuine patriot indeed!"

"Now," continued Bunyon, with that settled, "Johnny Notlob could be a good candidate to consider in the future. His goatee beard is reason enough. Chump loves a good beard."

Notlob had a reputation for taking counter-intuitive, contrary stances to conventional thinking, yet nonetheless brought an essential wisdom to his interactions through his paradoxical positions. He expressed himself candidly, palindromically, without pulling any punches. "Dammit, I'm mad!" he would say when angry, leaving no room for ambiguity.

He had a strong track record working in youth services, helping rogue, drug-addicted teenagers come clean, particularly through breaking up drug deals in the City of Washintown. Almost like a human sniffer dog, he would point at the youths' bulging pockets and screech "Xanax!".

When questioned as to whether his frequent low grunting during policy discussions amounted to an expression of agreement, Notlob would candidly state: "No, it is opposition." Yet he was known to carry a boundless optimism and hope for the future. "Are we not drawn onward to new era?" Johnny had famously asked when he had first heard of Chump's win. While deeply engaged in political ruminations, Notlob would walk around in circles with headphones on, playing Weird Al's "Bob" on repeat.

Chump had sought Bunyon's help to hire a crack team of barristers and solicitors for the new administration. So far, Bunyon hadn't had much trouble finding willing solicitors. He had apparently misheard Chump, however, for he had placed a half-page advertisement in the Washintown Sentinel seeking applications for "a crack team of barrators". Thankfully, the advertisement had nevertheless prompted a wave of responses from eager applicants and supplicants.

Curly-haired office clerk Ponce Rebus, a distant relative of serious actor Larry Fine, was an obvious choice for the role of undersecretary, a position he could job-share with Bunyon, sharing the same toolkit of props for management of the new staff, including rubber mallets and a balsa-wood plumber's wrench. Rebus came out of his first meeting with Chump thinking it had been a stellar experience, with just a small lump on his head. Chump remained quiet, taciturn and reflective, barely uttering a word, before giving curly Ponce a feisty double-finger-poke in the eyes and an instructive knee in the groin.

With the Rebus appointment, Bunyon found a new friend, though not exactly on an equal footing, due to Bunyon's anatomical unevenness in the podiatric department. The latter's large red, inflamed osteophytes and bony outgrowths remained a slightly embarrassing, unspoken difference between the two, and was apparently an anatomical anomaly not only present within his shoes, but also starting to show up on other parts of his anatomy.

* * *

Friend Tommy Brick chipped in, cementing one of the previous suggestions. "Paula Moneyport! Paula would be a great catch. You will never regret having Paula on board! What a team player, a real player! Her networking skills are to die for! She will really have you going places!" It was true: Paula Moneyport was indeed highly skilled, and had friends all over the world who would spread the Chump name and who would help forge creative partnerships with the City of Washintown. Forging was one of Paula's key strengths.

He couldn't help adding other suggestions. "There are advantages to Mattress too", he went on. "Mattress is firm and supportive, and will never talk back to you. And he's straight-up; he won't go lying on you. If you hire him, you'll always be able to sleep well at night." Barry Kabana had also hired Mattress several years earlier due to his dovish attitudes concerning peaceful parklands, libraries and noise reduction in the City of Washintown. "And Mattress will spring into action if any crisis occurs. He'd be a dream to have on staff."

Mattress himself was virtually illiterate and reputed to be a little rowdy in his personal behavior, but Chump was determined to "give him a go" on staff, despite him being a hangover from the Kabana mayorship. Bunyon had taken a while to get used to Mattress, as he initially thought he was a little lightweight, full of fluff. Over time, though, Bunyon would begin to appreciate old Mattress's good qualities: his supportiveness and his inner steely nature.

Mattress found alliances and partnerships annoying and irrelevant, believing that Washintown should make decisions independent of other legislatures. He was known for showing a rather contemptuous attitude to Washintown's civic counterparts. Nevertheless Chump, being a man of true honor, felt that Mattress could learn to be softer and more giving, if afforded the right position.

Given Ronnie Chump's background of overcoming his setbacks and handicaps, Ogles was as unsurprised as anyone else that Ronnie had won the municipal election. He loved Chump's humility and his common touch. He loved his famed wit, which, back in Ronnie's elementary school days, a particularly hard-marking teacher had once graded as an "F" wit. Having suffered in those times from recurrent head lice (and wood lice), and having learned how to manage them, Ronnie had also been held in high regard as the class's nit wit. Thankfully his observant teachers had noticed that Ronnie's big head was lousy, and had recommended him for serious treatment even back then. These early experiences set Ronnie in good stead for similarly managing his busy staff and the crawling collection of fellow city councilors who now inhabited his headspace and his cabinet.

After establishing Moose FM, Ogles had been one of the town's most respected broadcasters, known for giving women in the industry a 'leg up'. This was a shared area of interest between himself and the inspirational Chump.

Ogles knew that having helped the winning Chump team to cross the line there would be an eternal place for him, too, among the stars.

* * *

Bunyon and Ogles fondly reflected on the lead-up to the election. Their great buddy, Ronnie Chump - a seasoned social justice advocate who had spent frustrating years occupying obscure roles on city council, had finally tackled his nagging self-doubts and had mustered the courage to run for mayor. Long marginalized by more vocal but less talented councilors, Ronnie had beavered away throughout his spasmodic career, drafting legislation which rarely saw the light of day or which had ever attracted any notice in its own right. Yet now, like the old adage 'every dog has his day', Ronnie's day had arrived. He was determined to make a great big mark on the city and to pursue the greater good of the community.

Bunyon and Ogles had planned to decorate the back wall of the diner, like at an office farewell party, with a large photo of Ronnie, some streamers and a celebratory and supportive festoon of lettering, aimed at cheering the new team onwards with Ronnie's upcoming policy plan. The wall banner was meant to say: 'WE ARE ALL FOR THIS! GO ON!' with each letter on an individual A4 sheet, hand-drawn by the boys. Unfortunately, the absent-minded Ogles had forgotten to include the non-alphabetic characters, which resulted in the sign instead reading:

WE ARE ALL FOR THIS GOON

Chump had been perennially self-deprecating, often describing himself as an "unstable knucklehead" despite his obvious talents in city administration and his clear proficiency in his main hobby, mini-golf. But beneath his modest exterior was an even humbler talent, waiting to emerge like a moth larva from a packet of oats: a philanthropy and an egalitarian heart like you just wouldn't believe.

With his lovable personality and radiant orange skin, Chump stood out like a beacon, or at least an amber warning light, of lovability.

Since, to use Ronnie's metaphor, the "motor vehicle of municipal governance" had, he believed, been careering out of control under previous mayor Barry Kabana, Ronnie was determined that his own legacy would be a giant skid mark. His skid mark would, he said, be a clear sign of him braking the vehicle of governance so that its wheels no longer turned, and its engine could ultimately be shut down for the safety of all. His skid mark would be right there in the middle of the legislative road, indicating a reversal in society's forward journey. Yes, in a sense Chump was seeking to revolt against Kabana's form of governance. Indeed, Chump was revolting.

All the more, with Ronnie now having prevailed in the municipal election, not only would the community be in for the surprise and delight of the ascendant Chump as their 'main course', but also, thrown in as a bonus like complimentary prawn crackers, would be Ronnie's delightful family members:

There was his stunning, fruity wife Melony, as fragrant as a ripe durian, a plain dresser and, though born an alien, one with a deeply caring heart, now loyal to her new municipality. Melony, born Melanoma K'nivin in Munni, Hungary, had toiled in sweatshops as a child so she understood the value of freedom and what it was like to be enslaved to an odious money-grubber. She recognized the value of finding a quality husband, a virtual Einstein, who could change her life in a relatively quantum way and lead her to a life which allowed her to break out of her shell, and to charge energetically out into the world. She found she could have deep theoretical conversations with Chump about the Universe, and let loose her ideas on bosons, winos and sleptons.

Next in the Chump lineage was his camera-shy, nail-biting son Iwanker. Never far away from Iwanker was his terrific wife, Janey Kushynird. And who could leave out Ronnie's lovable daughters, Dinah and Erika, ever-enthusiastic and brimming with a fresh take on ethics. And finally, young reclusive Bruno.

Not since the Duke family of Washintown North in 1939 had there been such a charming klan destined for the City Hall. If ever there had been an incentive to vote, this had really been it! The community would certainly have a lot of joy to digest at once. So much to digest, in fact, that they might even get sick of digesting.

Yes, thinking back on that time made Ogles and Bunyon realize they were now part of a unique moment in history where the stars had aligned for Ronnie, their special friend, and his crew.

* * *

Now Ogles, close to permanent retirement - perhaps even more permanent than he expected - knew that he was bequeathing his left-wing ambitions to Bunyon. Moose FM, which handed out millions to abused pets, had been one of the city's leading charities. Now Bunyon's Dimbrat Press had surpassed even the shining success of Ogles' Moose FM by a successful mass mailout of flyers encouraging both pet owners and their pets to forgo their own needs for the sake of animal liberation by donating to their kitty. Ogles felt his audience was in safe hands with Dimbrat.

Ogles deeply respected Chump's poise and moral authority, and his ability to engage public policy with conviction, or even multiple convictions. Chump was determined that his triumph would result in more sweeping reforms for the municipality. These would include more frequently-rostered street-sweepers and the increased brushing of cobwebs from Washintown's public edifices.

Some months earlier, Ogles had been presented an award for the advancement of women's issues and had been celebrated over the airwaves via Moose FM for his progressive stance on female advancement. Bestowing the well-earned award was Robbie's rather sickly and pallid-looking work colleague Regan Mordorc, who worked as Program Director at Moose News, having risen through the ranks from the position of janitor over many years. Mordorc himself was a selfless humanitarian whose face looked nothing like the back of a bulldog's ass.

Then Chump, barely three months later, won even more prestigious citywide acclaim for his groundbreaking, live 'hot mic' broadcast aboard Bushy Bill's Beaver Bus while on the road to help narrate a nature documentary on the habits of the elusive furry riverine critters. With his passions inflamed by seeing the shrinking forest cover on display, Chump skillfully segued into a revealing broadside on the marginalization of women. He passionately called upon all members of society to grab every opportunity to champion, to fight relentlessly for, and to never give up on, the goal of elevating women to higher roles in society, starting with a culture of respect and ending only when their every need had been serviced. Quite predictably, this stirring and unforgettable oration marked a never-to-be-repeated moment in history, and would remain in the hearts and minds of many, playing a pivotal role in his success in being elected mayor.

It also elevated the beavers' endangered plight in the public consciousness.

On hearing this broadcast, his wife Melony who, at the time, had been at home doing dishes as sternly directed by her loving Chump, was brought to tears. We can only guess these were tears of intense joy, knowing that her sweet Chump was now publicly recognized as one who could put his hand up for women.

* * *

Ogles, similarly inclined to espouse women's affairs, was certain that Chump's long experience in other municipal issues, particularly waste removal, would serve him well in his new role if he were to be successful. Chump had proven himself with a solid track record in civic sanitation and migrant affairs, establishing a fine public laundry service for the City of Washintown, and assisting the settlement of Eastern European and Russian émigrés into the community. He had helped them establish their business skills, tax matters and networks in the US, via his key roles in the civic public health and social services sectors.

Chump's deep practical experience with women's issues sealed his reputation and gave him a hands-down advantage among female constituents. His philanthropy and pro-feminist tendencies knew no bounds, and he inspired others to emulate him. He had even encouraged his local mechanic, Mickey Crohney, to reach out and financially assist a number of young women who had strayed into difficult times or needed medical assistance for large bilateral chest abnormalities. Chump did so by funneling helpful funds to them via Crohney through an old colleague in the waste removal business, Dick Pickles of Associated Motor-oil Industries (AMI) Inc.

Crohney was Chump's long-time mechanic, a loyal guy who could always be relied upon to give Chump honest car service and tune-ups. Crohney had an arrangement with bulk oil recycler Dick Pickles, who regularly collected the endless drums of dirty, dripping oil produced in Crohney's workshop in what they called a kind of 'catch and fill' operation, making sure the tarry waste oil products were stored in a safe location, never to be at risk of polluting the public space. The diminutive but wily Pickles, through extensive lobbying of Chump and other councilors on environmental grounds, had secured a contract with Washintown City Council to store the waste oil drums in the hitherto unused basement rooms of City Hall, for later cleansing and sale back to Saudi Arabia.

Crohney ran a small auto repair shop and oil recycling service down on Mulberry Street, right next door to Bert's Clam House. He was a trusty mechanic, although his workshop was rather grungy and bug-infested, with customer invoices and documents stacked all over the place in higgledy-piggledy heaps, and fly-strips hanging from the ceiling. These sticky tapes caught all sorts of creepy critters which crawled about or flew past. While visitors to his workshop found the dangling pest strips filthy and grotesque, Mickey, clearly somewhat of a hoarder, would insist - as he dragged on a ciggy and ran his fingers back through his greasy hair - that the fly-strips needed to stay, citing a future wish to create a world-class bug collection. He declared that one day he would hand them all over to the public.

Chump could always be counted upon to help those in need, whether a poor tenant facing eviction or, like these young women, a constituent requiring significant assistance with medical or legal bills. He frequently stated how much he loved assisting women, and was thrilled when he could give them a lift in their personal circumstances. He wished he could give them everything he had. But failing this, he would at least give them a hand, or at the very least a finger. In this way, Chump personified the absolute best in humankind. The women who met him never forgot him.

Crohney looked after Chump's old Moskvitch 412 sedan which needed the occasional tune-up, and made sure that any oily drips were plugged up promptly, with excess oil or grease shipped off to Dick Pickles for safe off-site storage.

As it turned out, Crohney had played an important role in Chump's success in the mayoral race, by making sure the mayor's Moskvitch was always reliable and in good service, or as Chump affectionately said, "in tippy-top shape". This vehicle had been a centerpiece of the Chump campaign as he tootled around town with a large speaker on the roof, just like Jake and Elwood Blues drumming up an audience; in Chump's case, waving to potential voters, handing out leaflets, and tossing out free canine whistles, albeit blowing some black smoke and asbestos dust out the rear of the jalopy. It was a charming bucolic scene: "You! On the motorcycle!", "You, two girls!" No-one in Washintown had missed out on seeing Chump's trusty vehicle belching its smoke through the suburban streets.

* * *

Apart from his motor vehicle repair shop, Crohney - a true genius and multi-talented Renaissance man, some would even say a modern-day DaVinci, Michelangelo or Jeanne de Valois-Saint-Rémy - ran a number of other businesses. He had small businesses, he had large businesses, he had businesses with cashflow, he had businesses with outgoings. Many had profits, which were gross. Crohney knew accounting was accrual business which had entangled many a budding entrepreneur, but nevertheless continued tallying up these gross profits, and had his books vetted and checked by his bookkeeper, Heath, who was quite a joker as he would juggle a few of the numbers just to keep Mickey on his toes and to amuse any overly-serious IRS auditors.

He had all sorts of businesses: a tuk-tuk business, a steam cleaning business, a confectionery business, a stain removal business, even a communications and data collection business. Businesses, businesses, businesses. He was a truly gifted businessman. One had to constantly remind oneself that he was the local mechanic, yet he bore the qualities of a Thomas Edison, a Nikola Tesla or a Napoleon Hill.

As an army veteran and a patriot, Crohney had suffered injuries during a nuclear test in the late fifties at Tahoe, near the Nevada nuclear test range. Working as a young field officer for the US Army who had ridden out with his troop onto the test ground on trained military mules, Crohney was left behind not far from ground zero when his senior officer rode off to save his own ass just before the device's detonation. Crohney's direct exposure to the ensuing blast - not to mention its subsequent fallout - had not only melted all his equipment, causing a melted walkie-talkie and fusion of his GPS, but had also irradiated his whole persona with damaging alpha particles, fission products and isotopes. This left him carrying an extremely high background level of radiation, strongly detectable on a Geiger counter all these years later. Consequently, it wasn't advisable for his customers these days to shake his hands or even share his cups, telephone or hand sanitizer. Unfortunately, Crohney was quite literally "radioactive". Some said he might stay that way for many years, or would likely need admission to a special facility for treatment.

Yet Crohney was a charming, honest and ethical guy, like a brother to Chump, and always 'at the ready' to help, like a diligent boy scout with a length of rope.

One of his businesses outside his workshop involved the procurement of fish carcasses, beets, offal and other offcuts from market stall holders, which he passed on to local restaurants for soup stock, and of course to his great friend Ronnie Chump for use in making Chump's signature family dish: Chump Chowder, a broth of beets, thin fluid and tangy aged verdure. As I will elucidate further in the following chapter, for Chump this brought back fond memories of his good old Dad, so Crohney occupied a special place in Chump's heart for providing this nostalgic service, for which Chump was of course charged very little indeed. Chump received regularly-couriered drop-offs of the chowder ingredients direct to his back door, at night, thanks to Crohney's generosity and close ties to stall-holders, mainly southern Italian and Russian émigrés, who were in possession of more beets and green stuff than they knew what to do with. Mickey was indeed a treasured life-long friend, far more than just a mechanic.

Mickey, in fact, once literally took a bullet for Chump when, working back late in the workshop one night, some local hooligans had attempted to steal Chump's Moskvitch, booked in at the time for a clogged oil filter. Mickey had repelled the gang but took a .22 caliber pellet in his shoulder for the trouble. It would take Mickey several years to recover from his bullet injury. "Awww, with friends like Mickey," Chump thought after that incident, "it would be unpardonable not to support his businesses. He will always be there for me."

Another of Mickey's businesses was called Car-Tar, named after a sticky black tarry substance, patent pending, made by mixing a proprietary oil-based liquid, trademarked 'black water', with various glues, horse chaff, bull dust and binding agents. The multi-purpose formula was excellent as an auto body filler, put to great use for example when Chump's Moskvitch sustained any kind of dint; but it was also useful for use in covering byways, sewer pits and multi-story fabrications. The tar needed to be handled with great circumspection because, like Lady Macbeth's infamous spot, it had a tendency to stick to one's skin and be very difficult to remove without interventions. Mickey received a steady income stream from Car-Tar which facilitated his humanitarian ventures. His exposure to the 'black water' had soiled Mickey's hands in a way which would take about three years to rub off.

To thank Chump for his loyal support in the establishment of Car-Tar, Mickey presented Ronnie with a glistening tar suit. Kind Mickey was not to know this in advance, but the tar suit would later cause an enormous stir in the Washintown press when first boldly worn by Chump to a press conference. The tar suit was enormously controversial. The suit's gleaming appearance, akin to Sonny Corleone's shiny black Lincoln Continental, stunned some analysts and horrified others. It dashingly (and a little drippingly) broke long-standing fashion conventions in the town for civic leaders, and certainly put to shame any of the dreary beige suits worn by Barry Kabana. Commentators debated at length whether a tar suit was entirely appropriate for a mayor, or was needed to project a slick impression. Though indeed an eye-catching and truly innovative fashion statement, it was catching in other ways too, for it was slightly prone to picking up stray feathers, dirt and the like. But Chump wore it with style, as though it had been tailor-made for him.

Oddly enough, Mickey Crohney only ever seemed to have the same three cars in his workshop, including the collapsed Ford Edsel of Sean Henutty and Billy Tootride's VW Bus; yet he exuded great confidence when seen in his repair shop, leaning on these cars, polishing them and talking about all things mechanical.   After interviewing several of Chump's colleagues and conducting further late-night research I was able to discover that Crohney was supplementing the passive income from his businesses by way of yet another part-time job: a nightshift at a diner, where he flipped burgers with Pickles, and helped customers to buy large buns.

Through his extensive experience with old motor vehicles, combined with his razor-sharp intellect, Crohney had quite naturally become an expert in a wide range of fields: in restructuring the accounting systems of major aerospace manufacturers, in healthcare and in telephony. As a result, he became an Essential Consultant to anyone with any problem from a sore toe to a broken space vehicle. Fixing Chump's old Moskvitch 412, therefore, was of course child's play and it purred like a well-fed pussy after being serviced by Crohney (though unfortunately oily leaks persisted).

* * *

Like Chump, Crohney was a remarkable philanthropist, spurred on to ever greater deeds by his inspirational customer, Ronnie.

Early in his career, Chump had established the Chump Foundation. This remarkable charitable foundation disbursed funds to a wide variety of other charities, including the Iwanker Trust for

Impoverished Children, the Dinah and Erika Community Fund for Struggling Startups, the Melony Chump Haute Couture Supply and Refugee Shelter for Aliens, and Chumpy Kids, aimed at providing fresh healthy food to youth offenders in cages. The Foundation also provided generous donations totaling around $6 million to veterans' causes, though, due to Chump's well-known humility in not disclosing donations, this figure might have been much higher. Iwanker, Erika and Dinah together ran training classes to teach people the fiduciary skills needed to run a charity like the Chump Foundation.

As a true investigative professional, I devoted time to training my young journalism colleague, Davy Fahrenheit, through a series of masterclasses I ran from my sidewalk stake-out, on how to verify these Chump donations. With my help, and that of his editor, Barty Marrowbone, Davy was able to confirm their veracity, and wrote a powerful series of articles shining a Spotlight on this wonderful largesse, which would otherwise have gone unrecognized. The Chump Foundation had implemented a powerful marketing strategy, reproduced on mugs and T-shirts, which exhorted donors to emulate Ronnie by following his philanthropic spirit with encouraging mottos, including "Be a Chump, donate bigly" and "Chump Foundation - where good money gets thrown."

In fact, the Chump Foundation truly serves as a model of good governance for charities right across the country, and organizations would do well to implement its probity measures. No-one expects a charity to be as exceptional as the Chump Foundation. Its chief weapon is surprise.

In yet another example of his bottomless generosity and impeccable character, a long-standing friend and mini-golf partner, Sylvie Clittafford, had encouraged Chump, in turn, to encourage his friend Mickey to donate $130,000 to the Hush Foundation, a registered charity promoting the use of calming music in hospitals to assist children undergoing painful medical procedures. This was of course a suggestion which Chump very eagerly complied with, enthusiastically discussing with his long-time confidant, Alvin McWeaselberger.

Yet knowing Mickey to be a very humble and private person, Chump was keen for Mickey's donation to remain anonymous, and in fact, motivated by his impeccable humility, intervened to restrain Sylvie from publishing details of the donation in the hospital newsletter. Such was the way of the great man: assisting a worthy cause while taking care of a close friend at the same time. It is also a measure of the caliber of his friends that Mickey would, without a moment's hesitation, pull out his check book and write a check, made out to Sylvie's preferred charity, just on a word from his dear friend Ronnie. Such was the moral force of this man and those who surrounded him.

Chump subsequently hit upon the idea of introducing Sylvie to some of the well-known personalities in Philanthropy 500 magazine, so she could further her fundraising efforts for the children. Teeing her up for a private meeting after a particularly grueling round of mini-golf, he pulled out a copy and bent over backwards to assist her in her charity work, with his own bottom line taking quite a walloping in the process. He gave what little he had, and in Chump's true gentlemanly style, like a culinary artist, he even brought out a little cock-a-leekie for her.

* * *

Bunyon was one of the few who had taken Chump seriously long before he had decided to run for mayor. He had first attached himself to Chump in September 2001 when they had worked together as volunteers in one of the city's soup kitchens run by an Honored Society charity, aimed at providing meals for underprivileged families and immigrants. Chump had been handing out stale bread and lukewarm tea while Bunyon was manning the soup-pot, dishing out a hot watery broth. As Bunyon stood there with his ladle, Chump was again reminded of his dear father's chewy chowder and how Chump the Elder would serve out the warm gray mixture to the shivering young Ronnie in his hour of need.

When they struck up conversation, they realized that they had much in common, right down to their shared bony outgrowths, Bunyon on his toes and Chump in his rear passage, where there had been calcification around an old injury where some metal fragments had once pierced his gluteus maximus.

They had compared notes about their congenital defects, for Bunyon had the foot issue which had stubbed his chances to be great on the soccer field. Ronnie, on the other hand, had been born with a problem in which a certain appendage oscillated in size by many more standard deviations than one would usually expect. In his case, it swung wildly from an almost microscopic size, which left him with frequent feelings of shame and inadequacy, to something of elephantine proportions which became a regular embarrassment and inconvenience in public. Its standing seemed to be linked to what was coming out his mouth at a given moment.

They had bonded over these common qualities.

From that moment, Bunyon had really grown on Chump and had become a standout feature of Chump's base, even following him around on foot as Chump did the hard yards on the hustings.

Due to Ronnie and Stevie sharing a visual likeness, they actually looked like two Chumps, or one double-Chump, though were in no way related, at least not to anyone's knowledge. The two had struck up conversation in their volunteer capacity and realized that, just like two brothers from another mother, they shared values of compassion for those less fortunate than themselves.

I daren't spread scurrilous innuendo, as that would be far beneath a professional journalist such as your beloved Martha. There were, however, some in Washintown society who openly wondered whether Ronnie and Stevie may have also shared that other mother. It would, of course, be utterly preposterous to even suggest that Ronnie's beloved mother MaryLou Chump could have had wild, unprotected floor-shaking hayloft intimacy with the great Marvin Bunyon. That simply could never have happened, and their likeness must have been purely perchance, rather than the product of an illicit and passionate polyamorous pairing.

Now, through this deep bond forged with Chump, a bright new day had dawned in Bunyon's career and he could see years ahead of him in faithful service to Ronnie Chump and to the public good. Bunyon believed that the city needed to foster peace, root out corruption and cronyism, and tear down the divisions between social groups in order to further fortify its strong public institutions.

Chump embodied that message.

Like a moth at the outdoor light of a roadhouse toilet block, Bunyon had been captivated by Chump's predictability and the methodical nature with which he progressed his agenda, of public policy.

Bunyon willingly flapped around that light, only occasionally banging his head on it, charged with a steamy cocktail of political pheromones and an inner lust for brightness.

* * *

"Does he *get* it?" Ogles asked with a pause, staring a little weirdly at Bunyon.

He was wondering if Chump got the significance of now being the mayor, rather than a just a nondescript, run-of-the-mill councilor dealing mainly with parking infringements, rubbish collection and stray dog laws. Now he could help set council's social agenda, improve the plight of immigrants and low-income earners throughout the municipality and enact powerful bylaws. Did Chump get it? Hello?

Bunyon took another sip of herbal tea. "No, he doesn't get it yet. Ronnie is so focused on others that he hasn't stopped to consider what this means for his broader ability to enact meaningful progressive social change."

"Good old Ronnie, what an incredible altruist."

"But you know what?" continued Bunyon. "For years Ronnie has nurtured a great vision for the public good, one he's confided in me, even way back, when we worked together at the soup kitchen. It's a dream he has kept alive in his heart, a kind of large-scale IT Project, to unite the city of Washintown through a sophisticated public works and IT renewal project, to renew the city's aging water, IT and electricity networks, and to bring all of Washintown's services together in one central hub. He even came up with a name for his pet project years ago, hoping that one day it could become a reality. I think he wanted to call it the 'Secure Hub IT Project'.

"I guess that would make it the 'S.H. IT Project' for short then, right?" added an intrigued Ogles.

"Yeah I... I guess you're right. But whatever you call it, it's a doozy of a plan," replied a thoughtful Bunyon.

"Well now he might not have realized that dream yet, but his chance has finally arrived!" quipped Ogles.

"Yes, Ronnie has not only longed to see it come about, but actually wants to head it up, so now he'll be the S.H. IT Head. He really deserves that title. He'll be the main guy! The Grand Poobah! Can you believe it?"

"Good old Ronnie. He so deserves it" Ogles echoed.

* * *

After that discussion, Bunyon went off to the toilet and was gone for an exceedingly long time, as though the talk of Chump had stirred up or unblocked something deep within his system.

As the large group waited for Bunyon to return, the distant bathroom to which he had retired in the bowels of the building could be heard resounding with what sounded like moaning explosions, then screaming jets punctuated with loud rapid-fire bomb blasts, with crackling pops. Finally, several giant, thundering 'raspberry' sounds echoed down the corridor through the restaurant, shuddering the wine glasses on their racks and rattling the light-fittings, causing the lights to flicker, as if due to an earth tremor. The guests shuffled their feet in an embarrassed way, and changed the subject a few times.

Finally, Bunyon wafted back, looking much fresher and a few pounds lighter. A pungent, fishy odor accompanied him back up from the unkempt rear of the establishment.

He gave an entertaining soliloquy on the predictability and dynamic nature of politics, and shrewd observations that, as with a bucket of pondwater, a candidate with the obvious qualities of a Chump would naturally rise to the top, with the unfolding beauty of a lotus, or, perhaps more fittingly, a DeLorean.

*　*　*

There was one thing perplexing Ogles.

"Why is he so unfriendly to Russians?"

"Mainly due to a run-in he once had with a tradesman, a guy called Viktor Punkin," replied Bunyon. "The guy's a Russian plumber and electrician, delightful but lacking a bit of talent. Chump hired the guy to do some plumbing at his old place, before he bought the new one, and the job didn't exactly work out. He heads up a home maintenance franchise, Fix-It Services Business, FSB, y'know, a bit like Weed Man Lawn Care."

"Anyway, Ronnie asked the guy to fix a bronze shower and a ceramic toilet, seemed easy enough, and the guy and his lads come out to Ronnie's to do the job. But get this: somehow Punkin and his apprentices manage to connect the toilet directly to the shower, and Ronnie found himself covered in shit next time he took a shower! Can you believe that?! It even got in his mouth and bits have been coming out ever since! Ronnie, bless his soul, sought to forgive, but just couldn't quite do it. I mean, who could? Even a lesser man couldn't."

"That's Ronnie for you, heart of gold".

"It's magnificent" said Bunyon, beaming. "But he's been shy of Russians ever since."

"And you know what?" added Ogles rhetorically. "The Viktor Punkin guy tried to make it up to Ronnie at the time, he delivered him a whole stack, like a whole tower, of his old Russian Penthouse magazines wrapped in brown paper, plus a dried Russian fish and a fifty ruble note. It was a really nice gesture, especially the fish. Chump's mechanic Mickey Crohney helped arrange the Penthouse delivery to Ronnie, through FSB's marketing secretary Dmitrov Pesky. But you know Ronnie - he's so clean-livin', that only incensed him more. He couldn't believe the filth and audacity of it, and sent it all back. Can you believe it? Ronnie accepting a stack of Penthouse magazines?! Who does that Punkin guy think he's dealing with? This isn't Barry Kabana! Punkin and Pesky really crossed a red line. Anyway, I think it'll take Ronnie a long time to get over the whole thing, the poor soul."

* * *

The two pals spent the rest of the evening planning out policies for the new city council, including purchase of new plates for the catering division. Ogles insisted that they didn't want to just look as though they were serving up Chump food on camping plates.

"China's everything. Nothing else matters." said Ogles.

"If we can't get the china right, we can't get anything right" Bunyon laughed. "The catering staff would all be groaning 'China by Bunyon'".

"Who'd have thought I'd end up being an expert on crockery!" he exclaimed after a brief pause, with a mixture of mock grandiosity and self-deprecation. "Which reminds me, Rob, we really need to come up with a whole new set of crocks."

"Ronnie will be so proud of you", said Ogles. "He is always brimming with gratitude. Just like his father, and his father's father, and his father's father's father..."

"Ok, I get the picture," Bunyon interrupted. "He's a Chump alright. Chump is definitely a giant among Chumps."

"Yeah, he's a Chump alright" seconded Ogles, referring to the fine historical lineage of Chumps, dating back to their early Caucasian origins in Nuremberg, a long dynasty of nomadic Eurasian Chumps, who had survived centuries living only on turnips and dung, and who had passed on their resultant DNA to make Ronnie the resilient man he was.

"And what a fine Chump! He's even taller, broader in girth and perhaps more honorable than his forebears, and that makes him the greatest Chump of all time!"

And with that they clinked glasses and downed their Mojitos.

Stevie then rubbed his hands together with relish and pulled out a wad of manila folders from his briefcase.

"Right, now let's look at all these resumés."

1

EVICTION NIGHT

On the day of the council elections, about two weeks prior to Bunyon and Ogles' celebratory post-election lunch, Kylie-Jo Connard - Chump's articulate and compelling political strategist, an intelligent and polished media performer and campaign manager - was looking rather pallid, disheartened and slightly nauseous. She was settling in to an unappetizing, gray-looking glassful of "Chump Chowder" which the aspiring mayor, an avid chef (at least in his own mind) had whipped up from an old sturgeon gifted to him by some wealthy Muscovite friends who had visited him earlier in the campaign.

These foreign friends of his had come bearing the fishy tidbit in discrete packaging, tied with a pretty ribbon. Late that afternoon, Chump had dismissed his immigrant kitchenhand for the day, sending her home with a jovial pat on the bottom and a fifty ruble note to spend as she wished. He then rubbed his hands together as he headed for the fridge in search of fish bones, stock and carrots. He had spent the next few hours frenetically chopping fish carcasses and boiling them up into a nondescript glutinous, oleaginous gel which was then slopped out into bowls for anyone present - the famous "Chump Chowder".

* * *

Chump had been raised in a ghetto where his poor father had taught him to make questionably delicious soups from the most sparing of morsels: pumpkin soup from an old moldy pumpkin rind; "mushroom" soup from moistened brown paper bags run through a blender with water; minestrone from vegetable leftovers found in restaurants' dumpsters, and - most notably - "Chump Chowder" from offcuts donated to the poor family by benevolent fishmongers and vegetable stall holders at the local market. This family staple consisted mainly of fish heads, turnips, yams, beets and carrot stumps.

Ronnie never forgot these humble roots, and - at times to the dismay of his company - he would suddenly invite all his colleagues to share in a sitting of Chump Chowder, occasionally with other unexpected guests, for example passing Russian lawyers, building developers or orphanage operators.

These Chump Chowder meetings often resulted in a heart-warming round-table ritual whereby Chump would seek the opinion of his co-workers on the quality of his fishy chowder. This would typically be followed by a procession around the table of weak smiles and obsequious comments on the wonders and deliciousness of the chowder, and on the mayoral candidate's unparalleled culinary skills, as the staff simultaneously sought to suppress their gag reflexes. Still, Chump was held in such high esteem by his fellow council workers that this seemed to them a small price to pay to keep their beloved colleague happy and feeling loved.

Chump's daughter Dinah had grown up her entire life ingesting the gray chowder and had acquired quite a taste for her father's fishy concoction. Young Dinah relished every sitting of Chump Chowder, lapping it up eagerly with her large Winnie-the-Pooh-themed plastic spoon, regularly exclaiming "I love it!" as it stained her teeth red, dribbled down her chin, and oozed all over the front of her pretty blouse. "Especially in the Summer!"

Keen to emulate her dad, she had started learning to cook up her own Chump Chowder, though she still had a way to go before producing as rich and gamey a flavor as his.

* * *

Though based on fish, Chump Chowder had a complex bouquet with a full body, a musty nose and surprising overtones of borscht, with a peppery, smoky structure and a spicy finish. The fish, however, remained the overriding flavor on the palette no matter how subtly it was disguised under the roots and other oily ingredients. In its preparation, Chump Chowder required a fine balance between letting the fish "cure" for several days or weeks, and, on the other hand, allowing it to age too much when it could - like the notorious Japanese 'fugu', the delicious but potentially deadly pufferfish - actually become toxic. Luckily Chump was skilled in knowing exactly when and how to serve it up to his 'customers'.

Chump Chowder was best quaffed rather than sipped. Kylie-Jo's error that day had been to sip.

Unfortunately, when dished out, Chump Chowder was a rather sloppy, goopy substance with a consistency like engine oil, and all those who partook of it with Ronnie were invariably left carrying a noticeable stain of one kind or another, some in the form of a splatter mark, some in the form of a dribble, others in the form of oily spots or drip-marks. Some suffered from indelible staining to their teeth due to the high beetroot content. All, however, left bearing the signature fishy odor and greasy smears which almost impossible to remove from their fabrics. All were permanently stained.

Being ever faithful to Ronnie though, this never dissuaded his team members from partaking in a hearty serving of the chowder, and one could always rely on seeing his colleagues bearing a stuffed grin as they came away from a swilling session, despite the indelible stains on their Hugo Boss suits and Christian Dior skirts.

* * *

Chump's father Freddy had worked as a cobbler who made a scant living for the family by setting up a small stall outside the city's first supermarkets where he carried out shoe repairs for passing shoppers, earning just a penny or two for each shoe repair. Ronnie learned the value of hard work and honesty by watching his dad performing this humble vocation. Each day without fail, Freddy would diligently attend to the masses, despite his own intractable poverty. He always sported a grin and was quick with a witty comment, serving his customers with a sparkle in the eye. His work-worn hands, textured like leather itself from constantly working with black shoe polish, and nimble with a thick leather-needle, could make otherwise-costly shoe damage simply disappear, like magic. His customers' loose coins, similarly, vanished, seemingly transformed into a black glossy shine in the blink of an eye!

A tragic yet formative event for Ronnie had occurred when he was only seven years old. His father, leaving his shoe repair kiosk one wintry evening to head home, was - in a scene reminiscent of **Romper Stomper** - confronted in the darkness by an angry mob of white supremacists who mistook his dirty skin and blackened hands as a sign of him being a filthy, rotten, lousy, disease-ridden immigrant. Despite Freddy's protestations, he was dragged into a lane and severely beaten by the mob with sticks, stale baguettes, golf clubs and a croissant.

To be fair, Ronnie always said that there was probably some blame on both sides, as Freddy never knew when not to irritate a white supremacist with his irrepressible repartee - for example with a witty comeback echoing the Omo washing powder advertisement about their white sheets needing to be run through the wash one more time "for even brighter whites". But in this instance it was Freddy who came off second best. A passing florist on her way home found him slumped in a heap and left for dead in the alleyway, and cried out for a horse-drawn wagon to rush Freddy to the city hospital, but sadly Freddy died during the wagon trip. He ceased to be. He was an ex-Freddy.

Ronnie was left devastated and near-penniless, yet he carried the imprint of his father's noble and virtuous ethic in his heart.

This incident powered young Ronnie's desire to forge a safe and tolerant city, where strong public institutions served to educate the populace, provide sound universal health care and welcome people from all nations to contribute to a vibrant unified community, free of discrimination. He sought a society with strong underpinnings of social justice, with healthcare for all, a society where wealth was shared fairly and in which people seeking refuge were treated with respect and dignity. As Freddy used to say to Ronnie, as he did to his old cobbler mate Alf Lennon: "Imagine", referring to people living their lives in peace, free from any harassment by evil régimes.

Thankfully, Freddy, as though having had some prescience regarding his own fate, had safeguarded Ronnie's moral development by nominating his close confidant, the wonderful Alvin McWeaselberger, as Ronnie's Godfather and guardian in the event of any such tragedy. In the years which followed, Alvin would play a key role throughout Ronnie's ongoing adolescence by teaching him the highest principles of family trust, equity, prudent financial records management, and how to manage perfidy and parsimony.

Ronnie was also emotionally consoled by another stroke of good fortune after the terrible accident: finding $4.13 in loose coins in the pockets of Freddy's threadbare work-pants as he scoured dead Freddy's possessions looking for mementos and other valuables.

Maintaining his dad's legacy and ensuring that his death had not been in vain - or at least not worth only a measly $4.13 - spurred Ronnie to take up the cause of social justice with extraordinary passion. During his lonely teenage years, when other kids were playing baseball with their dads, Ronnie made two commitments to himself: firstly, to one day enter public life and strive to make his city a fair and equitable place to live; secondly, to flip his hair back and improve his tan so that he could more easily blend in with the minority groups he wished to represent. These remarkable early pledges would chart the course of Ronnie's life for decades to come.

The pain of Freddy's death left Ronnie desperate for activities which would take his mind from his huge personal loss. In the ensuing period, he took up a number of pastimes to dull the deep hole in his heart and wallet. Following in the footsteps of his father's nimble hands, he picked up the art of prestidigitation, purchasing a mail-order magic kit and learning to perform neat tricks with his own tiny balls and a mere thimble, which he found gave huge entertainment to little kiddies and those with some level of mental impairment. Wherever he went, Ronnie would pull out his bag of tricks, which he saved for certain occasions. They didn't necessarily apply to the occasion, but when he felt the need he would produce his thimble and tiny balls to confound onlookers, firstly covering them up with a black cloak as he was well-practiced at doing, then stunning everyone by having them appear in another location (after some brief fumbling under the cloak). He got a lot of claps. In fact, he had the clap from hundreds of different people. Kindly, Chump charged only a meager fee for his spellbinding entertainment, payable fortnightly, terms and conditions available on request.

Striving to overcome adversity at every turn, Ronnie as a grieving young boy had learned, and received great solace from, the art of bootscooting, introduced to him by the wife of the undertaker at his dad's funeral, who took the sad boy to her bosom and showed him everything there was to know. Since then, he had developed a great love for that comforting bosom, and an aptitude for the activity, using it to express not only his own personal anguish through classics such as "Achy Breaky Heart" but also to guide his nascent social justice policies which would become the hallmark on the Chump name. Ronnie loved playing his favorite bootscooting tunes on repeat, inspired by "Asleep at the Wheel".

In the years to come, Chump's strong sense of social justice saw him spend significant efforts, and much of his own personal assets, in trying to fight against the gambling industry, working to drive casinos into the ground and to run these crime-ridden businesses out of town, and into other towns, along with all their lousy employees.

* * *

Chump's opponent in the mayoral race, Hildegard Glintin, had been a cruel and relentless foe, almost as bad a foe as a European, and with a heart as hard as diamond but less easily converted into cash. Throughout the campaign she had mercilessly taunted Chump, like an evil puppeteer, with highly personal insults, both verbally and via her Twitler account, implying that the Glintin name was squeaky clean and implied strength, brilliance and steely resolve, whereas the Chump name evoked the banal, the carnal, the venal, soupy, and flaccid. She had mocked his overgrown hands and his enormous schwangdoodle which barely managed to keep itself contained during press conferences. These taunts hurt Chump immensely and forced him to seek counsel with his dearest friends. These included his old school friend, the gentle soul and human rights activist Roddy Duedirte; the reformed Asian crime boss Kimmy "Long Gun" (now a Christian preacher who had handed in his weapon collection, and with whom Chump had "fallen in love"); his high-school tutor Ronald Mugbaby, and a former overseas travel buddy, Christopher Stainless. These great friends had guided Ronnie's every action, helping his decision-making and policy formulation. Christopher steeled Ronnie's resolve to shrug off the taunts, to ignore Glintin's cruel criticisms, and to put his best foot forward in the election.

"When she goes low, I'll buy a submarine" Chump had resolved after having sought the counsel of his friends in relation to Glintin. They all agreed that would be a good way to handle Hildegard, and that it would be wonderful to see Ronnie frequenting the sea floor in a sealed vessel.

* * *

As the campaign progressed, Melony Chump had been elated when a candidly-recorded tape was revealed by the press, in which Chump was overheard expounding his strong feminist views and his determination to improve the plight of women. He had expressed his values with such conviction and heartfelt honesty that she had sat, unmoving, by the television with tears of pride and joy streaming down her face. From that moment she intrinsically knew without a shadow of doubt that not only was her wonderful husband destined to claim the mayoral position in the coming election, but that he would execute that responsibility in the most exceptional way, just as the Philippines might execute an industrious suspected drug dealer.

To further strengthen Chump's reputation, BuzzyBee magazine published a 53-page article in its print edition, highlighting Chump's magnificent overseas work helping foreign aid agencies; for example, assisting struggling working women in Moscow to produce legumes - most notably, yellow peas - in raised beds.

* * *

"If I win, I'll be the most devoted public servant this city has seen," Chump had told his trusty aide Sid Nutberger towards the end of the campaign. Nutberger was a long-time colleague of the illustrious Roddy Pebble, an outstanding campaign networker, collaborator and renowned dog lover, who had built a reputation for making ripples in the briny ponds of Washintown politics since helping former Mayor Dicky Nicksoff reach heady heights of fame in the 1970s. Pebble had often lobbied for increased police presence and more police weaponry at crime scenes, particularly around the time of arresting 'vermicious knids', his pet name for low-life, treasonous criminals. These days, Pebble also worked closely with Jeremy Corsidid, a disarmingly honest young man who possessed an uncanny ability to predict future events, as if endowed with a connection to the matrix.

Nicksoff had been so impressed with Pebble's assistance all those years ago that he had commissioned an image of Roddy to be engraved on his chest.

Between Pebble and Bunyon, Chump felt he was surrounded by a pair of firm yet forgiving supporters, as relieving and well-fitting as a pair of Dr Scholl's inserts.

* * *

"But how many times do you want to be mayor?" Nutberger had asked (a quantitatively different question to the usual candidate test: "Do you want to be mayor?"). Nutberger received a compelling answer by way of Chump's blank look in response. Ronnie had just realized that - like George Bailey in "It's a Wonderful Life" - he was so loved by his community that he had a virtual Monopoly on being mayor as long as he liked, and as long as he paid Income Tax, Luxury Tax and his dues on Pennsylvania Avenue, Washintown. The community had bestowed an incredible privilege upon him, a veritable Community Chest of goodwill, which he recognized with a great sense of honor, humility and a strong desire to serve. Never on Earth would he consider cheating them of everything they possessed, their civility, even their dignity, or of shaming them in front of international visitors. Never. No way. Never on Earth would he sell them out for self-interest. No way! This was Ronnie Chump, not some lousy, despicable, venal and egocentric traitor!

The point was, the answer to Nutberger's question didn't matter because Chump was going to be the best mayor he could be, every day serving up his constituents new wonders, new servings of Chump Chowder, new sources of joy-filled "shock and awe", elevating them to new heights of self-awareness and connectedness. He would wrestle the truth like a Supreme Court nominee would wrestle the truth and bring it down to the canvas. He would model only the very best behavior, using the very best models; he would handle women and women's proclivities with the deftness of a master prestidigitator, and give refugees and asylum seekers the kind of treatment they would not easily forget.

Each day he would regale the community and its cherished institutions with an exciting BOOM of new events, new talking points, new sources of legal and legislative debate. What a spectacular ride the community would enjoy! Boy, would they get a ride. Like on an antique roller-coaster at Coney Island, Freddy's old haunt, with a few loose bolts here or there just adding to the thrill. They had no idea what kind of a ride they were in for. What great pride he would bring the city and its people! I don't think anyone had brought so much pride for a long, long time. There was such a happiness about this sense of pride that one could indeed call it a very gay pride.

What honor and integrity would shine, like a gas light on a stormy night from a creaky windswept shed, or like the glowing spectacle of Notre Dame's roof, illuminating Paris with its warming radiance.

* * *

After years of obscurity, Chump's time in the spotlight had finally arrived. He stood poised now to swoop upon the mayoralty of Washintown, population two hundred and forty-nine, riding on a wave of popular apathy. His opponent, Hildegard Glintin, while swanky and showy, would be lucky to muster a meager fifty votes.

As results started trickling in through the evening, it started to become clear that this, at last, would be the eviction night for previous mayor Barry Kabana and his crooked cabal of town councilors. A new, fresh administration would wipe away the stain of the Kabana years and herald a new era of corruption-free and treason-free government, skilled diplomacy and statesmanship, and - most importantly - mighty fine rootin' tootin' bootscootin'.

* * *

That evening, Chump and Melony were attending one of their favorite hangouts, the Washintown Regional Ethics Field Office, where election night drinks, cakes, caviar and canapés were being served and a large wall TV was turned on in a corner of the room. Chump had found the television's remote control and had flicked the TV over to Moose TV, as he knew that his favorite cartoon - Boris and Natasha - was screening at the time.

Chump, always a health fanatic and a firm believer that "you are what you eat", was chomping down on a huge chunk of fruit cake. He was firmly hanging on to his piece of cake on this occasion, having fresh memories of a crumby experience at a recent Christmas party when his cake had been Stollen. Melony, in heavy-applied makeup, was sipping on a leggy glass of Zonin Prosecco Brut, the stem of the flute balanced on her large implants. On screen, Boris was just about to punch a moose in the snoot when the scrolling banner at the bottom of the screen suddenly flashed with the election result: "CHUMP WINS!"

Chump knew they had some great pranksters in the Ethics Office, such as Wally Schlobb, so at first he thought this may have been a prank by some such jester on the council staff. Yet I can exclusively report here, as I managed to get some comments directly from Chump as he sought to evade me the next day, that this theory was quickly debunked:

"So I turned to Wally Schlobb and said 'Someone put a lot of work into that!'" Chump reported. "And then I continued chatting with Melony and other staffers. I really didn't think a thing of it."

"But Wally looked just as shocked as me," he continued, "in fact he needed to take a seat and be treated with oxygen and a defibrillator, so I knew that it wasn't a prank after all. The news came as a great shock to us all. Now can you please move away, Madam, and stop camping outside my house?"

Ronnie had won the mayoral race, and Hildegard Glintin had been trounced fairly and decisively. This was yuge.

And on that victorious night, as they stood with their apéritifs having just been apprised of the news, Chump and Melony looked at each other, cake face to caked face, with jaws dropped, utterly stunned that the people of Washintown had elected him to be their representative on Earth.

Melony was so excited at the prospect of Ronnie becoming mayor that she again wept tears of unbridled joy. Her mascara ran, and although this resulted in her looking like the sweet transvestite from the Rocky Horror Picture Show, she knew in the deep, dark recesses of her heart that Ronnie's mayoralty would be no such horror show, but a spectacle of a totally different kind!

Almost in sympathy, Ronnie's personal secretary, Madeline Washherout, sitting alongside Melony, began similarly "tearing up" with pride at the news of her employer's win. She saw a bright future ahead now (due to the prospective glare of media lights), where she would stand by Ronnie for the long term, always close enough to hear even his whispered requests. She would guard his, and his family's, most intimate privacies with the utmost safekeeping, with the same ultra-high level of security and unassailability one would expect to be applied to, say, a detained pedophile in a high-security prison. These thoughts got the better of her, and her tears, with Melony's, flowed freely on the floor, then down a corridor and out onto the street.

Ronnie's team gathered around and there was more generalized weeping (and some gnashing of teeth) as the apparent joy of the moment overwhelmed them all. In my observation, the team was experiencing such an intense experience of joyfulness stemming from their shared bonds (and other overseas holdings) that the scene was characterized by what sociologists would term as a rare, mass event of "ugly crying".

* * *

Chump had prevailed because he was committed to getting on top of corruption within the city and further, a broad. He had prevailed because he was a vocal advocate for open reporting of finances. Chump had prevailed because he aimed to be the most transparent mayor in the history of Washintown: 'nothing to see here'. He had prevailed because he stood for youth development, particularly through his strong desire to support the advancement of women, regardless of age, by way of his 'affirmative action' approaches.

Demonstrating this commitment, Ronnie and his old friend Jimmy Ekkswine, affectionately known as 'Ekky', would always take care of the elderly ladies at social events. Ronnie and Ekky were the kind of men to whom you could safely entrust your granny, and whom every parent would consider as ideal role models and protectors for their children. Their appeal transcended the generations.

* * *

And so, it came to pass that within the weeks ahead, after a transition period as short as Melony's resumé, the first sittings of the new council would be held. Chump at last would rise up from council's rear, from his position of relative obscurity, now to head up proceedings, proud to be wearing the fine ermine gowns of the mayoralty. He would bear the mace to show everyone - particularly new migrants - who was now in charge. He would monopolize the airwaves with regular talk show appearances, and once in office would have the police and army do regular celebratory marches down Main St, brandishing his powerful mace. There was so much to look forward to!

And though, dear reader, I am bursting to describe in coming pages the sheer magic of Chump's inauguration, it is hard to refrain from offering you first some sneak peaks at what was in store on the floor of City Hall: some background on the pumped Chump team he was able to cobble together, and a preview of their early gifts to the people.

* * *

For what his staff had perhaps least expected was that, immediately after his elevation into office, Chump had insisted on Chump Chowder being regularly promoted via the media and distributed among the populace (with free crackers and food stamps exchangeable for more chowder). So, despite the good intention which lay behind this great generosity of spirit, the public too was to experience the same nauseous malaise experienced by Kylie-Jo Connard on that November afternoon, possibly for as long as four years.

During one of the first group sittings of the new council, Chump suddenly hit upon the idea of extending the impact of Chump Chowder by sending out batches of fresh Chowder via a new Blue-

Apron-type program for low-income families, in what would be called a "Chump Happy Harvest Hamper", including dry bread sticks and a sprig of parsley to go with the sloppy gray mixture. In addition to having perfected his signature chowder, Chump had spent many months working away after hours to develop his own environmentally-friendly Chump(TM) drinking straws, which he now insisted should be packed along with each 'Happy Harvest' shipment. These small drinking tubes, made from highly compacted cow dung and lined on the inside with a thin veneer of smooth cheese to soften their aftertaste, were totally biodegradable and would make it much easier for townsfolk to suck down their chowder without the need for other utensils.

With a loud SNAP of his fingers, he called across the table to Ponce: "Rebus, tomorrow help me draw up some legislation for this!"

Within a matter of days it had become law, and early in the administration the soup shipments were arriving in gray aluminum buckets on thousands of doorsteps.   As hamper program administrator, Joy Hickey had arranged to have a decal of her smiling face emblazoned on the side of each bucket. Though a valuable public service, these home deliveries of soup were also something of a boon to the blowfly population of Washintown when residents forgot to bring their special "Happy Harvest Hamper" indoors.

Washintown was in for some dégustations like it had never expected.

* * *

Chump's campaign had, quite deliberately, duplicated the plot of the award-winning movie *Aliens*, in which a group of highly evolved and well-equipped beings, possessing a strong intent to govern their surroundings, take complete charge of a vehicle of civilization and seek, in an orderly and methodical way, to subtly influence its direction and the destinies of its inhabitants.

The campaign, similarly, had adapted to a changed environment (the calling of the local council elections) and Ronnie's top staffers had thereafter fully embraced a worldview quite different to their own. Many had had distinguished careers outside the rough-and-tumble of municipal bureaucracy (i.e. were aliens), and now were devoting themselves entirely to the betterment of society (fixing the ship the way they wanted it to be) while their previous careers were put on the back-burner (absence from home planet). They would all share in the unexpected thrills of the new administration (jump scares).

His staff were also eminently capable, impeccably credentialed, and well organized. Sergeant Mickey Flout, for example, Chump's new Head of Policing had - without a word to anyone - arranged an unbelievably kind donation of $45,000 to Chump's favorite charity for orphans in Russia. A lovable rogue ex-cop, Mickey was often seen around Town Hall with white powder all around his lips, and the other staffers would joke "Hey Mickey, been hitting the cocaine again today?" when actually they knew full well that Mickey was just an incorrigible sweet-tooth, hooked on Turkish delight and other confections that left icing sugar dust all over him and his suits, like fingerprint dust. Quite a scallywag, Mickey loved going along with the joke and would quip back: "Yeah, just got a new shipment in from Colombia, high-grade!"

At one point, Chump overheard similar jests by Flout, and didn't appreciate him making light of the serious issue of drug dependence. As he wandered off down the hall, Chump was heard to mumble "the guy has serious judgement issues."

* * *

Mickey scoffed boxes of Turkish delight in obscene quantities, risking near-certain complications to his long-term wellbeing, but generally kept this vice to himself in his own office. With a face covered in sugar-dust (and while struggling, straight-faced, trying not to explode with laughter), he maintained to Chump's assistant Mikey Pancedown that he had never touched a single slab of Turkish delight in his life. Poor old Mikey was such an uncomplicated and ingenuous soul that he took this seriously and believed Mickey at face value. Between them, these two were like a funny man and a straight man, like the original Abbott and Costello doing "Who's on First?": Mickey knew he could set gullible Mikey up, and when Mikey finally caught on to having his leg pulled, he would exclaim "Oh dang, Mickey, you've done it again! Lordy me!". This provided enormous fun in the office for everyone else, almost as a spectator sport.

Mickey also loved messing with people's minds in jest, for example admitting in serious, hushed tones that he had accepted bribes from motorists he had pulled over, then - after inserting a brief delay to ensure perfect comic timing - suddenly laughing at you uproariously saying "Sucker! Got you with that one!" and almost falling on the floor in hysterics, as of course Mickey would never have behaved in that kind of corrupt or illegal way. His personal motto, after all, as expressed on his Twitler bio, was "to stand for American principles and values". What a fine and funny character was Mickey Flout!

Mickey was fiercely devoted to the City of Washintown and its public institutions. Not long after joining the Chump team, he had experienced a medical emergency when he had choked on a large slab of Turkish delight containing a number of foreign bodies, which, following X-ray, turned out to be low-value Turkish lira coins which had somehow been incorporated into the sugary mix. Though Mickey swore until he was literally black and blue that he hadn't noticed any coins in his Turkish delight as he gulped it down, his desperate gasping and flailing in the corridor degenerated to such a point that an ambulance was called and he was rushed to hospital with sirens and lights blaring. Doctors at Washintown Emergency Department (E.D.) were forced to perform an emergency tracheotomy to remove the offending coins.

Once out of Recovery, Mickey, eternally grateful to the hospital staff who had saved his life, arranged for a beautifully-designed tattoo to be permanently inked onto his belly, proudly stating

I ♥ WASHINTOWN E.D.

Yet ignoring doctors' advice, when discharged from hospital Mickey soon reverted to his compulsive pattern of ongoing and incessant scoffing of Eastern delicacies. This resulted in him developing several new rolls of belly fat, so even just a few weeks post-operatively, the tattoo, now partly obscured by freshly-deposited blubber, unfortunately appeared to read:

I WAS OWNED

* * *

As you can see, with performers such as Mickey Flout at its core, the team being assembled was of such a caliber as to be 'off the charts' in the history of Washintown politics. In fact, Flout was quite the norm in being a role model for this administration. Chump had such faith in Mickey that he was known to refrain, by way of calling out for the succor of his trusty appointee: "When in doubt, Flout!" Indeed, there were a lot of Mikeys and Mickeys in this administration, and quite a few Dicks too (most notably, as we will see, Dicky Fences and Dick Pickles). Chump was indeed blessed, some might even say inoculated, by those who surrounded and enabled him, all of a similar kind of mold.

Consider this for luck: a willing Spinner would always mount the podium. The Connards had helped finance Chump's putsch for the leadership position. And of course, Chump could rely on Crohneys, for it was not just Mickey, but also his extended family, who had experience servicing a Moskvitch; an entire mob of Crohneys at his disposal.

Sure, funding the team's ambitious programs could at times be tricky, but one certainty held the administration in good stead:

There was always a Moneyport.

* * *

Paula Moneyport, a highly talented woman from an engineering family with a successful career as an intercity drainage specialist and sluice designer, whom Chump had demoted from a higher role to run his campaign after Ruineddogski was promoted out of the role - had spent years doing *pro bono* work on behalf of the underprivileged in Russia. There, working with the great philanthropist Lusa Yankyuinaditch and her loyal assistants, the punctilious bookkeeper Dicky Fences and personal assistant Konstantli Kriminiki, she had spent millions of her own hard-earned income to ensure the health and wellbeing of disadvantaged children, buying them toy cars, dolls' houses, rugs they sorely needed, furniture and life-saving medical equipment. True to her name, Paula was skilled at sloshing funds across international borders for the purposes of charity and selfless economic development.

So abundant were Paula's donations that she had been required to store them in a large storage locker before shipment to the underprivileged. She had even quietly donated $17 million buying a home for a single impoverished Russian, Dreg Oripackya, who had previously been living 'on the smell of an oily rag' by scrounging used aluminum cans in the streets and alleyways of his village for their meager scrap value. Never seeking accolades or attention, Paula worked away quietly in the background helping needy mendicants such as Dreg. It was hard to withhold praise for Paula - her generosity was as free-flowing as a Summerbreeze. This kind of unbelievable philanthropy was "standard kit" in Chump's exceptional team, which embraced no-hopers like Dreg and made them feel like "immediate family".

Paula was always charming, helpful and considerate to others, yet her altruistic exterior could be misleading, perhaps masking her own deeper inability for self-love and a Jungian quest for affirmation. For despite the intervention of her friends, Paula could not be persuaded to take care of her own wellbeing. So committed was she to her charity and fundraising work, that she exercised very little - often staying indoors for up to twenty-three hours a day - and chain-smoked cigars imported from Havana, living and working in a virtual cloud of smoke from this foreign vice as she sought to bring about the most beneficial policy and philanthropic outcomes.

Paula's devotion to her friends was exemplified by the selfless assistance she rendered in times of need. When Lusa Yankyuinaditch had put out a 'maidan (sic) in distress' call following an assault in her home town, Paula rushed to donate her own blood. Unfortunately, despite her good intentions, in her haste she incautiously dislodged the cannula, and had ended up with blood all over her hands.

She had perhaps been overly generous throughout her life, as these days Paula's clothes were worn and tatty, in a limited color palette: saffron, tangerine, peach, amber and rust; her home was a simple and humble abode, sparsely decorated, in the hamlet of Alexandra, just north of Washintown. She confined herself to a monastic diet consisting of staples such as cornbread, beans and gruel. Paradoxically, though a skilled charity networker, she had become something of a homebody in her private life, who couldn't bear the prospect of travel or any change in her living conditions. Yet her contribution to the reputation of the Chump administration would shine on for years to come.

* * *

Like Mickey Crohney, Paula ran very successful businesses alongside her drainage firm and related charities.

One of Paula's businesses was the successful U-Crane "lift and shift" towing and crane hire business, which offered a great service hauling in heavy loads and depositing them anywhere one liked. U-Crane could, for example, shift a large dining table into one's beach house, even through the back door if needed, or a heavy freight container full of banknotes to the 17th floor of a German bank's skyscraper. The enterprise had operated flawlessly for many years, on good margins, and remained a viable business with registered charity status and never an accident. Though Paula had stepped back significantly in her role, during the time she was involved it had been a healthy money-spinner for her, allowing her to expand her philanthropic ventures and supply furniture to the needy in Palm Beach Gardens.

The business had even achieved what many thought impossible: helping to lift an enormous lead weight - a dull effigy of Washintown's most wanted criminal - into an office with small oval windows in the dilapidated Washintown Museum in Pennsylvania Avenue. The lifeless orange-gray statue, covered in gaudy but worthless gold leaf, had to be jammed through sideways, damaging the architraves, but its successful installation was nonetheless a great achievement for Paula's business.

Paula's ever-helpful sister-in-law Jenny Yuhoo had helped Paulie get her U-Crane business off the ground by selling off her own cherished possessions, including her electric guitar, piano accordion and her tickets to Spamalot. The Bonds of love were indeed strong in the Moneyport family, and Paula's loved ones bore the Moneyport name with pride, just as an enlightened mosquito joyfully bears a dose of dengue fever.

Yet business for U-Crane had dried up somewhat, leaving Paula to scout for other humanitarian opportunities. She developed a plan to bring kindness and good cheer through karaoke to the inmates of her local correctional facility. She knew that she would really need to put her heart into it to achieve this altruistic goal, so worked hard over many months to achieve this dream in cooperation with the local authorities. Day-to-day running of the business would gradually be handed over to other skilled operatives while Paula planned out this inmate assistance program which would, she hoped, become her life's devotion in the long term.

In the meantime, Paula was also still hard at work in her day job, konstantly on the phone with her personal assistant Konstantli Kriminiki, who helped Paula with office paperwork, press releases, even her laundry and banking. In fact, Paula, somewhat addicted to both her cell phone and her laptop, could hardly be stopped from networking with her friends even from the most unlikely places, such as when she sojourned at her favorite country-club hangout or performed her charity karaoke sessions. In this regard, however, she was a great asset to the Chump administration while also being of value to Konstantli Kriminiki's many friends in overseas media organizations.

By sheer coincidence - or, as Ronnie might say "happy happenstance" - all these wonderful friendship networks had cross-pollinated and interwoven like a beautiful spider's web glistening in the morning dew. Viktor Punkin's building maintenance and plumbing company was in a helpful partnership with a similar enterprise, known as the Renovate Group, a charitable trust headed up by the dynamic Hektor Vexyaburgh, with a mission to provide low-cost housing to veteran widows. Hektor's cousin Andie Traiterin, who headed up CalamityBus Nogo, shared Hektor's charitable visions, and worked hand-in-glove with Hektor to provide microloans to developing countries, while also giving all the love, support, and funding they could muster for Mickey Crohney's fledgling businesses.

Mickey also loved to involve his family in sharing the many fruits of his businesses, so several of the Crohneys, even his mother-in-law, worked together on his altruistic enterprises.

Bunyon of course was not out of the charity loop. Together with fundraiser Becky Onceler, he worked on a cake stall to raise donations for a charity known as Oxford Rectalitchyca, a spin-off of Oxfam, which provided educational materials, medicaments and foods to illiterate and undernourished populations worldwide. Oxford Rectalitchyca funded a natural olive-oil-based hemorrhoid creme whose profits were channeled to assist small businesses in the third world, including a plumbing startup, FixyaLeaks, supplier of plumbing accessories. FixyaLeaks, in turn, provided parts and accessories to Viktor Punkin's Fix-it Services Business.

Mickey Crohney, driven by his strong social conscience, similarly funneled some of the profits from his motor repair shop back into these wonderful social enterprises. The circle of love was complete.

And Chump was like the spectacular orbweaver which held all these gossamer threads together.

* * *

Yet Chump would be nothing were it not for the love, support and protection of his family, his beloved klan, a highly organized, disciplined association, as tight-knit as a hyena pack.

Chump's marriage made complete sense to all who had contact with the couple: Ronnie Chump loved Melony with an unwavering devotion, and reciprocally, Melony held Ronnie in the highest esteem and would go to the ends of the Earth just to hold his hand.

The couple were inseparable and were often to be seen hugging publicly or staring deeply into each other's eyes. Whether in private or in official company, Ronnie would always look around for his wife, catch her eye with a warm smile and make sure she was included at all times. She would seize his hand with affection, pull him towards her and embrace him tenderly, like a teenage girl who has just been reunited with her boyfriend after an absence.

She always held such tender memories of when her youngest was just a newborn, and Ronnie with his hallmark thoughtfulness would dash off to a charity mini-golf event to allow her special time to bond with the baby while he donated his services to others.

When they danced, sparks flew, and the sensual heat generated by them being physically close to one another was palpable to all, and made one mindful of the saying "Get a room!".

After any prolonged absence for travel, Melony would scream out and rush to greet Ronnie at the first sight of him, literally pouncing onto him in delight, wrapping her arms and legs around him in the style of Natalie from Love Actually in the airport arrival scene, and smothering the surprised Chump in warm kisses. Melony felt that Chump filled her soul with hope. Chump, in return, thought of Melony as a shining wit.

* * *

Chump was intensely faithful to those close to him. His marriage to his previous wife, a Nigerian charity worker called Iwanga - who of course took the Chump name and would, within their first married year, give birth to their first child Iwanker - had only ended when Iwanga died suddenly while on a charity camping trip in Canada with newly-arrived refugees, after being struck by a tall maple tree, sadly eroded by termites.

Thankfully she had left Chump with her lasting legacy: their beautiful son Iwanker; although in fairness to the truth, beauty was not exactly on the side of Iwanker, for he grew up as a nervous and spotty youth with gappy teeth, oddly-proportioned features and a limp. Iwanker would remain media-shy and had a difficult relationship with his father, never wanting to feel the warm paternal touch.

As a teenager, Iwanker grew his frizzy hair into a quite a large bush partly obscuring his face in order to avoid the media scrutiny involved in being the mixed-race son of a much-loved town councilor. He clearly lacked confidence and social graces, and on those rare occasions when spotted in public, Iwanker would invariably be seen gnawing at his fingernails and displaying a nervous head-twitch. He was most often spotted, due to his intractable acne.

Yet keen to learn from his father, Iwanker followed, closely watched and eventually mimicked his father's masterful negotiations and policy-making. Iwanker gradually became a formidable policy wonk in his own right, to the extent that if in future he should ever decide to run for mayor, he would, like a congealed cake mix, indeed be very hard to beat.

Due to Iwanker's burgeoning reputation for precocious leadership skills and penetrating insights into complex societal issues, other visiting municipal leaders and leading dignitaries literally begged (on their knees, once the mischievous Chump got involved) for him to be allowed to insert himself into their intimate meetings and conversations. In this way, they could take pleasure and benefit from the flow of wisdom which now oozed liberally not only from the paternal Chump, but also - thanks to the strange fruit of his loins - from Iwanker too.

Although Iwanker had little business acumen and struggled financially, he had found his place in philanthropic fundraising, particularly via the Chump Foundation, and was known throughout Washintown as a quiet achiever for good causes. He had also taught himself how to use a sewing machine, and spent many hours at home stitching together outfits for refugees and other disadvantaged members of society, donating these handmade clothes to various charities.

Thankfully, in his early twenties, Iwanker had met Janey Kushynird who similarly hailed from a reputable family with high aspirations for the betterment of society. Although the pair looked intensely awkward together in public, their strong relationship and shared values in private made them a morally formidable couple who could take on any social challenge, local or far-flung, and defeat it: whether homelessness in the city, global poverty, world peace or corruption in the Middle East. Local council issues such as dog-on-leash bylaws were therefore almost too easy for this power couple, known affectionately throughout Washintown by the amalgam of their two names as 'Kushywanker'.

* * *

Chump himself had risen through the ranks of law and ethics, with years of specialty work in the areas of tax evasion and money laundering. His daughter-in-law Janey Kushynird had similarly excelled in human rights law with an exemplary career representing stateless immigrants, unjustly evicted tenement tenants and oppressed sweatshop workers. Chump's twin daughters Dinah and Erika and his son Iwanker had all worked in legal aid services for the local community, having based their public-spirited careers on the inspiring model of their father.

Indeed, Iwanker saw himself as an understudy to the great Chump, for despite his own spotty skin, gappy teeth, halitosis, and body odor, he knew deep in his bowels that a future may one day await him too as a remarkable mayor, just like his father, or at the very least one who could do much for the needy in society, such as spending long hours working amongst the prison population.

Also just like their great father, the Chump spawn and all those around them eschewed the shallow trappings of materialism. Even Chucky Kushynird, Janey's father and father-in-law to Iwanker, a lawyer working for the UN, had chosen his principles over his personal safety in pursuing the legal defense of displaced tribesmen in Uganda against a despotic government, and had spent several years in a Ugandan prison as a result.

Now Chump, with his principled and strong moral background, was finally on the cusp of evicting the nefarious Kabana from his high office.

Washintown City Council's strict regulations stipulated that a losing mayor needed to vacate City Hall within a short time of a final election result being announced on Moose TV. As a result, that very night, Chump had the pleasure of knocking on the great oaken doors of City Hall where Kabana was holed up with his mangy supporters. Kabana knew why. He skulked to the door.

Chump had rung ahead, requesting a mayoral handover session, complete with tea and snacks to be provided by the soon-departing former mayor, in which Kabana would show him around the mayor's quarters at City Hall. Kabana showed Chump which keys to the city to use, where to make coffee, and where the bulk supplies of toilet paper were stored.

The handover of course included a tour of the Square Office itself, including an explanation of the purpose of the bookshelves, the chairs and of the giant carved oak desk, famously known as the Irresolute Desk. Most importantly, Kabana went into great detail about the giant red button installed on the desk since the early 1960s, with a faded Dymo label spelling out a word starting with N. Chump read the word to himself, letter by letter. "I wonder what that's all about?" he asked his inner Chump. There was no reply. As Chump tried respelling the word in the recesses of his own brain, Kabana kept talking about how the button had been wired up by Jim from Washintown Electrics to link down to some kind of underground silo, somehow connected to the military. Kabana rambled on that the button was only to be used under special circumstances, for risk of annihilating civilization as we know it. Chump hadn't seen that all-caps N-word before, but he liked the ring of N-words. Yet in that moment he was even more distracted by the shiny pen next to the button, and thought to himself "I wonder if I get to keep that pen once he's left the office."

Kabana seemed to go on and on and on about the great importance of the red button. Despite the repetition, Chump later wondered whether Kabana had said "should not press it" ... or had he actually said "should press it"? Chump had been even further distracted by the entrance of a slim secretary bearing buns and other titbits, and as she bent over he had completely missed that part of the delicate briefs.

But regardless of these minor details, and with the hasty (and tasty, some would say nasty) transition out of the way, Kabana's time was up. This was no time for nostalgia. Chump ordered him to pack his bags, then showed him and his highly disreputable family to the door, and out onto the street. A cold wind blew, like a hurricane. Chump looked out the window after them. "A hard rain's gonna fall" he mused, noting the advancing stormclouds. Within minutes Kabana was already feeling a kind of subterranean homesick blues. But times were a-changin'. Though it was not dark yet, the Kabanas receded into the imminent night, and sought shelter from the storm.

"Can't wait," said Chump as he surveyed his new domain from behind the Irresolute Desk, his feet up on the desk.

* * *

The ducks were lined up. The dream team was in place.

There was Flout, devoted to sniffing out crime and dark money, and getting really stuck into it.

There was Moneyport, clearly an organizational and networking genius. Together with Roddy Pebble, these two were as formidable a pair as the testicles of a prize bull, whether or not said bull be destined for the knackery.

There was Mattress, with an inner spring in his step, who would come down on any opponents if he were put up against a wall. He believed Chump to have unlimited cognitive ability, and to be of the most noble and ethical character. Endlessly loyal, he couldn't stand the idea of ever leaving Chump. Chump, in return, of course felt he should reciprocate and would similarly stand by Mattress through thick or thin, like a kind of Mattress protector.

There was Crohney, keeping Chump's vehicle and his philanthropic ventures in impeccable shape, and keeper of all receipts.

There was Spinner, who would nail every press conference.

There was Nutberger, who had a real "gas" putting the wind up journalists with his strong, if artful, interviews which always left a lingering impression of the Chump administration.

And similarly, there was Odorosa Animalgut, a seasoned policy analyst and the first albino member of City Hall. Odorosa brought tremendous depth to the team and her great sense of fun and personal passions into the work environment. A budding recording artist in her spare time, she would weave her hobby into her day job, singing in the office at every opportunity and road-testing different types of recording equipment in meetings and as she wandered the corridors of City Hall, bristling with microphones, sound filters, graphic equalizers, Dictaphones, cables, cassette decks and even Edison-like wax cylinders.

This was an exceptionally strong team, like a firm, well-layered Black Forest cake, or Deutsche bank Schwarzwälder Kirschtorte (with a file baked into it), filled with dark cashew fondue. And on top of it all, like full-fat cream, were Bunyon and Ponce...

... and of course, like a chunky cherry on top, Chump.

2

CHUMP CHOWDER

The day after his election, Ronnie Chump entertained a group of supporters in the humble garage of his recently-purchased family home, nestled above a swampy lake.

Chump - renowned not only for his moral leadership but also for his sound money management - had recently acquired the new home, an exquisite residence at 2245 Mt View Place, Ganacostya, only a short walk from Washintown City Hall, using nothing but cash.

The property featured a beautiful historic house, painted white in color, which had been built by master craftsmen over two hundred and forty years ago. It boasted a spacious entrance hall and ample accommodation, fine oak paneling throughout, ornate chandeliers, a fully stocked library, a map room, several fireplaces, 35 bathrooms, even a grand staircase and a custom Steinway piano. So proud was he of his purchase, that Chump had a new front gate installed, featuring two large steel eagles gripping a stack of hay.

Regan Mordorc and his new wife Jagli Hills came to pay a visit to the new mayor, along with a few close fiends and some reporters Chump had invited from the Washintown Handbasin, a local plumbing trade journal. That afternoon I had spotted Chump in his driveway, nailing up a homemade wooden sign over his garden archway to guide his guests around to the party in the garage. Showcasing Chump's Dantesque poetic skills, it read:

"THROUGH HERE TO A WORLD OF FUN,
THROUGH HERE TO LASTING GOOD TIMES,
THROUGH HERE IF YOU'RE LOST, PEOPLE.
LEAVE BEHIND ALL YOUR WORRIES, YE WHO ENTER."

Guests began arriving in dribs and drabs. They were brimming with enthusiasm, evidenced by the large Duchenne smiles pasted on their faces as they dragged their tired bodies up the driveway.

That evening, as the party got underway, there too in the shadows was I, your dear Martha, intrepid reporter, positioned just outside on the sidewalk, straining my ears to hear the goings-on behind the garage door. The Moskvitch was parked outside, quietly dripping oil which trickled peacefully into the stormwater drain. A fox skulked by in the cool night air.

Mordorc, resembling Squidward Q. Tentacles but with a wig, worked as a producer at the local FM station, Moose FM, producing quality content for broadcast to the Washintown community. Like Chump, he was a man of strong ethics and a lush head of glued-on hair. He was also a person whose respect for Chump knew no bounds, as they both envisaged a world where wealth and prosperity would be shared fairly among all people.

Mordorc, who, with his previous rather Windy wife, had often shared gassy ales with Janey and Iwanker, had always showered Chump with care and attention, seeing him as a kindred soul.

Melony had organized a wonderful housewarming party, including a delicious spread, as she was wont to do, and for which she was well known in several magazines. The table was set with a delightful assortment of nibbles, including vinegar in cups, Marmite, croutons, unshelled Brazil nuts, whole raw coconuts, lychees (unshelled), sandwiches, more unshelled brazil nuts, tripe, black pudding, fried fruit bats, spam and hamberders.

Chump had promised Melony he would bake some pies, but had run out of time and only managed to churn out a few before guests started arriving.

The sandwiches alone covered an impressive variety of tastes: there was egg and bacon; egg, sausage and bacon; egg and spam; egg, bacon and spam; egg, bacon, sausage and spam; spam, bacon, sausage and spam; spam, egg, spam, spam, bacon and spam; spam, spam, spam and spam; and spam, bacon and lobster. As usual, Chump also served up his own pork pies. Copious quantities of Chump Chowder graced the tables in large plastic buckets for the visitors and media. A fly landed on the bar. I guess you could call it a barfly.

The guests mingled happily. The bar was buzzing. Johnny Notlob was spotted at the bar, ordering himself a glass of punch somewhat fussily: "No lemon, no melon" he requested. Mickey Flout was already down at the dessert table, tucking into the sweetbreads. Paula Moneyport drifted around on the other side of the garage, looking to make connections and new contacts whom she could later introduce to Konstantli Kriminiki.

Chump's culinary expertise with Chump Chowder was on full display that night. Chump had skillfully aged fish heads in a deep bucket with vegie offcuts and wilted greens, old enough to add a strong gamey flavor but young enough to just precede the rotting process. Chump had totally mastered this signature gloopy watered goulash, garnished with a floating fish head, as his kids would say in the parlance of the younger generation, "You totally killed it, Dad!"

Over the years, Chump Chowder had been instrumental in cracking some incredibly artful deals with otherwise reluctant parties, so it featured as a central dish on the menu at Chump social events such as these. There was something about its unique glugginess that seemed to attract a certain type of discerning scoffer or quaffer to the powerful substance. It would be served to an unsuspecting business partner, lobbyist or pollster, and within a short time they would be under its influence, helping Chump achieve his goals for the betterment of society and for the remarkable Chump Foundation, just before they needed to rush off to use the conveniences.

* * *

It was at this garage gathering, surrounded by removalists' boxes yet to be unpacked, that Chump first had the courage to enunciate his bold plans for Washintown that, as a young councilor, he had nurtured for years but had never previously felt were within his well-practiced grasp. Now, buoyed with a renewed confidence and several cups of the fermenting punch, Chump stood up on a milk crate at the back of the garage and took dear Melony's hand firmly, resisting her well-trained, secretive erotic flick-away action which usually drove him wild with passion. Melony stood there next to him on a slightly lower pile of old telephone books, a little deflated at the rejection of her clandestine advance. Chump tinkled a glass to gain the crowd's attention. He went on to thank his guests, and to raise a toast, then a crumpet. But most dramatically of all, as a gradually speeding-up Bouzouki played from his rear, he proceeded to spell out his vision for great and ambitious changes to the administration, services and public amenities of Greater Washintown.

"Dear friends", Chump orated. "Since boyhood I have fostered a dream for the city of Washintown, a dream of uniting our people via a municipal government supporting the citizens' needs. For many years prior to this election, I had dreamed of a project to unify the city's IT systems and infrastructure, and I had conceived a project, held close to my heart, known as but a hope, a mere wish, to myself and a few of my closest confidants, as the "Secure Hub IT Project". Its aim would be to centralize Washintown's IT for the benefit of all. I cradled this dream, and held it dear to my heart, never guessing that one day I might have the chance to bring it to reality. Now, having humbly won the election, an even broader vision has come to me, as if gifted from the heavens, as though I am the chosen one to deliver it for you."

"To you, my dearest friends, I would hereby like to announce an expanded version of my long-nurtured project, one which not only encompasses IT Services but which includes a holistic renewal on a much more ambitious scale."

The crowd stood, mouths agape. A pin could have been heard to drop, had someone dropped a pin. Luckily this didn't occur, as the garage floor was covered in balloons.

"As I stand here tonight, I commit to you all that I will launch an even bigger, brighter project than this city has ever seen. Friends, I hereby announce that I will seek to establish a truly ambitious project, to be known hereafter as the "Secure Hub Infrastructure Transformation Project", a project which will renew not only Washintown's IT services but also all our water, electricity, and data services. Yes, I know that's quite a mouthful, so we'll still just call it the S.H. IT Project for short."

The audience collectively issued an audible gasp.

"I will engage the brightest and best. Yes, only the best people, very fine people. I will hire teams of consultants and project managers. Many chiefs and a few Indians. I am not a racist. I will roll up my own sleeves, and even get into the thick of it myself. I will ensure that we renew and replace everything which holds our society together: the plumbing; the internal cabling of our beloved City Hall; the gas lines, the water pipes, the internet cables. We will plug up Barry Kabana's old sanitation system with cement, shut it down, and put in new PVC piping, eventually - Chump-grade. It will be awesome. You're gonna love it!"

"In addition," Chump went on, "I will be seeking to provide new state-of-the-art equipment to our emergency services personnel: protective clothing and other accessories like never seen before. The police department will also get a new bell."

* * *

The onlookers nearly fainted from the sheer genius, the audacity of hope, and the underpinning humanity, of Chump's grandiose promise. As a matter of fact, two of the more elderly members of the gathering needed to be escorted to couches in the drawing room to overcome the shock of the announcement, so stunning was the plan.

Unfortunately, these audience members missed the key policy announcement, the crème de la crème, the master-stroke which only a man like Chump could have conceived. For following his first momentous revelation, and taking a big breath before the final reveal, Chump went on to announce...

...wait for it...

... that as part of the project he would contract out the construction of a large central CUPBOARD in the basement of City Hall which would house the centralized services, all with a single lock and key, to centralize security.

Utter genius.

The centralized CUPBOARD - which would span the entire length of the City Hall's basement chamber, and would be called "Peaches" - would make control and maintenance far easier than it had ever been in the history of Washintown. He had even commissioned some early designs of the giant cupboard, featuring slatted air-vents, or vented slats, whatever you'd like to call them, which were wide enough to allow cooling of pipes and cables, while being narrow enough to prevent any invasion from vermin. It would be really important to keep pests out of Washintown's infrastructure hub, and the clever design of the cupboard, drafted by Chump himself, would achieve this. The new 'turnkey' cupboard would also house the special server, known as the Domain Name Controller (DNC) which would route electronic traffic all over the city.

Chump finished by thanking his guests and apologizing for the lack of pies, which had been noticed by some of the local journalists.

Chump's revelation at the party was a bombshell within the Washintown society, and having Melony at his side made it a double banger.

* * *

He stepped down from the milk crate to rapturous applause from his audience. Quite humbled by the response, he then slunk back into the crowd with his typical humility, seeking no glory, just anonymity. But his guests would have none of that, and milled around him like ants to a beaver carcass, eager to hear more details of his expanded dream project.

Finally Chump was able to blend back into the crowd. He circulated, chatting to his admirers, left, right and center.

* * *

Chump liked to say that one of the things that made life worth living was getting your friends' wives into public office, via affirmative action. Chump would engage in what was, for him, more or less constant mentoring and political banter. "Do you still believe that you are a candidate any less qualified than your male counterpart? Do you realize how talented and unique you are, and what beautiful eyes you have? Do you realize how society needs to hear your voice? Tell me about it. I have friends from Emily's List coming in from Los Angeles at three o'clock. We can go upstairs and discuss pre-selection options. I promise..." And all the while, Chump of course would maintain complete confidentiality, to ensure that his friend's wife felt safe and supported, both metaphorically and literally. They always left feeling that he had had a firm grasp of their most intimate issues.

That night, he did indeed go upstairs with several of his friend's wives, who were surprised by his chutzpah, his manhood and his unconventional mentoring techniques, giving them each a private and confidential session.

Chump had mastery of virtually any topic one could think of. Further to this, his deep knowledge on diverse subjects across all major disciplines was matched only by his personal poise and equanimity, his measured tone and his calm, respectful delivery. What a guy. Here indeed was a highly sought-after individual, a wanted man.

* * *

Chump had not long stepped down from the milk crate when the sound of a motorcycle was heard pulling up in the driveway of the new home, in front of the garage. Chump excused himself for a moment to investigate. A FedEx courier in a motorcycle helmet shoved a digital signature device at him and asked him to sign for the receipt of a package, which the delivery man then shoved into his hands. It was marked "From sender: Viktor Punkin" with a declaration slip listing "Two personal assistant. Two chocolate blok."

Chump was thrilled to receive the package and believed that Punkin must again be seeking to put aside their old grievance and was reaching out to make amends for their past altercation.

He put the package aside and went back into the party, looking forward to opening it later in the evening. From the cover of the packaging, it appeared to be a sort of electrical device, equipped with some kind of button.

When his guests had left and he was having some romantic downtime with Melony, Chump looked for the package. By then, the party had gone on for several hours, and there was, during that time, rumors of things going astray. There had been a great confusion as to where things really were. And nobody really knew where the package had been laid down. Chump scoured Melony's drawers, and, with her help, eventually located the mystery contraption with the button. He opened it with relish, and a handful of crackers. He was so caught up with the excitement of unboxing a gift from Punkin that he didn't even notice when a number of small black critters dropped from inside the package and climbed up the inside of his trouser leg.

There, inside the box, he was delighted to find a Special Edition boxed pair of a Russian-made version of the Amazon Echo, gleaming and glistening seductively. Each came with a custom-made wooden trim and with a sort of raffia-work base with an attachment, labeled 'made in Crimea' (though the 'a' had been slightly rubbed off in transit). There were also some dark Kis-Kis chocolate bars, a kind of Russian Bounty bar with a chewy center that encourages hard sucking, which he and Melony shared romantically in that special quiet moment as the gift lay exposed.

Chump was truly touched, as Melony had been before him, by Punkin's conciliatory gesture.

With great pride in the new gift, Chump installed one of the Echos, on its charming Crimean hand-made base, in the middle of his kitchen table. Melony peeled off the small label and playfully stuck in on his forehead. "Zere you go sveetie, now you is like King of Crimea".

They powered up the device, which came with inbuilt personal assistant technology called Alexei, and the two of them had fun late into the night asking it questions ranging from simple culinary tips right through to questions of social welfare, moral philosophy and advanced Buddhist Ethics.

Later that week, Chump asked Keith Schifter to arrange to have the other installed on the conference table in the chambers at City Hall.

The Alexei-powered Echos came with a handy "Synk" button which he duly pressed, allowing a range of synchronized bi-directional operations between the two devices, linking up their functions between Chump's new house and City Hall. He could listen to council proceedings while still at home, issue directives to his staff from home, or automatically order the porch light at home to be turned on from the council meeting room at City Hall.

Chump was thrilled to use the new technology, and could often be heard asking the device for guidance with his decision-making. In return, it performed with surprising effectiveness, helping with virtually everything from finding out the weather to formulating important policy and legislation, though it did display the odd glitch, occasionally blurting out a Russian phrase, such as "Алексей, Я не могу его правильно слышать" ("Alexei, I can't hear him properly.") or Идиот, ты выключил кнопку отключения звука! ("Idiot, you have taken us off Mute!")

* * *

Recruitment and candidate selection of staffers was going ahead at a cracking pace. Chump's friend Tommy Brick, who had a history of suggesting the very best people like Paula Moneyport, was excelling even his own high standards, nominating high performers such as Betty DeVious, Reg Fillexson and Scotty Proveit. The primordial, embryonic structure of a cohesive team was beginning to come together, like cement mix on a Chicago building site.

Within weeks, Chump was making considerable use of the Russian Amazon Echoes, due to his busy legislative schedule. By pressing various control buttons and invoking the right name, he enjoyed the power of using the impressive automation to initiate activities either at home, at work, or, when using the 'Synk' function, in both places at once. He became so familiar with the personal assistants that he had named each one after one of his favorite TV characters: "Natasha" for the home-based Echo and "Boris" for the City Hall-based one. He was so glad that someone in the Eastern Bloc was clearly as clever as his great friend Geoff Bezeus, the chief technician at his favorite US company.

The devices were proving to be a real godsend, and he felt grateful indeed for the kindness and conciliatory nature of Mr Viktor Punkin's gesture in having gifted them to him. In Ronnie's no-nonsense, straight-talking parlance, he referred to Punkin's kind gift as "a thing of value" as he held his heart with gratitude.

* * *

It was during these early days that the team also canvassed the hiring of General J.F.K. "Kitty" Malaise, one of the first female army generals. Bunyon in particular thought that having General Malaise on the team would encourage all to do their best. General Kitty was known for bringing a playful, youthful, fun-loving attitude to her work, and would mesh in well with Chump's lively policy agenda.

Chump was full of questions about what getting Punkin's crew working for them again could mean, if he chose to allow that. He even asked the Russian Amazon Echos, which reassured him by replying "Is alright."

Hobbies were an important form of stress relief and team morale-building for the busy Chump, who expertly wove these in to the work environment. These days Chump was keen to promote his passion for bootscooting in the office, and would often interrupt a meeting to get all his staff to line up, hands on hips and join in a bootscooting session to the tune of "Boot Scootin' Boogie", or "Achy Breaky Heart" (which he hummed for them, having dedicated to Melony). Despite the occasional eye-roll from one or two recalcitrant staffers, as one might see on 'The Office', there is no doubt that these sessions were a great boost to the team's attitude and physical fitness.

The initial hirings proceeded and the new communications office grew to include the former animal shelter worker Sally Muckabee Blathers.   Sally took an active role in the team's morale-building bootscooting strategy. Chump and Spinner trained her assiduously, and she quickly got up to speed with complex footwork. While giving press briefings up on the dais, Sally would often - unbeknownst to the media, and seen only from behind by fellow staffers - perform intricate bootscooting maneuvers, only from the waist down, under the podium, all the while presenting a straight face to the media. Her footwork became increasingly dexterous as she gained more experience in the job as Chump's spokesman, and she enjoyed the bootscooting to such an extent that she ramped up the frequency of her briefings, just to be able to cram more fun and exercise into the work week. She quickly learned how to independently move upper-body parts, while beneath the podium her legs were learning to fly around like Brer Rabbit's.

In a way this reminded me of some family folklore of my own. In the Skewermann family, following a tradition started, I believe, by Grandpa Skewermann, we had often joked that the family dog, Scooter, was "scooting his boot" when he (Scooter that is, not Grandpa Skewermann) dragged his butt along the carpet due to having itchy anal glands. Grandpa, by contrast, had always dragged his along the side of the kitchen bench due to itchy hemorrhoids.

Sally Muckabee Blathers of course exercised a much higher form of bootscooting than Scooter's, ultimately perfecting her fancy footwork while keeping the upper body totally still, and the face straight, in the manner of a soulless zombie, a skill which took months of practice to develop. Sally was indeed blessed to have had this one-on-one tuition out of hours from her dedicated master, Ronnie Chump himself, who had taken the time - above and beyond his mayoral duties, mace-bearing and what-not - to train Sally in correct bootscooting technique from her Day One on the team. Shawn Spinner had then further assisted her in perfecting her technique. The rewards of this double-banger tuition were that Sally's entire upper torso and facial muscles could remain completely still during a press conference while her legs and lower body were involved in wild gyrations beneath the lectern at a rate which no other living human would have survived.

Oddly enough though, when her press conferences were over, an odor hung in the room similar to the one our dear Scooter used to leave on the Skewermann family carpet.

* * *

As amazing as Sally's bootscooting was, she was not to know that in the months ahead, as the team became more diverse with the hiring of Micky Mullvenality, an even more brazen bootscooting approach would be taken in press conferences. For Mickey's strategy would be to bootscoot not only with his flailing legs on full display, but additionally with exploding strips of firecrackers strapped to them, ensuring that the press was fully alert to his message.

* * *

Around City Hall, Chump dabbled in amateur magic which was both enjoyable for the team, and energizing for their busy boss. He could make a coin, or even a lot of coins, disappear inside a handkerchief (sadly all too often forgetting that he had already blown his nose into it). Likewise, he could wave a dubiously-clean handkerchief over an Excel spreadsheet of campaign donations and have all the numbers suddenly disappear (probably using a combination of Excel macros and deft sleight-of-hand). These acts caused gasps of amazement among the delighted staffers who all wished to learn how to do the trick, and lined up to copy Ronnie in the hope this might bring them, too, a touch of his indelible magic.

Chump also scheduled a significant period of "executive time" to be blocked out each day for him to help elderly members of the community with gardening.

When free time allowed and Chump was not bootscooting, his other main passion - other than having fun with his magic thimble-and-balls tricks or putting in time for his community - was the challenging game of mini-golf - "putting" in a different sense of the word. During intermissions in council meetings, Chump would call up the mayoral limousine and together with a coterie of bodyguards would head out to the local amusement park to monopolize the mini-golf course. If any of the local kids were already playing, he was forced to pull rank and send the kiddies away, owing to an obscure mayoral precedence clause he had had added into council by-laws. Keith Schifter would act as his caddie and offer Ronnie encouragement at every hole through his dark sunglasses. Occasionally when Ronnie missed a hole, Keith, always with his heart in the right place when it came to his boss, would look around furtively, then subtly kick the mini-golf ball into the hole, and exclaim "Oh look Ronnie, you got it in! What a champion you are!" Ronnie would beam like a little kid who had just scoffed an entire bag of someone else's candies, and they would move on to the next hole.

Ronnie loved moving on to a new hole.

As his legislative schedule became busier, Chump found he had to evict groups of children from the mini-golf course more often, to allow him time to play through before the bell rang again for voting in City Hall. The evicted children, patient and respectful, then had to wait in a caged-off area behind reception until Chump and his entourage had played through. Though regrettable, this was, he felt, supported by the bible, where in a letter to the Corinthians, Matthew makes reference for the need to "suffer the little children, and forbid them" which Chump believed was surely was a reference to allowing space for his unencumbered round of mini-golf to proceed, by the grace of God.

Chump's favorite hole (other than the par-for-the-course training hole he shared with Sylvie Clittafford one day while Melony was busy buying Bruno a booby prize up at the front counter) was one which required hitting the golf ball through a plastic drainage pipe before it emerged unexpectedly near the putting green. He found that this one - due to the mystery disappearance and sudden reappearance of the ball - filled him with suspense and made him literally squeal with excitement like a five-year old. It seemed to focus his decision-making skills, for he always returned to his office with much more clarity and determination having played that challenging par four.

* * *

Chump's inevitable rise could be traced back to his indefatigable appetite for battle, and his propensity to pull out heroism when no-one around him could find it. He was an undisputed hero, a veteran of many battles.

He had battled school bullies who, threatened by his intelligence, had called him "Lumpy Chumpy" back in his school days.

He had battled the fact that, even though his father had left him near-penniless, he bore a huge responsibility to help others gain financial independence, navigating complex and demanding tax laws, probity and fiduciary requirements.

He had battled migraines throughout his teenage years and young adulthood, as his huge, possibly unbounded intelligence struggled to contain itself within the confines of the meager organ which had sprouted atop his shoulders.

Not only was he a hero in all of the above aspects of his personal life, he was an actual war hero too. No kidding.

He had battled the military establishment itself, starting with a war enrollment officer who had sought to exclude him from active duty due to his bilateral ingrown toenails. Ronnie had taken this battle to the chief army officer for the district. He had then battled the enlistment hierarchy by writing a stern letter insisting that he should be eligible to serve. He had even battled to unscrew the lid of the pen. A sense of being embattled was in his every move.

When finally written, the letter was so admirable and convincing, and finished with such an impressive signature, that it moved a senior Army official to step in on Ronnie's behalf and allow him to serve, as the officials finally concurred that it would, in fact, be a good idea to send him off to the front line.

It was thus - after an epic journey which started all the way back in his schooldays - that Ronnie finally prevailed in his battle against the military bureaucracy, and joined the 40th Infantry Division, known among the troops as the "Flaming Assholes".

Sadly for Ronnie, the Division's nickname would, ironically, bear unusual and long-lasting significance for him. During a mopping up operation at Mỹ Cao Dong, Chump, together with a brave friend Robin, had braved the stony, bony spur of a mountain ridge as the enemy lay in wait, and his deplorable platoon pals quivered in bushes behind him. Shots rang out, and as Robin's blood-curdling cry of "Run away!" echoed down the hillside, Chump scampered away bravely from the enemy fire, heading for the nearest bush. Luckily Chump was skilled at finding bush, as he had trained himself for years at that skill.

Chump's war diary detailed the level of heroism involved. In Chump's own words: "As a result of this supreme act of self-preservation, I received a Purple Heart. Yes, though hard to Beleive, I had exurted myself so much as to Cause some deprivation of Oxygen to MY Heart Muscle, causing MY Heart to go Slightly Purple until I could regain my Breath. As well as the Purple Heart I also received Red Cheeks, Shortness of Breath and one Sweaty Armpit. War is hell."

This stirring document is preserved in the Washintown Civic Memorial Hall, under bulletproof glass.

More importantly however, during the hasty retreat, a piece of shrapnel had glanced through Ronnie's rear end, impacting with the target of his oversized butt, and lacerating his gluteus maximus before nicking the small nerve controlling his anal sphincter. Unfortunately, this wound, though quite small, would leave Chump trailing around a mild stench for many years to come. This was due to the damaged parasympathetic nerve in the inferior hypogastric plexus of his rear end, resulting in ongoing small leaks, noises and inappropriate emissions in public. This heroism-induced injury had left Chump needing to change his underwear and adult incontinence pads several times a day at work, even - and in fact particularly - during legislative sittings. Doctors had sought to remove the shrapnel via a high-pressure enema, however Ronnie had steadfastly dodged this particular treatment, refusing to give his consent, based on an idiosyncratic protest he raised about "wildlife habitat destruction". When military histories are written, Ronnie will forever be remembered for his brave escape from the enema.

In later years, Chump had admitted in a candid interview: "Mỹ Cao Dong was very humbling. It taught me that it's not as easy being a real man as you might think."

"Indeed, mỹ Cao Dong has been a real burden, and for Melony too," he added, adjusting his trousers.

* * *

Chump now had brought much of this intense air of bravery and strategic expertise from his decorated military career to his management style: demanding loyalty to the truth, establishing strict chains of command, passing responsibility up the line, hatching escape plans, formulating systems of accountability as needed, and hiring armies of experts to wage his war, on behalf of us all, with his sights firmly set on corruption, iniquity, discrimination and entrenched privilege - all while attempting to stem nasty leaks.

* * *

With their noses proudly in the air, and strong winds of change now blowing through the corridors of City Hall, Chump's rusted-on retinue of followers and new staffers - like Chump before them - sought to remove the administrative stench which preceded them.

3

NIGHT LOST

Previous mayor Barry Kabana had been a total nutjob - constantly tweeting, spontaneously ringing up radio stations with inflammatory rhetoric, and tossing ill-considered policies into the public sphere. The community had expressed a collective sigh of relief when Chump had been elected and Kabana had finally been "shown the door" politically. Kabana had been voted the least admired man in Washintown for eleven years in a row.

Kabana was also a socially disconcerting individual: irrational, dressing shabbily and uninhibited, launching into unexpected hugs and giving inappropriate gestures and handshakes. Furthermore, he was a wicked prankster, having once tricked the ingenuous Chump into connecting polygraph wires to his own private parts, claiming that it would give an accurate measure of Chump's "political virulence". In fact, the resulting flatline (which occurred only after - mortifyingly - Ronnie had had much trouble fiddling around trying to find the relevant appendage onto which to attach the electrodes) caused Ronnie a considerable degree of personal embarrassment and shame, while Kabana had meanwhile literally laughed himself off his chair in hysterics.

To add insult to injury, the crocodile clips had left a series of lingering circular red marks and a toad-like swelling on a part of Ronnie's anatomy which he had otherwise kept in tippy-top shape.

Kabana had been known for years for his self-aggrandizing ways, ensuring his name was dropped into speeches and plastered on billboards.

Chump, on the other hand, took an understated approach to public life, rarely seeking praise or to have his name attached to good deeds or buildings.

Yet barely a moment went by when he did not have his eye out for a person or an animal less fortunate than himself.

At his weekend game-hunting retreat at Murky-Lako, where he pursued his animal passions for nature photography, wildlife and bird-watching, Chump was constantly seeking out furry beavers, vixens or birds such as little wrens and tits, creatures he cherished and hoped to help procreate, even in the face of the rampant denuding of the bush he had seen on Bushy Bill's Bus.

On several occasions while campaigning, Chump would insist that his council chauffeur pull over to assist an injured or stray animal. Despite a rare genetic mutation which resulted in his skin having the color of an Oompahloompah, Chump's humanity was written on his face as he was visibly pained by the suffering or hardship of any person or creature he saw wandering the streets without a home.

In one notable instance on a night-time drive through the coincidentally-named outlying suburb of Petworthy, Chump, suddenly spurting out a mouthful of Tic Tacs he had been chewing, urgently requested that his driver stop the vehicle to assist a small kitten wandering alone in the dark by a busy highway and about to be flattened by a large Greyhound bus.

Chump grabbed the pussy and held it close to his body for fear it should run away; he could not conceive of anything worse than a runaway pussy. The kitten seemed to feel it could do whatever it wanted, knowing little of the risk to its well-being. Having retrieved the pussy, Chump got back in the council limousine clutching the tiny animal and signaled to his driver to take him directly home so he could provide a place of refuge for the frightened feline.

The well-meaning Chump was mortified to find in coming days that a local model had gone to the press alleging that the kitten was in fact her beloved pet, accusing the mayor of having grabbed her pussy without first having made enquiries as to its ownership. The cat, meanwhile, in a manner reminiscent of the classic tale 'The King, The Mice and The Cheese', was already enjoying a life of luxury at Chump's new residence, as the inveterate animal-lover had set it up with its own toys, play-pen and penthouse pethouse. The hungry pussy was helping itself to his pantry at all hours. Little did he know that the cat he had so kindly saved threatened to ruin him.

Ronnie, being the 'softy' he was, had even made a special trip out to buy it its own scratching pole. The kitten hardly reciprocated the favor by getting into Chump's study where many of his work papers lay about, defecating on his CV and tearing up documents including a legislative Non-Disclosure Agreement. What a silly and ungrateful kitty!

This incident was mockingly reported in the media as "Pussygate" and stood to dog Chump for years, as he insisted that, in rescuing the animal that night, he had intervened in what had amounted to negligent treatment of the pet. He therefore sought to assert his strong love for the pussy through a protracted legal battle for the custody of the kitten. On the other side of the legal argument, the case was prosecuted that Chump had abused both his mayoral position and rules regarding the use of council vehicles to abscond with the furry pet without the consent of its owner. As we go to press, this is a legal question still in process. The cat meanwhile has grown into quite a fearsome adult beast and now occupies a significant wing in Chump's new home in Ganacostya.

Ronnie's reputation as a caring individual who would provide shelter for people or animals in need quickly became legendary throughout the city.

Local kids whose parents had refused to accept their pet snakes or rats in their homes would bring the creatures around to the Chump residence, and Chump would gently take the forsaken pets in his huge, altruistic hands and place them in his purpose-built animal shelter room.

When a particularly savage storm blew through Washintown in mid-2018, leaving several houses unroofed, Ronnie had been approached to take on a number of pythons, terrapins, domestic chickens, rabbits, rats and other rodents for families who could no longer house them. Not once did Ronnie complain or act as though there was a limit to his hospitality, he just gave a hearty laugh and said "Sure, bring them in - we can make a home for all creatures great and small!"

Similarly, stateless out-of-towners could show up at the Chump residence in the wee hours, without notice, and within moments of knocking on the door, having explained their difficult predicaments, would be met with a hearty welcome: the comforting Chump chuckle, a powerful handshake, a warm cup of Chump Chowder and a bed and potty for the night.

With the latest addition of the young rescue-cat to the Chump household, Chump was acquiring quite a menagerie of rescue animals at his home shelter, including dogs, a few pet rats, several snakes and even a couple of toads. Neighboring farmer Dobbin Moonez offered to drop by to regularly feed the rats and snakes with whatever food scraps he could gather. Chump's other neighbors at times joked that his home was itself starting to resemble something like a swamp, owing to the cacophony which emerged from it and wafted, like a miasma, across Washintown.

Yet Ronnie considered all these beasts his friends and colleagues.

* * *

Chump was so busy developing policy for his social programs that he decided to designate Janey Kushynird as his spokeswoman and intermediary with the press. Despite Janey's slightly scruffy hair and often smeared makeup, she had a genuineness and authenticity in her nature which was refreshing and disarming.

Several of her father-in-law's confidants had confided to Janey that they believed Chump was overworked, so Janey's new role seemed to alleviate some of the pressure on Chump.

Kushynird introduced herself to the team: "Hi! I'm Janey Kushynird. I'm here to help, just starting as a volunteer."

"Did you say Lenny Kuchma?" one of the staffers replied, struggling to catch the name.

"No, it's Janey, not Lenny. Janey with a J, like JAIL. Janey Kushynird."

"Apologies, Ms Kuchma." By now Janey was getting frustrated.

"No, the surname's Kushynird! I'm a Kushynird, do you hear? It's Kushynird! Kushy-nird! I'm a Kushy-nird! I'm not a Kuchma. They're a totally different family, ok?"

"Whew, that's lucky, for a moment I thought you were a corrupt foreign-dealing kakocrat! You had me worried there for a minute, Janey. Welcome aboard, Janey Krunchynird."

* * *

In her advisory capacity, Janey recommended to Chump that he make a visit to the city's penitentiary to address the prison population on the first day of his mayoral term. Chump thought this was an excellent idea as it addressed two of his highest values at once: an utter abhorrence for the life of crime, and a strong commitment to bettering the lives of all members of society, even hardened criminals, of which he knew a few.

Chump fully backed Janey's suggestion, being a great supporter of the incarcerated, but reminded Janey that following his huge electoral success, this would now have to wait until after his inauguration.

"Let's get the inauguration out of the way first, Janey" said Chump, casually scratching his armpit, "though I'm really itching to spend time with the prisoners."

For indeed Chump's inauguration was looming at an ungodly rate. Excitement in Washintown could barely be suppressed.

Such was the demand for tickets that C-grade actors were even seen trading tickets in broad daylight to ensure their spot at the town's biggest event since Washintown's Monster Truck Show a few months back. Billy Bob McGraw, virtual royalty in Washintown due to his delectable jelly rolls at the Washintown Diner, and Sam Boner who runs the Washintown Central Car Wash on Main St, were seen engaging in actual fisticuffs on Pennsylvania Avenue, or so it was reported to me by several slightly inebriated eyewitnesses.

Ethel May Phillips of West Washintown ran the Chump Inaugural Fundraising Committee, and, through the sale of baked goods and conserves, was able to raise a whopping $107, more than had ever been raised before in the history of Washintown.

* * *

The great day finally arrived and, as history will record, Chump would go on to love every moment of his inauguration.

Chump had hoped for a subdued affair, but Washintown turned out in full force. Margery Jones, ninety-two, who lives on Main St, festooned her fence with some balloons and ribbons.

Chump stayed overnight at Blain House, across the road from City Hall. He woke in a cheerful mood, whistling and hugging all those who passed, praising and complimenting everyone. His truly lovable spirit was shining through. He felt invigorated by the establishment's fresh cold water, strong showers and comfortable beds. There was nothing that didn't evoke joy and enthusiasm from Chump, so energized and optimistic was the mayor-elect. Even the chilly Blain House water gave him a spring in his step (and, oddly, a small itchy lump on his foot), only matched by the excited Bunyon who was skipping gleefully through the corridors of the rooming house in bare feet, like a toddler. Bunyon was ever-present (at times, truth be told, even a bit of a pain), never far from the 'Big Guy'.

Melony too was in fine spirits, her eyes twinkling and her walk bouncy. She was seen in small gatherings of the staff, laughing with the joy of this special day. Her teeth remained ungritted all day. Chump would pull her away gently and speak to her softly and intimately. She willingly acquiesced, in a most sensual way.

Kylie-Jo Connard had taken to helping Melony choose an outfit for the ceremony, selecting a puce Dior jacket featuring embroidered white Greek pillars, representing Melony's unwavering support for her husband, underneath which she sported a flapping pussybow blouse in salmon pink. This was topped with a broad vermilion sombrero-style hat from the celebrated Scottish milliner Phillip Treacly, featuring - in a world first - an actual miniaturized fountain with running water atop the hat, requiring a small pump to be secreted just above Melony's left ear, and a complex filtration and chlorination system.

This haute couture artwork symbolized Ronnie's all-encompassing and protective personality, bathed by his bubbly, refreshing nature. The unique visual statement was capped off, in a dashing éclat of fashion panache, with Australian-style bobbing corks on strings around the rim of the hat. These served not only to evoke a rustic insouciance, but also captured the essence of Ronnie's 'no flies on me' honesty and ensured that no gnats or other buzzing insects would ruin Melony's photo opportunities. Although the variegated RED HAT did obscure her eyesight, in this pretty get-up Melony presented as an inspiration to all young women in society, and to budding fish tank technicians. She indeed looked like a real Chump, and not at all like an impersonator flown in from overseas on a dubious visa, which of course would have been outrageous.

Topping off Melony's fashion statement was graffiti which she herself had excitedly sprayed onto the back of her dress using a spray-can she found in their shed, much to her dress designer's shock, proudly exclaiming "Ronnie won!" Bless Melony's soul, what a cunning stunt!

There was so much joy in the air that day. People seemed to be drunk with joy. Most were drunk with alcohol. Some were just people who looked drunk at the best of times, even when sober. Some were regular town drunks. Some were recovering drunks. Some had once recovered, but then had lapsed back into drunkenness. It was indeed a diverse crowd.

The size of the crowd was enormous, or at least quite a lot bigger than usually seen in Washintown. There were at least thirty Washintown residents and a few members of the press. Some pets attended too.

Melony herself was again in tears of joy seeing her husband so fulfilled and alive. His long-held dream of shaping the city into a beacon of fairness and progressiveness, a sanctuary for those needing shelter, and a humming metropolis with a rich cultural life, well-preserved public buildings and strong institutions, was one step closer to reality.

* * *

At the ceremonial meeting between the incoming mayor and the departing one, Barry Kabana, Chump waited respectfully for Melony who was adjusting her corks, then strolled hand-in-hand with her up the steps of City Hall, just like young lovers, to meet the nefarious Kabana and his iniquitous wife Mercedes. At that meeting, Chump believed that the Kabanas were suitably dignified and respectful towards him and Melony, which was surprising as Barry was generally known as a messy, uncouth and disrespectful boor, who had reportedly even stooped to groping women. He was known, for example, to wipe his mouth on his sleeves when eating at official functions, talking with his mouth full as semi-masticated peas and carrots dropped out, or flew out hitting his interlocutors, and for rubbing spilt food into his clothes when it dripped. Quite frankly, Kabana had been an utter embarrassment as mayor.

Thankfully, Chump had arrived to restore dignity.

The inauguration was indeed a love-in, a celebration of the joy the town felt at finally having an ethical and public-spirited mayor after years of cronyism and rampant corruption under the slovenly Barry Kabana.

The crowd size made Barry Kabana's inauguration look feeble and pathetic. Townsfolk were packed literally shoulder to shoulder across Main Street, so that even emergency vehicles could not squeeze through unless people obligingly moved aside. There were so many people that press reports began to trickle through that this was the biggest crowd turnout ever seen in any rural city in modern history. The crush to catch a glimpse of the passing Chump led to some dangerous scenes, including a stroller nearly being bumped off a curb, and one chilling report of a dropped ice-cream. Thankfully there were no injuries. Officials from the Guinness Book of Records confirmed that never before had a crowd of this magnitude been seen in the City of Washintown, population 247. It was insane.

Chump, who had written his speech entirely on his own, struck a harmonious and collaborative tone. His inspirational oration laid out a vision of sharing society's riches, encouraging the flourishing of public services such as universal health and education, and taking on organized crime, corruption and bribery with relish. Many believe it was the best speech given in the history of speeches. Famous notables in the crowd referred to the address as "truly historic", "spiritually uplifting" and, in the words of the Arizona Daily Bugle's editorial, "the speech by which all other speeches should be measured". A Washintown Sentinel reader poll in the ensuing weeks voted that the speech should be given its own name, the winning recommendation being 'Speechy McSpeech Speech'.

After the formalities, he embedded himself in the crowd - with Melony by his side of course - for over an hour, mingling with his Russian friends and getting friendly with corporate leaders from all walks of life, plus a few townsfolk. In the evening, there were wild bacchanalian scenes of celebration as Ronnie performed the David Brent office dance with his wife in the town hall ballroom, managed a convincing lip-pouting and strutting impersonation of Mick Jagger, and made a mess of himself by sloshing punch down the front of his shirt as he tried to drink it directly from the ladle. On his way out at the end of the night, he tripped in the gutter, laughing with delight as he ended up in a planter box on the sidewalk, looking up at the stars. In his sozzled mind, a stellar future was ahead for Washintown.

The next morning though, Chump had a cracking migraine, and needed Melony to bring him a double dose of Berocca to be able to get out of bed.

As he meandered to the bathroom, he noticed that the answering machine in the hall was blinking with a message he must have missed the previous night. He hit the play button and was taken aback to hear a Russian voice in crackly tones, with a brief message saying: "Ronnie, I sorry I miss you. Here is my message. Is Viktor. Viktor Punkin, you know, I help you with pipes in you house. We fix you shower, you know, you shitty shower. OK I sorry we mix up and we not agree last time on job. I have gift for you, for say sorry we make mistake on pipes. I send it to you. Is a gift from me, from Viktor. Da svidania." Then the call cut off with a click and the answering machine made its usual "Beep, Beep, Beep" to indicate no more messages.

Melony, who had been adjusting her face at the bathroom mirror, overheard the message and took her husband's hand gently. "Ronnie, you mustn't hold a grudge against zeese verkmen, Ronnie. Be best, Ronnie. Vee who come from zee East of Europe, vee know you must krumble away any wall in your heart. Forgive zem, Ronnie. Krumble your heart's wall, Ronnie. Be best, my love. Be best."

There was such depth and soul to Melony's entreaty, and such genuineness in her eyes, like a genuine Gucci bag from a Bangkok alley vendor, that Ronnie could not help but be moved. After returning from the toilet, he immediately picked up the phone and rang Joy Hickey in the office at City Hall.

"Joy", he said. "I know I've been harsh on them, those FSB fellows from East of the Ukraine, but you know what, Joy? I've decided that they need to be allowed to participate in the contract process for the services upgrade and information hub I've been dreaming of for Washintown, that's going to become a reality now. Accept their submission, Joy, if they make one. I have decided to forgive them. I've decided to Be Best."

This was classic Chump. Despite his strong antipathy for Russians and his desire not to do business with them, Chump, like no other leader - with Meloný's unwavering support and encouragement - had the magnanimity of character, the decency and the humility to reach out a large hand of forgiveness, to seek a spirit of unity where once there was hostility, a spirit of kinship where once there was estrangement. Indeed, now, in its place, a strange love had been kindled.

* * *

With the success of the inauguration leaving its great mark on the history books, Chump now tackled the future with this desire to work together.

* * *

Finally in a position to enact Janey's earlier suggestion to chat with prison inmates, Chump went on that day to give a stirring speech, just as an old friend would do, to the prisoners and hardened criminals at the Longley Correctional Internment Annex, a prison facility in West Washintown. His heart went out to his audience as he stated, with a cheery visage which looked just a little like a suppressed smirk, that although they were locked up, some for the rest of their lives, he would never ever forget them. With his hand on his heart and another on his wallet, he pledged that his sincerest thoughts and prayers would always be with them to give them succor, and to aid and abet them in their life's pursuits. He let it be known that he cared deeply for them, stating "there is no-one that cares more about the welfare of prisoners, such as you scum (I'm joking, folks), than Ronnie S. Chump. Yes, you may indeed be the utter scum of society, and I'll never relate to that, but you have my thoughts and prayers for self-betterment, that you may one day become more like me." His hearty laugh echoed through the cold stone establishment, bringing, one might hope, a kind of incipient internal cheer to the ashen-faced inmates.

He expressed that he could 'feel for' each one of them, and was aghast at the inconvenience of their detention. He said he shared many of their goals and ambitions, even if, in his case, for more noble means: to do well and reap rewards for his family, to develop clever and creative strategies for self-betterment, to reach into Houses one was not expected to reach into, and to hunt down crime networks. He wanted them to know that they had his backing, that they could see him as "one of their own", since, owing to his work for the State over many years, he knew many who worked in the correctional field and who had deep experience in the area of criminality. They were like family to him, or as they say in Italian, "Famiglia". He knew clever lawyers, editors and cunning linguists who could help offenders such as themselves to avoid long, drawn-out or even extended sentences. Easy.

Yet, as a fair and balanced leader, he made it clear that he also firmly believed in the rule of law, and that if they had been idiotic enough to break it without having found a good enough lawyer, well "you've gotta do the time, my good fellas". This was met with a tremendous round of applause and rattling of the inmates' tin cups on their rough-hewn wooden trestle tables. He seemed to have a striking resonance with the dastardly inmates, such was Chump's ubiquitous magic.

It was yet another truly respectful and inspiring oration, one in which Chump fostered an uncanny connection with his literally captive audience, and in return for his brotherly patronage, patronizing them as he did, the prisoners gave him another warm and hearty round of applause when it was finally over. They lined up to present the mayor with a laurel, and hardy handshake, before returning to their cells, with some grumbling reluctance, yet newly invigorated with his ideas and with fresh plans for the future. In parting, they slipped him many gifts to take beyond the prison walls. In return, Chump had his staff hand out a small rectangular Chump cake, one to each inmate, which Chump had personally made, but must have rather overcooked, as they were all decidedly stiff.

Later, at a meeting of inmates held down in the prison laundry, they voted together to form a club, and to make Ronnie an honorary member of their Internment Annex, offering him an open invitation to return as soon as possible for a protracted visit. They wanted him to know that there was a club waiting for him if he ever came back. They were kind enough even to agree they would make sure they 'looked after' Ronnie, their deep chuckles and toothless grins confirming this heartfelt wish.

* * *

Chump's first move as a newly installed mayor was to have a series of Barry Kabana's self-aggrandizing photographs taken down and replaced with inspirational photos of common people from all walks of life performing humble but fulfilling service and responsibilities for others: nurses tending to patients, aid workers feeding hurricane victims and refugees, people working hand in hand to achieve a greater goal. Ronnie suggested calling the display the "City Hall's Uplifting Municipal Photographs", and to arrange for the exhibition's acronym - which some noticed happened to spell out, by sheer coincidence of course, the mayor's surname - to be emblazoned over the entrance to the public building. The corridors of City Hall suddenly lifted with a lightness of spirit and a sense of unbounded hope that was palpable to all. Walking through there was suddenly like walking on sunshine.

Kabana's exaggeration, boasting and uncouthness would be a thing of the past.

Among Chump's other first acts in the mayoral role was to demand that a day care center be established at City Hall, ostensibly to support new mothers working in the council and to set an example to the city's employers. In an unprecedented display of emotion, he pounded the table and howled his case in the council meeting to the point of bringing himself to tears of frustration, insisting that what he wanted was desperately important and that there would be hell to pay if he didn't get it. Then, to this end, he passed a motion on the floor of the council chambers.

Once the initial shock had died down, and the cleaner had again spruced up and deodorized the chambers, councilors on the Parent Subcommittee attempted to pacify Chump. After a long tussle over the gavel, a new agreement was finally struck, backed unanimously by council; namely, that an unused wing of City Hall would, from here on, host the inaugural Chump Day Care Center, which was would come to be informally and unofficially christened "Chumpy Tots Day Care", or just "Chumpy Care". Joy Hickey would act as matriarch to oversee the day care center, and hiring of child-care workers would begin immediately. Chump, his tears now dried on his face, sat up high in his chair and beamed, having won a significant legislative victory, at which point one of his minders finally brought him some lunch on a tray, with warm milk in a bunny cup. This fiery resolve was a sign of things to come in the Chump administration. No challenge would rattle Ronnie's strong will.

There was absolutely no doubt - to Ronnie, child care was a top priority.

Within a week, work to prepare the new day care center was in full swing. The halls of the council building buzzed with activity as fresh new diapers, delicately scented with eucalyptus oil, were brought in to be stored in what had previously served as document shelving, now converted into linen cupboards for diapers and as storage for toys stuffed with polyester filling. Natural straw-based soundproofing was layered on the ceiling, making the whole day care Center quiet and restful. The previously disused wing of the city hall was given a fresh coat of paint, and the rooms which were to serve as 'day care central' were given decals depicting a large bunny rabbit, a weasel and some dinosaurs. This greatly impressed the mayor, to the point where he joked about having second thoughts about giving out this space to little kids because "maybe I should use this myself." Chump in fact put in a special request for a tortoise decal to be added, in honor of his favorite animal, spotted in the lake at his new home.

As the day care center gradually took shape, some visiting children with an elementary school tour group happened to pass a whistling Ronnie in the corridor. When he saw the young visitors, Ronnie crouched down on his haunches, looked them in the eye and said "You know what kids? One day, this will all be yours."

Once the day care center was up and running, the mayor paid frequent visits, as he was intensely proud of having taken his first baby steps in his new role as mayor; once there, he would call out for the staff, ask for some lunch or to see their new toys. At times he even took a nap in one of the spare nursery rooms between council voting sessions.

Conveniently, there was even a room where, upon waking up, he could change the adult Depends® he used to deal with his gluteal war wound.

* * *

So, dear reader, we can see that in no time, following Chump's spectacular inauguration, he had achieved a string of enviable achievements: he had rid Washintown of the stinking residue of Barry Kabana's time at the helm, engaged in numerous animal welfare rescues for pets and stray pussies, fostered camaraderie and hope amongst the prison population. He had even rekindled a stricken relationship with his former Russian contractor. To top it off, he had opened a child care center where the future of our society would be nurtured among the fun animal decals. Things were looking good for Washintown.

4

BUNYON

Stevie Bunyon was the last of Chump's supporters to find an office in City Hall. After the inauguration ceremony he had grabbed the new office manager Kitty Welsher, just as Mayor Chump had taught him to do, and, while other staff were choosing offices, had whisked her down to the local ice-cream parlor for a celebratory treat.

Stevie ordered a pure white vanilla, insisting on no choc sprinkles, whereas Kitty, since joining the Chump administration, had opted for Rocky Road. Like Grease's Danny Zuko and Sandy down at the Frosty Palace, they engaged in heated policy discourse, so when they returned like naughty schoolchildren their ice-creams were dripping down their faces and all over the City Hall carpet. Stevie had selflessly convened a private meeting with her and Ponce Rebus to discuss social policy development in a vacant room down the East corridor.

When Bunyon finally got out of that meeting he was lucky to find the last empty office, quite a large and impressive room with a splendid mantelpiece and a view out onto the rosy garden.

The carpet would now need to be shampooed owing to dripped ice-cream, and it needed many changes, but Bunyon had at last found his feet, with a new office surrounded by his dearest friends like Janey, Ponce, Flout and General Malaise.

Bunyon claimed this space and immediately set up a series of whiteboards to plan out his social reform agenda, making sure Kabana's blackboards were moved to the basement storeroom. He brought in additional new comfy furniture, and decorated it with pretty flowers and daisy chains. A large poster of Mahatma Gandhi was Plasti-Tacked to the wall. Incense was burned. This was to be a room for peace. This was a peace room.

Many who had worked with Bunyon on the campaign initially noticed that he was absolutely no different, a little dreamy and distracted as he had always been. Rather boring.

* * *

A few on the staff noticed the changes Bunyon had effected to his office. He drifted around the space in a dreamy state, scattering rose petals and, arms out, twirling around through trails of incense smoke like a Whirling Dervish.

"What's up with Steve?" Kushynird asked. "Is he OK? He is just so friendly these days, and I feel so close to him." Then he finally understood - Steve was obviously in the midst of a peak life experience, a moment of pure self-actualization, as he fully aligned with his new capacity to bring good to society. Settled in his new, if somewhat smoky, office, Steve had finally realized that he was literally incensed at the very notion of social injustice. His eyes watered. He coughed, and opened a window. This was a stunning moment to see.

Within a week though, Steve had put away the incense and was down to business, in full commander mode, not wafting or drifting but totally accessible to all others on the team, a vision of mindfulness.

Bunyon had become even more gregarious and intimate than ever before. To some, this may have appeared slightly creepy, but those who knew him knew Bunyon understood that his devotion to the community, even ahead of his singular devotion to the Chump local government, drove him to reach out and spread what he himself called his "focused shit" on as many people as he could.

Usually, Steve was a plodder. But not now. Now, he was a ninja of social justice, anticipating, performing Taekwondo moves in the office as he planned out progressive new policies. Hi-ya! Take that, injustice! Karate chop! Not so fast, private housing estate!

* * *

In these crucial early days, Bunyon had encouraged all the staff on the Chump team to watch "Dumb and Dumber" for its inspiring story about comradeship, teamwork, moral leadership, the need to seize life's opportunities and the importance of strong law enforcement.

But the movie also served as a kind of official guide to his policy development, insofar as it exhibited such a genuineness of performance, such a levity of spirit and such tenacity in the face of difficulties. It became a handbook (as much as a movie can be a handbook) for the style of administration he and Ronnie would forge together, and just like Paula Moneyport, forge it with skill indeed they would.

The movie defined the look and feel - the fun, the heady heights and joie de vivre - that City Hall could experience if the Right team was in place. It would set the tone for the next fifty years of municipal governance for Washintown and its surrounds, scorching the earth of other incompetent, shoddy administrations, and sowing the seeds of enjoyment and wit.

Following its plot lines and casting as a model, the hiring of inspirational characters like high-level Transylvanian strategist Sebaceous Gawker would bring peace and dignity to the Rosy Garden and bring great honor to the administration. Only the most hard-hearted moviegoer would not envy a scenario in which they were a player in this most life-affirming and fun-filled piece of dramatic theater which the Chump administration would epitomize. This cast of very fine people would immerse Washintown in a deep rinse of professionalism and toe-tapping entertainment.

Stevie Bunyon was one such stellar entertainer as he waved his boater hat and tap-danced away down the hall in glee from his new office, singing "Ronnie, how I love you, how I love you..." to the tune of Swanee, with his Star Wars stormtrooper figurines jiggling on the mantelpiece.

* * *

If, in "Dumb and Dumber", Peter Farrelly's archetypical oeuvre defined the ideal moral characteristics of the mayor and his team, Chump not only adhered to these, but exceeded them in a stratospheric fashion, placing him in the rarefied company of Washintown's leading exemplars of character and power. These included Washintown luminaries such as Granny May Moses (known in town for her scrumdiddlyumptious vittles) and Johnny 'The Ant' Lucchese from the Washintown Pizzeria (famous for offering a free lunch on Tuesdays, and reduced rates on bulk cement, via his cousin Tony).

* * *

It was a fluky career that got Bunyon here.

When he was still quite young, his parents had made the difficult decision to home-school the lad, recognizing him as a boy with special needs, and such a blazing charisma that he would surely distract other students with his compelling aura and affability if sent to a conventional school. Since both his parents needed to go to work themselves, they then passed responsibility for Steve's pedagogy onto his beloved Jewish grandmother, Granny Bunyon.

He had thereafter been home-schooled by his grandmother while his parents worked to provide for them both, glad to have Stevie in good hands, albeit arthritic ones. Granny Bunyon proved to be a formidable educator for the burgeoning Bunyon, toiling to have

Stevie develop through repetitive overuse of her comprehensive, manually-intensive curriculum of essential life skills. These included Copperplate handwriting (on slate), cow-milking, butter churning, tater cooking, operating a moonshine still and a spinning wheel, needlework, chicken husbandry and how to build a well from first principles.

Espousing a globalist world view with her own hillbilly twist, hyper-intelligent Granny Bunyon taught Stevie everything he needed to know about international politics and what she referred to as 'farn relations'. For example, when he needed to urinate out in the field during an outdoor education class, she would holler the instructive phrase, "Ay, European own mah boot, boor!" Cleverly embedded in such seemingly simple, rustic messages were, in fact, highly crafted communications about world issues and global politics, including the injustices of colonialization, the usurping of property and international human rights. You couldn't mess with Granny Bunyon.

Yet Stevie struggled with the complexity of the tasks Granny set at home school, demonstrating consistently low grades and a high level of truancy. She had been forced to pull him aside with her shepherd's crook, and suggest that if he didn't pull up his socks, he could be expelled from home-school and may need to join the military.

Unfortunately, this warning went unheeded. Stevie went on to fail each and every subject, doing particularly poorly in Cobbling, and became the first student ever to be 'let go' from home-school. It was a real pity, as he had shown promise in her self-defense classes, which included neck-grabbing and wrist-twisting.

From then he was on his own, living on the street, wandering, barefoot, lonely as a cloud, in search of his foothold in society. Yet his determination to succeed could not easily be crushed underfoot, despite his scholastic handicaps. It was during this period that he discovered his natural proficiency for street dance and musical theater, and that an underlying gregariousness gained a foothold in his life. Granny's "tough love" had ultimately paid off, and Stevie would, in the end, be fine. He established Bunyon & Co, providing entertainment services to the finance industry such as tap-dancing, mime and interpretive dance, later branching out into media and print. The rest is history. It was but a small hop for Bunyon from alleyway breakdancing to the rigors of municipal politics and the media.

Granny's regular encouragements for Stevie to study hard, and her often-hollered moniker for him during those years, would in fact be the inspiration for the naming of the publication that he would go on to found in later years: Dimbrat.

* * *

Described as "honest and caring" by colleagues in the liberal media, Bunyon, once let loose on the world, collected friends like a belly button collects lint. He had friends all over town, and not a soul would hear a word against him. He was so absolutely lovable. His smooth baby face made people just want to pinch his cherry cheeks and smooch him. Indeed, even in the writing of this book, I have had folk coming up to me as I shivered out on the street and say to me "Lady, are you the one writing that book on Stevie Bunyon?"

As I would start to explain, by stating that "well actually my book is not specifically about Stevie but is much more a reflective, long-form investigative piece on the entire Ch..." they would cut me off and say "Man, I love that guy! Ain't he just so cool!"

In fact, having developed into a seasoned local council officer and buttoned-down bureaucrat, he was, if anything, just slightly dull, insofar as he insisted on all policy being planned out meticulously, with no surprises for the community, even insisting on everyone in the office having the same type of coffee mug. He was a great defender of the principle of equality for all people, and became annoyed, for example, if a white person received any perceived benefit over a person of color. Steeped in human rights and telling all equally and in no uncertain terms not to step on his toes, he treated all people the same, regardless of color.

And after a string of successful marriages, Bunyon was well placed not only to show his prowess in the policy development stakes, but also to offer valuable relationship advice to other staffers.

* * *

Bunyon skimmed the council records relating to mayoral decrees and discovered that Ronnie could in fact accelerate some of his planned social reforms if he were to implement them via the hitherto rarely-used mayoral decree. Yet Bunyon was a man of such high ethics that he also knew that neither he nor Chump could never stoop to such an undemocratic legislative mechanism, so firmly parked that idea in the trashcan, at least for a day or two.

Still, the Chump administration was sufficiently open-minded and innovative that even ideas from the trash could rise up again to become legislation, even if bearing the slight pong of a moldy banana or damp, half-eaten sandwich.

It was around this time that, following my repeated requests to staffers and high-pitched calls over the boundary fence for an audience with the mayor, that Mayor Chump finally gave in, at least to the degree of having one of his minions come out to the sidewalk and hand me one of Mayor Chump's prized menus, his famous Fruity Scone Recipe.

* * *

Chump and his colleague Slobodan Milersevic, who had previously worked for hot gay lawyer Jess Fessin, spent hundreds of hours crafting progressive legislation to bring greater social justice to the community, ready for the first sitting of the town council.

At the same time, Chump was weighing up whether to declassify several of his previously unreleased vegetarian recipes for public consumption. In this I have played an important role as in intermediary, by accepting printouts and leeks over the fence. For you, dear reader, I have striven in my research to gain exclusive access to some of these original Chump recipes. In a world first, with the release of this book, I am now making them available for the first time on my website.

There could be little doubt that Bunyon's remarkable unifying characteristics, his ability to bring people of all backgrounds and colors together in a spirit of cooperation and Amity, would, like the movie "Jaws", secure him a timeless place in history.

Stevie came from a long line of Bunyons, originally small corn farmers, who had, over the years, risen in stature from mere b-listers in society and had implanted themselves in the foundations of local government. The Bunyons irritated many, and although not pretty or photogenic, they were really a swell bunch, always held firm to their principles as an outgrowth of the Left, and it would have taken quite a concerted operation to remove them from this position.

* * *

There was a glut of other talent on offer among the senior council executives too, with Kushynird, Ponce and Connard, not to mention the mayor-elect, working in unison to put forward a set of cohesive policy positions. Around these bright stars, like satellites - here one could evoke the image of celestial bodies such as Miranda the satellite of Uranus or asteroid TB1456 - were other fine contributors such as Odorosa Animalgut, attentive and diligent, her iPhone always at the ready to take notes; Shawn Spinner, master wordsmith, keen topiarist, and General Kitty Malaise who brought a great sense of fun and youthfulness to the team, always playing the role of the 'kid in the room'.

Connard, a key player in both the Policy Development and Ethics teams, sought to contribute more deeply to these heavyweight think-tanks by seeking out quiet moments on the lawn outside City Hall. She would clear her mind of all thoughts and mental activity, and just allow unprecedented new ideas for the administration develop within her head, like baby chicks about to Hatch in an incubator.

Though I myself remained out on the sidewalk, so had little direct experience of their interchanges, the word filtered out to the street that the synergies of the team within City Hall were, quite literally, a sight for sore eyes. I also often saw Kylie-Jo suddenly run back inside, calling to herself when struck by divine inspiration, "Oooh, I've just had a good one!" so I knew that ideas were coming thick and fast, though possibly more thick than fast.

With such an idea-laden team and a host of Russian friends willing to help, there was not so much competition, but more what one could call collaboration, among the top staffers, to create a team which altered the very definition of the word team, so tightly bonded as to be more like a 'gang'. Kushynird, Rebus, Connard and the mayor-elect Chump all shared the same ability to take coherent perceptions or narratives and create a mash-up of them for public digestion.

The resulting confection was then piped out, fresh daily, particularly via Moose News.

* * *

Chump had heard stories of people risking their lives to get to the safety of Washintown from life-threatening situations in their own countries. They came seeking safety and refuge, and brought with them incredible strengths and capabilities with which they would repay the community which lovingly welcomed them. Chump knew well that the strongest societies are ones which are composed of a wide range of cultures. He wanted to increase Washintown's diversity and its respect for women and downtrodden losers in general.

* * *

As his new team congealed around him like junket, Chump's heroic thoughts naturally turned to the poor and the disenfranchised.

Chump asked his team to gather for an emergency meeting on the subject, and the team sat around discussing the arrival of refugees and what could be done to assist them further in resettling promptly and safely. Chump asked the team to provide an alphabetical list of the places from which these refugees came. Sally Muckabee Blathers raised her hand saying "Mayor, sir, that is one diggety-dog long word, 'alf-a-hehaw-betty-colly'. Chump patiently explained that this meant lining the words up via juxtaposition in order from shortest to longest according to the known modern English alphabet, as originally developed by the Semitic people of the Levant area, principally derived through Phoenician and Aramaic, during the early first millennium BCE.

After dang-near spittin' out her plug of chewin' 'bacca right there, Sally's eyes rolled back in her head while Chump spoke as though she was either having an intimate moment with herself, a frisson of amazement at Chump's dazzling intellect, or a mild epileptic seizure. There proceeded something of a squabble between Kylie-Jo Connard and Sally Muckabee Blathers as they wrestled over the Sharpie® permanent marker pen at the whiteboard, both keen to impress the totally ripped and intelligent Chump.

Finally the talented team came up with the following list, scribbled with the Sharpie on the whiteboard:

> Mexico
> East Asia
> Nicaraguan
> Democratick Republick of Congo
> Asian

(later the cleaner would need a high-powered solvent to remove this)

Blathers stood there with her hands on her hips and her jaw dropped. Her blotchy mouth, incidentally, was showing signs of leukoplakia - a precursor to full-blown cancer of the oral cavity - due to her entrenched habit of chewing on unsound "bites" of loose-leaf tobacco, and on her own used plugs.

Chump looked for a long time at that list. He looked again, and blinked. Then he looked at the first letter of each name on the whiteboard, and what it spelt out:

M
E
N
D
A

M-E-N-D-A.

Tears welled up in Chump's eyes. Something about this had clearly affected him.

"These people," he spoke with a wavering voice, "these people cross deserts and oceans to make Washintown their home, and to contribute to our society. We owe them something more than just safe refuge." Chump's giant humanitarian heart was obviously pumping overtime, sending excess blood to his peripheral organs, some more than others. He was excited. He was calculating if there would be enough spare chowder buckets in Washintown to give these refugees a treat they would never forget. His raw genius was at work.

Then suddenly he spoke: "Team, increase our refugee intake. Get it done! Ponce, draft up another mayoral decree."

Chump, clearly a man of action, then stood up and reached for his chef's apron.

"And someone, Connard you'll do - bring me a fresh fish. And make it snappy!"

Connard darted to the kitchen, looking to fulfil Chump's fishy desire.

The new refugees were about to be welcomed with one of Chump's finest gastronomic, or at least gastric, treatments.

5

KUSHYWANKER

On the Monday after the order to increase the city's refugee intake, Josh Scaboff and his partner on the local FM radio station show *Afternoon Scaboff*, Mayka Zebraski, arrived for dinner at the Town Hall.

Only the previous day, excited by the prospect of welcoming more refugees, Chump had donned Junior's galoshes and rummaged through the removalists' boxes in his garage looking for his largest net, in effect abandoning any sense of net neutrality. He needed the big net.

Now, in preparation for dishing up a treat to the refugees, Chump had wanted to trial some of his latest recipes on his media visitors, based on critters he had just hauled from his marshy lake with the net. He simply adored members of the media, almost as much as he did refugees, calling them 'The Friend of the Populace'.

Yet as we will see, he couldn't help himself also trialing some of his own hilarious practical jokes. What a funny Chump!

Scaboff was a former city councilor, and Zebraski, a woman with an exceptionally high IQ, was the daughter of the notorious ex-mayor Bzwgniwnwkl Zxcmhlewjk-Zebraski. Sadly, their show was spectacularly unpopular among the local community, however this engendered sympathy and tenderness on the part of Chump, who embraced losers and always stepped in in support of the underdog. Truth be told, Chump himself also actively disliked their talentless radio show, but being endlessly kind-hearted, nevertheless welcomed the hosts warmly into his chambers.

When they arrived at Town Hall, Chump showed them into his Square Office and was thrilled when Zebraski mentioned that she had been in square offices before, with her mother, from about the age of five. Chump showed them some of his favorite mayoral trinkets and the Jackson Pollock which he had installed, symbolic of the structure he wanted for his administration.

Chump excused himself for a moment, indicating that he had a small errand to run in the kitchen. The guests sat down, the meal was promptly served and they began dining without waiting for Chump, who had said he would only be a minute. From my vantage point on the street, I could see through the window that he tarried momentarily around the servery, fiddling with what looked like the hot paprika jar. I had a momentary flash of *déjà vu*, as though I had seen this moment before, but then a dispelling doubt fired up in my mind to counter this, and the moment passed.

At lunch - fish, which Scaboff loves with a passion and wolfs down in large chunks - things progressed smoothly at first, with quiet conversation proceeding once the waiters had served the meals. Zebraski seemed relaxed, aside from the occasional glance at Scaboff's rather off-putting eating habits, for rudely he had not only started ahead of the others, but was chewing with vexatious squelching sounds, which reminded her of Bunyon adjusting himself in a chair.

Chump finally appeared, bearing pepper and salt shakers, and took a seat at the table. He was in an upbeat mood, excitedly relating how he had succeeded in providing instant employment placements for some of the refugees and their young children, whom he had arranged to all work in the City Hall kitchens this very day. It was a policy masterstroke which resolved four issues at once: the welcoming of refugees, low-cost care of their children, securing meaningful employment both for parents and progeny, and increasing the production of Chump Chowder for the Happy Harvest Hampers.

As the meal progressed, Scaboff asked for the salt and pepper to be passed down. With a boyish grin, Chump obliged.

Though the Scaboff-Zebraski household (like their radio show) was usually something of a war zone, with regular screaming matches and crockery flying against the walls, today the couple were in a cooperative mood with one another, and were even sharing their meals. Mayka gave Josh a slice of her crispy quinoa fish fritter and Josh too shared a few of his buttered scallops with Mayka. In doing so they were too busy to talk to the Mayor who was chomping down on a Caesar and Brutus salad, prattling on about upcoming policy decisions during gaps in his chewing.

Meanwhile, Scaboff, who obviously cared little for his colleague, was still blithely tucking into his meal, the scallops loosely arranged around Lobster mornay with a light sauce and tarragon sprigs from Chump's own garden. He sprinkled some extra salt over his scallops.

During a lull in the conversation, just after Chump had managed to elucidate how the new immigrant employment program would work, Zebraski happened to notice that Scaboff had gone unusually quiet and in fact was turning blue in the face while frantically waving his arms for attention, looking somewhat like a puffer fish.

Mayka gave Scaboff a confused look, patting him on the back before suddenly realizing the gravity of the situation.

"Oh, he's choking, he's choking" she exclaimed. "He's choking! Help!"

Chump mumbled something under his breath, inaudible to his visitors, though it sounded a little like "Oh no, I killed the bastard." Since there is no way that Chump would have been saying that, he is much more likely to have been exclaiming "Oh no! It's the Dijon mustard"

Then he seemed to gather his wits, and cried out "Help is on the way! Help is on the way!" before running around the table

Before anyone else could figure out what was happening, Chump had pushed out his chair and was racing to the back of Scaboff's chair where he began grabbing him and hoisting him out of his seat in an attempt to apply the Heimlich maneuver. Bunyon, following his natural impulse to help, launched himself across the lunch table, sending plates, glasses and crockery flying to the ground with a tinkle of breakages. Chump, meanwhile, had successfully wrapped his arms around Scaboff's waist from behind and was physically lifting him off the ground with loud grunts while he grew ever more blue in the face, until his color began to fade to more of an ashen grey. Thankfully Chump, performing a final dramatic lift and a sharp compression of Scaboff's waist, achieved success when a large chunk of the now-highly-spiced scallop suddenly flew out of Scaboff's mouth following a loud pop, and hurtled across the table skidding over Chump's draft refugee policy in a goopy trail.

At the end of this heart-stopping episode, Chump comforted Scaboff, holding his hand and sitting with him compassionately until his breathing had returned to normal, then, in a calm and relaxed way, walked back around the table, with all the coolness and suavity of Britain's James Bond, to retake his original seat. In doing so, he had even adroitly rescued the offending scallop from the carpet with a paper napkin and returned it to Scaboff's plate (though admittedly it was now covered in carpet fluff), ready for him to have a second attempt at chewing it properly. As Chump taught his citizens: "Waste not, want not."

Yet despite Chump's understated suavity at that moment, there was nothing which could downplay the enormous sense of respect felt by all the onlooking patrons for his heroism. Chump emerged from that incident with an even more elevated reputation as one who could deftly handle a fishy situation, as though he had a lifetime of experience in handling fishy situations.

* * *

Everyone advised Janey to take the secretarial job, confident that due to her obvious integrity there would be no risk of any perceived nepotism. Chump, due to his impeccable ethical standards, would not have a bar of this. When he heard that some of the staff had been even contemplating this idea, he was understandably outraged and upbraided them severely. It took several calm aides, some physical restraint and several of Ronnie's calmative pills (Subtracterall®), quietly stirred into his glass of water, to placate Ronnie and to convince him that Janey's input would be both of immense value and of little ethical concern. As he finally sank into his chair after his protests, Chump naturally insisted on getting a full clearance from the ethics branch, and finally a totally ethical compromise was struck.

So instead of an actual, real job, rather, Kushynird took up an informal and unpaid "virtual assistant" role in Chump's orbit, involving little real content, though a lot of strutting around, a role which, had it been within, say, the scouting movement, one would refer to as a more of a "parent helper". This would involve being just available at any time just over Chump's shoulder, when needed acting as a courier for important documents, for example carrying reports between the mayor's office and the council chambers, without reading them of course.

Chump had considered taking Janey down to the office of Security Clearance Uniformity Manager, Karl Krime, but all the staff knew that Janey was implicitly trustworthy, so the informal nature of her role was never an issue and security clearances were "red tape overkill". Even the ex-Vietnam vet police chief, Major General Kitty Malaise, was happy to turn a blind eye to Janey's comings and goings through the city's treasury, cafeteria and document archives, knowing Janey to be of the highest integrity and unlikely to steal much, except perhaps a donut. Besides, Janey was known to have a healthy bank balance so would not be one to be compromised by the lure of anything less than totally "kosher" (such as a donut). That settled, there was general merriment in the Chump ranks - "Hip, Hip, Hooray!" came the voices down the carpeted halls of a City Hall - a delightful, miracle-working helper had been found! And so it was: Janey Kushynird to the rescue.

* * *

Janey's successful integration into the team motivated Iwanker to consider a future as a mayor one day himself. Bunyon, who had coined the 'Kushywanker' conflation, was delighted with this idea.

Janey turned out to be a dedicated office worker, but due to her poor eyesight (requiring thick glasses) and her quaint lack of organizational skills, she had enormous trouble filling out forms. With her tongue perched halfway out of her mouth like The Peanuts' Charlie Brown, she would try her hardest to fill out each question and each checkbox, but - dang! - every time she would either scribble in the wrong area or just leave something out. Luckily she could call on the assistance of her accountant Abby Normal to help out, just a phone call away! Abby had a cerebral mind and had helped several high-profile clients such as the psychic medium John Edward and the Menendez family. He and his colleague Jude Sinkulow were endlessly helpful with reviewing and editing any of Janey's erroneously-completed forms or written communications.

Over and over Janey's forgetfulness would recur, but the infinitely forgiving Mayor Chump maintained his composure and allowed Janey another try each time, after all she was indeed trying. Very trying. Chump lent Janey some of his own special crayons to help her with learning to fill out forms through the use of primary colors. He himself had also experienced difficulty with forms in his younger years, struggling to accurately complete his 1040 forms without an enormous amount of assistance from his own lawyer and accountant, Ray Con, so he empathized with Janey's plight. To be fair, Ronnie would be nowhere without the great Con, who was like a member of the Family and who had, in the Golden Age when Freddy Chump was still alive, mastered form-filling (quite unlike Janey), and had even helped with spring cleaning.

Gerry Conehead was one staffer who was extremely helpful to Janey as she became familiar with her new role. Gerry would help arrange all the documents for signing on the mayor's desk, making sure everything was in place ready for the mayor's black, indeed very black, marker pen. As a show of solidarity for minority communities, Chump had shunned all use of white marker pens.

Yet, like Barry Kabana before him, Gerry Conehead was also quite an office prankster, and needed to be watched like a hawk, as he loved office levities of all sorts. He particularly enjoyed swapping documents on the mayor's desk, both for the adrenalin rush it provoked, and to make sure Chump was paying attention to his weighty legislative duties. On several occasions, Gerry replaced a formal piece of legislation ready for signing with an unsigned check, made out to himself, for (say) $35,000, which the mayor then unwittingly signed. At that moment, Gerry, as ethical as every other Chump staffer, would jump out from behind the drapes of the Square Office, teasing Ronnie with the cutest smile, saying "I tricked you again, Mr. Chump! What a silly Chump! Pay more observance to my wit-filled activities!" before tearing up the check and tossing it like confetti, or dandruff, over Chump's hairpiece.

Some of Gerry's unexpected office tricks caused Chump to experience palpitations of the heart, which sent Ronnie's staffers racing back to his prescription medicine bottle to soothe their rattled leader.

* * *

Chump greeted everyone he met with a heartfelt smile and warm handshake, never weird, creepy or inappropriate. He listened to every word spoken to him, processed it deeply, held the other's interest in the forefront of his mind, as though all your life's cares and concerns were kept in the palm of his giant, noble hands, and as though nothing in the world mattered more. He considered and deliberated with singular focus, often with a gentle nod and an endearing pursing of the lips, then gave profound, well-reasoned and moving responses. He treated his interlocutors with the utmost respect. It was, therefore, no wonder he was popular across all wards of the city, regardless of political persuasion.

These deeply authentic yet all-too-rare human qualities - the ability to listen wholeheartedly and to put the interests of the other ahead of himself - lay at the heart of the man's exceptional character.

Chump cared deeply for his staff. Not long after Janey's hiring, he had noticed a small pus-filled welt on the side of her face. Sensitively and caringly, Chump took her aside and said to her in soft tones: "Janey - listen. That massive disgusting thing on the side of your face. It looks like it's a little pussy. There's actual pus dripping out of it. You need to get that looked at. I know when something's a little pussy, believe me. And when I give you advice about something being a little pussy, grab onto it. That's honest advice. Please, go see my friend and ex-physician, Dr Goney. That's unsightly." Chump's incredible kindness was like a salve on any wound, whether physical or emotional.

* * *

Early on, Chump, in a remarkable humanitarian act, had given work at the city council to a man by the name of Dr Jeb Goney, who had had an unfortunately checkered employment history.

A short, stumpy man with a furtive nature and scant regard for the conventions of the law, Dr Jeb Goney had previously been working as a family doctor, including for the Chump family, and in those days had been a trusted member of the community, specializing in Irritable Bowel Syndrome (IBS). In dramatic circumstances, however, he had been struck off the medical register by the AMA for a series of egregious incidents involving unethical conduct. These included: abusing access to his patients' medical records, 'upskirting' Councilor Hildegard Glintin and using the names of deceased patients to book himself raunchy golf weekends with golf-loving sex workers and lap-dancers at Murky-Lako in Florida.

Further compounding these transgressions, Goney had then thumbed his nose at the medical profession by refusing to give up his honorific title "Doctor" despite having been stripped of his medical registration. This brazen anti-establishmentarianism had branded Goney as a rebel and a troublemaker, and no longer an IBS doctor to be trusted.

Having suffered this very public fall from grace, Goney had been forced to find work in any field which would hire a disgraced, stumpy ethics violator. Fortunately the world of New York building- and pest- inspection greeted him with open arms, and for a while he was able to avoid further scrutiny by the authorities, working as a contractor for several honest mob bosses in the building trade.

From his previous routine in a busy medical practice rendering help to members of the community of all ages, Goney's life had been reduced to a kind of ghostly existence. Like a spook, he roamed alone, with nothing but a clipboard, through the empty corridors of cement skyscrapers and apartment buildings, looking for shoddy wiring, leaks or rats' nests. His loneliness and hollowness of soul resonated through his entire existence, creating an existential angst of Dantesque proportions.

It was midway through this darkest period in the man's life that, Ronnie Chump, true to form, had come to his moral succor, just as Virgil had once led Dante from the dark, tangled forest.

Over several days Goney had harassed Chump to allow him to meet for lunch. Chump had initially refused outright, then softened a little and proposed that, if Goney were to get down on his knees, crawl and beg, Ronnie would think about it. Ronnie couldn't help himself bring some levity to the poor man's situation. For Ronnie, with his keen sense of humor and comic sensibility, knew that there is indeed nothing funnier than seeing a former IBS doctor crawling and begging like a worm.

Chump had invited Goney to share a meal at a busy diner, and in front of multiple witnesses, finally had the pleasure of seeing

Goney desperately beg for forgiveness and crawl on knees among the patrons, beseeching Chump to forget about him, to cut him loose, acknowledging that he deserved all the consequences coming to him for his malpractices.

Finally Chump relented.

"Look, I don't want any dishonesty or any disloyalty to our noble City Council, so Jeb you need to change your ways and become an honest, upstanding citizen just like me. Do you think you can do that, Jeb, do you think so, huh?"

Jeb looked deep into his dark soul for a moment then grudgingly agreed that he could try to be honest.

"Alright Mr. Chump, if you could just please help me. Help me, I need somebody. Help me, not just anybody."

At this point, Chump's natural compassion and humanity gushed forth like one of FSB's defective shower fittings had once done, and he offered to call the City of Washintown H.R. Department - staying at arm's length of course - to see if any positions could be offered to Dr. Goney.

Though innately dishonest and untrustworthy, Goney had always been, and remained, intensely loyal to Chump, having built a strong relationship through attending to Chump's rear-facing war wound over many years. Chump, cognizant of this, in turn reciprocated at that moment, standing by the broken and dispirited Goney. He pulled out his wallet, set aside twenty dollars in an empty glass for a tip, then put in an order for a veritable feast to be brought to the table: burgers, drinks, hot dogs and donuts. Having been down on his luck and struggling to afford groceries, Goney could not believe his eyes. Chump then offered to help Goney find new work, even promising to put in some calls on his behalf to the HR office at City Hall. Goney nearly choked on his burger, so overtaken he was with emotion at Chump's kind offer, and partly due to the amount of burger he had bitten off. The moving incident, the first step on Goney's road to redemption, was recorded on smartphones by several of the diner's patrons. When the dinner was over, the twenty-dollar bill Chump had intended as a tip had somehow disappeared, never to be seen again.

And so it was, several weeks later, that Dr Jeb Goney reported for duty at City Hall in his new dual role as Council Building and Pest Inspector. Although no longer officially registered as a doctor, Goney, due to his lengthy medical training, was nevertheless still in position to give unofficial medical advice to City Hall staff, while also fulfilling his new role rooting out fleas, termites, rodents and structural defects on council property. Chump, ever conscious of probity, had of course remained at arm's length from Goney's recruitment process, apart from his initial phone calls to establish the possibility of the arrangement, a few follow-up discussions with the HR office, suggesting his pay rate and drafting Jeb's Letter of Offer.

Though unbeknown to Goney at the time, in offering the disgraced IBS doctor an opportunity to apply for work with the city council, Chump had again exercised his unique flair for administrative excellence. In this case, by combining both his characteristic generosity and his strategic foresight in the same gesture, not only was this an act of essential humanity in reaching out to a broken loser, but it also served to further the strength of the administration by giving that man a purpose ideally suited to his talents.

Since the inauguration, a number of staffers had reported unusual issues in the office with bugs and creepy-crawlies. A few had reported seeing unusual black spiders scurrying along into crevices in their offices. Chump had identified Goney as a person with the diagnostic skillset needed to tackle this. Dedicated to providing a safe and vermin-free working environment for his team, Ronnie naturally wished to address this issue with haste. Compassion and utility came together as one, and Chump had masterfully engineered a situation in which Goney's soul could be redeemed from a life of crime, while at the same time he would be gainfully employed looking for insects, rodents and building defects.

Goney had in fact spotted one of the spiders himself as it raced into Ronnie's office one day and found a hiding place behind the bookcase. "Oh yeah, that's a Karakurt, that one," Jeb had mentioned laconically, so familiar he was with creepy critters. "Good ol' *Latrodectus tredecimguttatus*, the Russian Karakurt. They're little beauties, those ones. Dangerous as f*** though, Ronnie. You'll want to watch out for those. They can really... wait for it... *'gettatus.* You get it, Ronnie? *'Gettatus?'*" he laughed. Ronnie was unimpressed, wanting this to be taken seriously. Unfortunately, this was not the last to be seen of the Karakurts, which seemed to have been imported along with FSB's building materials for the Washintown project. They had apparently taken up residence in the heart of City Hall. Or had they arrived through Chump's Russian-built Echos, hidden in the raffia-work base? We may never know for sure.

Odorosa in particular had come to Ronnie complaining of being infested with some kind of bug too, perhaps not a spider, but something itchy. This was possibly head lice or horse flies, she thought. But after an unofficial check-up by Dr Goney, nothing unusual could be found and she went back to roaming the corridors testing out the sound equipment wired up all over her body, in preparation for her next gig on the weekend.

There had even been a troubling incident in the Square Office when Chump noticed a baby Karakurt spider scampering across the floor of the Square Office. Chump quite politely asked Jess Fessin to get down on her knees and investigate where the hell the dark critter had ended up. Yes, admittedly, Ronnie's "get down on your knees" ploy was always a running joke of his, in liberal use, which his staffers needed to watch out for. Yet on this occasion he had been genuinely asking for assistance with the lowly Russian infiltrator.

Ronnie was not to know this, for he would never deign to look up a colleague's skirt, but Jess at the time happened to be suffering from an intense itch of her own, having been overtaken with a raging case of genital thrush. As a result, unbeknownst to her City Hall colleagues, she had been opting not to wear underwear to work, in an attempt to air out the problem. She was, therefore, understandably reluctant to comply with Chump's request to bend over for her boss and elevate her butt-cheeks in the office.

What ensued was that Jess issued a stern refusal and stormed out of the office, looking offended.

Shortly after Fessin announced her refusal to get down on her knees in her short skirt, Chump called Dan Imgone into the Square Office in the presence of Ponce and Rebus, to see if Dan could encourage Jess to comply and really get down on her knees. To Chump this had seemed like a reasonable office request, for the spider was an imminent threat, and he was not the type to look while she was in a compromising position. This incident would have ongoing ramifications.

Chump himself had experienced unusual itching sensations, an armpit rash and development of a cobweb-like substance in his groin area and butt cheeks. He had put this down to heat rash, but had been forced to admit, at least to himself, that he was starting to have doubts about its cause.

* * *

Iwanker, meanwhile, felt that he needed to hire more quality staffers for his own support and wellbeing. Having taken an additional, demanding role in the administration as Acting Head of Recreation, he was keen to cushion himself from becoming overworked, and hence overtired in the chamber. One name that kept coming up was Edna Pillow. Pillow, raised on an Egyptian cotton farm, was fluent in hieroglyphics. She had at one stage tried to teach Chump the alphabet, but of course it was too difficult for Ronnie, perhaps due to the deep spirituality and symbolism of the timeless script, though his brain was well suited to simple pictograms.

Pillow was brought on board to ease the burden on the Acting Recreation Head, and to help generate fresh, unconventional ideas for the administration to carry forward each new day. This turned out to be an inspirational hiring choice, and Pillow was quickly put to good use in recreation policy development. She felt she had landed a dream job.

6

NEW HOME

Within the first few weeks of the new mayoral term, Chump moved into his new family home, thereby marking a new phase in his inseparable, intertwined political and domestic lives.

The house sat in a quiet court, and had an air of tranquility as it had little passing traffic and backed onto a forest reserve, so birdsong and the gentle whisper of wind through the trees could be heard throughout the day. A true lover of peace and nature, Chump had been keen to locate a home where regular tweeting could be heard, and in the kind of quiet district where mob bosses and criminal gangs wouldn't normally venture. The Eastern side of the property abutted a semi-rural dairy farm.

The rear of the property featured a grassy knoll with a direct view to City Hall, leading down to a dark and slimy lake, more of a swamp, which provided a home to innumerable life-forms, including Newt-like bottom-dwellers, a fat old turtle, alligators and a host of other slithery reptiles. The deepest parts of the swamp were even purported to contain Stonefish, sprat and catfish. A keen environmentalist, Chump loved the lake for its biodiversity, affectionately calling it "my murky lako". It was this visceral bond to his algal lake which had inspired him to name his holiday home after it: "Murky-Lako".

An old row-boat sat tied up at the swamp's edge, yet the water was generally only knee high. When any visitor to the property sought to cross the swamp, the difficult decision would come up: row versus wade? For the lake was tremendously big, and tremendously wet, one of the wettest many had seen from the standpoint of water, Chump said, knowledgeably.

The house itself was remarkable in that it was not just white, but a dazzling, pure white which, when lit up, shone out across the other houses in the area, almost like a Stalag's searchlight. Chump was intensely proud of the shiny new house, which he quickly dubbed "House of Chump", and was determined not to allow its pristine clap boards to be stained with any kind of discoloration.

Even before moving in, he had purchased an array of new cleaning implements and cleaning chemicals - scrubbing brushes on poles, chamois cloths, buffing agents and so on - to ensure that not a speck of brown filth should soil its fine white slats. He was determined that this house and its unique color would continue to shine out with a resplendent supremacy over the neighboring houses which had let their clapboards deteriorate. To Chump, pride in one's home was a duty and a priority; this was a personal affinity which made him all the more lovable and relatable.

On the day Chump moved in to his new home, he invited Shawn Spinner to join him in taking a quiet, reflective stroll around the property with him. Together they inspected the house, swamp and surrounding gardens of the new home, with Spinner remarking in particular on the beautiful shrubbery which graced the gardens of the property. Chump pointed towards the perimeter of the garden.

"You know, Spinner" he mused. "One day I'd like to erect a stone wall around this place, to keep the pesky donkeys out." They sat out in the golden afternoon light around Chump's outdoor campfire, overlooking the city as some clouds rolled in. Chump mixed up some rustic bread ingredients, wrapped in foil, to cook a loaf on the fire. He was hoping to produce a more crusty loaf, but with a light drizzle falling as he unwrapped the campfire-cooked bread, it turned out to be damper.

He confided in Spinner his ambitious dream to rewire Washintown and all its public institutions and services, including the water supply. Spinner, having done some home electrical work himself, offered some wise advice regarding the wiring: "You're going to need a few strippers, boss." Chump appreciated Spinner's suggestion, and made a note to himself to remind Viktor Punkin and any of the other applicants.

One of the other projects which Chump championed with Spinner in the administration's early days was the establishment of a new fiscal division of City Hall, known as the Financial Investment Branch (FIB). Chump was a huge supporter of the FIB concept and frequently promoted, via the press and his Twit account, the cause of FIB and FIB's work. He then sought to further expand FIBs influence by having multiple FIBs running at the same time, out of both urban and regional centers as well as his own office. He and his communications staff such as Spinner made regular FIB presentations to the media and the public, emphasizing the need to rely on FIBs for social stability and economic growth. Together they stressed the importance of promoting the extensive spread of FIBs through Greater Washintown society.

Chump and Spinner worked seamlessly together, like Bonnie and Clyde. As my colleague Erika Wimpole, reporter at the Washintown Guardrail noted: "Shawn Spinner had a relationship with Chump like a family member in a mutually supportive relationship." Spinner would follow Chump around, learning how to weave his words like magic to maximize their impact on the public. They were often seen laughing together, enjoying quality time by the lake or the hedge, and were known to share deep and intimate conversations. This closeness was reflected in the fact that Chump allocated Spinner his own shrubbery out near the east fence, which Spinner would frequent in the twilight hours, practicing his bootscooting and other dance maneuvers.

* * *

Rather than treat his elevation to mayor as a mundane electoral event, Chump was deeply reverent of the solemnity and gravitas of his new role, and realized that his actions and his words now held increased weight in the community so needed to be considered with prudence.

He therefore met with prudence, a busty young policy analyst (with an admittedly pretentious lowercase name styled after e e cummings), once or twice a month to engage in feisty social and policy discussions whenever Melony was out of the house at her regular child welfare forum and would therefore not interrupt their heated, liberal intercourse.

* * *

Inside, Chump's new home was neat as a pin, with not a mouse or cockroach in sight.

According to staffers who provided me with inside information of the mayor's quotidian life at home, Chump lived a wholesome and virtuous life, starting each day with an hour-long yoga session and a period of silent meditation, finishing with an ancient yogic practice chanting the mantra "Ummm". He also chanted this at regular intervals throughout the day, particularly on phone calls or during important policy decisions. His yogic practice had clearly infiltrated his life in a profound way, and to share its essential wisdom he trained his communications staff to begin press conferences, and answer policy questions, with many invocations of this timeless mantra.

After his morning yoga, he would tackle the day with verve and prudence again, before taking a long shower then heading out for a brief game of mini-golf to focus his mental abilities. Once revved up, there was no stopping Chump. When he arrived at City Hall around lunchtime, he then had to spend a while checking that his recliner chair was in a comfortable position, then make a few calls to other leaders before taking a much-needed mid-afternoon break to fit in a muffin and some more meditative mini-golf with Sylvie Clittafford. He was then primed to put in a good half-afternoon for the community. Chump's efficiency levels were so high that his busy afternoon was equivalent to what others achieve in a week.

* * *

At home, he never watched TV, and as the day wore on was usually to be found reading Shakespeare, Rumi and other great modern authors, whether Western, Asian or Arabic, and pawing over policy documents, passionately looking for ways to improve the community. Each night into the late hours, he would excitedly discuss all his ideas with Melony, always seeking the soft touch of her hand and her cherished intellectual input in his decision-making. Melony, it must be said, came up with some of his policy masterstrokes, such as increasing the bucket size for Chump Chowder deliveries up to two gallons per family; developing the concept of "Chump Chowder concentrate" by having the chowder buckets left out in the Sun to thicken up; and significantly reducing expenses of the food aid program by dispensing with lids for the soup deliveries. Some additional mops were needed for the delivery trucks.

Although generally speaking a fine, well-adjusted person, Chump by nature did have a few obsessive quirks. As a particularly avid reader, he was rarely seen without a book in hand, and could spend hours devouring anything from fine literature or poetry to detailed technical or political white papers, departmental reports and policy documents. As a result, his general knowledge was encyclopedic, matched only by his spelling abilitties and his deep wisdom on issues of humanity and social advancement.

He was particularly sensitive about his personal security at home, so in the first few days after having moved in, had over a dozen locks fitted to his study door, in the manner of Maxwell Smart. Chump would lock himself in the study for long periods with nothing but books and, more often than not, his family, whom he loved so dearly that the thought of being without them for a few hours was akin to death.

All four walls of the study were fitted with beautiful oak bookshelves from floor to ceiling, the only exception being the gap for the doorway itself. Melony and his beautiful kids were of course always welcome to join him in the study, though they were also locked in once he triple-bolted the doors from the inside. Though one might expect them to be a little old for such amusements at ages 34 and 40 respectively, Erika and Dinah would quietly play on the carpet with trucks and other toys, while the devoted Melony took up a position on a comfy chair in the corner to knit Ronnie a scratchy wool sweater, sweetly emblazoned with his initials "R.S."

As Melony had grown up as a sewer and stitcher, she took great pride in her crewelwork, often donating it to children's refuges. She lovingly stored her needles in a pincushion which she had jocularly, or at least semi-jocularly, fashioned in the form of Ronnie himself, by way of a small effigy doll, full of cheap synthetic stuffing from a two-dollar shop. Ronnie loved Melony's cheeky wit (or in this case half-wit) in this family joke, and would chuckle heartily on seeing her at work with his 'mini-me', although admittedly, for some reason, he did feel odd pangs in his body when she sat in the corner using it with gusto. When, on occasions, she became over-enthused or inaccurate in the use of her pincushion, she needed to exercise great caution in order to not experience a painful prick herself.

In addition to her inherent mastery of sewing and needlecraft, Melony had, in her younger years, been intensely involved in cross-country running, even having been known to sprint across countries. She could therefore be considered a "running sewer". She had patiently imparted her sewing skills to all the children, who - unlike her - showed a tendency to take up the pastime amongst the pleasures of Nature. So, whereas Melony preferred sewing indoors, in closed, confined spaces within eyeshot of Ronnie, the children on the other hand enjoyed sewing outdoors, so could therefore all be considered "open sewers".

Among his other idiosyncrasies, Chump also had a fascination with cooking, and would often confect conglomerations of unexpected ingredients to the amazement of those around him. The most celebrated example was of course the traditional Chump Chowder, but Ronnie could whip up a range of equally palatable foodstuffs at a moment's notice, for example pickled liverwurst smoothie, oyster and cabbage pâté á la Niçoise, black pudding fried in aged lard, a load of hearty borscht, and even anchovy jam.

* * *

Chump had always been a sucker for a good bathrobe, and owned an extensive collection of them. With his move into his new house, he was more tempted than ever to slip into a bathrobe and saunter around like a young David Hasselhoff. Yet there was one more thing he enjoyed even more than his collection of bathrobes, and that was **not** wearing one, to ditch the robe and allow the Washintown breeze to waft around his nether regions.

"I'm the kind of guy who just adores not wearing one" he confessed to a group of local paparazzi as he stood on his doorstep taking an interview with them, possibly forgetting that this was one of the times when he was, in fact, not wearing one. Thankfully he was safe from any scurrilous reporting that day as the crews had left their telephoto lenses behind.

He only just finished the interview with the paparazzi when the phone rang. It was Regan Mordorc, live streaming on Discord, with a studio audience and a set of questions on civic administration. The call went on for sixty-two minutes. It was a perfect call.

7

RUSSIA, MY LOVE

Just as Chump's office had reached out in a spirit of compassion and charity to enable the appointment of medical miscreant Dr Jeb Goney, it had similarly given a chance to a rather sloppy and inexperienced sixty-five-year-old law clerk, Shelley Yeats. Shelley was a former factory worker at well-known sports equipment manufacturer Queen and Slazavenger, who had managed to scrape her way through law school by studying at night. Chump, ever supportive of women in the workplace, both literally and figuratively, adored Shelley like a daughter and was keen for her to 'get a good feel' for her job and to develop in her role. He always wanted to give a hand to any woman prepared to work through the night.

Through her studies, Shelley had shown promise as a brilliant wordsmith, producing eloquent essays, rhyming reports and alliterative affidavits which resonated with a poetic quality; however she was unfortunately plagued by something of an inferiority complex, a kind of existential angst. As such, she felt insecure about her own abilities in City Council and was actively looking to pursue a quiet, dreamy desk job in a private law firm.

That was, of course, until the day she first spied Head of Policing, Sergeant Mickey Flout, who worked in the office just across the hallway from her. His mischievous, outgoing nature, broad biceps, slack jaw and brazen jocularity contrasted with her waif-like physique and her cool, meek introversion. From that day, a fire and fury of sweet passion was kindled in her heart, and she began lingering longer than needed in the corridor, equipped with her poetry notebook, eager to steal glances at Mickey Flout as he diligently went about his policing duties, his face habitually smeared with sugar-dust. Pausing, rendered spellbound and breathless by Cupid's arrow and Mickey's sweet visage, a picture of innocence as he was, she would jot down romantic sonnets in his honor, inspired by his cherub cheeks and the honesty which shone from his eyes like a drone's laser beam. To any outside observer however, she had the appearance of a slightly creepy stalker.

As the weeks went on, even a short absence from Flout had her reaching for her poetry notebook and penning a somber poem, starting with pained words such as "The darkness drops again".

Flout had been overindulging again in Turkish delight and Chak-chak, the baked dessert especially popular in Tratarstan, to the point of developing a large pot-belly and significant signs of tooth decay which, to anyone else, risked ruining his boyish smile. The deep black enamel erosion, which had even infiltrated his pulp, was now plainly visible when he grinned or bared his teeth. Yet Yeats could see past these external imperfections, and saw Mickey's true inner being, his true self, his *Ātman*, even if it was betrayed by his outward actions, necrotic teeth and pungent halitosis as he ventured into the hallway having just scoffed more sweet delights in the privacy of his office.

* * *

With her office directly opposite Flout's, Yeats was often in a position to observe the comings-and-goings of Mickey and his visitors, and to overhear some of his conversations in the corridor.

Although the tender process for Washintown's public works project had not officially started yet, Mickey had initiated several intimate tender meetings with the saucy sales secretary from Punkin's Fix-It Services Business, Shirley Kissayak. These catch-ups were, ostensibly, aimed at hammering out fine details of security requirements in the hypothetical scenario that FSB should, perchance, ever win the contract for the S.H. IT Project.

In nailing down the Scope of Works (SOW), Flout had been insisting that, as Acting Chief Security Officer, he needed to remain in close collaboration with law enforcement agencies worldwide, including, for example, the British and French police (the latter known colloquially as '*les flics*'). To this end, he claimed he would need the winning bidder to install a high-speed cable connection to his beach house for fast access to the French police information system, NetFlics. Negotiations such as this seemed to require repeated hookups between Mickey and Shirley.

Shelley Yeats' loving emotions had been pushed to breaking point as time and again she had seen her beloved Mickey and the burly Shirley chatting and giggling in the corridor like high-school sweethearts.

Chump, by contrast, getting wind of these meetings, some might say dalliances, had expressed his delight that Flout was getting along so well, and so proactively, with someone who might help with Washintown's infrastructure rebuild.

These dangerous liaisons, however, drove Shelley wild with jealousy. She had endured the indignity of catching snippets of their intercourse, often as they were just wrapping up various intimate *sotto voce* exchanges, such as:

* "Oh, my sweet, I won't tell Mikey Pancedown."

* "Can you arrange a bigger one?"

* "Meet me after dark and let's do the business."

Yeats sought to express her pained feelings through her poetry, but she could not shake off the intuitive sense that she needed to look out for Mickey's best interests, to hold him in her custody, in her lawful, loving care.

Tensions in the corridor came to a head one day after she overheard the two engaging in intense negotiations in the photocopying room, which clearly climaxed in some form of firm agreement as Shirley repeatedly squealed "Yes, Yes" at the top of her voice even as Flout undoubtedly drove a hard bargain. Shelley then spied them emerging from the room with flushed faces, having sealed the deal amongst the reams.

"And don't call me Shirley", Shirley whispered flirtatiously, with a coquettish flick of her golden locks as she exeunted the room. "*Mon chérie* would be nice."

With that, she was gone, though her Muscovite perfume lingered.

Flout emerged and adjusted his ruffled shirt, looking sheepish.

"Why, good mornin', Miss Shelley" he said as Shelley stood there, notebook in hand, flooded with a rush of conflicting emotions, from the fire of fury to the ice of jealousy.

* * *

So livid she was ere she saw Flout with Kissayak on that occasion, so wracked by the agony of an unrequited love, that not even a word's worth of poesy would flow forth upon her poetry notebook that day. Love indeed Burns. Her pencil point snapped with the rage poured through it. Then, in another moment, she suddenly was overcome with Frost:

> *"Some say the world will end in fire,*
> *Some say in ice.*
> *From what I've tasted of desire*
> *I hold with those who favor fire. "*

She was all over the place. Bursting into tears, Shelley raced for the exit. For a moment or two, she was totally Wilde again. *"The heart was made to be broken!*" she fulminated to herself as she fled down the corridor, tears streaming down her face.

Shelley ran across the street from City Hall and raced right past me, to the quiet parklands of Chump's white house, where she sought solace for her troubled soul in the field looking down upon the murky lake. Out in the field, she sat and sobbed under a particularly exquisite tree, a poem as lovely as which I think I shall never see. Kind and intuitive Dan Imgone approached to comfort her and to offer her advice on dealing with her intense emotions. Shelley was inconsolable.

Finally, through his gentle counsel, Imgone managed to get through to her that she should seek the sage advice of Dr Jeb Goney, for Jeb seemed to know the ways of foreign women and, though he was known to be somewhat shady, was nonetheless a man of great intelligence. She could do so, he suggested, under the valid pretext of raising her heartfelt concerns for Mickey's health, in regards to his overconsumption of sweet treats. This was the defining moment which convinced Shelley to approach Dr Goney, which she did in the coming days.

* * *

The team dynamic became quite complex. Yeats' passion for Flout appeared to inspire further office romances, some of which flourished in the pheromone-laden environment of the Chump administration.

Paula Moneyport was becoming increasingly intimate with her colleague Konstantli Kriminiki, exchanging ever-more-sensitive notes via email, having sweet phone conversations and obviously holding each other's deepest secrets. Kristya Nosoulson had taken a shine to Slobodan Milersevic, as they shared the same value system, both believing that Work Brings Freedom, and loved hanging out together in the dark quadrangle discussing refugee policy while staring blankly into each other's eyes.

Jess Fessin began showing a love interest in Mr Chump, writing sweet notes of resignation to his hypnotic charms, even though she knew how very wrong this was, given Chump's status as a loyal, faithful, non-prostitute-bonking husband. True to form, when Fessin managed to slip one such tempting note into Chump's coat pocket, Chump sternly returned it with a black pen mark saying "Not accepted!"

Shirley Kissayak, though primarily showing a fancy for Flout in the perilous love triangle with Yeats, proved that she was something of a floozy, as she was regularly seen hovering around several other offices, including Fessin's, Chump's and Nutberger's. When I pressed her to specify her meetings with Chump staffers as she raced out to her vehicle one day - a waiting Soviet T-34 tank - she admitted to me "the list is so long that I'm not going to be able to go through it in 20 minutes." With that, she sped off in a cloud of obfuscating dust and diesel fumes.

* * *

So Shelley Yeats, aware of Dr Goney's medical background and genuinely concerned for Mickey's wellbeing, at last approached Dr Goney, ostensibly seeking Jeb's advice about Mickey's gourmandise of confections. While initially not wishing to reveal her intimate feelings for Mickey or her accompanying jealousies, Shelley's deep, damp eyes belied a concern far greater than that of the average work colleague. When she had tapped on his door and been invited in, Goney was pleasantly struck by the flattering cut of her light floral dress and the intoxicating scent of her perfume.

While Shelley unloaded her concerns regarding Mickey's diet, barely able to conceal her unbridled envy of Shirley Kissayak, the amoral Goney allowed his wandering eye to remain mainly focused on Shelley's pleasing cleavage. Shelley provided extensive details of Mickey's intake of treats, with just a passing reference to the sweet gifts from Shirley.

Though highly distracted by Shelley's pleasant and shapely presentation, enough of her message got through to the dissolute Dr

Goney that he did start to appraise some real risk to Mickey's overall health, and his dental wellbeing, thanks to this discreet meet-and-greet re sweet-treat eating habits.

Shelley relayed to Goney some of the conversations she had overheard in the corridor, and, by way of obliquely expressing her jealousy, mentioned that Mickey still seemed to be receiving further gifts of chak-chak from the seductive Shirley Kissayak, who had been offering her sweetnesses to the ingenuous Mickey like a diabetes-inducing temptress.

"Shirley, you can't be serious."

"I am serious, Dr. Goney. And don't call me Shirley. I'm Shelley, not Shirley."

Ignoring Goney's distractedness, she went on to give further details of everything she had witnessed, and conversations overheard.

"Jeb, listen. I heard him talking to Janey once Shirley had left, and he flatly denied that he was overconsuming Turkish Delight. I couldn't believe it, Dr Goney! He still had sugar-dust all over his sweet little mouth."

"Mmmm" replied Goney, looking intense, transfixed, even a little creepy, obviously trying to grasp the gravity of what was being presented before him.

"We must do what's breast, I mean what's best, in this situation" he responded thoughtfully.

Shelley continued in earnest to explain her second point, for she had two outstanding points: "And then, Dr Goney, would you believe it? He went on to say that Kissayak had only brought him some promotional brochures. I was sure I saw her passing him chak-chak, a whole big box of it! I did, Dr. Goney. I did!" she asserted breathlessly. Her breasts jiggled lightly as she spoke in animated tones of Mickey's twin lies.

"Well, those are obviously two giant whoppers." Goney conceded. "Something needs to be done about this. I will need to take these things into my own hands. But don't dwell on it, Ms Yeats, let me deal with it. I hope you can see your way clear to letting this go. I hope you can let this go. I'll see to it that Mickey is ok. I'll get him to cut back. That's definitely too much chak-chak."

As their meeting concluded, Shelley turned on her heels and left with a flourishing swish of her low-cut dress. Dr Goney thanked her for having given him the opportunity to look into it.

* * *

When Shelley had left, Goney, with his two new titular responsibilities weighing on his mind, juggled whether or not to involve Chump, who was known for his firm grasp of female sensitivities. Chump and his friend Ekky would have had been furious with Jeb had they witnessed his disgraceful, disrespectful comportment towards Shelley.

Chump, however, was far too busy in his office, focused on social policy.

As part of his "Youth off the Streets" initiative, Chump had requested Dan Imgone to contact the troubled teen Bobby Mauler to see if Bobby could be convinced to participate in a youth diversionary program involving quiet meditation and chanting at a remote youth camp in the woods. Chump hoped that this process - designed to quieten the teen's unruly, crime-obsessed mind - would set Bobby on the path of one day becoming a useful contributor to society, just like Chump himself.

He then asked Dan Imgone, who was always keen to fulfill the Mayor's requests, to draft up a beautiful letter inviting Jess Fessin to join in a Saturday Night Masquerade party with Chump. It would be quite a romantic affair. Jess was thrilled, and immediately began choosing frocks for the party.

* * *

Emerging daily from his hedge, Shawn Spinner had been hellishly busy training Sally Muckabee Blathers in her role as his new assistant. Deep in the foliage they worked on presentation skills and on the fancy footwork Sally could use beneath the podium to make her feel at ease in front of the probing press. Shawn reiterated that Sally could do as much bootscooting as she liked from the waist down, as long as her jiggling remained confined to her lower half and she could still present a stationary face and eyes to the media. Shawn suggested that she dab some cigarette ash around her eye sockets, not unlike The Joker, so that the press could focus on her message rather than her bewitching eyes. Sally complied. She seemed to be a great learner, and like just The Joker, her presentations were always a blast.

* * *

Council - though slightly short of the required funds - unanimously passed Ronnie's proposal for the huge infrastructure project, based on it having Chump's moral backing, and the tendering process officially began. Joy Hickey worked diligently to type up the Request for Proposal (RFP) for the project.

In hindsight, the proposal contained a little 'overbundling' as it sought a very broad range of services, including wireless access, plumbing works and testing of IT security breaches by way of realistic network penetration. Yet Joy was very pleased with the font and cheery floral cover she had chosen and the RFP document itself presented as a very impressive document indeed, amounting to over 200 pages.

It was now just a matter of waiting for the proposals to start rolling in.

* * *

The date soon arrived whereby submission of proposals for the Secure Hub IT project would be open, and the process for accepting proposals began in earnest.   Unfortunately, this happened to coincide with a period of significant apathy in the Washintown business community.

At the same time, in preparation for getting the tender selection process finalized for the Secure Hub IT Project, Chump gathered a crack team of his most talented, experienced and objective staff members to form the selection committee to determine the awarding of the contract.

This team, brilliantly chosen for its impartiality and expertise, consisted of Paula Moneyport, Mickey Flout, Janey Kushynird, Dicky Fences, Grigor Ganadobonus and Jess Fessin. They were tasked with assessing the proposals and making a prompt decision, in order to get the project off the ground as quickly as possible.

* * *

Not long after the publication of the formal Request for Tender (RFT), minxy Jess Fessin slinked up to the door of Joy's office, bearing a large envelope. "Oh Joy" she exclaimed, "Oh Joy of joys, lookie here - we have our first tender response!" Joy squealed with delight, knowing how glad Ronnie would be to be receiving tender responses.   Sure enough, there in clear print on the envelope was written: "Яesponse to Яequest for Tender for Kommunity Central Hub Wiringk and Good Qvality IT service."

"Joy do you think it matters if it has a Moscow stamp on it?"

"Show me that, Jess." Joy took the envelope.

"No that'll be fine, we know those boys. That's the FSB crew. Ronnie's forgiven them for their last shitty job. Such a sweetie, our Ronnie."

Sure enough, on the back of the envelope, the sender was listed as "Viktor Punkin, Fix-It Services Business", with a hammer and sickle embossed on the envelope's wax seal.

* * *

FSB's proposal contained pretty pictures which caught Chump's eye and immediately made it stand out as the leading proposal, although, to be fair, at that point there had only been one submission. The package also included several complimentary bags of sweets, one could say sweeteners, which greatly pleased the committee.

The proposal was concise, and the pricing appeared reasonable. It included a detailed plan of action to really rig up a great IT system at the heart of the city's operations. This first proposal was shown around the office to great excitement. Joy, who had flicked through the submission before the others, described what she had already read of it to Dinah. Dinah took it in and processed what she had just heard from Joy.

Seventeen minutes later, Dinah expressed her strong approval, exclaiming: "If it's what you say, I love it!" That level of enthusiasm could really help clinch a decision on the critical project. For overhearing this, Ronnie was inclined to think, as he rarely did, that if his daughter so liked the proposal, it must indeed be a good one.

"It really must be time to let bygones be bygones as far as Viktor Punkin is concerned", thought a ruminating Chump. "Just look at the Qvality of this" he added as he stroked the images of the young women pictured on its cover. "But let's follow due process and see if any of the other applicants can match this."

For the first time, now with a real proposal in his hands, Chump could at last allow himself to dare to believe that his dream project would actually become a reality. A lump formed in his throat, and a small tear of civic pride rolled from the corner of one eye.

8

DISORDER CHART

In the initial phases of the mayoral incumbency, there were three dedicated and talented staff members literally falling over each other to assist Chump: Bunyon, Ponce and Kushynird.

Chump, with Stevie Bunyon's companionship, ran his new administration with military precision and the wisdom of an enlightened being like Sadhguru. There was a strict hierarchy with clearly defined roles for all his staff.

As soon as Chump moved in to the Square Office, he had removed any symbols of pomp and ceremony which had been installed by previous administrations - dusty brass cups, photos of dignitaries, flags and other memorabilia - and in their place installed maps of the city highlighting areas of need for housing, public transport and other social services.

He instigated a strict regime of meetings with him to ensure that information flowed smoothly between departments, whose staffing levels were bolstered to unbelievable levels, truly incredible, like you just wouldn't believe. Staff were systematically slotted into only the meetings they needed to attend, and the mayor's time was partitioned out according to well-defined priorities.

It was as though Chump had fitted a revolving door of deeply skilled individuals, who were shoehorned into jobs they were always destined for, sometimes with a detailed background check via Google or Wikipedia. In Chump's own words, the administration was 'like a Lazy Susan at a Japanese Yum Cha'. As soon as one person left a room or a meeting, another would enter who had a similar skill level.

Chump viewed efficiency as an essential element of good governance. He had not been long installed in his office when, to assist with operational efficiency (and partly to copy what he had seen in Barry Kabana's handover session) he insisted that a large red 'UNCLEAR' button be installed on his desk, just an inch or two adjacent to the other enormous red emergency button with its own label in small font. His dyslexia had been showing some signs of improving lately so he was fairly confident he could hit the right button when needed. Echoing Kabana's parting admonitions, General Malaise had again advised him never to push the other red button except in a real, life-threatening emergency, but this new button - Chump's own idea, of which he was immensely proud, and not AT ALL Kabana's idea - would be Ronnie's personal addition to the efficiency of city administration. "One day this will be called the R.S. CHUMP button" Ronnie asserted with a swelling chest.

His plan was faultless: whenever he was unclear on a point of policy, he would quickly bang on the new UNCLEAR button and - in a blinding flash - one of his highly capable assistants, usually Kylie-Jo Connard or Joy Hickey - would immediately present at the office door to explain whatever he needed to know. He once accidentally hit the other enormous red N-button when he was on the phone to the Mayor of Hawaii, but thankfully it was malfunctioning at the time so only caused a partial evacuation at Ronnie's end. Ronnie's staff all laughed nervously and breathed a huge sigh of relief on that occasion, once they had worked out how to turn off the sirens and klaxons. Some grimaces and white faces, drained of blood, were momentarily observed. Ronnie, bless his sweet soul, couldn't see what all the fuss was about.

"I'll be more careful next time" he promised as he headed to the bathroom.

* * *

Only weeks into the new administration, staff were seen to be strutting the corridors with a renewed sense of confidence and purpose. An air of excitement and great promise circulated through City Hall. The UNCLEAR button was getting a good workout, and the team was learning how to work with a Chump.

As the staff grew more accustomed to the new dynamics in place, they quickly learned that Ronnie could not stand dishonesty in any form, and was known to excoriate staff or fellow councilors who even dared tell even the slightest falsehood. He brought a new sense of ethics and morality to the office.

Regular huddles were formed in the mayor's office which included Chump at his dual-button oak table, surrounded by Bunyon, Ponce, Mickey, Kushynird, Joy, Iwanker, General Malaise, Kitty Welsher, Rod Hurther, Melony, Dinah, Erika, Paula, Odorosa Animalgut and the tea lady. Wilbert Robbs would have been there too but was busy on the phone stitching up a lucrative procurement deal for the council, insisting that it be ethically watertight. With so many great minds gathered in one spot it was no wonder that the administration could put out such high-quality legislation at such a rapid rate.

When not involved in huddle meetings, the team was a textbook model of collaboration and ingenuity at work: Bunyon invariably developed policy over in one corner, flipping through papers like a Vegas card-shuffler; Rebus sat with his chair towards a wall, seeking inspiration as he rocked back and forth, repeatedly voicing the Hindu sound "Ummm" and avoiding looking at Bunyon who had a "thing" about people looking over his shoulder. Kushynird walked around the room adding deep insights into each person's thinking process, suddenly dropping phrases such as "Simplify!" and "Shhh!" to prevent anyone falling into conventional modes of thinking; meanwhile Chump sat with Joy Hickey, Connard and Odorosa Animalgut untangling the intricacies of upcoming legislation, or on the phone with Viktor Punkin giving a few friendly advance details about the upcoming contract for Washintown's essential services rebuild.

It was from these wonderful collaborations with his team - and Viktor Punkin on the end of the phone occasionally adding some new suggestions - that the finer details of minor amendments to the Secure Hub Infrastructure Transformation Project's Request for Tender (RFT) documents were gradually hammered and sickled out by the Chump administration. The Chump team were indeed skilled collaborators.

Following the example set by Flout, who had arranged special cabling to his beach house, Janey was similarly moved to negotiate inclusion into the tender documents of an additional high-speed cable back to her own residence too, in her case exactly a mile out of town. She had made it clear to everyone in The Office that she needed this urgently, as she had been working extended hours at home downloading critical video materials for the administration in her important research work for the High Business Overhead project (HBO), the sub-project she had initiated as her contribution to the city council's broader Start-up Assistance Program.

* * *

Thanks to Joy's nifty typing, the city had been able to quickly reissue updated tender documents for the new work, which, as we have heard, would involve extensive rewiring of City Hall and the provision of new IT systems and software to run all the social programs, plus renewal of water and gas piping and communications systems - in short, a comprehensive overhaul of the city.

The contract would require the winning applicants to peel back the housing on all the old wiring in City Hall. FSB had estimated that the job to re-peel and replace the wiring for the entire City of Washintown would take about four years in total.

In an ominous sign for the future replumbing and renewal project, a leak occurred as the tender process continued.

Some annoying killjoys hanging over from Barry Kabana's administration, about 16 in total, headed up by Frank Allen, a former straight man, and his pals from the probity office, plus a few reporters from the Washintown Sentinel, had somehow gotten wind of the FSB submission. Like a posse of cowboys, they wandered down the hall one day to send a message to Chump, through Joy. They were keen to make the point that the FSB gang had been found to have done some substandard work on other government projects and really shouldn't be allowed to tender for the S.H. IT Project. They even wanted Jess Fessin to make contact with the Russians and run checks on their work history. When they arrived at the office, Jess Fessin herself happened to be there with Joy, chatting about the young men they liked.

When Jess heard the message the group was wanting to convey, she immediately said "Now wait up, you fellas. I've met the FSB boys on a few occasions, includin' once at a rodeo bar, and they were mighty fine boys. They 'r gonna do us proud with all their, you know, wirin' and plumbin' an' stuff. I think you fellas should keep y'all big sticky noses right outta the mayor's business."

The group shuffled off disconsolately and Jess turned back to Joy.

"Why, how dare they come on down here with such a trivial, nit-picky little complaint! They should be ashamed of themselves. What would their mommas think of them?"

* * *

As the tender submission period rolled on over the following weeks, another submission arrived from a highly-respected U.S. company, Centralized Infrastructure Associates (CIA LLC). This company listed extensive experience in the successful supply, rollout and maintenance of complex IT systems, cabling operations, high-tech security systems and data storage, very similar to the requirements of the Washintown S.H. IT Project.

Whereas the FSB proposal had contained stunning imagery, the U.S. company's application, by contrast, contained a lot of quite boring words, detailing the intricacies of their successful projects and proof of their skills, certifications and compliance with industry standards and best practices. It included a dry appendix listing multiple reference sites of their similar, successfully-completed projects which had been rolled out with 24x7 uptime, availability and redundancy.

Jess Fessin just didn't like the look of it, and besides, she thought: who would want to risk such an important job to a local company?

She sniffed the envelope suspiciously, then showed the application to Joy.

"I hardly want to bother Ronnie with this." said Jess. "This project is his life's work, why would he risk it with this mob?"

"It looks a little tatty anyway, don't you think, Jess? And that round logo with the decapitated bird is pretty lame." said Joy. "I should just stay out of this whole process, but I'm so tempted to bin this one. Do you think we should even pass it on to Ronnie?"

"You know Ronnie" replied Jess. "He's so even-handed. He will want to give them a fair chance."

They reluctantly passed this latest submission on to Chump and his selection committee, having simply redacted some of the more boring bits, however their initial assessments proved not to have been far wrong. When going through the application in fine detail, as he did with all official paperwork, it reminded Chump of Barry Kabana blowing his own trumpet. Showboats. The CIA proposal also did not seem to provide employment opportunities for marginalized groups or other people of color, or for losers, for it seemed the organization was run solely by white cis males, with no women, or at least none pictured.

The FSB submission, by contrast, had indicated that in addition to its on-the-ground Russian technicians, the team would also provide multicultural human resourcing, through the services of a world-leading Pakistani specialist in server installations. A supplementary appendix in the form of a yellow Post-it® Note at the back of the Russian submission had further offered, succinctly: "Ve vill also fix up all ze other infra**Strzok**ture, Яeal good." Finally, FSB had also promised extra giveaways in the form of a set of real American McNugget Buddies to eligible customers. They had even agreed to run the additional requested optic-fiber cable the 1760 yards to Janey Kushynird's home, north by northwest of City Hall. This is what Chump called "going the extra mile."

* * *

As the tender requirements documentation was fleshed out further, even after submissions had already started rolling in, Animalgut, for her part, with a strong background in online shopping, was able to provide valuable inputs on network topology, encryption (mainly via message scrambling), cashless transactions and the laying of large cables.

She was a quick and perceptive judge of character, and had Chump pegged from day one as a wonderful human being who had a strong sense of fairness and respect for all. She was much beloved for her qualities by General Kitty Malaise in particular, who sought her out at every turn for advice and woman-to-woman guidance. General Malaise was starting to feel she, the General, and not the Mayor, ruled over the entire staff, and she made that very clear to all; but she had a soft spot when it came to Animalgut and would take her into the Washintown Situation Room, lock the door and have intimate discussions with her for hours at a time. Together they would chat for hours on topics from the latest shoe trends to creating the perfect smoky eye; but these intimate chats were also a way for General Kitty to let Odorosa know how much she treasured her input to the team and never wanted her to leave.

Despite Odorosa's superlative skills in assessing people, she had nevertheless taken some time to fully warm to Chump because she needed time to develop a rounded sense of his remarkable character, such were its exceptional depths. This could be likened to how a new parent might take a while to develop an awareness that their baby's diaper needs changing, while still being a brilliant parent all the while.

Pending finalization of the tendering process, Chump embarked on a rigorous program of fiscal responsibility. He was adamant that the city would not be allowed to get into a toxic debt situation, so ensured that each and every one of the council's spending proposals was fully costed and fully funded, with no reliance on debt. Ronnie knew from personal experience that a misuse of "debit card" could lead to "bad credit". Council therefore found that accountability was now expected even when submitting relatively small expenses. As an example, even to repair the small picket fence which ran along the side of City Hall between the council offices and the restaurant next door, Enrique's Mexican Cantina, Chump insisted that the fence expense should not be borne by council, and offered to fund the repairs from his own pocket.

Good management acts as an enema to the ills of an organization, and in the Chump administration, juices were flowing at such a rate that no enema was needed, hence no need for such a prescription.

* * *

Chump was thrilled that Washintown had an $81 billion annual trade surplus with its sister city in North Korea, and was also earning $5.30 a day from North Korean tourism to the city.

Despite almost daily reports of the smooth running and harmony in City Hall, the public didn't know how great the internal situation actually was. Chump was never shifting from sheer excellence. He was fixed, resolute, dependable and determined in his decision-making. He would get in a happy mood - something medium-sized would delight him - and he would sing out a resounding chorus:

"We're going in today!" though no-one quite understood what that meant.

* * *

The internal efficiency of the office, including the processing of significant amounts of paperwork, was incredible. Gerry Conehead was particularly keen for Chump to sign all the letters that had been lined up on his desk and wanted to make sure that he saw them all. He had entered the Square Office, moving cautiously towards the famous Irresolute Desk, intent on helping to organize the steady stream of important correspondence and legislation flowing across Chump's desktop. Having granted himself walk-in privileges to Chump's office, he surveyed the daunting task and took a deep breath. He knew he could do it.

The documents which Chump had let fall onto the floor around his desk, Conehead placed into the yellow container marked "OUT" to imply that the documents needed to be signed and then go out, rather than remain on the floor where they might be overlooked. They had obviously already come "IN" earlier. He was fairly sure, too, that the ones spread out on the desk belonged in the same category, so they also went into "OUT".

Noticing the plastic bucket which Chump had marked "IN" with his Sharpie, Conehead moved the documents from this bucket, into the yellow container marked "OUT", using the logic that surely anything which had come "IN" should then efficiently go "OUT". 'He's going to see all his documents now,' Gerry thought to himself.

On the desk were several smiling photos of Chump, on Summer vacation with his friend Kimmy 'Long Gun', and with Viktor Punkin in early negotiations for the S.H. IT Project contract. He took the photos and placed them in the blue folder marked "KEEP". Finally, he stood back to assess his handiwork. As if enchanted by the Irresolute Desk, he had a moment of vacillation. Seeing the container marked "OUT" again, he wondered: maybe "OUT" really means, like, "throw out"? He paused, then, after looking furtively over his shoulder, quickly transferred these documents to the waste bin, since, let's face it, "OUT" means "OUT". The "IN" bucket was ready for new incomings, "OUT" was out, and "KEEP" had retained the precious memories. It was the perfect call.

The office now looked clean and efficient, and Conehead knew Chump would be pleased with his day's work.

Ordinarily Rob Hurther, the organizer of mayoral paperwork, would have been responsible for managing the mayoral paperwork, but Hurther had been tied up with Joy Hickey lately. Conehead, an enthusiastic team player, intent on loyally and diligently serving the mayor, and bursting with eagerness to help, had politely offered to Hurther "Don't worry, I've got this Robbie. Leave it to me." It was truly inspiring to hear of such dedicated staff members hard at work, sharing the load, within the heart of the Chump administration. This was teamwork at its finest!

Hurther, 4-foot-6, broad as a freight train, 20 years old and raised as a Norman (despite having an Anglo-Saxon heritage and traces of Viking in his DNA) was a colorful character: a slightly anarchic lad with loads of pizzazz who had attended a Harlem criminology school, where he had been a top student. He and Joy Hickey had been putting in a lot of overtime, including weekend work.

On his return, Hurther discovered that Conehead had done a brilliant job tidying up the mayor's desk, making sure no mess was left behind.

* * *

Firm in his role as a guiding influence to the administration, Ponce Rebus commanded the respect and attention of all as he delighted in issuing well-planned meeting schedules and detailed daily directives to the staff, guaranteeing the smooth functioning of the mayoral office.

The mayor himself, confident in the competence of his leadership team, consulted widely among them and Bunyon and Rebus worked hand-in-glove to ensure that each and every press release, quote and legislative document was drafted to the highest standard. Rebus, at the epicenter of such a word factory, felt that he had secured the dream job, and wished to never leave.

Chump was often heard making friendly, encouraging or congratulatory quips to Ponce Rebus. He both adored Ponce and respected him deeply.

Among the three staffers with top ranking in the Chump administration - Rebus, Bunyon and Kushynird - a shared sense of respect kept them forever united and working together cooperatively. The love and respect flowed like the waters of North Carolina after Florence was downgraded to a tropical storm.

The situation seemed clear to everyone: these three in particular were so dedicated to achieving lasting outcomes for society that they selflessly shared their workloads and responsibilities, and worked together like a family in a crisis refuge. Chump himself, similarly, stayed up into the wee hours of the night sending out important messages.

With such a great Chump at the helm, and a list of staff as loyal and disciplined as Baldrick, how could this ship of city-state do anything but shove off majestically with such a list into the deep, unexplored and rocky waters of municipal politics, taking on more as it drifted along, as nobody wanted to bail, and new crew joined to plumb new depths.

* * *

In addition to new hirings, Chump had achieved another magnificent outcome; over a period of weeks he had finalized the shortlist of contractors for the Secure Hub IT Project, whittling it down to just two finalists from the total of two applications. This had only come about after an exhaustive process undertaken with Ronnie's hands-on guidance and involvement.

At the closure of the application period, Chump had rung a bell and announced that he would begin the task of tallying up all the proposals received. He retired into the Square Office with the applications collected by Joy, and emerged half an hour later, proudly stating that by his count there had been a total of three applications. On hearing this, Joy Hickey gently took the mayor aside, and following a moment of whispering between themselves, Ronnie humbly corrected himself, stating that Joy advised him there had been a total of two applications, and that he must have accidentally double-counted. Math had never been Ronnie's strongest subject, for his focus throughout his education had always been on Ethics and Jurisprudence.

Of the applications which had been submitted, there were two in particular which stood out as exceptional: the FSB submission, addressed directly to Chump himself, which, loaded with pretty pictures, appeared to have been prepared at a very high-end print shop in central Moscow; and one from the local company, Centralized Infrastructure Associates (CIA LLC), with their impressive, if boastful, track record. The latter, however, had incorrectly addressed their submission to the Public Services Department, City of Washintown, not to Ronnie. This had cost them points in terms of credibility.

The shortlisted submissions were passed on to Ronnie's hand-picked, highly-objective selection committee for evaluation and final determination.

Ronnie played only an advisory role to the selection committee, though the final decision would rest on his shoulders. Still bearing a slight reluctance to engage the Muscovites after his incident with the bronze shower plumbing, he initially had a slight preference for the U.S.-based specialists, CIA LLC. His selection committee, while acknowledging this company as a viable contender, strongly urged consideration of the budgetary benefits to his bottom line if Chump were to choose the cheaper Chernobyl-based challengers.

Melony's "Be Best" pep talk was ringing in Ronnie's ears. The FSB application's high-quality graphics showing happy people typing at keyboards or looking knowingly at screens, were also certainly swaying Chump with their compelling subtext of near-certain success, and clean implementation. This would not be an easy decision.

Chump thought over the alternatives just one more time in his own noggin, straining to get the decision right: so, on the one hand, there was the rather dreary CIA submission. Up against this was the colorful FSB submission, with crisp images, the added Pakistani expert and free giveaways. Chump felt that this offered great value for his party, and for the people of Washintown, who had not previously had such compelling offers on collectibles.

Chump's review committee virtually mirrored his thinking: they also particularly liked the additional free giveaways offered by FSB, plus FSB's multicultural human resourcing which included the world-class Himalayan server expert.

* * *

With these factors in mind, and with the strong persuasion of Chump's independent and objective committee, Chump finally saw the light and together, the committee, along with Chump and his veto vote as the committee chair, made their final decision to unanimously nominate FSB as the successful bidder for the project.

It had come down to some difficult choices, without a doubt, but the appealing FSB proposal looked clearly stronger than CIA's anodyne offering.

The city was about to have a major wiring upgrade, and its IT, health and communications systems would be out of this world! FSB was awarded the contract. Party poppers were popped and streamers slung over seats in the office. Fizzy drinks were shared around. This was a great day for Washintown.

* * *

Habitually cautious, Chump conferred one final time with his team before preparing to make any public statement. He didn't want to make a fool of himself. In honor of his forebears, Teddy, Baloo, Paddington and Fozzie Chump, he too wanted to be a fine example of a Chump. He wanted a speech which was honest, no-nonsense, not tainted with ego, and with no hidden meanings or any trace of sarcasm or other literary devices. He didn't want his announcement speech to be full of "I, Ronnie..."

Soon after the tender decision was finalized, Chump called a press conference to announce the successful bidder, making sure to arrange a roaring, whirring helicopter in the background to minimize the focus upon himself as a great leader, and to showcase, indeed to symbolize, the city council's cutting-edge technological ambitions. He did not want this to be about him, at least not after the initial announcement. The press and others in attendance waited nervously, buffeted by the blowback thrown up by the chopper's blades, to hear - or rather, to lipread - the long-awaited announcement of the company which would be entrusted to renew the city's key infrastructure. "It looks like a Sikorsky Cyclone" my prescient colleague Jimmy Acostya screamed out to me over the noise of the chopper's turboshaft jet engines. "Yes, it is a Cyclone" I screamed back to Jimmy as the upward billowing of my skirt, Marilyn Monroe style, risked causing front page news in itself.

Chump always made sure his press conferences were homely and welcoming, by providing the media with vats of Chump Chowder and a number of pork pies. The press and others in attendance waited nervously to hear the long-awaited announcement of the company which would be entrusted to renew the city's key infrastructure. The chopper was throwing some bulldust into the soup vats.

Today he had let Sally Muckabee Blathers be off-duty at the podium and instead she was out the back dishing up Chump Chowder to the team. Having a background in catering for overfed felines at a cattery before joining the administration, Sally had earlier helped with preparations for the press conference, filling the vats and lining up bowls of chowder plus a number of Chump's specialty pies for the press on a small table next to the mayor. Chump drew the inspiration for his pie recipes - which included specialty pies filled with ingredients such as tripe and baloney, flavor-enhanced by dill - from celebrity chef Kel Knight. Dill was in fact a chief component of many a Chump confection, as he felt it 'represented' him both metaphorically and literally.

Finally, Chump mounted the podium.

With television lights glaring, Chump stood grandly before the press (though unfortunately not noticing that he had a giant oily stain down the front of his shirt, plain to see, from sampling the bowls of Chump Chowder which Sally had been lovingly preparing for the waiting media):

"Punkin, if you're listening, I'm prepared to set aside old grievances. I think you'll do a tremendous job. I urge you to build a system that will be capable of transmitting thirty thousand emails in a week. Washintown has faith in you guys. All is forgiven. You have won the contract!

A huge roar broke out from the crowd, and loud cheering. A group of civics enthusiasts rushed the stage and lifted Chump high on their shoulders, transporting him over the crowd like a rock star. Everything was certainly going peachy-dory.

Not many people noticed, but as Chump was carried aloft that day, on his way to his next appointment, at the Municipal Tip, he was trailed by a mysterious gossamer thread, as though a fine silk stitch from his Boss suit has been pulled and was trailing through the air behind him. He scratched his armpit a little, then was put down and shown the exit, directed swiftly to the waiting mayoral armored car and whisked away, with only a slight lingering pong reminding the audience of his presence.

* * *

So, as you can see, the remarkable Chump, having set aside his old grievance, and in a spirit of good will and forgiveness, and based on the dispassionate advice of his objective panel, had decided to award the rewiring and replumbing contract to none other than Viktor Punkin's Fix-It Services Business. In doing so, he had opened the way for Punkin's FSB group to show their true expertise in laying cable all over Washintown.

* * *

As the celebrations continued after Ronnie's triumphant exit, Chump's mystical advisor, Elrond Resinstone, wandered the corridors in a dreamy state offering sage advice and pithy aphorisms to the staff to keep their moral compasses aligned with the South, and inspiring the team with ad hoc speeches.

One of the more flamboyant staffers, Elrond was known for wearing a large plastic daffodil on his lapel. Oddly enough, it looked like a series of thin cables dangled from the flower, and apparently led to a small device in his pocket. Whenever he stood close to Chump, he would thrust his chest and his daffodil forward, encouraging Chump to "SPEAK UP, SIR! I'm a little hard of hearing."

Not receiving much attention from the excited staffers that particular day, he finally resorted to standing up on a chair in the staff cafeteria, tapping a glass instead, before clearing his throat and delivering an epic oration, as an ancient Greek may have done, eloquently summarizing the zeitgeist:

"Fellow staffers, gather round and lend me your ears. We have just witnessed a watershed moment in the history of our town, Washintown. For that watershed, we owe much to our beloved Mayor Chump, without whose vision and guidance none of this would have been possible."

As the staff became restless, partly due to his interminable verbosity, he continued: "As the famous historian Robbie L. Jackson once noted: 'The qualities of a fine mayor are as elusive and impossible to define as those which mark a gentleman; and those who need to be told would not understand it anyway. A sensitiveness to fair play and sportsmanship is perhaps the best protection against the abuse of power, and the citizen's safety relies in the mayor who tempers zeal with kindness, who seeks truth and not victims, who serves the law, and not factional purposes, and who approaches his task with humility.' Our fabulous Mayor Chump has nailed these principles, utterly nailed them!"

This drew an enormous round of applause and general back-slapping as the staff knew they had all played their part in allowing Chump to get into the position he had. They were all responsible for this! The staff in the cafeteria then went back to their hamberders and covfefe.

Elrond glided back out of the cafeteria, after having picked up a soy latte and a cherry Danish, and levitated back down the hall to his office like Luke in his Star Wars Landspeeder (minus the Landspeeder).

* * *

The enormous S.H. IT Project was about to get underway on a massive scale, like nothing seen since the great Stickney wastewater project.

9

CRAPI

On October 7, a 57-degree day in Washintown, Chump went to sleep in a house with a broken-down heating system. Throughout the night he shivered and had broken dreams about being one of the greatest Chumps the world had ever seen. The freezing conditions brought home the reality that he had done the right thing engaging the FSB experts, experienced in similar Siberian conditions, who would soon be making a start on reinvigorating Washintown's services infrastructure.

Only three weeks into his new term, the mayor had been due to give a keynote speech at the Convention for Regional and Provincial Investment (CRAPI), one of Washintown's premier annual events, where it was expected he would be up against a tough crowd of centrist liberal fat-cats openly hostile to his agenda for a more socially progressive municipality.

In the meantime, however, Chump had been awarded the prestigious Freddie Chump Humanitarian Award for Services to Child Welfare. He had reworked his busy schedule to attend the award ceremony after attending a prior engagement honoring immigrant and refugee families at Ellis Island, but it did not appear that he would be able to make it back in time for his CRAPI keynote speech.

In his place, Chump ordered Bunyon and Ponce to attend the convention, and to speak on his behalf of the terrific work being undertaken by his administration. Since they were both undertakers of this work, he felt it only fair that they should both have to share the heavy burden of addressing the potentially hostile CRAPI audience while he dined on canapés at his award ceremony in New York. Kylie-Jo Connard would be attending with her two sons and an aged care worker, as well as Becky Onceler from the Chump fundraising cake stall, so there was no doubt the boys would be in great company.

The venue for CRAPI was to be Bob's Country Bunker, a graceful lakeside establishment frequented by 'chardonnay socialists' and other hand-wringing, left-leaning snowflakes.

The conference was sponsored by a number of small-name organizations including the National Retardation Association, Imprisonment Aged Care, and Cock Industries, a family-run recycled sausage company.

Thankfully, the organizers had arranged for the installation of chicken-wire between the audience and the stage.

* * *

Meanwhile, the Russian crew were setting up their digging equipment.

The FSB team had extensive experience in the trench-digging, earth-moving and soil removal required for large-scale cable-laying and wiring installations. As for Washintown, the historical city of elegance, once known as the 'grand old dame' of North-East Arizona, with Chump's coordination and blessing, they moved quickly on her. They moved on her like a ditch. They moved on her very heavily. All of a sudden, they got into her phone pits. They got into her underground spaces, streets, and even the airport. They got to work on her landing strip. They rammed the ramparts. They got to work on her outskirts. They totally changed the look of her. They dug. They excavated. They drilled. Boy, did they drill. When you're a contractor, they let you do it.

FSB excavators got to work in the alleyways and avenues, ripping up concrete and digging new pits for the planned cabling. With the final sign-off from Chump and a brief ribbon-cutting ceremony outside City Hall, boring machines were sent deep into her cavities and could be heard hammering away all night long. For the Chump team, this was a dream come true. In a masterstroke of fiscal negotiation written deep in their contract, Chump and Moneyport had arranged that the excavated soil would be sold back from the Russian team at a heavily discounted price, thereby somehow helping to finance the whole project via some complicated offshore structures which Paula said she was "on top of".

IT systems were powered down in preparation for the city-wide upgrade. Chump had assisted in arranging a fast-tracked visa for FSB's Pakistani server expert, due to be flown in from Chump's favorite Pakistani city, Lahore, on Soviet Airlines Flight 175 the following Thursday.

Monstrous MAN trucks motored through the malls and marketplaces, marking the might and muscle of the Muscovites' machinery. They gouged out vast quantities of soil from beneath the once-sleepy city, and from Day One began to dump it in a growing slag-heap on the outskirts of town, causing significant disruption to Washintown's road traffic, IT networks and infrastructure with their extensive excavation and slag-dumping works. Roddy Pebble, coordinating closely with the FSB team, encouraged further dumps under cover of darkness. As a result of the ongoing noise, many residents found they #staywoke for much of the night.

* * *

Back at CRAPI, the conference was just starting, in the late evening. Bunyon, already looking dapper, was ushered into the make-up room behind the stage, just to correct a few lumps and bumps, the event officials told him. The early-arriving Ponce was already in the makeup chair, being made up for the impending appearance with a team from Washintown Cosmetics.

Ponce had gone to great lengths before going on stage to ensure that he was coiffed adequately, asking the conference organizers' best make-up artiste to apply ample hairspray to him, and to allow just a few strategic curls to dangle loose for a kind of Michael Jackson "Thriller" look, matching the theme of his planned speech that night, on the thrilling news coming from the administration.

In faraway Zacatecas, Dick Singlet, a strong proponent of tolerance and multiculturalism, was arranging his own transport to CRAPI. Singlet, a leader in the liberal peace movement, was famous for once punching a neo-Nazi at a similar convention. On this occasion, Singlet had no plans other than to support the Chump team, but then he always kept things close to his chest. His participation among all the other attendees wielding their pamphlets and origami promotional giveaways would prove to be somewhat of an omen for what would later unfold. He came as an emissary for peace.

The registration and snack sessions had gone on for several hours during the afternoon before attendees had filled their seats and Kylie-Jo Connard, acting as MC, took the microphone to warm up the waiting crowd. With the eager crowd desperate to see Chump himself, the first news of the S.H. IT Project hitting the fans was instead to have come from the great Connard. That was, if she could get to it.

She began by giving a moving introductory speech in which she thanked the Chump team, consisting of remarkable talent such as Joy Hickey and Sid Nutberger. She went on to excoriate Hildegard Glintin for her distorted focus on private enterprise and vested business interests over the public service which characterized their team.

Finally, she got to a slightly awkward part of her introductions.

"Tonight, folks, you are going to hear some wonderful news from the city administration. I think you will be really, really impressed.

Now I know you're all bustin' to see Ronnie Chump. He was going to give you a special announcement." The crowd sensed a let-down coming. Kylie-Jo could feel hostility in the air.

"However there is one big but." The crowd groaned, not impressed. "Look, like I said, there is one big but" she said. "And this one's on Chump's head, not mine."

"Unfortunately, Mr. Chump is being presented with an award today, so he can't be here himself. But he has sent two of his finest representatives, Messrs Bunyon and Ponce, and they will fill you in on all the latest from the Chump admin team."

Angry participants booed at the thought of being cheated from seeing their dear Ronnie. Champagne glasses were thrown at the chicken-wire. Connard closed her eyes tightly, fearing she might cop a foreign object to her noggin. Things hadn't started smoothly. She sought to rapidly move on, to introduce her next guests, Bunyon and Ponce.

* * *

About the same time that Connard had been explaining her own left-wing ideologies during the warm-up, Dick Singlet finally arrived at the convention, slightly underdressed. Not particularly keen to attend the breakout session running at the time, "The Left Ain't Left Enough", he instead positioned himself at the front of the conference cafeteria queue to get the first of the fresh donuts which had just been delivered, right beside a heating vent.

In the green room, Bunyon - in white shirt, light jacket and black pants - now stood berating his assistant, Alexander Prostate, for limiting the flow of liquids. Stevie, after all, only wanted a mere slug of water before facing the crowd. Ponce still sat in the makeup chair, making sure that before going on stage that he would be looking really good, having had ample hairspray applied all over.

Finally, once Kylie-Jo had wrapped up her oration to the tetchy crowd, Bunyon and Ponce mounted the stairs together and were welcomed up to the stage, to a faltering round of applause from the gathering of lefties.

Bunyon warmed up the crowd with his signature wit. "Y'all must be the biggest bunch of tree-huggers I ever doggone seen!

There was silence, and a pause.

"You're not a bunch of loony champagne liberals are you?" he joked.

"Oh hell yes we are!" came the thundering reply, along with a volley of champagne glasses which sprayed into fragments as they hit the chicken-wire. Bunyon and Ponce recoiled, shielding their eyes from the fine spray of glass fragments. They then regained their composure and prepared to address the audience again as the last tinkles of shattered glassware died down.

"I think you should go first, Ponce" Bunyon offered, always one to think of others before himself.

And it was thus, here at CRAPI, that one of the first and only signs of any disunity in the Chump camp appeared on public display. One of the largest scandals of the Chump administration was about to play out.

For you see, dear reader, as I strove to bring you this truthful tale, I, your intrepid Martha, had managed to slip in to CRAPI by hanging very close to Dick Singlet as he entered the conference hall, and evading officials checking tickets by claiming, 'I'm with Mr. Singlet'. I was able to witness these events first-hand, while also being fortunate enough to get my hands on some of the CRAPI food.

* * *

Stevie Bunyon and Ponce Rebus had been assigned consecutive slots in the program schedule, however each wanted to extend the kindness to the other of letting the other go first. Since the event was nationally televised, there was also, I believe, an element of wanting to make a good impression on Chump, who they knew would be watching via Moose News, as the broadcast was going to air just after the cartoons.

What followed was an initially polite tussle over who would be holding the microphone. In the struggle which ensued, the microphone struck Ponce on the bonce, right in the middle of his forehead, where he had a little curl. It then dropped directly onto Bunyon's swollen, gnarly toes.

The two of them were then both writhing in fits of pain on stage. Ponce, his face now dripping with blood from a gash on the forehead where the microphone's ON/OFF switch had scraped over his epidermis, was openly weeping, calling out for tissues and crying out "Will I be blind? Will I be blind?" Bunyon, meanwhile, was hopping around the stage on his one good Right foot, knocking over the microphone stand and the two glasses of water which had been neatly set out for the presenters, all the while screaming out on live television "F***, F***, F***, F***, that really hurt! My f***ing toe is bent now!"

On his second pained lap around the stage, he circled back around and was about to take a swiping left hook at the bloody Ponce, who he was sure had intentionally dropped the mic on his bony toes.

At precisely the wrong moment to be doing so, Connard stepped in to break up the argument, when Bunyon's swinging Right hook suddenly floored her, with the side of her pumpkin and her thin, surgically-altered lips taking quite a bruising in the process. Ponce jumped to Connard's defense, grabbing Bunyon's osteophytic arm bones firmly, with one hand seizing his wrist and the other firmly grasping Bunyon's radius and ulna, to immobilize his flailing forearm. It was by no means a humerus situation.

* * *

Just as the incident appeared to be on the brink of degenerating into full-on fisticuffs, who should suddenly appear on the stage to be the savior of this situation but the almighty Chump, who had managed to fly back early from his award ceremony and who, now draped in an impressive medal and matching sash, luckily popped out, just as a giant pustule on a teenager's forehead might pop, onto the scene to save the day. He had hurried back to assist at the CRAPI presentation, but would never in a million years have expected to find his staffers quarreling openly in public.

"Gentlemen, peace be with you!" he ordered assertively. "Lay down your arms."

Immediately the two stopped their brawling, and with shamed and downcast faces, stood quietly as Chump took charge of the situation.

Symbolic of his heroic stature, Chump had arrived with almost divine timing, to bring peace where there was hostility, to bring calm where there was disturbance, and to bring wisdom where human folly was on full display.

Chump himself became the highlight of the whole CRAPI presentation.

10

SILVER LADY

Kushywanker and Bunyon were getting on better than ever before, like a pair of well-matched carving knives sharing the same velvety decorative case. Janey felt that Bunyon always "had her back".

A convivial atmosphere reigned in the office following the announcement of the tender. Stevie Bunyon told me that he would call everyone into his office and start up a Horah dance (or had he perhaps said "horror" dance?), using a rendition of Hava Nagila he had adapted on his balalaika. His office was often eerily reminiscent of the Party Animals official video of the classic celebratory ditty, as it attracted a host of vibrant and colorful staffers from all parts of City Hall, and Steve similarly re-enacted this with the same fake beard, red plastic saxophone and pre-wrapped gifts for the other staffers.

* * *

Chump, raised by an inclusive father who in the 1920's had formed an early hip-hop crew in the South Bronx area near his shoe-shine stand, has music in his blood and was therefore no exception when it came to the festive spirit. He was often known, on hearing the music drifting down the corridor, to shimmy down the hall and join in the party. Chump loved the inclusion of all races in the dancing, whether white folk or any of those other kinds of folk.

Janey, it must be said though, dominated the dance floor, with moves rivaling Napoleon Dynamite's "Vote for Pedro" dance.

After the election, Moose News intern Funker Cunson had jested that Chump had done his daughter-in-law Janey (as opposed to his daughter), a kind favor in giving her a role carrying documents around, as it gave Janey a sense of being useful which she so needed, being good-hearted but otherwise slightly incompetent and gormless.

"I know" replied Chump, "I love bringing meaning to people's lives."

Just like Stevie Bunyon with his decorative, though empty, gift-wrapped boxes intended to gladden the team's spirits, so too Janey, through her additional qualities as a jive artist, had brought along her own unique gifts which would benefit the whole administration. Well, at least metaphorically.

* * *

In the very early days of the new administration, Kushynird had suggested that Gerry Conehead, a former volunteer for the charity Feeding America, should advise the council on finance matters. This is how Conehead had landed a job in the team, bringing with him new perspectives, like rock samples from another planet.

Conehead had headed up a food relief program, so brought a wealth of experience to the team and - as soon as he hit the ground - worked smoothly with Bunyon and Kushynird in delivering on Chump's agenda, never once having to sell out his principles or the unfortunates in society whom he hoped to represent.

Conehead's original appearance in Washintown all those years ago had, coincidentally, occurred around the same time as the discovery of some kind of bizarre winged aircraft, possibly a large experimental Air Force drone, which had crash-landed in a field just outside town. Conehead, similarly, brought an air of mystery and wonderment to the team, and was such fun to have around that he, too, seemed almost heaven-sent. Seeing his cheery face and his bald, if somewhat conical head, arriving at work, suitcase at hand, was enough to lift the spirits of his colleagues in the administration, with his witty quips such as "I trust I have arrived at the predesignated time coordinates."

In those early days many years ago, Bunyon and Conehead, like Bunyon and Chump, had worked together packing food relief boxes for the homeless, however Conehead had stayed on with the charity, where he had gone on to pack many more boxes while Bunyon had moved on to other selfless community work. With Gerry having acquired a reputation for a voracious appetite, there were some in the charity who joked that he must have been consuming a few of the relief boxes, so rapidly was he "processing" them.

Being old colleagues, Bunyon and Conehead were inseparable. Within weeks of Conehead's arrival on the team, Bunyon had helped advance Conehead's plan to expand the Social Welfare team by about thirty people.

Sid Nutberger, meanwhile, gave frequent updates to the press regarding the incredible work being done by the powerhouse team of Bunyon, Conehead and Kushynird.

Janey in particular was adamant that in her new secretarial-style role she would single-handedly annihilate all poverty within the city. She had some pretty good ideas too, just needing to be workshopped a little more, as to how to cure cancer, free all sentient beings from suffering and, in the words of the famous John Lenin, to "stop all the fright", prior to the next election. This inspired her to bring out the whiteboard again and brainstorm these other issues she felt she could resolve in her role.

The media lapped up the constant drip-feed of reportable, if non-potable, events emanating from City Hall. Some of the city's most seasoned reporters kept Moose News constantly stoked with news fresh from the Chump headquarters.

Sean Henutty was one such ageless journalist documenting Chump daily news, whereas I personally was more focused on longer-term analysis. Sean, though sixty-five, still lived at home with his mom and his grandma. Prodigiously talented behind a camera, he had never learned to feed himself, to change his (now-adult) diapers, nor to sit in a normal chair at the dinner table, so would sit up in his high chair while his mom or grandmom spooned him fortified baby cereal or, when a good boy, some Chump Chowder from their Happy Hamper.

"Look at that cute little pumpkin you've got on top of your shoulders! What a pretty boy. You should be on the radio for Mommy" Shawn's mom cooed to her son with pride.

This happy home life had obviously encouraged Sean to be the very best he could. He was, in fact, a living representation of Melony's call for us all to "Be Best".

* * *

Kylie-Jo Connard acted as Chump's female mouthpiece, using her finesse and classiness to present the mayor's visions and policies in a - mostly - delightful way. The only slightly disconcerting aspect of Kylie-Jo's presentation was that due to an unfortunate accident several years prior when she had gotten her lips caught in a left-leaning printing press, she had needed to undergo a labial transplant to supplant alternative lips. This had been a delicate operation in which another, lower, part of her body was shifted upwards to swap out her injured lips.

Naturally, I'm referring here to a skin flap made from the skin on top of her kneecaps. This made it slightly distracting to listen to and watch her press interviews, as the movements of her reconstructed silvery, slivery orifice did not always match the words which emerged from it, possibly due to the accidental incomplete surgical inclusion of the knee-jerk nerve, or just the jerk nerve. Having said that, other than this minor blight, she was a tremendous, and appropriate spokesman for Ronnie. Ronnie, after all, had always had a hankering for alternative lips.

* * *

Stevie Bunyon thought to himself:

Ronnie Chump needed no shining, no polishing - what you saw was what you got. Like something which flowed naturally from a pipe, Chump's virtues flowed naturally out at every juncture, instilling enormous optimism in all those around him.

Yes, Bunyon thought, some things cannot be shined. And Chump was certainly one of those.

* * *

Based on his strong interest in youth outreach programs and his experience working with troubled youth on the streets, Chump rang Dan Imgone, imploring him to contact Elrond Resinstone, so that they could work together to offer special counselling to local punk Bobby Mauler. Bobby had recently been engaged in a series of violent street-fights with about eighteen angry members of a rival gang, the Demon Rats. These conflicts in the streets of Washintown had risked spilling over into public spaces, so Chump was particularly keen for this egregious behavior to be shut down in the interests of the wider community, and for Bobby's own betterment.

"You've gotta do this," Chump encouraged Imgone. "You've gotta call Elrond."

Imgone was very happy with the call and said he would see what he could do. He intended to act quickly and decisively on the request. Being a stickler for privacy, he promised to keep his mouth shut about anything Chump had said to him. He and Chump's other advisors believed the gang conflicts were "serious" and "real", and they had previously communicated these concerns to Chump. Chump himself believed that the Washintown Counselling Office should be involved in every effort to help Bobby resolve his conflicts peacefully, without resorting to sticks and stones.

11

WIRING

Over Summer, the mayor had been working on developing his key platform for social reform, reading up to three books at a time. Joy Hickey had been helping, typing out drafts of the policy, which focused around streamlined technology services within the city. As mentioned, a centralized IT hub for the city, to be known as the Secure Hub IT Project, would be established in a new server room at City Hall. The mayor's intention was to speed up services and payments to schools, hospitals and other civic organizations by linking them all to the central IT hub at City Hall. This would remove a range of barriers, for example: reducing delays in payments to teachers or to the unemployed, allowing childcare bookings to be centrally managed across the city, and providing efficient logistics for hospitals, to name just of few of the benefits. It was a first-rate plan, which now just needed execution (and several billion dollars).

Thankfully, the fine details of the project were being nutted out by Sid Nutberger, Crohney, Pebble and Moneyport.

Eighty-two-year-old Joy Hickey was Ronnie Chump's right-hand man in the secretarial role. She felt that the demands of the job as Ronnie's assistant had aged her twenty years. To some, she seemed a little too old and a little too experienced. True, she smelt like a poorly-run nursing home, still had the libido of an amorous rabbit, and wore floor-scrapingly long dresses, but she was striking in her confidence, in her agility with a typewriter, and in her swiftness in leaping from the keyboard to chat up any passing male.

Often going missing for long periods, usually to be found flirting with young men in the corridor or the tea room, Joy would often cause Ronnie to be calling out "Where's Joy? Where's Joy?" leading a few in City Hall, mistakenly interpreting this as a cry of existential angst on his part, to wonder if Ronnie was starting to feel the heavy burden of high office. There had certainly been recent occasions in city council meetings when Chump had looked so tired that Johnny Notlob had needed to prompt him with a gentle nudge, saying "Rise to vote, Sir".

Chump was rather untrusting of Joy's dalliances in the tea room, but with such a strong retinue of staff, how on Earth could he be anything but brimming with gratitude and appreciation for his team? "Hickey by name, hickey by nature!" Ronnie would quip as Joy frequently emerged from her office with a flushed face and fresh red marks on her neck after briefings with her much younger single, or married, male colleagues. Of course, Ronnie knew that she suffered from a nervous eczema, nothing more, but in the spirit of office fun which prevailed in his administration, he was ever the Joker around the office.

With Spring in the air, sexual tension seemed to abound. FSB sales girl Shirley Kissayak had now started coming on to young Jess Fessin. Jess naturally told everyone in the office. There were reports that, not unlike the recent steamy sessions with Flout, they had been seen smooching in the back of the photocopier room. Chump was a proponent of love regardless of one's gender, age or country of origin, so would not have been judgmental of these couplings. Around this time, Joy Hickey had detained several young men including Rob Hurther and Gorby Ruineddogski, clearly invading their personal space and crossing social boundaries which one would normally respect, as one might respect, say, a basic law of society or a fellow human being seeking asylum. Chump felt that Joy's advancing age warranted cutting her some slack in this regard. Hickey herself thought Gorby was the best piece of tail she would ever have, if only she could somehow, seductively, get him to ignore her massive granny-pants and nursing-home odor.

Disturbingly, Shirley Kissayak would hang about in the corridor with her legs akimbo seeking to engage anyone who would stop with her for a while. The ingenuous Mickey Flout could never escape Shirley's attentions. Initially she would display FSB sales brochures, but it wouldn't take long before her blouse buttons became mysteriously loose with some tempting cleavage on show for him, and before a sweet box of Russian treats was being proffered.

* * *

While all this was going on, however, Chump's fellow councilors, with Bunyon's help, were meanwhile kicking goals on the legislative front. A number of the councilors were intent on ensuring that Chump's landmark Universal Healthcare legislation pass quickly through voting sessions. One, a Pauline Rynitis, had usually been dreaded in chambers as a phlegmatic whistle-stopper, known to have chronically blocked the passage of important bills.

Yet under Chump, there was no such obstruction or congestion on her part. With Chump having given her a spray at the start of the Spring season, Rynitis dampened her usual inflammatory tendencies, and worked cooperatively with fellow councilor Mitzi McCon'emall to make sure the big bill was not blocked.

With the rapid passage of this key legislation, Rynitis's efforts were not to be sneezed at.

12

CEASE AND DESIST

A document marked UNCLASSIFIED flew past me in the street, having blown out a window of City Hall. I picked it up. It looked like some kind of A Warning, though its writer was apparently Anonymous. I stopped everything to read it in detail.

It reminded me of a theater script, written by a tormented playwright. Had someone in there lost the plot?
It simply read, on both sides of an otherwise blank sheet:.

It simply read, on both sides of a blank sheet:

Shit, shit, shit. This is serious.

Shit, shit, shit. This is serious.

13

BUNYON JOY

Bunyon had never felt a greater sense of freedom, he had told Kitty Welsher when she came to tell him that she planned to never leave, such was her devotion.

"I feel the same", said Bunyon. "Being here is like being in Heaven. I loved the campaign and all the new foreigners we met. None of them was a rapist! I loved the transition and I love being here in City Hall" said Bunyon, standing one morning in Ponce Rebus's office on a typically chilly morning with the door onto the alleyway, left right open just in case their great friends 'Kushywanker' wandered by and wanted to drop in.

His current joy was multi-faceted like a sparkling diamond. His smooth baby face, devoid of giant crevices, blotches, crags, skin cancers, rotting chunks and the like, beamed like a Kardashian butt-cheek.

* * *

During my long hours in the street, I was lucky enough to receive a leak of Chump's private schedules, filled with hundreds of hours of his relentless break-free work time, which - other than a very short period watching Moose News and playing mini-golf - were packed with legislative activities and private meetings with young women to promote the feminist cause. People inside his orbit were genuinely impressed that he was able to complete such a busy schedule and devote such enormous efforts to feminist policy.

I believe Chump was assisted in his tireless drive and vigor by the frequent visits made to him by his dear friend and mentor George Nüder, a luminary in the field of women's and children's rights, who clearly guided Chump's policy-making and assisted him in policy development. I often witnessed George arrive to visit the Chump residence late in the evening, bearing tins of high-energy candies, and the two would stay up late into the night sharing each other's company, watching movies and feeling like underage kids again.

The leaked Chump timetables, which Chump had developed hastily on the back of a pad but which covered every working day since the inauguration, showed Mayor Chump spending hundreds of hours of his scheduled time in structured 'executive time' which consisted of meetings, policy development and direct 'hands-on' involvement in social programs and female affairs, in particular the #FreeTheNipple campaign. He had even needed an additional skilled secretary to help manage this. Only a few breaks were scheduled for watching Moose News, taking a shower and playing mini-golf. Few novice staffers would be able to match a talented secretary, or a work schedule, such as the one Chump knocked up. It seemed impossible that Chump could keep it up, at least not without medication.

Chump thrived on differences of opinion, relishing the prospect of listening deeply to ideas which stood in opposition to his own. He would then reflect deeply, and arrive at insightful, unexpected outcomes which both included, and paid respect to, the inputs of others. This thoughtful and caring approach left all those around him with a sense of having been listened to and meaningfully consulted. It lay at the beating heart of Chump's success as a civic leader, with a reputation to match even the Confederate Major General Gideon Pillow, perhaps one of Edna Pillow's distant relatives. In a world reliant on accurate information, Chump was full of it.

Bunyon was playing an ever more important role 'on the ground' in assisting Chump to fulfil his Utopian social agenda. He was going from strength to strength with tidying up his office paperwork, decorating his mantelpiece and rearranging his Star Wars figurines. He felt elated that his philanthropic philosophies were able to be implemented so easily, and that he could fit over a dozen figurines along the mantelpiece. As an experienced policy wonk, he been excelling in putting out wonky policies.

He was a sociable young man, fundamentally altruistic, eternally optimistic and a die-hard supporter of multiculturalism, who got on effortlessly with other people. He bore the self-assurance of a developed soul who knew that all people - women, men, and those of all other gender identities, including intersex and transgender - are created equal.

Bunyon was also naturally gregarious, which bore fruit - some might say even strange fruit - more often than not in terms of his quirky but successful relationships. Bunyon had a faithful following of diverse and colorful characters from all parts of Washintown. Most notably, he was particularly touched by the constant supportive comments being made by his wonderful boss Ronnie Chump whose kindnesses and casual compliments on his excellent work were a great source of inspiration and eternal succor.

* * *

Around November, the anniversary of Washintown's foundation was fast approaching, and Chump had been keen to mark the occasion with another one of his grand announcements, which both long-time residents and newcomers would remember for a long time. Yes, Chump thought, this would definitely call for another press conference. Again, the press gathered, and again, the Mayor's hospitality was on display with ample home-cooked sustenance wheeled out from the busy Chump kitchen.

In a surprise move, Chump stunned the crowd with an additional announcement, typical of the great leader's ever-latent genius. Behind the scenes, he had been working on this with his colleagues for several weeks, and his fellow councilors had fully backed what he was about to reveal to the public.

Harking back to his team's work discussing the refugee issue at the whiteboard several weeks previously, Chump drew a deep breath and announced, "I hereby announce that I will be making every effort, exerting myself and straining, to put forward a motion to Council, that in order to show our respect and gratitude to those who seek refuge in our community, we will move to officially rename our city from 'City of Washintown' to the 'City of MENDA' ".

"Yes, citizens," he reiterated, "having considered this long and hard after consultation with my team, and out of profound deference for the people of all nations who seek refuge in our great city, I put forward to you today that I plan to rename our town, from the City of Washintown to the City of MENDA. That's M-E-N-D-A, folks, honoring the diverse nations from which our newest citizens arrive, seeking refuge."

"In future I will be known as the Mayor of Menda City". There was a hubbub throughout the crowd, either suppressed joy or slight annoyance, and some sporadic clapping. Finally, the applause built to a crescendo and the mayor descended from the podium. The public had clearly been blindsided by Chump's daring, history-making plan.

There was a huge round of applause, and a few gasps.

A huge moment in Washintown's history had just taken place. Washintown would be no more. It would cease to be. It would be an ex-City.

* * *

Over the ensuing weeks, the Chump administration rolled out a public campaign to promote Menda City in the press and in live interviews. Chump initiated a public information and advertising campaign, featuring blanket coverage of the city's new name across all forms of media. He signed off on engaging a leading ad agency,

OmniCon Group, to create a funky italicized and compressed logo for Menda City, which looked something like this:

MendaCity

The whole team was on board with promoting *MendaCity*, as Menda City would come to be informally known, through use of the new logo. Chump ordered Kylie-Jo Connard to send out a series of press releases via fax, letting media outlets know in detail the plan for changing the city's official name.

Just like Nutbush City, Chump wanted to extend *MendaCity*'s limits and promote the project through song and a redrawing of municipal boundaries. He asked Ruineddogski to help draw up new extended boundaries for *MendaCity* and to get Kelly-Jo Connard to fax across to the city's urban planning department urgently, along with the press releases to the media.

Half an hour later, Connard returned indicating that the fax machine was jammed with outbound documents Gerry Conehead had stuffed into it. For some odd reason which she didn't hang about to find out, Gerry had apparently been trying to cram it with important documents for faxing to the secure fax machine on board NASA's Voyager spacecraft, bound for the outer solar system. He waved her away, stating, without expression, "My intergalactic messaging is incomplete, Ms Connard."

Connard, a quick thinker, indicated to Chump that she would have to use an alternative fax.

* * *

To some it felt like a dream, but to Chump it was a dream come true: a city, with modernized infrastructure and a name to reflect its compassionate ideals.

Chump was elated. At last this lengthy process was over and his visions for enhanced social equity would be advanced with his new and exciting urban transformation project now able to get underway, along with this brand new, socially progressive name for the city. He planned to make Menda City known throughout the world. He felt it was much cleaner than Washintown, which had always reminded him of laundering, something he rarely did himself.

Chump ordered the town's church bells to be rung out, for wet dishrags to be wrung out, for schools and workplaces to be closed for the day in celebration, for government workers to be sent home for a lengthy break, and a parade to be held down the main street of Washintown, featuring the town's rusty military jeep and Kylie-Jo Connard's old horse, Molly, saddled with a floppy Menda City banner and beautiful pink bows along her mane.

Kylie-Jo, with Sally Muckabee tucked up right behind her in the saddle, rode down Main St together, like the Four Horsemen of the Apocalypse, except that they were both women and that there were only two of them. In any case, they rode together down Main St, proudly promoting Menda City, trailed by a line of Chump's staffers performing a live bootscooting demonstration as they dodged Molly's regular issuances of manure. Willing staffer Stevie Manurechin followed up with a shovel, though some splashback ended up on the bottom of his face. Chump arranged a guest appearance with local celebrity bagpipe artiste Kimmikah Duzyahedin, to help spread the word about Menda City.

This was indeed a glorious and glamorous moment for the city formerly known as Washintown, perhaps even more illustrious than Chump's inauguration (though the crowd was smaller), a day which will forever be burnt into the city's memory. It signaled the start of the transformation of the city to a new era of Menda City, glaring out like a mercury street-lamp from this zenith in the Chump administration's endeavors to chart the highest heavens.

* * *

Chump paid for a Premium advertising package, which included the development of a number of slogans, as well as an extensive range of merchandise, including lapel pins, coffee cups and T-shirts bearing the *MendaCity* logo, plus horse ribbons, '*MendaCity* Crime

Scene' ribbons and extensive advertising coverage across television, print publications and outdoor media.

As a result, giant outdoor billboards through the former City of Washintown now proclaimed:

"MendaCity - where it's at!",

"MendaCity: UNBELIEVABLE"

and

"MendaCity - you're living in it!"

A tourism-focused billboard was commissioned in eight of the surrounding towns, encouraging tourists to visit with the catchphrase:

"MendaCity: The perfect call!"

Washintown's previously dreary buses sported giant decals featuring the new logo and slogans including *"Welcome to MendaCity, Get on board"* and *"Ronnie Chump - Bringing you the best in MendaCity"* with a giant picture of Chump wearing a cheesy, toothy grin, subtitled in small font: "Mayor of Menda City, R.S. Chump".

New legislation coming out of City Hall was all to be stamped with "Menda City", the italicized slogan tagline 'Unbelievable' in 6-point font underneath, and signed on the bottom as such with Chump's new title as mayor of the renamed city.

Oxford Rectalitchyca was brought in to ensure that advertising and informational messages on Facehook were targeted appropriately at Washintown's urban and rural populations. For farmers on the city's outskirts, advertisements were pushed out which said "Howdy y'all, did y'all know that Washintown is now 'Menda City'? Well diggety-dog, it is. There ya go!". For city-dwellers, the Facehook message simply read: "Washintown has a new name! We're now the City of Menda. Get used to it!" To ensure accessibility to the announcements for blind and vision-impaired residents, new braille signage was posted on public toilets and the like, with messages such as: "You may be blind, but you can still enjoy our great Menda City".

Additionally, Chump paid a further $200 to have Dick Pickles' crop-duster hired to fly in circles around the city trailing a **MendaCity** banner. Thanks to Chump, no-one in town failed to spot Dick's giant appendage looming over their heads as it sputtered diesel fumes.

The advertising blitz was total, "*über alles*" one might say in German. On that note, some in the advertising industry would go so far as to call it an advertising Blitzkrieg. The city's spend on the campaign put a degree of strain on the municipal budget, yet Chump was certain every penny had been wisely spent, and that none had gone down the drain. He was indeed Penny-wise. He claimed that all the spending had been worth it, just as he said that building the Taj Mahal had been worth it for Pakistan when that tourist attraction and its water-slide were first proposed by Mahatma Gandhi in the late 1970s.

Within weeks, no inhabitant of the community was unaware that they were now living in Menda City.

13 3/4

OTHER VARIOUS GOINGS-ON

It is at this point, dear reader, that I feel I must hug you close to my bosom and confide in you some of my deepest concerns as I faced the dark night of my investigative research efforts. Midway through a documentary project such as this, it is easy to lose faith in the worth of one's undertaking. Am I heading in the right direction? Am I gaining your love and affection? Are my efforts bearing fruit? Am I gaining sufficient insight into this incredible administration and its colorful characters? Am I doing justice to their extraordinary efforts to enhance the public good? At times during the penning of this explosive work, these and other questions have risked disrupting my usual journalistic equanimity and sending me into a scone-scoffing tizzy.

I had been particularly concerned that my rival, Michael Bearr, was getting the upper hand on me due to his much higher level of access to Chump and his team, possibly for the purposes of his own tell-all book, which - scandalously - was rumored to mimic my own book's title. I had seen Bearr breezing past me, sticking close to Chump, with a visible smirk as he enjoyed the privilege of being admitted as a 'fly on the wall' for various meetings to which I, stranded outside on the sidewalk, was not privy. Shawn Spinner had emerged from his hedge a few times with the occasional leak, however for the most part I found myself needing to draw upon my talents of intuition, my strong binoculars and some downright fabrication to piece together my account of the history-making events occurring around me.

Even more galling was hearing rumors that various staff had been sneaking out the side entrance of Chump's house, totally bypassing your dear Martha Skewermann, and leaking directly to Karl Goodword, a fresh young journalist of no repute whatsoever who was claiming to be an experienced investigative journalist - my ass! Had I not already eaten all the cream scones in my survival kit the day I heard that, I would have had no fear in marching around to that side gate and pushing one or two creamy scones right into the presumptuous Mr Goodword's face to express my outrage at his flagrant flouting of the Journalists' Code of Honor and his utter disrespect to a female colleague many years his senior.

By that stage I had been camping out on the street for several weeks, whereas Goodword had only just blown in.

He, too, was apparently working on a book, chronicling the role of Joy Hickey, aptly to be titled "Joy". Goodword's book project was in fact only one of a spate of publications being produced on the topic of Chump and his unpresidented team, including one being worked on by my dear friend and colleague Ricky Swilloff, entitled "Everything Chump Touches Thrives", and Debbie K. Jackson's fictional romp "It's Even Better Than You Think - What the Chump Administration Is Doing for MendaCity". Yet I was adamant that it would be my own work which would be the definitive recounting of the Chump administration, even in the face of this stiff competition from my fellow authors. Yes, dear reader: this very book that you now hold most preciously in your hands, in your heart and in your mind; it is this very work, brought to you through my tenacious street-side toiling, which I intended to make shine out from its origins in the gutter, and to resonate throughout history, leaving the tawdry and hackneyed writings of my desperate competitors to languish in relative obscurity. Their obstructions would not hinder or discourage your beloved Martha Skewermann. The truth needed to get out.

* * *

My frustrated sense of being undermined by other members of my own profession was dampened down somewhat when I noticed Shawn Spinner emerging once again from his hedge, looking around furtively. He whispered to me over the fence that I needed to be '*en garde*' over near the Eastern Annex, as an important event was likely to be unfolding soon.

Later that day, true to Spinner's tip-off, I noticed a heavy armored vehicle pull up outside Chump's residence, and a number of Middle Eastern men wearing Saudi headgear (known as the *ghutra*), emerge carrying large gifts, soup bowls, chowder ladles and what appeared to be cases of medical and forensic equipment. And who should I see guiding them towards Chump's gate? None other than the delightful, hospitable George Nüder.

I recognized their chief character as Prince Bin-and-Slaiman, a wise and gentle soul with a wicked sense of humor and a love of kittens. Several of his Saudi helpers were carrying bone-saws, bone-cutters and other surgical paraphernalia, and I managed to catch a glance of one of the attendants carrying an open casket of high-quality stainless steel toe-cutters, finger-crimpers and industrial-scale scalpels, clearly a trade delegation seeking a deal on medical supplies for Chump's impending public hospital upgrade. The Saudis were leaders in the manufacture and global distribution of this type of high-tech medical implement, with a quality of design and function not seen since the Middle Ages. Chump only wanted the best medical equipment suppliers for Washintown's universal healthcare system, and wouldn't deal with any second-rate charlatans, fraudsters, creeps or scumbags.

Several of the Saudis appeared to be ghutra-less, totally ghutra-less. Others, rather than wearing the traditional "*keffiyeh*", had opted to wear the more modern "*kuttya*". Prince Bin-and-Slaiman sported a decorative tribal "*kuttya-up*" in gay colors with a floral trimming and a sparkling adornment of decorative Saudi razor-blades.

I was aware that there had previously been several important Chump Chowder meetings with the likes of Janey, Dinah, Paula and some of Viktor Punkin's apprentices, and I also knew that Michael Bearr had obtained a good record of at least some of those meetings. On this particular day, however, Karl Goodword was nowhere to be seen. Similarly, Mikey Bearr was away, filing a story back at the newsroom, so it appeared that right here, unfolding before your dear Martha Skewermann, was another clandestine meeting, of which neither Karl Goodword nor Mikey Bearr would have any advance knowledge. I realized immediately that this would be a Martha Skewermann scoop, vindicating my many days standing out in the cold, windswept street in the service of my beloved readers.

Here, I thought, I might finally have the story needed to impress my demanding and punctilious editor at the Washintown Sentinel who, throughout my long career, has suppressed many of your dear Martha's articles, at times even pretending to have accidentally dropped them into the office shredder or down the back of the filing cabinet.

Here, I thought, I might finally have found the story needed to garner a faithful and loving readership, appreciative of my long hours waiting out on the street to bring them this tale of truth about Chump and his team.

Here, I thought, could be my big break. My big exclusive. My own choc-topped scoop. Front page of the Washintown Sentinel. Special Correspondent: Martha Skewermann. My Dad would be proud if he were alive.

* * *

The Middle Eastern men headed across the lawn of Chump's private residence and into his garden shed at the bottom of the garden, not far from the swamp, headed by Prince Bin-and-Slaiman, bearing their saws and a tall stack of hospital-grade cotton cleaning towels. It looked like this was indeed an important sales deal being struck, one of Janey's master-strokes no doubt.

Sure enough, Janey appeared at the door of the shed and welcomed the delegation in with their medical equipment, a broad helpful grin pasted on her cherub face. Unfortunately, there had been some spread of the pus-filled welt which had recently appeared the side of her face and top lip. This was now throbbing, ready to burst in the face of the kind Prince, as though her soul were screaming to get out of that body. There was no shortage of irony that she should be doing a healthcare deal with the Prince that day when she herself looked so ghastly in the deal-making.

She was well enough, however, to pander to Prince Bin-and-Slaiman's every need, asking "Can I carry that heavy equipment for you, O Precious Prince?" and running back to open the gates and door ahead of the prince's retinue to facilitate their ingress into the shed. She then took a subservient place against the door jamb, head bowed in reverence, allowing George Nüder in last before closing the shed door.

Chump had often raised the issue that to achieve healthcare for all, Washintown hospitals needed to be equipped with the finest medical equipment, so he was clearly pursuing a clever negotiating strategy to impress the visiting Saudi salesfolk with a sitting of Chump Chowder to clinch an artful deal for high-quality bone-saws at a discount rate.

I could overhear from the street that the Saudis had quickly adopted a complete changeover to 'Menda City' in a flattering show of respect for their host and trading partner. Indeed, I noticed that their sample instruments had already been stamped all over with 'Menda City', demonstrating the prince's true character, which spoke for itself through such acts.

Within a few minutes I noticed Dinah, Iwanker and Erika also crossing the lawn headed for the garden shed. Before long I could hear hearty discussions, laughter, then the slurping of soup coming from the shed. "Bingo!" I thought to myself. "This is indeed another Chump Chowder meeting and neither Karl nor Mikey is here to report it. Finally, a genuine exclusive! I could make a book from this! Finally, I might be taken seriously."

I could sense that there was great significance to this meeting. Clearly the Chump administration was seeking to expand its reach to assist not only the residents of our own city, but also to extend its trade prestige to far-flung dynasties such as Saudi Arabia, an emerging leader in world ethics, surgical equipment manufacture and free association.

I proceeded to take copious notes, and some video on my old Super 8 home movie camera, of everything I saw, all of which is now reflected in the ground-breaking publication you are now reading.

14

FIELD OF PEACE

Just after five o'clock on the afternoon of Friday, October 26, the forty-seventh day of the Chump mayoralty, in the field beside Chump's house where the tweeting of birds could be heard, appropriately known as Tweetstock, hundreds of amorous students gathered for a Woodstock-style 'Love-in'.

Inspired to crawl out like peckish cockroaches from their filthy bedrooms by Chump's musky, sweaty, life-affirming influence on society, dozens of local and interstate teenagers participated. They descended on Tweetstock in droves, bringing flowers, fresh fruit and other signs of fecundity with the aim of engaging in a kind of steamy, bacchanalian revelry. It was the first time a major local event like this had reflected the effect the Chump candidacy was having on the hearts, minds and passions of Washintown's impressionable youth. Driven to action by the loving vibes of the Chump administration, they had swarmed over the fields of Tweetstock like Russian mobsters over a casino-apartment complex.

Chump's broadcast desire to spread love throughout the world, through a kind of viral ripple effect, had spontaneously erupted into this remarkable demonstration of universal love among the teenage population, who, like migratory birds, had descended on

Tweetstock, possibly to then reproduce in large numbers like starlings or Common Shags.

Almost everyone in the Chump administration knew how the mayor would react. Chump's response was characteristically, wise, swift and compassionate.

He had already received a full briefing from Gerry Conehead and Private Mickey Flout about the risk of a Sexually Transmitted Infection (STI) and teen pregnancy epidemic. Chump saw this not as a crisis, but as an opportunity to calibrate the moral compasses of the city's libidinous teenagers. He refused to allow these kids to become broken, morally dissolute children. He felt he could show them, as a role model, how to control one's primal urges.

In consultation with his team, he immediately implemented a multi-pronged strategy to deal with the issue, announcing it proudly over a loudspeaker to the Tweetstock crowd. Speaking over the excited whoops and hollers of the loving crowd, Ronnie stated to the crowd: "Children and youngsters standing here today, my administration has great news for you all, really great news. As part of our commitment to your wellbeing and your very important sexual health, we will be establishing a 'test, treat and cure' program for any of the diseases you might happen to pick up here during this splendid event. Believe me, you're gonna love our program."

"Now wait for it, folks, for we are also going to provide for you all of the following services, at absolutely no cost."

"Are you ready to hear it?" he boomed.

The crowd cheered in response. Chump went on to explain that the new strategy would provide:

* thorough contact tracing and partner notification processes with specialist nurses on the ground 24 hours a day.

* full support of prospective teen mothers regarding their reproductive rights and options

* financial aid and food packages, including vouchers for Spam and extra Chump Chowder packs

* peer support of potential teen fathers, also including extra chowder packs

* sexual health education (chowder optional)

* legal support, with chowder, and some additional legal funding kindly kicked in by Mickey Crohney

* advocacy and nursing outreach, including midwifery support, plus maternal and child health nursing postnatally

* youth chat line and 24 x 7 email support (with mandatory Spam)

Of course, LGBTQI kids would be prioritized too.

Many loving and amorous teens took up these support services, advertised via a Chump-funded social awareness campaign.

Here was the kind of call to action which normally might make for a morally murky scenario, but in this case, it would be handled in a whole new way: people in the Chump administration were trying to respond creatively, unconventionally, and in a modern, Bohemian fashion to the similarly modern issue of teen-like promiscuity and twisted morality. This new strategy involved a commitment to harm reduction and a human rights-based approach to public health, particularly sexual and reproductive health, areas in which Chump had made huge personal contributions over the years. Chump particularly loved the 'nurses on the ground' idea, which he had come up with himself. To Ronnie, this went hand-in-glove with the 'peer' program he had also been the one to propose.

* * *

Unsurprisingly, there were many such people, including Chump, Hickey, Ruineddogski and Hurther, who wanted to join in the response to the 'Love In', if not the 'Love In' itself.

Edna Pillow was one such staffer.

Pillow, had always gotten on well with Mattress. They both felt that, particularly given the cold weather out on the field, the kids needed to be supported through the supply of blankets and other warm comforters. Bunyon, being a stiff, was concerned that this could encourage some hanky-panky among the impromptu festivalgoers ("goers" being the operative syllables, he warned).

Chump, fearing Stormy conditions and concerned that, once wet, the youth may contract some nasty infectious disease, insisted that some prophylactic measures should be taken, by way of an airdrop of additional waterproof rubber protection (galoshes).

Bunyon, arguing calmly and respectfully against what he perceived as Chump's 'soft response', was more inclined to favor a 'tough love' approach involving giving them a 'kick in the butt' with a firm police boot and sending them trudging back home, yes perhaps footweary and throbbing, but having learned a good life lesson from the bottom up. Chump didn't favor a military-style response in this instance.

Even more impressive was that Chump had actually walked down onto the field at Tweetstock to address the youth audience directly. He spoke frankly, and laid his heart on the line, telling the kids through a megaphone, while fighting off tears of happiness, how his monogamous devotion to Melony Chump had resulted in bonds so strong, and family connections so deep, that they would be hard to sever. Even his lawyer couldn't quite see a way to dissolve them, if ever, God forbid, that were ever to be needed, which he very much doubted. The mayoralty only further cemented their bond, for it gave them shared activities to care about, and a purpose which they previously had lacked.

Just as they had gathered, the teenagers again dispersed. Once again, Chump had put his moral stamp on affairs of the city, while providing a kind of wholehearted paternal, or perhaps paternalistic, support for its citizens.

* * *

In October an anonymous email circulated around the office which described the exuberant feeling of working in this thrilling administration:

"It's better than you could ever imagine. A genius surrounded by super-talented staffers. Chump diligently reads everything, from the one-page memos to the thousand-page reports; everything! He persists through the toughest meetings and is forever engaged, never bored. His staff are equally inspirational. Kushynird is gracious and mature, with deep knowledge spanning a wide variety of subjects. Bunyon is a humble gentleman who is smarter than anyone can imagine. Chump himself is more than a man, more a demi-god, with his collection of admirable traits.

I love the work, and I intend to stay as long as I can with this super-duper team where everyone has a clear idea of what they are doing. The reason so many jobs have been filled is that despite the high standards expected, we are blessed to have a surplus of excellent candidates continually applying on account of our team's unparalleled reputation, even for the most complex and demanding legal and policy-making jobs. I am in a constant state of delight and gratitude."

It was indeed true that a position in this administration left a significant mark on the reputations of those lucky enough to have a place on the Chump team, by dint (after dint) of the levels of competence and professionalism shown at every moment.

Iwanker Chump - who had previously been quite introverted - was quite the social butterfly now (or at least a social moth, or at the very least an emergent grub), as these days he was networking with everyone in the administration - even foreign dignitaries - and interacting freely with staff on all levels. He had really come out of his shell now, and flapped around the office and the staffers, attracted by their desk-lamps and only occasionally getting in their hair.

Iwanker had become increasingly thrilled about the direction in which the Chump administration was heading, seeing huge progress in social programs, refugee housing, as well as in crime enforcement-prevention and healthcare. He had tentatively suggested to his father that, with the greatest of humility of course, the new healthcare system might perhaps be named after him, namely: IwankerCare. Ronnie himself had already been examining naming proposals which included ChumpyCARE (named not selfishly after himself, but in honor of his father), SCARE (short for "Super" Care) and IDONTCARE (short for "Integrated Dental, Orthopedic, Naturopathic & Therapeutic Care").

Iwanker and his wife Janey attributed much of this success they were seeing to the masterful Stevie Bunyon, whose presence could be keenly felt as the administration marched towards its goals, like a Berliner goose stepping towards a pond. The couple had come to see Bunyon as more heaven-sent than Michael Bublé's ukulele. He brought life, he brought laughter, he brought tap-dancing - in short, he brought "Bunyon Joy". He lit up the corridors of City Hall with his wisecracks, his camaraderie, his pocket torch, his ukulele and his infectious spirit, as contagious as Ebola to those in its midst, or when enveloped by his incense and its misty miasma.

* * *

The unique problem here was that Ronnie Chump was reading and processing material at a rate never seen before. He digested and summarized information - reports, charts, graphics, or the current affairs he saw on Moose News - then was able to distil the essence of what he had read or seen to then produce stunning draft legislation whose qualities rang like a crystal glass at night. Joy Hickey was having to type at a rate of hundreds of pages per hour just to keep up with Chump's prolific output, which highlighted his unparalleled intellect and left most people in awe, if not utterly gobsmacked. His mini-golf bag lay unused in a cupboard, gathering dust. Ronnie's devotion to his high office meant that his own personal pursuits took a distant back seat in relation to his work for the community. His humble holiday house at Murky-Lako grew weedy and overgrown, and could not even be rented out at half the usual rate.

The citizens of Washintown would be forever grateful that Chump had intervened directly into their lives, and the lives of their young adult children, as a glowing role model, leading the way in teaching them how to avoid the perils of promiscuity, moral depravity and STI-induced dementia.

15

PRESS

On October 11, Willy O'Rally had followed in the footsteps of his colleague Robbie Ogles and had been promoted within the Moose News organization for his inspirational speeches on the subject of feminism. The ascendency of these wonderful men had given a new stature to the organization, and the event had been recognized with a front-page special showing a delighted Regan Mordorc celebrating with a limbo dance under his newest wife, less windy. Along with these successes, Moose News synergized with the Chump administration through the negotiation of some exclusive broadcast rights and a series of planned documentary specials on their shared involvement in promoting women's affairs.

A few of the staff in council agreed with Bunyon's view that they should similarly encourage good relations with the local print media, for the better the relationship with the press, the more easily council could advance its socially progressive agenda. To this end, Chump poured significant personal effort into developing a strong communications team, headed up by the delightful Shawn Spinner, who could feed stories to the press to then be churned out in the Washintown Sentinel or the new *MendaCity Times*. The team treated reporters with the kind of respect made famous by hip-hop culture expert Ali G.

Spinner had been feeling slightly despondent after accidentally understating some of Chump's achievements and crowd numbers in two of his recent press conferences. In a rare oversight, Shawn had wrongly reported that a post-inaugural canapé party attended by at least twenty-three participants had only been attended by eighteen. Chump, however, unconditionally supportive of his team, overlooked this misrepresentation and consistently praised Spinner for his expert handling of the press regardless of this atrocious blunder, by providing kind, encouraging words to Shawn at every opportunity, keen to put him out of his misery, just as one might similarly do for a suffering horse. He took Shawn aside and gave him a private viewing of some of the team's most cherished internal communication devices, particularly the business end of a balsa-wood mallet.

It was during this period that the idea was first floated to bring yet another helper on board to assist Spinner and Blathers, such as a member of Washintown's great communicative dynasties, like a Scummaratti, or a Willy Shiner. Shiner had been a reporter over at Moose News who had also been attracted to work for the Chumps. Ogles meanwhile was helping Bunyon get his Dimbrat News magazine into the public sphere by developing an 'app' that could be freely downloaded on all platforms. With its captivating local news articles and strong emphasis on Community Relations (CR), the administration's new app was billed as the total package needed for Community Relations, and was available through the play store as the "Complete CR App". The team's press and media reach was clearly expanding into exciting new areas. Ominously, however, beneath the radar of the administration's extensive achievements, some less-desirable critters were also expanding into new areas. Some of these will, quite literally, come out in the ensuing chapters, should you dare to face them, brave reader.

* * *

Like the calm before a storm, signs for the administration were looking mainly positive around that time as the staff assembled for a team photograph, though a few issues were beginning to creep into the picture.

As the team stood together on what remained of the steps of City Hall, beside the Russian slagheaps, Joy Hickey brushed some cobwebs from Ronnie's shoulder. Stevie picked a small spider off his own shirt and flattened his hair. He wanted to look his best when the picture was put up on the web. There were smiles all round, then a mighty "whoompf" of the photographer's old-style magnesium powder flash, a cloud of magnesium smoke, and the team was immortalized.

Ogles was speaking to Chump more regularly, aware that Chump had been praising him and keen to take this opportunity to further influence him with progressive feminist ideas. At the same time, Chump was basking in the lavish treatment he was receiving from the Washintown media on the back of the strategies described above. The feeling in the administration was decidedly upbeat, particularly due to the heavy use being made of Bunyon's ghetto-blaster.

Chump had been in an effervescent mood in the period following his Menda City announcement, particularly after downing an entire bottle of soda in celebration. He loved to poke fun at himself and was sensationally amusing. He loved joking with his staff, and at the end of a team meeting would often quip something like "Now get out or I'll have to legislate you out of here!" and would then proceed to work himself into a laughing fit so intense that he went red in the face, had tears of joy streaming down his face and occasionally had to gasp for air as he repeated his own funny line to himself "Legislate you out, what a corker!"

Of late, however, staff had noticed that Ronnie's jests had invariably been accompanied or followed by some concerted and unsightly itching of his private parts and underarm areas. There was no doubt that further investigation would be needed in this regard. Something creepy was up.

* * *

Ronnie's team members were fiercely loyal. Some had known him since he was a mere rug rat, others knew him well as a juvenile. A few had even known him since he was 'knee-high to a grasshopper'.

Kylie-Jo Connard, for example, had first met Ronnie Chump at the opening of the Chump Hostel, a soup kitchen which Ronnie had funded for homeless and employed students in the city back in the early 2000s. Kylie-Jo at that stage in her career was already a successful boot-scooter whose family organized itself around her public performances, while her husband, a 'Mister Mom', was something of an irrelevant sidekick as Kylie-Jo bootscooted her way to prominence.

The complexity of her foot movements back in her formative years had indicated an intelligence well beyond the norm. At a bootscooting competition in the 1990s, she had been talent-spotted by a college administrator and offered a scholarship to a prestigious university where she enrolled in advanced quantum physics, pure mathematics, theoretical bootscooting and philosophy, while still enjoying line dancing in her spare time as a social activity. Her final year thesis, entitled 'Alternate Universes and their Influence on Contemporary Wittgensteinian Theories of Bootscooting', was highly acclaimed, and she received her Masters *cum laude*.

Kylie-Jo had grown up on a ranch raised by two mothers in a lesbian relationship and, after a lackluster primary school education, began to exhibit signs of precocious intelligence as she grew into a young adult. Having grown up closely observing the perching and vocal antics of chickens in the family coop, Connard herself began making TV appearances while working as a new graduate for Randy Cluntz, an important figure in TV advertising for the Washintown Revolutionary Party.

* * *

Way back in the early days of the transition, when Connard had been out of action with a sprained ankle from over-energetic bootscooting, Chump had been determined to find someone quiet and understated to be his mouthpiece: someone who could unabashedly face the media with reservation, yet placidly give them a good serving of the information they needed from council.

But there was a counterview: there should perhaps be a media star.

As the search for job applicants continued, Rebus had suggested Shawn Spinner, a slightly unpopular bureaucrat, a keen topiarist and tap-dancer, who had undergone a lengthy period of unemployment. Spinner was a known master of understatement, and had a strong personality which would suit the position, and work well with Chump's friendly, collegial attitude.

Spinner, getting wind of the proposal, had been highly enthusiastic and was overheard to exclaim: "If I land this, my job opportunities will be endless!"

There was absolutely no doubt this was the role for him.

* * *

Chump was constantly supportive of Spinner, with gentle words of advice and encouragement on a daily basis, one-on-one mentoring sessions and peaceful debriefs together in the Rosy Garden.

It was thus that a Spinner had been added to the administration, with Chump and Spinner forming a duo as impressive and competent as Beany and Cecil.

* * *

Joy Hickey, then aged sixty-two, had been one of the later hires of the campaign, having turned up over an hour overdue for her initial job interview, which had been arranged to take the form of an informal Chump Chowder meeting. Finding herself short of a valid bus ticket en route to the interview, Joy had been hauled up by angry and ill-trained ticket inspectors at her bus stop. They had manhandled her (that part not completely to her displeasure), even roughly grabbing her gray locks for her alleged fare evasion when she had darted off, claiming that an unpresented ticket lay somewhere in the bottom of her handbag.

The bus had arrived, and as she had attempted to get on board, the hair force one of them rudely applied to her had yanked her back, pulling her up on the spot. She had been forced to come clean, and as a result, had needed to wait for the next bus, but only after purchasing a valid fare from the tousle-tugging transport-ticket-trackers. Only then would the inspectors let it be, satisfied that she had a ticket to ride.

Upon hearing this shaggy dog story in her job interview, Ronnie thought it was the best tale he'd ever heard. He admired her pluck, but also understood the shock taken by the inspectors when she had sought to cut and run. The tugging of the forelocks, after all, had played an important role in suppressing a crime.

"You've had a bad hair day, old lady, but I've got news for you, and my decision's cut-and-dried, as good as any sham-poo... You're hired!"

* * *

It was these devoted team members who fronted the press on a regular basis on behalf of Ronnie, taking the pressure off the great man to allow him to focus on policy development. Yet not for a moment did Ronnie take any of this loyalty for granted. In fact, he decided one memorable weekend to pull out all stops and - benefiting from early prompts from Janey to expand his overseas cuisine - to start work on a new type of chowdery stew. Cooked up specially in honor of his trusty team, this tongue-scalding hot concoction, laden with chili, allowed him to express his gratitude for their fierce cooperation, by way of a new recipe from Northern Syria.

Inspired by the well-known Russian fermented cabbage soup known as Shchi, and influenced heavily by shellfish Ukha, another favorite Russian soup, he began it with a stock of watery broth, mixed in some dill and carrots, then dropped in some small pieces of honey-basted Turkey for good measure.

Chump's personal touch in trying the new recipe was then to add an aged fish head and about one cup of a strained liquid, a kind of curdled milk product, into the mixture. This was made by first placing milk in a cup, then squeezing out a twist of something truly bitter, such as a blood orange, into the cup, causing the milk to separate, and straining out the solids and tipping the tangy fluid residue in with the other soup ingredients, before mixing the whole lot up. It looked messy, and left a terrible mess in the kitchen, but it had the Chump aroma.

He made sure to discard the curds first.

The resulting soup was another Chump specialty; it was lapped up by his team, who had demonstrated that they loved turkey and were prepared to handle some strong spice to support Ronnie. Members of the press corps couldn't believe that an outcome as rich as this had been possible at such short notice. The new, curd-free soup was featured in Menda City's main restaurants.

It was a total sellout.

16

GONEY

CONTENT WARNING:

As a professional journalist well-trained in ethics and good taste,
I feel obliged to alert my readers that I will be discussing sensitive
medical procedures and must respect the privacy and decorum of
Mayor Chump. I will therefore seek, by way of sensitive
circumlocution, to maintain the dignity of the mayor while not
holding back at all from truthfully reporting the critical events which
unfolded in City Hall. Readers who may become squeamish upon
the revelation of private medical details would be well advised to
hurry through the coming passages or to "close your eyes and think
of England".

* * *

If you are still with me, dear reader, and have not skipped ahead
to Chapter 17, forgive me as I describe, without fear or favor, events
which transcend traditional investigative journalism and cross the
line into what some may perceive as more like horror writing, in the
style of that great Chump supporter and writer of thrillers, Stephen
Queen.

"It's impossible to make him understand that he needs these
investigations" Ogles had said, visiting Chump's home one day, as

he stood at Chump's kitchen cabinet, his voice tinged with frustration. Chump had been noticed, particularly in the media, regularly seeming to feel the need to extract something irritating from his rear end, and clumps of a sticky web-like substance were being found wherever Chump had last been seen sitting. His regular, almost obsessive behavior pattern of itching his nether regions had started to gain attention, having been caught on camera innumerable times, and was beginning to distract from the team's otherwise inspiring policy agenda. "In days gone by we used to say 'Leave it alone, leave that area alone'. Now, if you leave it alone, you are even more likely to need an investigation at some point, or it will build up to a point where it's just gonna blow. Chump just doesn't understand."

Several of the mayor's friends such as reformed crime boss Kimmy "Long Gun" had tried over and over to persuade the mayor to take due care of his own wellbeing and to get this looked into, but Chump was such an altruistic soul that he paid little attention to their exhortations and persisted with his busy schedule of humanitarian work and selfless toil for those in need. Still, this slightly disturbing and off-putting behavior persisted through many press conferences and even public meetings. In some ways it may have been a subconscious cry for help.

At the root of the issue, and not without accompanying irony, was that although Chump was a very private person, quite averse to contact with the press, he appeared to suffer from an unfortunate constellation of conditions which now were manifesting themselves very publicly. These were resulting in frequent yet unpredictable unchecked rectal emissions into his own pants, invariably in the presence of the media, and often spilling into the public sphere. A bizarre additional symptom was that when he went to speak, the mayor often found his mouth full of a fresh sticky web, very similar to, if not the same as, a spider's web. As you can imagine, this was more than a little disconcerting for the mayor. He would often need to cough and swallow to dislodge the sticky web-like substance regularly clagging up his cakehole and making him sound like a slurring, drug-addled blow-in at a public speaking course.

The gluey web also appeared to be altering Ronnie's pronunciation of words, as his tongue, like a reptile's, could not adequately enunciate certain syllables, so he frequently sounded as though he was eating his own words, just as reptiles sometimes eat their own eggs.

The team's low-level volunteer and coffee boy, Grigor Ganadobonus, an observant and compassionate young man, had been one of the first to seek assistance for the mayor's health predicament. When out for drinks with one of his former girlfriends, crazy Austrian Instagrammer Alexandra Upper, Grigor raised his concerns about the mayor's health, seeking Alexandra's advice. Alexandra, a girl who, coincidentally, was blessed with considerable experience in both otolaryngology and arachnology, in turn recommended seeking the assistance of none other than... wait for it... circle of love... six degrees of separation... none other than Dr. Jeb Goney, who in her mind had exactly the right combination of skills.

Mickey Flout had also been among the first to try to convince Ronnie to have his apparent infestations and leaky rear-end investigated. Then Paula Moneyport had made it very clear that she would even help him organize it. Chump was so lucky to have friends like these. His intractable incontinence - suspected of being a rare condition known medically as *incontinentia buttocks*, first described in Roman times - risked sullying not only his adult diapers but also his team's excellent track record for delivering progressive public policy outcomes. Perhaps the stress of hosting parasites had somewhat enfeebled Chump's rectal musculature.

Truth be told, Chump did in fact already frequently soil his diapers due to the leakage created by his war wound, which may in part explain the mild stench which followed him about. Yet even when sitting in his own fecal matter, as was more often the case than his aides let on, Chump still had the capacity to produce startling legislation and to take a keen interest in broad topics, particularly if the broads in question were blonde.

All these worried staffers had been dropping subtle hints while referring obliquely to the much-needed colonoscopy which Dr Jeb Goney, the now-former IBS doctor, had been recommending for Chump for several months, with limited success. Goney considered Chump one of the healthiest individuals he had ever examined, with excellent genes. He nonetheless was suggesting that Chump undergo not just one, but a healthy regime of checks: one during Ronnie's upcoming trip to Russia, another in one of the Atlantic coast cities, and yet another one at Murky-Lako. Chump was in fact very fond of colonoscopies, and had enjoyed several really amazing ones that he had even twitted about. Yet he felt that his commitments to his busy community service agenda did not allow his schedule to accommodate the time for further investigations, despite a gnawing in the belly and conscience which had troubled him since he had first been out to a free lunch several years ago in Moscow. It was possibly at that very lunch that the suspected parasites had first taken hold of him.

Even in the past few weeks, Chump had been openly calling for someone, including his own staffers, to look into all the itchin', scratchin' and bitin' that had been going on with various insects in the office, especially those on his own person. He had already flagged to the media, in reference to his own administration, that if they were to be honest about it, "they should start a major investigation into the bitin's." Then, in a very specific reference to the great local news reporter, Willy Shiner (who, by the way, was being seriously considered as a new hire for his Comms team) Chump had similarly told reporters: "Likewise, Shiner should start an investigation into the bitin's."

For some reason, the bitin's seemed to bother Ronnie much more than the itchin's and the scratchin's.

* * *

Goney, as we have seen, was a short, pudgy man, a highly disreputable medico with an erratic character and a long history of malpractice cases and fraudulence. Just to recap: disbarred from the medical profession after being exposed for unethical behavior,

Goney had confected a second career in the pest extermination business, an industry which seemed well suited to a man of his character. In spite of this troubled past, Chump's unbounded compassion had allowed Ronnie to reach out a hand to assist him in starting afresh. That kindness was about to be repaid, for Jeb's unique skillset was about to come in handy.

Despite Jeb Goney's appalling reputation, littered as it was with episodes of dishonesty, malpractice and *mea culpa*, not to mention his halitosis and shabby dress sense, Chump remained unshakably loyal to his long-standing physician. Goney in return, however, did not himself hold A Higher Loyalty other than to his own bank account, his own depraved urges and narcissistic craving for public attention. Goney was known to regularly conduct unnecessary investigations and interventions, and even to fabricate medical evidence to justify more tests. He had even once doxxed Hildegard Glintin after she had complained about his behavior during consultations. In spite of this shady history, Chump maintained such a pure and innocent faith in Dr Goney that he had even proposed offering him a promotion to the position as head of the city's Department of Youth Services, overseeing the many programs aimed at improving the health and wellbeing of teenagers. Chump implored Goney to follow up on notorious Bobby Mauler, as the lad was a liability to the community.

Goney floated the theory that Chump may have picked up an exotic intestinal worm during his stay in Russia, and that the worm, or worms, seemed particularly tenacious, resisting many conventional interventions. These were causing Ronnie not only considerable physical torment but also resulting in the regular public embarrassment of leaky emissions from the anus and rectum, often accompanied by tweety or squawky gas sounds, which brought endless unpleasantness to those who followed him.

When approached on the sensitive issue at the bottom of his health concerns and malodorous policy dumps, Ronnie brushed Goney off, and told him not to worry. He was fine, he asserted. Selflessness was a Chump attribute. He did not want to trouble Goney with his own trivial infestations, leeches and leakages.

Ever altruistic, Chump had insisted that instead, it was his great friend Mickey Flout who had an even worse rectal problem which would require Dr. Goney's urgent attention, to the point where Mickey, too, had been forced to wear huge adult diapers, or to be more politically correct, adult 'incontinence underwear'. Again, in Mickey's case, the symptoms had appeared after having had lavish lunches when invited to Moscow by Punkin on behalf of the home maintenance company. An exotic parasite and Punkin's dinner table certainly did seem to be the common culprits.

Janey and Iwanker were increasingly nervous that Chump's worsening IBS symptoms - which included bloating, hair loss and foul emissions - could, if left unchecked, even be detrimental to Chump's charity work for the Chump Foundation. An empathetic Bunyon noted with tenderness: "Iwanker is really worried."

Chump's most faithful friends, knowledgeable of Goney's checkered history, began suggesting to him that perhaps he should part ways with Doctor Goney, seeking to influence him by reminding Ronnie of Goney's messy, chair-deficient waiting room when he had been in practice, where Ronnie had been left standing up for protracted periods. However, Chump was utterly loyal to Jeb and absolutely determined that it was Doctor Jeb Goney himself who should be the one on hand to provide a thorough investigation of his nether regions, should the time be right. His enormous bravery and commitment to long-standing relationships were again on display, along with his soiled trousers.

* * *

To take the focus away from his troublesome trousers, Chump decided it would be wise to have an Open Day at City Hall, to allow members of the public to see, and feel involved in, the working of the municipal administration. This was an idea unpresidented in the history of City Hall.

Chump issued an impressive press release to stir the imagination of the populace:

"Townsfolk, I have today issued an Order to throw open the Doors of our grate City Hall for all Members of the pubic for a day. We will have an "Open Day"! This is unpresidented in the history of City Hall. Come on down and visit. My team and I will be honered to have you stroll through the Halls of the building plus the librery and Day Care Center too, and see us at Work. You can all play a roll in you're City Hall. Come on Down! You have nothing to loose!"

The response was overwhelming.

* * *

The day arrived and crowds began gathering among the trenches, mud piles and exposed cabling from the ongoing public works project. It was a busy day in City Hall, with many visitors roaming the corridors, including a group of visiting teachers, some lawyers, many members of the general public and their children. One visitor, an Appeals Court Justice, was particularly interested in visiting the council chambers and the adjoining City Hall library, keen to see the Chump administration's samples of legislation which the team had displayed on Post-it® notes on hastily-installed corkboards in the main halls for the public to inspect, in line with the Chump administration's '*glasnost*' policy.

In the mayoral chambers, after everyone else had left the room following the public tour, Chump asked Goney if he would mind conducting a thorough examination right there on the spot, as Chump had been feeling particularly uncomfortable about his "Russian worms" and other itchy bites which had been driving him nuts. Goney had willingly agreed, and, after his departing for a moment to consult his toolbox, reappeared, glove in hand, ready to proceed, with privacy guaranteed since even Jess Fessin had been asked to leave, he prepared the mayoral butt for inspection.

Chump, ever a strong advocate of transparency and openness in government, suddenly called "Wait! We are an open administration" then insisted that everyone present should be ushered back into the room to observe the procedure. To preserve the mayor's modesty, Jude Sinkulow had arranged that, when ready to prosecute the examination, a series of large screens would be raised around the mayor, a little ominously reminiscent of what one might do for an injured racehorse.

Everyone, including most of the City Hall visitors, came into the room as the examination was about to proceed, however just as the last visitor, the Appeals Court Justice, approached the door, Chump's patience with the dawdling crowd appeared to evaporate, and Chump pushed him away roughly with his elbow, saying "That's enough of you! The room's full. You can stay out." then slammed the door in his face and locked him out, leaving the other visitors shocked, though somewhat glad to have been allowed in themselves.

Unusually, Chump then went a step further, not only pushing a large table up sideways against the door, thereby fully obstructing the entrance, but somewhat obsessively going to find multiple ways, I think about ten, to make sure that the entry remained blocked, while the dismayed Justice thumped on the door begging to be let in with his wife to witness the event. Chump's active measures were highly reminiscent of Elwood Blues' sterling efforts at blocking the entrance of the Chicago City Hall to the Chicago police similarly wishing to ask a few questions. In Chump's case, these actions included sliding all the following in front of the door: several small tables, a candy dispensing machine, one coat-stand, a small child, a number of armchairs and two large "ash and trash" lobby bins. Last of all, number ten, he asked Jess Fessin to push herself physically against the door like a kind of giant human bollard with no underpants, as we are soon to discover.

Yet, as always, there was a legitimate reason for Chump's strange actions that day. As the Justice had neared him, Ronnie had suddenly recognized him as Bart Kravenheart who, together with another cruel boy at his elementary school, had bullied poor Ronnie back in his days in the playground, mocking Ronnie and forcing large peppercorns up his nostrils.

"Not on your Nelly!" shouted Chump through the blocked door. "You are not coming in, by hook or by crook!"

* * *

As he began the examination, Dr Goney noticed some strange red markings on Ronnie's rear, as though councilor Chump had been struck by a rolled-up magazine. These had left some sizeable welts which looked a little like ON/OFF buttons. Deciding this was curious but not medically important, Jeb decided to press on and poked around for a few minutes with some suspicion, although not coming up with anything firm. What transpired, however, was quite unexpected.

Early in the examination, the signs started to look unusual. Goney noticed: things were moving. Things that shouldn't be moving.

Goney poked around. During the course of the procedure, Goney quite casually dropped into what would otherwise be an awkward conversation the fact that he had recently received great service from Viktor Punkin's FSB team with plumbing for a jacuzzi which he often shared with some of his southern Italian friends who worked in the cement and garbage industries. He felt strongly that Mayor Chump had made the right call in similarly taking up Viktor's services for the Washintown reconstruction project, to take advantage of the low cost of the works. Chump, ever cautious of Ethics, indicated that they should not discuss such matters due to potential conflicts of interest.

As if that wasn't bad enough, when Goney, armed with tongue depressor, asked Chump to say "Aah" in order to inspect his throat and tongue, he found, in a moment of unparalleled shock (cue violin music from Psycho shower scene…) that it was full of spiderwebs. The gathered members of the public issued a collective gasp and reeled back in horror as Goney himself recoiled. He had seen Karakurt spiders before, but never so brazenly overtaking their host.

Goney continued the examination and, though he had attended
to many difficult cases over the years, could barely contain his own
shock when even further infestations became evident as his probing
continued. He noticed a marching row of bedbugs, in single file, one
by one, clearly on a mission as they made their way down Chump's
back, no doubt heading for his adult diaper, where the warm, moist
environment would be ideal for their wanton, orgiastic breeding,
just like a conga-line of libidinous golfers after driving a hot round
with several birdies.

Goney lifted each of Chump's arms up, only to discover a
teeming nest of scabies which had taken up residence, rent free, in
both armpits. Even Chump's hair seemed to be alive with head lice,
wood lice and fleas. And inspecting Chump's ears with his medical
penlight torch, Dr. Jeb spotted a large moth who had taken up
residence in the left ear canal, and a slumbering cockroach in the
other ear canal. Neither was in a mood to be disturbed, each flicking
a leg to gesture to Jeb to buzz off.

It looked as though Chump had clearly been comprehensively
taken over by other life forms. The concern was that, even worse
than any personal discomfort, this might adversely affect the
mayor's overall popularity, as the townsfolk generally weren't too
thrilled about people in public office who were this heavily infested,
particularly with foreign invaders. It had only happened twice
before in history. It certainly seemed that the unfortunate Chump
had been fully compromised by exotic parasites of various kinds.

Goney continued the investigation, jotting down notes with
some intermittent grunts. As he probed each of the mayor's body
parts, not to mention a few dark places, Jeb found an amazing array
of microscopic, macroscopic and telescopic inhabitants seeking
asylum on Chump's person, or perhaps, one could say, seeking to
invade it, like pernicious, soul-sucking real estate developers
moving in on Steeplechase Park, Coney Island. There were
bedbugs, scabies, moths, worms; almost every conceivable type of
parasite. As he further checked with the tongue-depressor, a giant
tapeworm slithered over Ronnie's semi-protruding, slightly forked
tongue.

Jeb Goney was heard to exclaim under his breath: "Lordy, I hope there aren't more tapeworms."

With so many critters having been activated or awoken by Jeb's prodding and torchlight, Chump himself jolted with a spasm like one of Dr. Fronkensteen's creatures just brought to life, before settling down for the rest of, or one could say for the butt end of, the examination.

Finally, as the waiting members of the public stood, hushed and expectant, Dr. Goney stood back to announce his findings and proposed course of 'best practice' treatment.

"Look I've taken a few contemporaneous notes, there were quite a few issues, Mr Chump. And I hate to say it to you, Sir, but it's not looking too good there."

"OK, here we go: so, I found lice on your larynx and left leg, fleas in your follicles, flies in your pharynx, tapeworms on your trachea and twisted on your tonsils. You've got spiders in your sphincter, leeches in your liver, mites in your medulla and botflies in your bottom. Oh, and some weevils in your waterworks. That covers most of it I think."

He paused for a moment, checking his notes as he riffled through the pages. "No, hang on, I missed a few..." he added, before continuing, "... you've also got axolotls in your axilla, cockroaches in your cochlea, bedbugs on your back, *Baylisascaris* in your belly button, flukes in your phalangeal folds. Oh yes, plus scabies on your scalp, sclera and scrotum." He paused again, out of breath, to inhale deeply. "But that's not the worst of it. You've also got Karakurts in your cakehole." He stopped there, blinking.

"I think that's all of them, I think so, Ronnie. I think, therefore I am, fairly sure. Then again, I 'mite' have missed a few. Get it Ronnie? 'Mite have?'" Goney went into fits of hysterical laughter while doing his absolute best to maintain a straight face, saying to himself, as seriously as he could, to try to dampen down the hysterics: "It's actually pretty serious, it actually is," all the while trying to suppress the guffaws which were threatening to burst forth from his purposefully pursed lips. He couldn't help himself repeating the high point of his diagnosis: "Axolotls in your axilla - I have literally not come across that before, like wow."

Chump was seriously infested. For once being true to his word, Dr Goney indeed hadn't seen anything like this, at least not since having to condemn a vermin-ridden building at 725 5th Avenue, Old York, a hamlet north of Washintown. On the upside, other than this major infestation, Ronnie appeared to have an apparently clean bill of health.

Having delivered his diagnosis, Goney stood back and opined on the required treatment. In short, a full fumigation of City Hall would be needed, he stated, including a spraying of an insecticide strong enough to reverse this infestation, Agent Orange, into the buttcracks, armpits and other private spaces of all the Chump staffers. Thank God for Goney, for without him this infestation could have gone completely unchecked.

As he left the room, Goney was heard to mumble to himself "Yeah, shit, shit, shit. This is serious."

Trouble didn't quite end there, however. For once Goney had completed the examination and was long departed, it became evident that somehow, Chump - apparently due to something ghastly which had oozed from him - had left a nasty mess on the town hall carpet underneath the examination table, which no amount of subsequent scrubbing or steam cleaning could seem to remove. In fact, the more the stain was scrubbed, the more indelible and dark it appeared. In the days ahead, the frustrated cleaner would be overheard to shout "Out damned spot!" but to no avail; the stain remained firmly embedded in the fabric of the great edifice. The handwoven carpet of City Hall, crafted by the early settlers and rolled out at the foundation of the city all those years ago, would unfortunately never be the same again. Yet little did anyone know at that time that even worse was in store for City Hall. Press on through your trepidation, dear reader, if your nerves can withstand the suspense.

* * *

With Open Day over, the office returned to normal and Chump did his best to keep his many unfortunate infestations 'under wraps' in order not to alarm his staff. He sought to return the fun and jovial working atmosphere which had, until then, defined his mayoralty. This was made a bit more difficult by the fact that he was still flicking off fleas, Karakurt spiders, lice, gnats and so on, at quite a noticeable rate.

It was around this time that Chump noticed a small black spider scampering across the floor of the Square Office, perhaps having fallen out of his shirt cuff or perhaps his rear sphincter. Chump politely asked Jess Fessin if she would kindly get down on her hands and knees and investigate where the hell the dark critter had ended up. Now admittedly, as we know, Chump was a little quirky, as genius tends to be, not to mention prone to office "horseplay", particularly with his idiosyncratic interest in getting people to go down on their hands and knees begging for various reasons, all in good-spirited workplace humor. On this occasion, however, there was in fact a perfectly valid cause for asking Jess to get down on the floor, as the spider seemed about to crawl up into the woodwork of the mayor's Irresolute Desk where it may have then interfered with the smooth functioning of his office. This one time, it was not a joke.

It seemed that poor Jess must have misunderstood though, for to the surprise of those in the office at the time, she issued a stern refusal and stormed out of the office, looking offended.

Chump was not to know this, for he would never stoop to looking up a colleague's skirt, but Jess's reluctance to bend over for her boss was based on a sound reason: namely, that she had taken the risk that day of "going commando" in the office due to intense itching in her 'downstairs' department, accompanied by a case of raging thrush. This was a set of conditions which - according to office gossip - appeared to have affected not only Jess but also, disturbingly, several of the other staff in the administration, some of whom appeared to be developing a similar itchy dermatitis on other body parts.

Shortly after Fessin announced her refusal to get down on her knees in her short skirt, Chump called Dan Imgone into the Square Office in the presence of Ponce Rebus, to see if Dan could convince Jess to comply and get down on her knees. He clarified that he had not said begging was needed this time. To Chump it had seemed like a reasonable office request, as he knew he was not the type to look inappropriately while she was down, with a fairly high degree of confidence. That would have been more like the dubious Goney. Chump himself was unimpeachable in that regard. He 'knew' himself, like someone who has a deep knowledge of the Bible.

But Chump was also not one to hold a grudge against Jess for this minor insubordination. In fact, Jess's resoluteness had so impressed him that he called Ruineddogski, asking Gorby to offer Jess a promotion if she would fulfil one simple prerequisite.

That weekend, Fessin and Imgone flew to Murky-Lako to meet with Chump on this topic. Chump revealed that he thought it might be character-building for Jess to make a public appearance and state, under the glare of media lights, something like "I know that I refused a recent request from my mayor, but I have realized now: that was treating Mayor Chump very unfairly as his request was quite reasonable. So in future I will seek to do better." Continuous improvement was one of the key mottos of the administration.

Jess, however, still annoyed about the spider incident, read the proposed script but again refused to happily oblige. Even the best teams can have their differences. And severe thrush can cause significant irritability.

* * *

At some point, Goney had run afoul of one of the local Washintown punks. Bobby Mauler was infamous throughout Washintown as a sloppy, ill-disciplined layabout, mischief-maker and occasional vandal, who used his copious free time to cause maximum chaos and disruption to the besieged citizens of the town.

In a classic display of his psychology skills, Chump also asked Gorby Ruineddogski to get Jess Fessin to ask Bobby Mauler to own up to, and take responsibility for, all his past acts of delinquency, in order that the boy may then move ahead with his life in a positive way. Chump intuitively knew that Ruineddogski's strong sense of ethics and his desire to cooperate with the rule of law would make him the ideal intermediary for sending this message to the troubled, antisocial punk.

Dan Imgone told Rob Hurther that he needed to record everything which had transpired in fine detail, for Chump had asked for a clear and honest account to be kept, so committed was Chump to a truthful account being available for posterity in council's record books.

Chump's admirable openness to the public, in conjunction with Dr Goney's pen torch, had allowed the creepy-crawly situation to come to light, where it could at last be addressed, little by little, by bathing it in the sterilizing radiation of the Chump administration.

17

ABOARD AND AT SEA

A week later, on November 18, Robbie Ogles was due to return to Washintown from his holiday at Kamilo Beach for a scheduled meeting with Pedro T. Heel.

He was bringing with him a bag full of mementos of his trip, mainly plastic knick-knacks.

Only two days before the meeting, just after parking his car, Ogles was out on the sidewalk watching workers unloading a giant white bathtub via a truck-mounted crane, into the apartment next door. As he watched the fascinating maneuver, a sudden, strong gust of wind caught the load, and the cable carrying the bathtub swung and dropped suddenly. As if possessed of a life of its own, the tub lurched towards the sidewalk, clipping the unsuspecting Ogles on the side of the head as it then continued its errant arc, taking out a number of the neighbor's fence palings and upending a letter-box. Ogles fell to the ground, temporarily rendered unconscious.

When he came to, only a few moments later, he took a moment to regain his bearings, then swept into lively action. Infuriated that the workmen could have allowed the damn bath to swing so dangerously towards him, he stormed into his garden shed and returned seconds later with a sledgehammer. Before anyone could do a thing to stop him, Ogles had wielded the sledgehammer at the bath over and over, until the enameled white nuisance was reduced to nothing but shattered fragments on the sidewalk. The bath was no more. It had ceased to be. It was an ex-bath.

Ogles went back inside and rested in peace, as the shocked workers were left to deal with the ceramic carnage he had left behind, which looked like the aftermath of a cat-fight in a pottery exhibition, or like a bad foreign policy decision.

* * *

Back at the office, Chump's team was similarly "smashing it" with the law statutes of Washintown, like an unhinged visitor reconfiguring Michelangelo's La Pietà. New legislation was flying off the shelves like fresh chips of marble. The folk of Washintown were feeling the effects of it, and of their regular feeds of Chump Chowder which now, due to another great idea from Melony, was being shipped out in troughs - one per street - for reasons of efficiency. Impromptu local gatherings around the Chump Chowder troughs was remarkably bonding for the community, prompting small campfires, hoedowns and general merriment aplenty.

Sally Muckabee Blathers sometimes rode her mule down to these informal street parties with Kristya Nosoulson, bringing down some of Chump's experimental "end-child-dadas" to roast on the fire. It was a long way from City Hall, but Kristya walked along with the mule, even though she didn't even have a water bottle.

Chump even attended some of these events himself, bringing some of his own pies, and played a wood pipe to join in the festivities, just like a regular wood piper would, but with pies, leading the children in an enchanting, almost hypnotic, dance line down the street and into the distance. Yet the merry folk were not to guess what might be looming ahead for Chump, nor their town, nor their children. It certainly took a while for some of the young ones to find their way back, at least those who were indeed lucky enough to find their way back. Thankfully, Kristya Nosoulson issued a lovely press release on behalf of the mayor to reassure citizens that any remaining kids would eventually get back, since the baked treats they had consumed on the way had surely left a clear trail of crumbs.

* * *

Civic leaders from around the world, particularly India, had lined up in vain attempts to curry favor with the new mayor after the election. Yet due to his impeccable sense of ethics, Chump insisted that each one of them follow proper process and submit detailed paperwork to ensure no risk of any undue influence-peddling, including full Conflict of Interest documentation and hefty application fees made out to the squeaky-clean R.S. Chump Foundation.

Regarding presents, persuasions and patronage from princes, presidents and pompous, pushy or popular prime ministers, Chump preferred to pursue the proper policies, principles and procedures practiced by prior politicians.

No-one was as meticulous as Chump on the ethics front.

At the same time Chump championed inclusiveness and transparency in any dealings with foreign dignitaries. His view was that we are all brothers and sisters, all fellow humans, and we all bleed the same color. Everybody hurts... (cue R.E.M.).

Kushynird was a passenger on board Chump's doctrine of global humanism, feeling that she had strong international credentials and, of course, not a jot of racism. She therefore felt very much '*au fait*' with greasy foreigners and many other types of non-white people. Being always keen to help out her beloved father-in-law, who clearly sought to expand his culinary range, she began introducing him to new dishes from abroad, such as pasta and sushi. Our dear Ronnie, although already known as a whiz in the kitchen, nevertheless had a fairly limited repertoire of dishes, mainly European staples such as chowder, spam, black pudding, tripe, casu marzu and spam.

(Apropos Chump's cooking, I have taken the liberty of making some of Mayor Chump's delicious recipes available on my website, the investigative journalism hub: www.marthaskewermann.com, with his permission)

Janey encouraged Chump to expose himself, indeed to expose himself widely, to a range of foreign dishes, delicious international cuisines and take-outs. She plied him with Saudi bread and irresistible Israeli treats. Janey's aim was to infuse substance and experience into Chump's globalist world views and to inspire the mayor's own culinary efforts beyond his standard menu of those delicious European staples which Ronnie, annoyingly, kept reminding everyone that he knew how to make: chowder, spam, black pudding, tripe, casu_marzu and spam.

At the same time, having him scoff from multiple foreign tables and exotic menus did risk causing Chump some bloat. Despite the manageable risk of this, Janey was adamant that she would instruct Chump on the ways of people whom some people referred to as 'curry-munchers' and 'illegal aliens' (though she would not use those terms herself, in public). To prove her comfort with such 'out-of-towners', Janey had even gone to the trouble of teaching herself some Canadian. She also knew all the lyrics to the celebrated song "I like Chinese" and was known to sing the ditty in her local Chinese restaurant, Pho Ho Chi Minh, to put the staff at ease and to show that she was accepting of all types of people and all skin colors, even yellow or off-white. With these skills, she coached Chump in similarly embracing a multicultural way of life, and gradually aimed to teach him white from Wong.

Unfortunately, Chump's success in wooing overseas interest in Washintown, or rather now Menda City, was not an easily won outcome, and he experienced several difficult episodes with foreign dignitaries who seemed intent on exhibiting their anti-Caucasian views and attitudes. Luckily though, Ronnie was up to the challenge, regularly getting on the phone to influence them in the right direction when not meeting them in person.

True city leadership had been all but paralyzed by the election of Barry Kabana. Kabana's irrationality and loose management had opened the way for Chump's kind, orderly and inclusive transformation of local government. He was deeply caring and humane, and endlessly patient with staff. He had only kicked a dog once or twice, allegedly in absolute self-defense.

After clearing it first with his Ethics committee, headed up by reformed grifter Wally Schlobb, Chump allowed a low-level Mexican diplomat to take him out to a Mexican restaurant for celebratory piña coladas, tacos and nachos one evening. Chump, after all, loved piña coladas, and getting caught in the rain. Yet in a controversy which would later become public, Chump, mistaking melting ribbons of grated cheese for live, wriggling worms on the plate, was unwilling to try the nachos, saying he was worried that they were "infested". Following this, an argument broke out in which he refused to pay the bill, insisting that his Mexican visitor had earlier promised to pay for the meal. This ended in an embarrassing scene in which Chump feigned payment, waving his empty wallet around like a magician with a pretense that he had "pay-waved".

Not long after this incident, Canada's newest supermodel, Justine Trubeau, came on an official visit to the city. Not known for her impulse control, she tackled Chump in an amorous embrace, much more ambitious than the gentle cheek-peck which had resulted in my ouster to the cold sidewalk at the start of this documentary project. Going in for the French kiss, habitually hot-blooded Justine somehow bit poor Chump's tongue. Chump, who deplored any kind of sexual harassment, was understandably outraged and the Canadian belle quickly became 'persona non grata' in the City of Washintown. Oddly, before she left town, Justine disappeared into the Square Office alone with Melony, who had offered to show her the antique etchings which graced the walls. She emerged ten minutes later looking quite flushed and flustered, with Melony following up behind, adjusting her garters. Somehow Chump's UNCLEAR button on the office desk had been pressed, so they had clearly been at work at the desk. It was indeed kind of Melony to put in this extra work in the area of foreign affairs under the circumstances.

A visiting Chinese politician was treated by Chump to a display of fireworks while they were having dinner together, with Chump earnestly teaching the official that, yes, you wouldn't believe it, fireworks were actually invented by the Chinese. In so many ways, Chump showed himself to be a man who not only had a broad general knowledge, but was also a person who would quite literally embrace anyone, even if they came from broken and crime-infested places, rife with jaundice. There was not a racist bone in his body, and he always acted in an ethically clean way.

Intent on further improving Chump's foreign relations and keen to 'mend the fence' with the Mexicans, Janey arranged for Mayor Chump to meet with a delegation of Mexican economics and law students, to participate in a celebratory *piñata*. Unfortunately, Chump did not understand the game, and when attempting to strike the *piñata* somehow managed to clobber one of the boys, a boy called Rico, across the back of the head with his giant stick.

The boy went home crying and bloodied, and this event had not ended well. The Mayor, deeply regretful but endlessly charitable, promised to pay for the boy's emergency medical treatment and rehabilitation, even though Chump intimated that he thought Rico's sore head may have been a pre-existing condition. The Washintown Sentinel carried a front-page image of the carnage which followed the mayor's inaccuracy with the stick. It was not a pretty sight. Chump would never forget Rico.

Following this PR blunder, Janey was keen to dispel the perception of the mayor as anti-"nacho-chompers" (which Chump, we can be sure, had only said in the most light-hearted way), issuing a press release to that effect. She felt it might be helpful for the mayor to invite some different dark-skinned foreigners to City Hall to repair the public image, and to do some odd jobs around the place at the same time such as sweeping the front steps, paid a pretty penny of course!

Chump's fledgling interactions with all these various foreigners of different colors, shapes and sizes prompted Janey Kushynird to organize a world trip to get him out of the country for a while, and to enhance the image of Chump's Menda City on the international scene. Janey worked wonders, thoughtfully developing the itinerary for an overseas trip for the mayor. She booked Chump to visit a number of quaint towns and smaller European cities before moving on to attend the Global Municipal Ethics Summit in Finland later that year as a keynote speaker.

* * *

Not known to many, not even to the Finnish themselves, about 185 miles south of Helsinki, on a small, windswept island, lies the historic village of Hellsinky, not to be confused with the country's capital city, with a similar-sounding name. Hellsinky was named after an ancient Viking settlement which in old Norse history, around 853 AD, had been incinerated in a hellish blaze, then sank into the swamp it had been built upon. The Global Ethics Summit was to be held there, in Hellsinky, a village which, although remote, for centuries had attracted great national heroes and activists outspoken against treachery and corruption. Chump was the obvious and quintessential emissary as a leading speaker at this pre-eminent global ethics event.

Janey's detailed itinerary, which she pointed out on a map for Ronnie as she explained it, had Chump starting his journey with a bus trip to the real-life town of Truth or Consequences in New Mexico to discuss civil and municipal law with the town burghers, and fries. He would then go on to the hometown of his ancestors, the town of Morón in South America, allowing him time to research his genealogy and DNA. Following this, he would fly via the town of Bastardo in central Italy, to visit the spot where, just prior to her marriage to Freddy, his mother MaryLou had been roughly abducted while out walking by an amorous orangutan who had escaped from the local zoo, and who dragged her, reluctantly, like Elizabeth from_*Young Frankenstein*, into the bushes. Thankfully MaryLou survived the terrifying incident, and about nine months later gave birth to Ronnie.

In Saudi Arabia, Chump was given a homely welcome with two falafels and pita bread on a plate, before being saddled up on a camel and sent out on what turned out to be a fifty-nine-day solo tour of the desert, before he was finally lucky enough to find his way back, seriously dehydrated. Sadly, at the last minute his hosts hadn't been able to accompany their cherished guest on this Odyssean tourism experience.

* * *

Meanwhile, FSB's renovation works continued apace. The team had already dug out most of the channels in the foundations of City Hall to be used for wiring and plumbing. Large dirt mounds were starting to pile up outside City Hall. Unfortunately, many of the visitors to City Hall found they had to trample over these clay piles, which brought messy, sticky clay in all over the historic hand-woven carpets and floor tapestries of the great municipal building, already stained by whatever it was Chump had exuded.

Though hopes were high for Chump's signature project, City Hall was already starting to look shabby and filthy as this dirt and clay was trampled into the fine floor fabrics of the city hall, or as they say in Germany, the **Rathaus**.

Punkin's workers claimed that to access the wiring trenches they had "unfortunate, we sorry comrade" had to dig out some of the foundations of the great civic building. To achieve this, heavy Russian earthmoving equipment had been brought in alongside the edifice, gouging enormous trenches alongside several of City Hall's heavy Ionic columns.

Johnny Notlob, itching to land a position on the team, had offered his services as a volunteer on the Quality Control Subcommittee. Touring the City Hall basement, he commented as he looked at all the equipment the Russian crew had installed on bicycle-powered generators intended to power the city's new energy infrastructure: "So many dynamos!" he exclaimed.

Notlob helped Chump with the latter's brilliant idea to put in a call to U-Crane to get them to subcontract some of the work already given to FSB, thereby freeing up the FSB workers to do more digging works. Notlob thought the call would be a huge success. He thought Judy should get involved in the negotiations too. "She's the bomb" he would have said, had there been a palindromic way of expressing that. "Boob" was the closest he could manage, but everyone knew what he meant.

Not long into the project, the team had similarly engaged, as a subcontractor, FSB's rewiring subsidiary, the Internet Rewiring Authority (IRA), which had shipped giant reels of cable from Saint Petersburg, delivering them into town where they lay in wait along the sidewalk of Main St, gathering cobwebs... or had they perhaps been shipped with cobwebs? We may never know for sure, but these giant cable reels are a suspected source of the Karakurts.

It was around this time that Chump received a complaint that local troublemaker Bobby Mauler had been seen openly interfering with the team's equipment and even stealing valuable copper, thereby threatening to disrupt project timelines. Chump of course immediately implored his aides Kris Krusty and Dan Imgone to engage with the troubled truant in an effort to convince him to 'lay off it' with the copper.

For here you had a hardworking crew of Russians dedicated to uprooting the city's infrastructure as swiftly and thoroughly as possible for the betterment of all, while Bobby and his band of thirteen angry punks was hell-bent on disrupting the operation. Chump would not stand for it. Hence, he sat, to discuss the problem.

As the project moved ahead, at first glance to the outside observer one relatively minor issue had arisen - namely, that a small but expanding sinkhole had started to open up on the lawns of City Hall, which, one could only guess, was somehow linked to the underground works occurring around the foundations of the building.

Yet if one were to stand further back, as I myself did out on the street, further issues became evident. Most notably, the deep digging works in front of Washintown City Hall's emblematic Greek columns were now resulting in a slight lean developing to the façade of the monumental stone structure. Similar diggings along the row of columns beside the building, known as the colonnade, had produced similarly higgledy-piggledy realignment of the columns as the ground beneath them sank due to the Russian team's over-enthusiastic trench digging.

From my post on the street, I observed a former city building inspector (unfortunately laid off by the Chump administration in order to help fund the works) who was questioning one of the Russian workers, busy leaning on a shovel.

"Why did you have to dig under the pillars out front? They don't even have any wiring!" asked the former inspector, who had lengthy knowledge of the town's infrastructure. "They've been perfectly good for two centuries!"

"Yeah ok that one we dig a bit too much but we straighten up later, is no problem." replied the project foreman.

"But comrade, it *is* a concern. Now they're leaning on this precarious angle. And look at that one! You're propping it up with a timber beam jammed into the clay." The Russian workers mumbled, had a discussion with the foreman in Russian while pointing at the timber beam and dragging on their cigarettes, then nailed another piece of timber onto the piece which was supporting City Hall's now-tilted classical columns.

"There, we fix it."

* * *

U-Crane trucks and cranes were rumbling into position, preparing to help dig up more dirt, while the Russians were busy with other priorities.

Chump, meanwhile, had flown overseas for his European tour, to forge friendships with other cities and boost friendly trade. He was loved and lauded in each city he visited, particularly London, his radiant personality warming the hearts of all those lucky enough to encounter him. Cheery gas-filled balloons modeled on Ronnie Chump dotted the skies to express the city-folks' shared affection for the visiting Mayor of MendaCity.

At the Global Municipal Ethics Summit in Hellsinky, Chump had not long arrived, and on approaching the podium got a sudden, rude shock when who should he see up on the stage between two of the speaking events but none other than his lead works manager, Mr Viktor Punkin!

Chump approached the stage and called up to Punkin who, in the black shirt of a roadie or a Northern Italian, was busy connecting some long microphone cables. He looked shocked, as though 'caught in the act', displaying this by virtue of the confused and diffident look on his face.

"Viktor, aren't you meant to be back in Washintown - I mean Menda City - working on the City Hall rewiring and plumbing job, guiding your team to renew our city's infrastructure, as per the Services Contract we signed with FSB?" Punkin knew he had been caught, like a miserable, two-timing "Joliet" Jake Blues caught in a tunnel. He shuffled his feet and tried some lame excuses in his thick Russian accent.

"Sir, Mr Ronald, is good see you. I j-just kome ovva to Hellsinky for is very short vizit, to do ah... ahnother reviringk job, is not very longk. Mebbee you could lend me some of your peoples, to help it speed up, zis other job. I just need about tvelve of your peoples."

Chump was appalled. The steely glare on Chump's visage indicated that there would be no escaping his laser-like calling-to-account. He glared at Punkin in the same way that Crocodile Dundee might glare at an offending water buffalo to bring it to its knees, minus the hand gesture. Punkin shrank back in obvious fear and embarrassment, intimidated by the strong and powerful Mayor

Chump wielding his raw assertiveness in front of the remaining audience members from around the world. A wet patch appeared in Punkin's groin area. He stammered and quivered. Chump, standing tall, radiated raw masculine power. He was no match for Punkin. Punkin made some pathetic whimpering sounds while Chump stood his ground glowering at the rattled Russian. Chump was clearly furious at the tradesman's breach of faith in moonlighting on another cabling job on the other side of the world. Punkin attempted apologizing feebly, looking around as though he wished the Earth would swallow him up, then slunk away, partly covering his soiled workpants in embarrassment.

My colleagues in the press corps informed me that Punkin was seen at Hellsinky Airport later that afternoon haggling to get a seat on the first flight back to Menda City. After the run-in with Chump, the only thing he had on his mind was Menda City.

Chump's withering take-down of Punkin on that stage at Hellsinky marked him as a formidable leader, utterly devoted to his own constituency, and one who could not be messed with. Punkin had cowered like a quivering coward at being caught moonlighting and had paid the ultimate price: severe embarrassment and $7.50 in dry cleaning expenses.

* * *

It really was after the trip to Hellsinky that events started turning ominously against Mayor Chump. There really was a "Finnish" air about Hellsinky.

Following the incident with Punkin, Chump risked falling into something of a depression. He felt he had been betrayed by the very chief workman to whom he had entrusted his most-cherished project. He kept mumbling to himself, as though trapped in an endless loop: "He told me he the wiring phase 'would be' completed by now. He should have said 'wouldn't be' finished it. He told me he 'would be', should have said 'wouldn't be'". "Would be... Wouldn't be... Would be... Wouldn't be..." On and on this went, on repeat, like the ramblings of a man in a straightjacket. His friends, colleagues and the press corps traveling with him began to worry about his mental stability. Chump had pinned his whole life on executing the S.H. IT Project. He had lived and breathed S.H. IT. Could he still deliver it to his people?

Everyone wanted him to continue his Finnish journey, where he was scheduled to visit other small Finnish villages such as Myrkky, Hevonenperse and Hellinahandbaskit. Even though all those who knew him particularly wanted him to go to Hellinahandbaskit, Chump unfortunately cut short his trip and returned posthaste to Menda City, hot on the heels of his aberrant project leader, Viktor Punkin.

* * *

After Hellsinky and the shock discovery of Punkin's moonlighting on the tech crew for the Ethics Conference, Chump risked falling into a great depression, one might even say a Great Depression. As with his previous blow to the head from the lintel, he had suffered yet another great whack, this time in the form of his huge loss of credibility, for Punkin. Chump had really putin efforts to overhaul the city's infrastructure 'big-time', and now the actions of this seemingly duplicitous ditch-digger was threatening to unravel the whole civic-minded project.

Chump headed back to Washintown, dejected but by no means beaten, as many thought he should have been.

Like many around him, Chump had the sense of having been betrayed, like there was a traitor in his midst. This traitorous sense invaded his very core and pumped through his veins. It felt almost palpable, like it was a part of him, or had invaded him. It seemed to hang about on his clothes, in his hair and seemed to assail his constitution. It was an uneasy feeling that even made those around him feel unwell, and which also seemed to increase his unfortunate gluteal leaking, as evidenced by a marked increase in the trail of fishy odor which now followed him everywhere. The airline stewards on his flight spent the journey trying to locate a strong pong, believing someone had smuggled a putrescing kipper on board.

Yet he was determined to channel his depressing energies into something of value, intended not for himself but for the public.

Whereas others in his state might simply give up and lounge in front of the TV, binge-watching trashy Moose News bulletins while scoffing hamberders, Chump was no such man.

On the flight back from Hellsinky, he started thinking, as he had never done before. Talking to himself, not unlike a florid psychotic, he ran through his options.

Then in typical Chump style, he had a moment of divine insight: he would fast-track the subcontracting by calling in U-Crane. They were bound to help. And Punkin would come good again, wouldn't he? He would, wouldn't he?

Hellsinky had been challenging. But with these thoughts going over and over in his mind, Ronnie fell asleep on the return flight, a flight which ended with a hard landing.

Chump arrived, slumped, with a thump and a bump, back in his familiar territory: Menda City.

When he got home, he sat in a darkened room, and meditated.

* * *

18

BUNYON REFLUX

Bunyon slid into the room to the tune of "Bad", but with intentionally butchered lyrics so as not to invoke a lawsuit for copyright infringement:

"I'm going to give you
Up to the count of about three
To close your mouth
Or maybe just let it be

I'm saying to you
Just keep an eye on your mouth
I know your tricks
What it is you're on about"

Bunyon moon-danced down the East corridor, showing a renewed confidence in his policy agenda as he karaoke'd his shredded version of Michael Jackson's "Bad". His footwork was phenomenal, despite the extra right foot.

"I'm bad, yes ah-hah, I ain't no good, I'm bad, come on
You know I'm pretty bad, ah-hah, yes I'm pretty bad, come on now
The word is about
That you're doing it all wrong
I'm thinkin' I'm gonna lock you all up
Before the night is long..."

A crowd of other staffers looked on, dismayed and slightly fearful that Bunyon would, in fact, lock them up.

Was Bunyon really meaning that he was bad? asked the worried members of staff - Janey and Iwanker, Edna Pillow, Gerry Conehead, Joy Hickey and O'Newbie.

If he was bad, that would fly in the face of the very ethics of the Chump administration!

Yet Bunyon hadn't stopped praising Janey and Iwanker recently. There were constant gracious and respectful nods to their skills. His overall behavior had been courteous, kind and considerate. This was confusing.

Surely he couldn't be serious?

The staffers stood there, looking gormlessly at one another, trying to make sense of Bunyon's disconcerting lyrics, gyrations and footwork.

As he finished his dance, his cheeky twinkle in the eye gave away the fact that he had in fact been kidding, and that of course he wasn't really "Bad", nor was he going to "lock them all up" before the night was long. Bunyon was singing 'tongue-in-cheek', for he had one of the sweetest hearts in Washintown, until now having only ever sung happy, optimistic songs like 'Volare' or 'Shiny Happy People'.

Bunyon explained that there were rumors that Ronnie had been deeply upset by events in Hellsinky with Punkin. This melodic interlude, he went on, was Stevie's attempt to cheer up the boss on his return, with a splash of musical theatricality, Bunyon style. He was thinking of adding a short tap-dancing routine. Stevie had also sought ideas among Washintown residents, who acknowledged Ronnie's powerful efforts berating Viktor Punkin at Hellsinky, and proposed nominating Chump for a Nobel Gelignite Prize, which was awarded annually with a decorative stick and a handy cigarette lighter.

Little did Bunyon know that the miraculous Ronnie had already talked himself out of a very dark place. Few would talk to themselves like Ronnie Chump.

There was a collective sigh of relief and some nervous laughs as the team realized that Bunyon's performance was, in part, what was known as "comical satire". These were such skilled political professionals that they had little experience with the arts and with such complex dramatic or metaphorical devices. They were also not familiar with the art of cheering people up, at least not in quite the ways Bunyon had mastered. In some ways, one could say they were artless. Slobodan Milersevic and Kristya Nosoulson were particularly artless. Truly artless. The team was so imbued with Ronnie Chump's honesty and straightforwardness that it was hard for them to conceive any form of artifice.

* * *

The team got back to work, inspired by Bunyon's Bad performance.

The mood was even better than before, and the sense of camaraderie, trust and confidence among the team members had been given a major boost. Bunyon, for example, felt a renewed faith that beneath Iwanker's overgrown curls and pimples, he was as sharp as a tack, with a deep understanding of the world and local politics, just like his father, Chucky. Janey, too, sensed immense pride that she had mastered world affairs in a very brief time, not bad considering she had only recently struggled to hold down a part-time job at the Kompromat Laundromat in Washintown. Bunyon's musical interlude had somehow encapsulated the team's hopes, dreams, achievements and future prospects.

* * *

On December 21, from a little after one in the afternoon to nearly ten in the evening, Dr Jeb Goney had testified to the City Hall's Human Resources Wellbeing Team, who had been looking into reported overconsumption of exotic treats. To protect his friend Mickey Flout from any criticism, Goney's performance was a tour de force of evasiveness, obfuscations, dishonor and misleading details, significantly underplaying Flout's addictions, particularly to Turkish Delight, Baklava, Acıbadem kurabiyesi (almond cookies) and Komposto. He had also been eating a lot of Lokma up.

Chump was later called in to correct the story, and gave a much more honest recount of Flout's tendencies to overconsume sweets, surely putting Mickey in a high-risk category for diabetes.

The contrast between the two men, Goney and Chump, highlighted the essence of Chump's personal qualities, which stood out like a police siren in a quiet residential street.

* * *

Bunyon believed the Chump administration was likely to succeed in fireworks-like fashion as long as Janey Kushynird and Iwanker remained involved in influencing, advising and delivering biscuits to the team as it powered heavenward, like a pair of peripheral wing flaps on a skyrocket, with cookies sticky-taped onto them. Their new-found experience had already elevated the mayoralty to heights never seen before, with only the occasional crumby outcome.

At the same time, the whole team believed that a large measure of their success lay with Ponce Rebus, who had helped forge an administration that had allowed Chump's qualities to spew forth freely for all to see.

In celebration of the team's standing and unity, Bunyon filled a disposable plastic takeout cup with a large serving of Chump Chowder from a grimy jug that had been in the bottom of his minibar since the inauguration. As the mixture bubbled with aliveness, he raised a toast and quaffed it down in one mighty gulp.

* * *

Twenty minutes later, a giant belch echoed throughout the corridors of City Hall and frightened several kiddies in the day care center.

This was Bunyon reflux.

19

BRAVER WHO?

As an experienced investigative journalist, one learns to dispel the corrosive voice of the inner demon and to push deep into the forests of research and truth-telling. Thankfully, your dear Martha is profoundly skilled in this regard, never allowing a moment of self-doubt to cloud her perspicacious wit and consciousness. I press on relentlessly, digging deep into the minutiae of daily affairs of the unfortunate politicians and public servants who - like tin ducks at a two-bit sideshow attended by a Navy SEAL sniper - find themselves caught in the crosshairs of my Commando typewriter. Long may they feel the steely sting of my rapid-fire commentary.

And so it was with the Chump administration. Despite my positioning on the cold sidewalk, beyond visible or even auditory range of many of the events I describe here, through the course of my shivery roadside stay, this administration was nonetheless subjected to the searing blowtorch of my intense analytical insights, fearsome long-form journalism and pleonastic verbiage.

My investigative techniques, though not to be revealed in detail here, often placed me in perilous positions: for example, wedged with binoculars in the boughs of the one small sapling which grew outside the Chump residence, or dodging on the sidewalk as large bundles of documents were thrown to (or at) me from high-speed passing trucks. At other times, great risks of unwanted revelation occurred, as evidence smuggled to me (including notebooks, folders and VHS video cassettes) - often passed to me by pedestrians - required discrete unbuttoning in public of my not-undersized knickerbockers in order to secrete the perquisites of my propositioning.

Voice recordings were leaked to me from Mickey Crohney's body shop, and on more than one occasion, from Chump's residence itself. From these, a clearer picture began to emerge of the Chump team's utter dedication to humanitarian causes and the progress of society towards greater fairness and equity, particularly fairness of skin color and equity in banking stocks.

Members of the Chump administration, were, however, meticulous in ensuring that they never engaged in any activity which could remotely be considered illegal or immoral. The ethics standards of the staff, thanks to the top-down modelling of their leader R.S. Chump, placed them well above any kind of misdemeanor, treasonous act or atrocity. Ronnie had always been a big fan of top-down modelling, especially since having the great honor of visiting the changing rooms while presiding over the judging of Washintown's Swimsuit and Beauty Pageant.

Wally Schlobb loved working for the administration's Ethics Office so much that he sought permanent tenure on staff, yet knew that the Chump team was already so ethical that his role was redundant.

* * *

A great example of the ethical practices of the Chump administration occurred over what would become known as the 'shoe incident'. It kicked off like this, I was told.

Dinah held to particularly high standards of ethics and was quick to find an occasion on which to pull the FSB team aside to demand proof that the team was strictly adhering to their construction contract. As the Winter season set in, she got wind of possible shortcuts occurring in the procurements process, in addition to having witnessed some improper handling of waste materials, in the form of damp soil residues from the underground diggings. Hildegard Glintin had sought to have these issues followed up. For a Chump steeped in ethics since birth, such oversights were unconscionable. Chumps were thorough people, and didn't like oversights.

When another staffer visited the diggings and filled her in with further details of these issues, Dinah was livid. "If it's what you say, I hate it! Especially early in the Winter." Dinah rang her Dad on his publicly-listed number and insisted that she would iron out any of the issues with the project by arranging a friendly and informal Chump Chowder meeting with key stakeholders, seeking to paper over any problems with a dose of the notorious family brew.

The meeting would bring together a formidable team of intellectual heavyweights: some Chumps and some other ring-ins. Ronnie Chump insisted on a broad agenda, particularly if the broad could be a Russian brunette this time. From the building inspectorate point of view, Dinah therefore called in a shapely Azerbaijani expert from a noise-cancelling business, Vora Lagasara, to hold the team to account in regards to the correct and compliant installation of sound-proofing and baffling. A musician - the talented trombone player Boris Leadbeetle - attended for the purpose of providing cheery background music for the meeting. To discuss the renovations and rewiring needed for the Chump Day Care Center, he called in a Russian-speaking expert on adopted children, Natalie Vevilskareya, to ensure that any adopted kids staying in the center would be appropriately catered for in terms of privacy, storage and amenities. Finally, Paula Moneyport was invited to ensure that funding for the project was being funneled to the relevant accounts, and Janey Kushynird to take minutes, later claiming she only took about ten.

One of the key items on the agenda would be discussion of damage to Hildegard Glintin's shoes.

In this Martha Skewermann special reporting, exclusive to my readers, I can now elaborate how this had unfolded.

* * *

Over at City Hall, progress on the S.H. IT Project had not been going particularly well. The Russian team had been digging cable trenches in the basement of the building but had found they had hit clay and basalt, slowing the cable roll-out and jeopardizing project timelines.

Goney, with his building inspection expertise, had also raised some concerns.

Disgruntled councilor Hildegard Glintin, already peeved following her unsuccessful tilt at the role of mayor, used the delay to conduct an impromptu audit on the progress and due diligence of the project, having heard of the equipment procurement anomalies. To this end, she had arranged to conduct a site visit along with Dinah and the council's own building surveyor. During that visit to the darkened basement, Hildegard had been outraged when the FSB workers, either not seeing or not caring that there was a visitor on site, shoveled wet clay and dirt onto her brand-new Christian Louboutin shoes. This had been the start of a major scandal, for these were shoes which were not for the 'down-at-heel'.

Hildegard, who had already been traumatized once by her incident with Dr Goney, stood in the dank darkness in utter dismay, looking down at her ruined shoes and catatonically repeating "Someone do something! Someone do something! What went wrong?!"

Dinah, thankfully fluent in Russian, had called the project foreman over and had immediately warned that an urgent meeting with the dig team would be forthcoming. But news quickly spread of the dirt on Hildegard Glintin.

Chump, on hearing all this through Dinah, ordered an immediate shutdown to the project until the issue was resolved.

And it was thus that the Chump Chowder meeting had unfolded. Considering the damage to Hildegard's whopping size 12 shoes, teeing up a meeting involved no small feat. Wanting to keep the meeting informal and friendly rather than confrontational, Dinah beckoned the FSB workers over to sit down on their familiar blue plastic stools around their steel-topped workers' table in the break-out area, and had them all served up a warm bowl of Chump Chowder ordered down from the council kitchens, along with a beer and a Bun Cha. Wanting representation of the Chump administration, she also called in Paula Moneyport and the other senior experts mentioned.

Hildegard, meanwhile, began to broach the issue of their workplace negligence and her ruined fashion footwear. As the workers settled in to their chowder, Dinah even sought to set them at ease with reassuring comments such as "Slurping is totally acceptable in this part of the world", even slurping herself to demonstrate its acceptability.

Unfortunately, although dragging on for close to an hour, this Chump Chowder meeting was not at all fruitful, for apart from the fact that the FSB workers struggled to understand due to their limited English, the loud trombone playing - as repetitive and annoying as the bouzouki one might hear in a cheese shop - was highly distracting and made it hard to hear the proceedings. Furthermore, the hot Chump Chowder, rather than setting them at ease, appeared to be causing them some consternation, expressed through a charade of cross-language gesticulations, scowls and generally displeased body language.

Seeing this was going nowhere, Dinah, using arm gestures, called an end to the meeting, then personally marched Punkin up to her father's office. By now, Mayor Chump was busy in his office dictating a letter to his office intern, Jude Sinkulow, but broke this off when his devoted daughter appeared with her acne-pocked face at the doorway of his office.

"Daddy, we need to resolve a situation with the tradesmen" Dinah piped up. "The meeting is all set."

Chump followed Dinah back down into the basement, using his pocket gas lighter to light the way. He participated wholeheartedly in the impromptu crisis meeting and took full responsibility for getting the hold-up settled. Despite his sketchy knowledge of Russian, it was thanks to these matchless negotiation skills, Chump's great propensity to sag acity, his gr eat humanity and his grea treason, that the issues were finally resolved happily and work was able to recommence on the digging. But first came the intense and ethically-driven mediation:

The Russians somewhat nervously explained that they were just installing new IT cables connected to a new Secure Hub IT switching system, using a complex arrangement of the latest valve radio vacuum tubes which had just arrived in from Pripyat. These in turn were connected to the dynamos on the exercise bikes in the new Asylum Seeker Resource Center Gymnasium, recently fitted out in the basement, thereby utilizing 100 percent green energy.

They apologized for the incident with the dirt, and in their own defense explained that the new system would make use of the latest in Multi-Factor Authentication (MFA). Chump, a technical wizard among his other many talents, stated that he didn't need to know all the technical details; yet he pulled them up forcefully on this point, grilling them in detail regarding the authentication strategy. He had been told by several tech-savvy residents of Washintown that the council should in fact be looking to implement the more recent **Improved Technology** Multi-Factor Authentication (ITMFA). In this, Chump was 'on the money', as discussions of #ITMFA had in fact been trending on social media. The FSB and IRA crew took notes in Russian and agreed to collaborate on this enhancement.

Chump then sternly discussed the issue of Hildegard's ruined shoes, seeking to negotiate an outcome which would keep all parties happy.

To the workers, he promised a personal guided tour through the corridors of City Hall, even through the usually high-security document archive, but ONLY IF they agreed to respectfully apologize and to cover the costs of Hildegard's shoe cleaning, and only once their work was completed. For Hildegard, he promised to have her Christian Louboutins professionally scrubbed, sanded and tumble-dried, through not just any laundromat, but - in a concession to the FSB workers' wounded pride - through one of the many fine *Russian* laundromats he was familiar with in Washintown. Everyone departed happy, and Chump's negotiating genius was, once again, indubitably confirmed.

This entire episode was emblematic of the rigorous ethical standards maintained within the Chump administration, standards rarely found in other governances.

Sadly though, as the meeting broke up, things suddenly took an unexpected turn for the worse. For as the mayor and his kind daughter escorted the dig team back down to the lower basement levels to resume their work, there was an almighty THWACK! as Chump's head smacked straight into the well-signposted lintel, a low beam over one of the basement doorways, when the mayor had failed to duck and weave under it appropriately. Everyone present stopped in shock having heard the sickening sound of his cranium reverberating for over a minute, like the American Freedom Bell, and the mayor stood dazed, looking utterly vacant, gobsmacked and feckless.

"Where am I?" said a confused Chump. "How the hell did I get here? This isn't possible."

It appeared that the blow to the head had erased from Chump's hitherto brilliant mind even the slightest recollection of the meeting they had just held.

"I suppose we should go downstairs and meet about this issue", Chump said, clearly flummoxed and disoriented. "The Russians will be waiting for us."

"No, Daddy, we just did that. I think you had better go upstairs and lie down. You really need to lie. Have a good lie, down. You've just had a collision with the Russians' wooden beam. You just hit the lintel Daddy."

"No, there was no collision! I don't recall... I don't believe the lintel" insisted Chump, dazed and half-chewing his words.

"I don't recall... I don't recall", he continued to mumble.

Dinah started to lead her father by the arm back up to his office when, in the darkness, THWACK! she too struck the overhead beam with her forehead with another sickening thud, having been so preoccupied with the wellbeing of her dear dad. The resonance of her more spongiform noggin made less of an echo than that of her father, more like a dull pumpkin infested with weevils, but unlike her dad she issued a shriek, similar to a distressed bird with diarrhea. The whole party necessarily stopped right behind her, with a few eye rolls, as immortalized by Maxwell Smart's Chief, knowing that Dinah had a tendency to be a drama queen.

There were now two Chumps staggering around in the basement, arms outstretched, with impaired memories, having injured their frontal cortices and lost their sense of any right direction, of any right way to go. The others present put in a phone call to the council's First Aid crew and to Dr Goney who thankfully arrived on the scene within minutes and proceeded to question the hapless pair repeatedly. Unfortunately they could not get consistent or meaningful answers from them, only a stream of mumbled drivel.

"You are such a brave pair of Chumps" he reassured them, with only a slightly patronizing tone.

"Now who's braver? Is it Daddy, or is it you, Dinah?" he prodded, talking to them like elementary school students.

The pair had however each sustained a blow which had, at least temporarily, dulled their rapier-like wits, and neither Chump the Elder nor Chump the Younger could muster a coherent response to the doctor's questioning, nor to his rapidly-deployed anal thermometers.

They were wheeled back to the surface on a pair of collapsible First Aid trolleys, face down flat on their stomachs with an icepack jammed under each of their foreheads. On the reverse side, their thermometers pointed upwards to the dark ceiling of the basement, jiggling like a pair of San Francisco seismographs to the swaying movement of the trolleys as the Chumps were wheeled to relative safety.

The emergency workers sought an appropriate exit from the subterranean worksite and finally emerged with their injured patients from a small door in the lane at the rear of City Hall, between a collection of dumpsters.

After this incident, just as Dinah had suggested, Chump took to lying, down, almost constantly. Lying became his default position; one could even say that he was prone to being prone.

He would lie on the floor. He would lie near a door. He would lie on a boat. He would lie on a float. He would lie on a mat. He would lie near the cat. Here and there, not on a chair, Chump was lying everywhere.

Chump's staffers became very worried about him, as he now never seemed to be able to be upright. When his handlers wanted him to be upstanding, he just couldn't bring himself to do it, and instead was prone to remaining prone, like a giant, brain-damaged worm in a diaper. He might initially stand to take a phone call, then would suddenly lie. Staffers found themselves constantly rushing to bring cushions to prevent him having a hard landing. They called for Jimmy Mattress and Edna Pillow for their assistance.

Chump writhed and wriggled, all the while voicing symptoms of cerebral edema by quoting the renowned T. F. Gumby: "My brain hurts". Dr. Jeb Goney, who, despite his own corrupt heart, had a deep understanding of Ayurvedic medicine, wasn't sure whether it was the human balance system in Chump's inner ear, or the one in his inner soul, which had been impacted by the collision with the lintel on the Russian worksite, and which was causing Chump to lie, in all kinds of settings, so recurrently.

Yet as the weeks progressed, Chump gradually learned to walk again. Advised by his rehabilitation specialist to dispense with clothing which could restrict limb movement, Chump at first toddled around the house in his Depends® adult diapers with the loving help of Melony, who would now flick his outstretched hand away both to jog old parts of his brain and to promote independent ambulation. Later, as his muscles strengthened and he was permitted back to work at City Hall, he was allocated a special recovery room in the Day Care Center where he could play, then have a sleep to further regain strength. Day by day, he developed the strength to stand up once again against a high chair, before taking his first unaided steps, to great applause from the day care center workers.

* * *

Before moving on to pay due respect to some of the key dynamics within the Chump team, it is worth our while to spend a moment reviewing the strong ties which bound Chump with his brood.

Ronnie's kids, Dinah, thirty-three, and Erika, thirty-seven, lived in an endearing guardianship role to their father, a role which made them immensely proud, but which they humbly kept from their public lives.

Their role was to be Ronnie Chump's mentors and carers, also attending to his unfortunate medical condition, now too his lumpy cranium, and occasionally helping to change his similarly lumpy adult diapers. Their father took great pride in making known that they had been blessed with extraordinary God-given talents and intelligence - then again, Chump tended to be highly deferential to anyone who could assist him intellectually. He respected, and always listened to, intelligence. Whether it was 17 or 4 intelligent people advising him, Ronnie would listen with great attentiveness, even when wearing his headphones playing loud hip-hop.

The Chumps were such an intelligent family that their brother Iwanker, a true genius by any conventional measure, was nevertheless considered just a little less bright than his siblings, who were even more towering giants of the intellect. Their sister-in-law Janey, though clumsy, clunky and poor at filling out forms, was effectively another Einstein herself (more specifically, an Elsa Einstein, Albert's wife and cousin). Dinah and Erika were given roles carrying huge complexity and responsibility, with their time largely devoted to developing serious social policy on behalf of the paternal Chump.

Though not (quite) a family member himself, Ruineddogski was like a beloved Uncle Fester. He adored Dinah, Erika and Janey as though they were his own siblings. Not only were they a bright bunch, and Janey so humble, but they were also all well-versed in politics. Indeed, they were a formidable trio to experience, as hard-hitting as a modern-day Moe, Larry and Shemp.

The kids sometimes reflected that one benefit of their father's run for office was that it kept him out of their houses, where in the past he would drop by unexpectedly and start cooking up a large pot of his fishy Chump Chowder. He had also been trying to perfect a Chump Peach Mint Salad, though continually struggled with the consistency and flavor balance due to his tendency to add too many fish-heads. Regardless of what he sought to cook up on a particular day, these impromptu visits had often left the kids' homes saturated with a strong fish odor for days on end, so there was some relief when Ronnie won the mayoralty and took his cooking activities over to the basement kitchens at City Hall.

In some ways, though, Ronnie's run for the City Hall leadership had caused a strengthening of the family dynamic.

The Chumps would get together regularly and discuss plans for "quality time" together, like a much-awaited family holiday to Alcatraz Island which the community felt they had well and truly earned after so many years of working hard for the public purse.

The Chumps had heard with some incredulity the adventurous tales of Mickey Flout and Paula Moneyport having tremendous vacations in exotic places such as the Underwood Lodge in the Southern District of New York, or the picturesque waterside accommodation - even fit for Prince Bin-and-Slaiman - with watery views along Cameron Run in Alexandria. It seemed only fair to the people of Washintown that the Chump family too had earned their time to kick back for a long stay at the taxpayers' expense.

* * *

But we must return with haste to our narrative, dear reader, for an important development was unfolding.

Bunyon rushed into the Situation Room in the bowels of Washintown City Hall and hastily powered up the giant flat-screen TV.

Dinah had secured a spot on a nationally-televised cooking show to demonstrate some of the Chump family recipes. She would be cracking an egg on national TV, and demonstrating how to cook up Chump's specialty pork pies for a hungry crowd, and even making a renewed attempt at Peach Mint Salad, with help from Ronnie and Joy Hickey. This would be too good to miss.

20

O'NEWBIE AND SCUMMARATTI

Chump was level-headed and loved making decisions that involved thorough research and analysis, particularly since he had slammed his head on the lintel in the basement. The workings inside his head became a source of interest, awe and fascination to all in the team.

On major issues of policy, his team was unequivocally united, and fell in behind his mental processes. And Chump's processes were indeed mental. On the Myers-Briggs Personality Type Indicator®, Chump had originally been rated as an ESTP personality type, however the severe blow from ignoring the lintel had scrambled his category rating, so he now rated more like a PEST.

His team was so tight that it was akin to them all being family members, a right bunch of Chumps. It was as though there were more Chumps than just his actual family members, who were already Chumps. In this sense, it was as though the whole of City Hall was overrun by Chumps.

Chump himself offered unparalleled certainty when it came to decision-making, and backing that up, he felt the incredible unity within his team. "Everyone's behind me!" he would say to himself as he strolled down the corridor of City Hall with his staff members walking in front of him, all on their phones, often to lawyers.

* * *

An unexpected crisis arose which gave Chump the opportunity to showcase his wise and sensible decision-making abilities, and the team's unbelievable unanimity. O'Newbie ran into Chump's office carrying a telegram, detailing a critical incident. Though already dealing with the infestation issue under the covers, Chump wanted to prove that he could both 'walk and chew gum', for until now he had usually needed to stop one or the other of those activities if attempted at the same time. He was fairly sure he could handle more than one serious issue. Several of his best supporters, including Melony, Dr. Goney, Dan Imgone and Jude Sinkulow had all advised him that he would one day need to deal with many concurrent crises. He stopped his doodling to listen to O'Newbie.

The urgent situation being reported involved a group of Afghan refugee students, whom Chump had previously helped resettle, and for whom he had arranged scholarships, at the city's main university. The students had apparently discovered Status Quo, and had been blaring the music from loudspeakers across campus throughout the night, disturbing nearby residents. The students' speakers dangled precariously from their dorm-rooms on flimsy power cords. Chump was under pressure to do something about it quickly. This Foreigner situation was Urgent. He gathered his team and told them in no uncertain terms that if they could resolve the issue peacefully, they could be "Heroes", though probably just for a day.

Bunyon had been keen to assign five more police to the scene, acting as moral support for one another, to knock on the students' door and to ask for the volume to be turned down. This police 'Sting' operation was a strategy initially backed by Chump. In Bunyon's opinion, nothing should stand between Ronnie Chump's resolute cranium and a deployment of additional police and mental health case workers into the college area, as it seemed an emergency may be developing with the upsetting Status Quo being played at high volume. "We're not gonna take it," asserted an inflamed Bunyon, who believed the errant students should toe the line with the authorities. Mattress, by contrast, had been inclined to just go soft and give in to the students' wishes. Writing my own ambivalent opinions on this subject, I was sitting on the fence, until Keith Schifter asked me to hop down and return to my tent.

Senior Constable H.R. O'Newbie, who had once been a tutor of Officer Dicky Patronus, a former security guard at the university dorms, was usually in full support of Bunyon, as was Kushynird. In return, these two were routinely praised in glowing terms by Bunyon. On this occasion, however, O'Newbie, meeting with Ronnie, Bunyon and some other Chumps, proposed a clever alternative to the police raid: adding surge protection to the music equipment being used by the students, to limit the sound output. "Wow! You're actually really smart!" came Bunyon's supportive reply, though his lip got stuck on a tooth, giving him a snarly look. O'Newbie had been worried that his idea might go down like a Led Zeppelin, but was pleased to find that there was a whole lotta love in the room, and his idea was backed up by Bunyon.

Ronnie adored O'Newbie and subsequently invited him into the Square Office several times to hear details of the new proposal. Each time he met with O'Newbie, Chump would exclaim, "You again? I couldn't wait to meet with you again!" Both Chump and Bunyon reveled in showering O'Newbie with compliments for his 'bright idea', while looking at each other intently.

They meanwhile had invited others to offer their ideas too. Edna Pillow further contributed to the think-tank, by proposing a more passive solution. The approach Edna Pillow suggested, which was also likely to improve the sleep situation across Washintown, was to install more soundproof baffling in the students' dormitory. Chump liked the idea of further baffling the educational establishment.

Such a cohesive team had not been seen in Washintown since the days of Dinsdale Piranha. As you can see, the team was synergistically aligned, and as harmonious as Blondie. They all believed that one way or another, the students should turn down the Status Quo they had blaring from the college dormitory windows like a bat out of hell. Chump, a lover of classical music, believed it would do well to introduce the refugee students to some of Kenny G's Best, or, for some more highbrow music, to operatic classics such as Stravinsky's *The Rake's Progress* or Gounod's *Faust*.

A flexible and creative O'Newbie kept proposing minor enhancements and amendments to the strategy, for example distributing protective ear-muffs for residents. Chump, testing out the proposed muffs, as always listened on respectfully and thoughtfully, nodding wistfully to the tune of Nirvana's "About A Girl" via a wireless earbud he had slipped underneath into his left ear. After about the 25th amendment, there was an almighty roar of approval from the team, as though that had been the idea they had been looking for all along.

Chump, though needing to be shaken from his apparent meditative state, was thoroughly impressed with O'Newbie's diligence and appeared to be crazy about his ideas, literally hugging O'Newbie in appreciation for his noteworthy contributions to the greater good.

As time went on with the crisis still unresolved, Chump grew in his love and admiration for O'Newbie, almost on a daily basis. Rebus similarly found O'Newbie to be cool-headed and a delight to be around. What emerged in the following days was a triumph of teamwork and cooperation, where all these heads came together to produce a winning outcome. Chump stepped in to veto all the preceding ideas, thereby breaking up the logjam of terrific suggestions, instead proposing a negotiated settlement with the students which would secure noise reduction in exchange for snacks delivered via drone.

Thanks to Chump's skillful intervention, the student emergency situation had at last been defused. For Bunyon in particular, who had directly faced the loud speakers during the negotiation phase, the successful resolution of the noise abatement measures with the students had been a ringing success.

* * *

Chump felt that the public needed to experience a display which symbolized the wonderful legislative gazpacho which characterized the Chump administration and its soaring, explosive achievement. He called a meeting of his team to workshop this issue at the whiteboard. Janey brought along some sliced carrots and celery on a tray with hummus, and the City Hall catering staff were ordered to deliver tea, then to make themselves scarce, as the team needed to focus on finding a way to press forward with Chump's inspired request.

Several ideas were thrown around, including a display of clay pottery made by the team, and an art show including a display of Steve Bunyon's Star Wars figurine collection. Connard suggested a detonation of the old Washintown Nuclear Power Station, followed up with a community sell-off of the rubble for charity, as Kylie-Jo reminded everyone had occurred with pieces of the Berlin Wall. This, she suggested, could be a kind of retro community "demolition party" like the one once held on Coney Island, where people had been invited to throw bricks at the facade of Steeplechase Park.

"Watching the detonation would be very unifying for the community, assuming they're not hit with the wreckage," she touted, "and, say at one dollar a piece, we could clean up on the rubble." No-one else backed her up so her detonation proposal fizzled out.

The whiteboard was starting to look quite messy, as the dizzying spray of thoughts being peppered across its surface began to cover almost every square inch of available white space. Disturbingly to some of them, the black seemed to be taking over from the white. The team engaged in lively, heated discussion on a range of ideas, with a flurry of new proposals being suggested while Sally Muckabee Blathers attempted to keep up, noting them all as fast as she could (that is, not particularly fast) on the assailed whiteboard, which was rapidly turning into a blackboard. As the team debated and rejected some of the ideas, the abandoned proposals were crossed out; and as they recognized connections between some of the good ideas, Sally would draw a solid line from one to the other, criss-crossing the whiteboard like a network of Los Angeles highways after a serious earthquake.

Just as Pollock used his whole body to paint, often in a frenetic dancing style, so too Chump and his team used the entirety of their collective brain cells in the frenzy of this kind of collaborative, colored—permanent-marker-pen-wielding team meeting, to arrive at masterpieces of legislation and public service.

This was the team at its finest, forming a huddle of gray and white matter, with carrot chunks in a dip, determined to produce an outcome which would reek of their raw, unprocessed talent, and benefit all those dear to them, determined to meld their competing ideas into a multi-million dollar gouache of civic mastery.

The result, if one were to stand back, was, in more ways than one, like the Jackson Pollock painting Chump had installed in his office in honor of his team. And in the same way that (to quote an art critic) "Pollock's paintings may appear to be the random product of a depressed and disturbed alcoholic without any real talent", it was only in stepping away to take stock of the team's combined thought processes from a distance - just another step or two back from where it looked like cat vomit - that one could begin to comprehend the sheer masterful distinctiveness and premeditation of this group of collaborators.

As the team began to run out of ideas, Chump did exactly that: he got up from the meeting table, went to the back of the room and took a seat at the far back of the room, with a view towards the whiteboard, to perceive that scribbled mastery as no other civic leader could. He sat there for a long moment, stroking his chin and imagining what he could see in the whiteboard.

A vision dawned upon his consciousness.

There, in the middle of the whiteboard, amid the swirls, scribbles, corrections and crossings-out, the concept rang out clearly. The answer was literally staring him in the face. With the rest of the room silent, it had become clear to him like a flash of inspiration, and Chump suddenly called out: "FIREWORKS!"

Once again, Chump's brilliance had saved the day. The team erupted in a cheer, and there were smiles and backslapping all around.

* * *

In the days that followed, Chump ordered negotiations to begin with Chinese fireworks suppliers for the event. He wanted nothing but the best for his incredible Menda City display, yet he drove such a hard bargain financially - seeking to maximize the use of the public purse - that the Chinese were forced not only to drop on price but also to make some shortcuts in regards to quality. Without telling Chump, they consigned container-loads of fireworks to the city, but some of these would have normally been categorized as 'seconds' or 'potential misfires'.

* * *

Bunyon was thrilled to hear on the day of the mediation meeting with the Afghan students, about a dazzling plan concocted by Kushywanker. They planned to hire as the chief public relations officer Angelo Scummaratti - affectionately known as "Scummi" - the genial, polished media commentator with a long history of high-profile appointments for major media organizations. The team was only getting better and stronger by the day!

Not long into his hiring, Scummaratti had blended into the team beautifully. He had even picked up Mickey Flout's habit of appearing with nostrils covered in icing sugar dust, ready to prank other staffers into thinking he was a raving crackhead.

Dovetailing gracefully into the Communications Team alongside Spinner and Blathers, Angelo was an absolute delight to listen to, a master of oratory who would delicately weave words into stirring speeches to appeal to community's highest values and ideals. Chump's team had only ever sought the most talented individuals, the most accomplished candidates, to fill their available roles; Angelo was one such sublime choice, who took this excellence to a whole new level, for his language was peppered with uplifting phrases and imagery, and he spoke with a dignity and poise which few could ever hope to achieve.

* * *

My colleague Lizzy Rana had gotten wind from me that additional team gatherings were taking place some evenings at the Chump residence, which was almost certainly acting as a kind of policy and culinary incubator. To research this story, Lizzy put in a call to Angelo Scummaratti, who described a lovely dinner which had recently taken place at Chump's house, attended by a collection of staffers including Chump, Melony, Sean Henutty and Willy Shiner.

The guests and their host had all worked together as a team to prepare the meal, consisting of a chilled Vichyssoise, and a salad topped with a white sauce. Several key ingredients had been chosen exclusively by Chump himself, including leeks, beetroot and a sturgeon. These had been combined in a blender, then boiled up on a gas cooker as the staff looked on and formulated social policy inspired by the simmering dish, the nomenclature of which caused some spirited debate among the team.

The resulting "Vichy", as Bunyon called it, had an unbelievable consistency, with overtones of borscht and pond gravy. Chump himself had trouble pronouncing such a long foreign word as 'Vichyssoise' so just called it 'sauce'. Several times during the call, Angelo referred to the dish as 'cock-a-leekie' owing to its similarity to the soup Chump had once made for his mini-golf partner, Sylvie Clittafford, though gastronomically I believe the team's effort was definitely more of a "Vichy".

Lizzy had asked Angelo to describe the sauce, hoping to publish a Chump recipe in the Sentinel. Angelo obliged with a spicy and detailed description of the sauce.

"And who provided the leeks to you?" Lizzy asked. Angelo admitted that they had been grown in Chump's own kitchen garden, just out the rear, and that they had been harvested only that afternoon by none other than Ponce Rebus, who loved getting his hands dirty, as did many other of the staffers. The leeks were therefore incredibly fresh, which had contributed to the quality of the "Vichy".

"It was such fun cooking this up with my colleagues," Scummaratti effused. "I so love these guys!" Angelo had exclaimed. "What a team. Making a potage like that together just sums them up."

"I'm going to see if I can arrange a pay raise for them all over the next few weeks," he added.

"Now you'll have to excuse me, Lizzy" Angelo concluded, wishing to wrap up the phone interview. "All this talk has made me famished. If there are any leftovers, I'm going to slurp on some of my own cock-a-leekie."

With that, amid sounds of vigorous slurping, Angelo hung up, and Lizzy did not hear back from him again.

Lizzy knew that Scummi was destined for a long and illustrious career with the Chump administration.

* * *

The Menda City fireworks night went off with a bang.

21

BUNYON AND SCUMMARATTI

Bunyon's family home was a bustling mansion, populated with a loving family and happy kids bouncing around in a spirit of *joie de vivre*. It was a humble but appealing multi-room home over a French restaurant, with just five or six books arranged neatly on clean shelves, true to Bunyon's well-known frugality and Zen-like character.

His PA, Alexander Prostate, happened to live next door, as did the agent for Nigel Grinstead, the aspiring Canadian politician and keen reader of Dimbrat magazine. They formed a close-knit community, often sharing each other's milk or other essential kitchen supplies. They also shared a lawnmower, and other garden implements such as rakes and leafblowers.

On the morning of Monday January 10, Bunyon was hosting a brunch for his colleagues. He was in a quiet, reserved mood, as he had originally ordered scallops for the brunch but was now concerned that one of his guests might suffer the same fate as Zebraski. Instead, he consulted his kitchen pantry and opted for bite-size wafers with anchovy paste on top, which seemed less of a choking hazard.

As he prepared the wafers, Bunyon took a call indicating that Scummaratti had landed the job of press secretary for the mayor.

"That is the best news I have had all year!" he exclaimed, punching the air with delight. "With this kind of talent representing the council, we're on easy street."

He got off the phone brimming with praise. "You guys have nailed it!"

As the call ended, a blob of the anchovy paste fell into the phone and worked its way into a crack along the edging. The phone became rather strong.

Bunyon was going from strength to strength. He had been receiving great press covfefe for his successful implementation of social welfare programs. A new book called *God's Premium* claimed, often in Chump's own words, that Bunyon had elevated the Chump team to achieve what had previously been considered impossible, to solve issues in society previously seen as intractable. The mayor was thrilled that one of his team was receiving such favorable treatment in the media, reflecting well on his agenda. To him, his own health concerns were not a priority by comparison.

Yet Bunyon felt that he still needed to break through to even higher levels of achievement. The mayor's office was running so smoothly that Janey and Iwanker were hitting new targets every day and reaching ever greater numbers of the underprivileged and downtrodden in the city. Chump Happy Hampers were being delivered by the hundreds, though admittedly there were some reports of hampers being left unopened, or being dumped in the canal.

* * *

The geniuses were reaching new heights of success. Chump himself was reaching new heights of success. Success was literally flowing through the corridors and offices of City Hall. Yet Bunyon still had some nagging self-doubt. Was he achieving enough? Was he helping enough? He thought for a moment, then came a flash of insight:

"I'm jolly well nailing it! The city's social welfare agenda? We're not just nailing it, we're stapling it! We're nail-gunning it! I'll be in this fab and fun job forever and a day." He then realized that he was talking to himself as the others had left the room.

During the brunch, Bunyon circulated an article from The National Enquirer about the widespread acceptance of the new social programs which the Chump administration was implementing. The article, by Nikitina Salival, showered praise on the administration and elevated Bunyon and Chump's policies to the status of history-making social advances. "Erstwhile supporters must agree that their policies have produced greater equality, more employment and an upward momentum for wages. Praise that economists only used to reserve for the most dry and arcane academic papers must finally be unleashed on these incredible architects of social improvement."

Now feeling confident and relaxed about their tremendous achievements, Bunyon recounted how Chump had praised O'Newbie and, as well, savored the perfection of the Scummaratti hiring.

In the same way that Shelley Yeats had romantically pursued Mickey Flout, Chump's own steamy charisma had attracted another fan by the name of Penny Social, a long-time Washintown resident who similarly followed Chump like a creepy stalker and exhibited disturbing behaviors such as making weird hand gestures towards him and wishing him Happy Holidays through gritted teeth. Penny, wise beyond her years yet scary as a gutter-clown, would at times stand with me on the sidewalk outside Chump's private residence, having emerged seemingly from nowhere, bearing food gifts for Chump, gifts he was reluctant to ingest himself in case they had in some way been tampered with.

As everyone knew, Chump had arranged to give an interview to Margie Haveherman (of the Washintown Sentinel), one of Chump's greatest supporters and a close colleague of your dear Martha Skewermann. Margie and I had often discussed Chump as we played darts in the newsroom, and had vied with one another to be the first to interview him. Margie had obviously prevailed in this instance (bitch!) In any case, Janey and Iwanker, along with Joy Hickey, had set it up. The result was one of the most memorable and inspiring interviews in the history of City Hall. The mayor in clear and concise terms had unequivocally showered praise on the young LGBTQI law intern Jess Fessin, even urging her to seek a promotion. Furthermore, in an act of unparalleled civil transparency, Chump had openly released his own tax returns and detailed records of his family finances to the media via Margie, and could even explain a few items on the returns which looked irregular but "really weren't".

Bunyon described the conversation he had had with Chump earlier that morning, after the Haveherman interview. "That was so honest and admirable of you to offer all your financial records so openly. I really love you, boss." Bunyon planted a wet smooch on Chump's orange peel-skinned cheek. This was the Chump administration at its finest.

Prostate, putting out Chinese chestnuts on the table as he listened intently, said, "Could you please pass the soy sauce?"

Bunyon then recounted another article detailing the respectworthy work of Chump's friend Fabrizio Stitcher, who together with Chump had arranged for used clothing to be sent to orphans in Kenya, and housing for refugees from Crimea. Reporter Andrew Wrightman had gotten wind of it and word was out that Chump and Stitcher were now likely nominees for another humanitarian award.

"Do you realise where this is going?" Bunyon asked as he passed down the sauce bottle. "If this goes on the tablecloth, it will need some serious laundering. You'll need to get Paula Moneyport to help you out there, she's very talented in that regard, has some powerful stain removers in her storage container. Pass this down carefully."

In fact, unwittingly, the team then made an enormous mess, and did indeed overturn the soy sauce bottle, over the top of what would otherwise have been a tablecloth laid out cleanly for members of the public. The public asset was smeared and stained almost beyond recognition.

To lighten up the situation, Bunyon piped up with office news from City Hall: "Dinah is going to be celebrated in the local paper! She's a good girl. She is going to be the talk of the town! O'Newbie is going overseas on holidays. And Gerry Conehead, well he's just having a ball paper-shuffling!"

Everyone at the table clapped and cheered. They all conspired to give Dinah a really warm round of applause. Dinah, going red in the cheeks, looked embarrassed and flattered. She did like being flattered. She had a real red look to her.

To relieve the stress of her busy work life, Moneyport had taken up semi-professional and competitive gymnastics to while away her otherwise long evenings in solitude.

She loved her new orange gym team leotard which was the same as the other girls'. It took Paula a while to warm up, but once going, her natural skills were clearly on display with this hobby, and she was proficient with many types of apparatus. When taking a dive roll, she somehow managed to squeeze in an aerial, which really impressed everyone! For most similar novices, that would have been unthinkable!

In preparing for competitive events, she had started to develop quite a repertoire of moves: she had several good vaults, which would attract much interest in the judges' eyes; she was in the early stages of perfecting an excellent 'flip' maneuver, and her 'back walkover' was also showing promise, though it still needed help from her five team members. The 'flyaway' from the parallel bars was one of the moves she just could not master, no matter how much hard labor she put in; sadly, in the long run, this, and the "flip" would be moves which continued to elude her.

Brave Paula had persisted with her gym work despite being regularly harassed after her sessions by local bully, Bobby Mauler, who hung around the gym menacingly, possibly wanting cash or to cut a drug deal. Paula would have no part in it.

* * *

Ten days into the Scummaratti hiring, Scummaratti and Shawn Spinner were collaborating better than ever before. Spinner was full of new energy, typical of his indomitable spirit, and wore a constant smile. Scummaratti's hiring had been a breathtaking move, and was already bringing in lot more media opportunities for the team.

Spinner came out of his office bearing a letter of thanks and praise to 'Scummi' for the wonderful qualities, new ideas, and innovative rhetoric he had brought to the team, featuring novel sound bites which had put the media in a frenzy. Spinner, one of the most admired men in Washintown, was determined to give Scummaratti a gift to show his enormous sense of appreciation. His days at City Hall, and visiting Chump's white house, had just begun and for that, Shawn was truly grateful.

For Scummaratti, it was a time to contribute. He in turn praised Ponce Rebus for giving him the opportunity to be a part of Washintown history. He had gained so much already from his experience in this high-performing team. Rebus was a living, breathing inspiration to Scummaratti, like a giant celery which had unexpectedly sprung up in the vegetable garden of Scummaratti's flourishing career.

The signal sent from the mayor to Scummaratti was that, although he was a relative newcomer, 'Scummi' was a valued team member, just like everyone else. In Chump's view, this team was so well-functioning and free of personnel issues that taking on a new Scummaratti was just part of the way they functioned. Scummaratti looked like he would have long tenure with the administration, up there with long-serving seasoned professionals like Rob Hurther, Kitty Welsher and Mickey Flout.

Bunyon recounted the details of a recent story from the Washintown Times about one of the brightest stars in the Chump orbit, Felicity Splatter, who had helped Chump over many years with fundraising for Chump's work for struggling housing tenement dwellers at risk of eviction. Splatter had also recently befriended Mickey Crohney in her work for a charity known as the RockyBay Group.

"Do you realize where this is all going? Our team is going to literally *clean up* with media coverage! All of our noble friends and colleagues are likely to get feature articles and TV appearances. It will be such a privilege! We can really advance our cause."

Bunyon's assessment yet again turned out to be prescient.

* * *

As he settled in to his new career, Scummaratti in turn began praising Ponce Rebus privately. Outside the french doors of the Eastern Annex, in the Rosy Garden, he mentioned in soft tones- "He is like a sacred cow to me". Mutual admiration and delight flowed freely in all directions, like the old Calcutta drainage network in monsoon season. Similarly, the loving feelings between the team members were palpable, like semi-solid objects floating in that very same old Calcutta drainage network.

According to evidence I gathered from Odorosa Animalgut, who recorded the following incident and leaked it to me on a reel-to-reel tape she had smuggled into the office disguised as a fashionable backpack, a heated round of self-congratulations and self-loving circulated among the staffers: Shawn Spinner first indicated, in mime approximating interpretive dance, that Scummaratti was like a son to him; the bastard son he never had. This was mimed with almost-Shakespearean looks of anguish, and hair-tearing. Then, aloud, he opined: "To me, you are just another Spinner", indicating his adoring familial sentiments.

Scummaratti, though not reciprocating directly to Spinner, in turn indicated via internationally-recognized hand gestures that he, similarly, was delighted with Chump, and pasted on a permanent toothy smile to forcefully demonstrate these loving feelings while his fingers said the rest. Chump then made it known to all that he was delighted with high-performing Janey and Iwanker; and of course everyone loved the pre-eminent Bunyon, even if he stood out somewhat. Scummaratti mused that they were all like family to him too, and that the whole workplace was like it was full of Scummarattis. Bunyon quickly countered, saying that No, he loved them all like family himself and that they were more like a bunch of Bunyons. Chump piped up saying, "No, you're all wonderful, and to me you're all Chumps, really great Chumps." The circle of love was completed when Chump hastily added, "Even you, Spinner, even you are a Chump!"

I believe they may all have been right, and that the team was, in fact, a great conglomeration of Chumps, Bunyons, Spinners and Scummarattis.

* * *

Bunyon and Rebus could not believe the cement-like bonds that had formed between the team members, like epoxy. "Epoxy team" they dubbed it, and were often heard mumbling that term *sottovoce* as they wandered the corridors. "Super glue" others called it. It was such a dream having Scummaratti on board; they wanted to open their eyes fully to appreciate this wonderful moment in time, and then to skip forth into a brilliant future. "Super glue" made this slightly difficult.

* * *

In fact, Shawn Spinner had been due to go on vacation, but was enjoying Scummaratti's company and expertise so much that he couldn't tear himself away and put his vacation on hold to spend more time around Angelo, learning tricks of public speaking which he could put into practice on his return.

* * *

Since Chump and Dinah had slammed their respective crania into the lintel in the City Hall basement, work by the FSB crew to re-peel and replace the wiring in the City Hall basement area had, at last, after a respectful delay, started to progress well. Peace reigned within the team. The stripping back of all the known infrastructure had gone exceedingly well, apart from knocking out all the dialysis and life-support machines in Washintown General Hospital, the refrigeration systems in the Washintown North dairy and the communication links to the outside world, for about two weeks over the "shutdown" period.

Regrettably, the incident also slowed Chump's completion of an important policy paper he had been working on. Brilliantly literate, he had been penning what could be a seminal document in which he propounded to other municipalities the strategy used in Washintown of ripping up their existing infrastructure in order to make a fresh start with highly skilled Eastern bloc contractors.

* * *

Janey, being the wonderful soul that she is, stepped up to the plate and took responsibility for the misunderstanding which had earlier led to the encounter in the basement.

Chump, meanwhile had traveled out of town to address a gathering of the Girl Guides, who were blown away by his stirring words on feminism, fairness and human rights. The speech prompted immediate praise from the Girl Guides Association. For such public presentations, Chump went to great lengths to ensure his appearance was impeccable, even scrubbing the undersides of his shoes with toilet paper to ensure that the dog droppings and associated stench which somehow regularly accompanied him after their 'bring you dog to the office' days had been wiped away before his oration.

* * *

It was not long after this that Willy Shiner joined the communications team. The team now had an added member of the Shiner family, an additional Willy Shiner, to add to the existing retinue of Spinner and Blathers. In the weeks ahead, Shiner would become central to the administration's messaging. Shiner covered many of the stories emanating from Chump's office. Chump was moving so quickly now that his communications team often couldn't keep up with him, so they asked him to slow down in the corridors, or even to amble rather than run, and were often forced to place small obstacles, such as cushions or office chairs, in his path to reduce his average velocity. Such was the nature of Chump, that the laws of physics almost needed to be rewritten.

22

GENERAL KITTY MALAISE

On February 26, Chump and some relatively minor staffers from the Eastern Annex left to play mini-golf in nearby Badmunster. Stevie Bunyon went along but General Kitty Malaise remained at City Hall due to a highly sensitive issue. The team had been under quite a deal of work pressure, and Chump was still recovering from the trauma of the episode with Punkin at Hellsinky, so the trip was seen as an excellent opportunity to regroup and take a much-need breather from the busy legislative and public works agenda.

As they drove off, I overheard, or at least I lip-read, General Kitty mumbling to herself, through only slightly clenched teeth, as she waved the others goodbye: "This is the best freakin' job I've ever had! Chump is a freakin' genius! I love Chump!" General Kitty may have been sad to see her team members driving away, but knew she had issues to attend to at City Hall.

Truth be told, Malaise had been experiencing ongoing, persistent diarrhea, and had had an 'accident' in the policy room, from overdoing it on the rancid chowder without having had the courage to decline additional servings. As a result, she needed to do a mop-up of her own smelly mess while the others enjoyed recreation at Badmunster. After she had wished her dear friends be departed, she entered the policy room with a bucket and gloves. In doing so, she stepped in her own mess, the malodorous result of her overindulgence, almost skidding, and realized that she had just ruined her own military boots, not to mention her reputation for smelling fresh, and her air of aloofness. Her day was not going well. Meanwhile, only a few miles down the road, the others had blown a tire and were standing by the roadside as Bunyon tried to work out how to take the wheel off.

Chump and his peripatetic team members were looking like they were in wheel trouble.

The staffing situation in the city council was starting to become problematic. Staff, just like General Malaise, absolutely loved working for Chump - some, such as Drew Meccaban, to the extent of delaying their retirement. In addition, a host of talented applicants were already due to be starting their induction, with yet others camping out on the lawns in the hope of securing a position in "Chumpworld".

Drew, in fact, had sought the wise counsel of Elrond Resinstone, to see if there was a way he could secretly arrange permanent tenure with the Chump administration, such was his devotion to Ronnie.

Meanwhile, new hires continued apace, often causing a doubling-up in important roles. To assist with his role dealing with migrants, H.R. O'Newbie willingly brought Johnny Notlob on board, a gentle and affable (though somewhat dreary) town planner sporting a distinctive goatee beard, who had just missed out on the initial intake. "You qualified for the role!" O'Newbie had excitedly exclaimed when announcing the position to Notlob, who coincidentally had dropped by to check whether there were any new openings at City Hall. He happened to be in luck, for the Russian workers let him into the building via a hole they had just punched through the western wall.

"Johnny, can you believe it? You qualified!" reiterated the excited O'Newbie, with a cough due to the building dust.

"I did, did I?" replied the ever-palindromic Notlob. "Wow!"

O'Newbie took what appeared to be two chilled Coronas from his bar fridge and poured them both a celebratory drink. "Regal lager!" pronounced the excited Notlob, clinking glasses. O'Newbie hadn't wanted to spoil Notlob's excitement by telling him that it was actually home-brew made by Muckabee Blathers' hillbilly first cousin (and half-brother) in Alabama.

The two sat enjoying their beers before O'Newbie, who had been running out of shelf space, got Johnny straight to work to help him put together his new iRack office storage, which he had been struggling to assemble.

* * *

The flurry of new hirings began to cause overcrowding in City Hall as the number of available offices was outstripped by the number of new recruits eagerly joining the administration to help fulfill its historic social visions. Offices which had previously accommodated a single desk with ease were now being cluttered with two, three or even four desks as the pace of new hirings showed no signs of abating.

Chump had needed to ask the FSB crew to knock out some walls and to install some additional temporary power cords, half-Amp electrical sockets, bar radiators and extension leads between offices to handle the influx of willing staffers. These snaked along the carpet of City Hall, as did the staffers. The power-boards hummed with the near-capacity electrical current they were drawing as the team produced torrents of socially-progressive legislation and Chump-inspired recipe leaflets for the Happy Harvest Hamper program.

Furthermore, several offices no longer had room for any more desks at all, so desks were now being placed in the corridors and side passages of the building, leading to a number of accidents in the corridors as staffers bumped into each other squeezing past the desks, tripped on chair legs or power cords, or collided with piles of legislative manila folders heaped up on the carpet on top of temporary cables.

Before long a spaghetti-like tangle of the electrical extension cords spread through the hallways to power the desk computers, lamps, printers, heaters and phone chargers of the supernumerary staff being set up in the corridors, all keen and devoted "Chumpsters". Plugs and power boards were heavily piggybacked. Several times coffee was spilled into, or all over, the power-boards. As a consequence, the place had a buzz to it like never before, as one might feel in an exciting police chase, or in a Soviet nuclear power station with a few control rods pulled out. It gave a new meaning to the term 'hot-desking'. The sense of activity and connection which filled the establishment was electric, just like the added cabling and the occasional spark it emitted in the corridor.

* * *

A day arrived when General Malaise again called Odorosa into the Washintown Situation Room for one of their regular one-on-one meetings, though this was to be a very special meeting indeed. Having left the door open as usual for the purposes of openness and honesty, Malaise was proud to offer Odorosa a promotion, showering her with praise for the incredible job she had done documenting all the happy times they had been sharing as a team. Odorosa was deeply touched and felt this sweet moment with General Malaise was one she wished she could preserve, cherish and play back forever, if only there were a way to capture such precious moments. She adjusted her head-mounted GoPro® as General Kitty explained how nothing could hold back her illustrious reputation, and that she had thoroughly deserved the promotion - which came with a pay rise of an astonishing $15,000 per month - because she had exhibited so much friendship and camaraderie to her fellow team members in the city council.

Kitty also explained that she had double-checked with The Boss and that yes, according to Chump, speak of the devil, it was indeed she, General Malaise herself, who had now taken over the internal running of the administration, as though she was "born to run" the office, Ronnie had said. In any case, Mayor Chump needed to focus on his external affairs such as the women's issues on his agenda when Melony was busy with their newborn, Bruno. These affairs were taxing, time-consuming and exhausting, requiring detailed legislative and timetable workarounds, extensive involvement from lawyers, and numerous press briefings, typically managed by the succinct Judy Ruelyini. Judy had done a superb job with all this additional work, all the more impressive as she was also doing some weekend work for U-Crane while Paula Moneyport had been focusing on fundraising for disabled children. Kitty promised endless office merriment, once they could get the aphids, coddling moths and weevils under control with some more Agent Orange.

* * *

The city's name change had not really taken off with members of the public or the media. People, through force of habit, were still referring to the city as Washintown, and Chump's great vision of having the city's inhabitants universally refer to his Menda City was failing to materialize.

It also seemed that there had been a fundamental problem with the design plan of the S.H. IT Project from Day One. It was the pits.

Yes, many of the pits had been undersized in the planning process as they had been drawn up in haste by Paula Moneyport without taking into account the large amount of effluent now regularly streaming from Chump's new white home, and from City Hall, due to all the additional staff.

* * *

Sadly, Ronnie's plans for the centralized Washintown Humanitarian IT Hub were rapidly falling apart as the Fix-It crew experienced a number of setbacks. Delivery of the custom-built Domain Name Controller, a dedicated server for routing emails, had at first been delayed due to ice in Vladivostok's port. Then, after it had arrived to be worked on by the server expert, a Mr Habib from Lahore, it had been accidentally corrupted during configuration, and taken to an unknown location by FSB agents who had been heard to state, "Is ok, we fix."

Furthermore, the crew working on the municipal building had dug up some of the wrong power cables, caused extensive tangling of cables in the roof spaces and had accidentally struck a large sewer main running underneath City Hall. Due to a surge of electricity, the council rates database crashed and several servers frizzled, scrambling many of the websites and the older automation processes which underpinned the normal running of city governance.

This in turn had caused an almighty flood - or, as we say in Arizona, an emmity flood - to appear in the hall, sweeping General Malaise along with it, just as the gang of 8 professional fireman was attempting to meet there, outside the server room, to discuss their combined knowledge of the unfolding emergency.

Chump, having donned a pair galoshes, trudged down to the basement to conduct a spot check of what was going on.

He hauled up several workers who were just seeking to escape the rising waters.

"Where is the server?" he demanded. "Where is the server? And what is the server saying? I really do want to see the server."

The FSB workers continued wading off into the distance, looking baffled.

"What happened to the servers of the Pakistani gentleman that worked on the DNC?" Chump called after them.

As the Russians disappeared into the distance, all they could hear was the gradually-fading sound of Chump calling out after them: "I don't think it can go on without finding out what happened to the server. What happened to the servers of the Pakistani gentleman that worked on the DNC? Where are those servers? They're missing. Where are they?"

* * *

It took a few days for the basement flooding to recede and project works to return to normal. It seemed that things were getting back on track. Chump had squeezed some answers out of the team with his strong and powerful questioning, yet some issues still lingered. The DNC server had apparently been sent back to a busy workshop in Karachi to have a new hard disk installed. It was due back within weeks, once Mr Abbas could arrange for his mother to move in with his brother-in-law Abdullah, and then get a flight back.

Some unappreciative members of the press were complaining yet again about the lack of pies they were being fed at Chump's press conferences, and that the chowder they were offered had been too cold and clammy. The media had picked up on the fact that Happy Harvest Hampers had been delivered to homes throughout Washintown - even homes with young children - which included complimentary bottles of vodka along with the other plastic-wrapped foodstuffs. Chump, a smart feller, countered quickly, saying "Look, I've had a bottle in front of me since I was much younger and look how I've turned out!" He thought the media were spending their time lighting a fire, making up a crisis that didn't really exist.

They were also reporting that some Washintown residents had grown sick from consuming infected Happy Harvest Hampers or putrescent Chump Chowder mixture delivered to their homes, but which they had failed to retrieve from the hot Summer sun.

Other batches appeared to be contaminated with offcuts of a toxic Russian fish which had somehow insinuated itself into the concoction. Even more disturbingly, unclaimed vats of Chump Chowder - delivered to poor families in Washintown or to abandoned residences but left for weeks on doorsteps - had caused an burgeoning outbreak of bubonic plague which was threatening Washintown's hospital system. A wide range of symptoms was being reported by those who had been unfortunate enough to consume a mess of the rotten Chump dégustation.

* * *

Things were also going wrong in other parts of town too. Roddy Pebble's beloved black shitzu, Nero, had fallen into the sinkhole which had opened up on Main St due to Russian tunneling beneath the surface, combined with the fact that here too the FSB crew had accidentally struck the water main under the road. Dangling on its very long, unretractable lead, the dog was still visible bobbing up and down, ten or twenty feet below the roadway, though it risked disappearing from view if not hauled up quickly by its still-protruding tail. "This was a screwup, I admit it," Roddy acknowledged as he looked into the deep, dark hole, realizing he had walked his furbaby too close to the Russian-made cave-in. Someone relayed this tale to Chump who already had his hands full.

Jeffrey Corsidid, on his morning stroll, had somehow just known, as though by a premonition or forewarning, that the black dog was in trouble. He had arrived on the scene and was attempting to help by tugging on the dog's lead, but actually was only making matters worse. Being flustered, in a panic growing like the sinkhole, he was scampering around the edge of the ever-widening sinkhole, causing the lead to get knotted. All the while he was babbling to himself "Pardon me, pardon me" as the barking pooch slipped deeper into the murky waters of the Russian-made cave-in beneath Main St.

Emergency crews had been called in an attempt to rescue the dog before it became irretrievably lost beneath the city. Roddy and his wife were beside themselves with anxiety as the emergency services arrived with numerous vehicles in attempts to haul the shitzu from the giant hole which had opened up and swallowed it up. Roddy, usually introverted, was in front of a local news crew, forcefully demanding more assistance, even though there were already seventeen vehicles and many officers in attendance. It was only with the arrival of Roddy's friend, Andy Critico, bringing a scooper on a long pole, that Nero was finally able to be fished out of the hole to safety.

* * *

Chump had been keen to stop the hemorrhaging of unfortunate news, for after the Hellsinky incident with Punkin, the administration had reeled from a run of bad luck which included, but were not limited to: the dual head-thwack, the developing sinkhole, the City Hall basement flooding, the dog in the hole, the toxic Happy Hamper deliveries and the Black Plague outbreak, to name a few.

As true professionals, Chump and General Kitty therefore wanted to 'prophylactically' head off any further misadventures, so worked together on a security review. They had met on regular occasions to discuss security of council documents and office materials. General Kitty was very comfortable that Janey had been using her security pass quite appropriately, and nothing much had gone missing from the stationery supply cupboard to the best of Kitty's knowledge, and only a few donuts from the staff cafeteria. Chump, on the other hand, perceptive as ever, had noticed that some of the more senior police chiefs based at City Hall had extremely suspicious looks on their faces at times, and occasionally used harsh words, particularly when talking about criminals (who, Chump reminded everyone, are people too), so he quietly arranged with General Kitty to have their security clearances revoked, something they would eventually discover over a period of time. Washintown was certainly being kept very safe! Thank God for Chump!

* * *

But then just when all were hoping the rough patch was over, another calamity was visited upon the administration, almost like a biblical catastrophe. Would this be the event that ultimately broke Chump? Many wondered.

Chump had been shocked and outraged following an audit of the Chump Foundation which had revealed a small discrepancy (around a penny) had been found in the Foundation's finances. He was furious that such an unpardonable error had been made when he had always been as scrupulous as the UN, literally UN scrupulous, about due diligence.

Since learning the tricks of the accounting trade from Alvin McWeaselberger all those years ago, Chump had aspired to punctilious accounting practices. Yet here, he thought, as he stroked his bonce, there was clearly something missing. Just as Alvin had warned him, it was accrual accounting incident. Chump tore out lumps and clumps of his hair in anguish, in spite of the strong glue. How could this happen? It just didn't add up. Going over the books, the phenomenal financial fail saddened Chump to such a degree that he felt was at risk of falling into a deep depreciation.

Like the single slip of an incompetent trickster which makes a house of cards fall down, this single oversight by this thoroughly virtuous man may have been a factor in the events that were to subsequently unfold in Washintown, for it greatly perturbed Chump and may have caused him to be far more distracted and error-prone than usual. Just as the wings of a butterfly in the Amazon Fulfillment Center can indirectly stir up a tropical cyclone, so this single discrepancy may have been a significant cause of the **DIRE** travails which were about to unfold in the City of Washintown, or as some still reluctantly called it, Menda City.

That night at home, mulling over the audit failure as rainclouds gathered, Chump was deeply troubled, thinking that his flawless reputation, developed over many years, would now be in tatters. He paced up and down the hall of his new home, tugging at what was left of his hair and asking in a plaintive tone, "How could this have happened?" Not sure whether he was asking himself rhetorically, or seeking her silky advice, Melony stood with a gormless confused look on her recently-botoxed face, then summoned up her wisest counsel. "I know nuthink, darleengk, I not know why. Ze numbers, zey rilly confuse me, Ronnie."

Lightning flashed outside. Melony's soothing words sought to quell his fires of shame and self-loathing, "Butt... you didn't do this, Ronnie. Butt... shin up, you are good man, Ronnie, you not fraudster, you rilly not, my sweet love. Please, let me flick you hand," she appealed, referring yet again to her favorite practice of secret intimacy with Ronnie, known to drive him wild with passion from this form of pleasured denial. But Ronnie was adamant that the appalling fiscal oversight could now hang like a cloud over his mayoralty, and over the virtuous Chump Foundation, for many years to come, and that the Chump name may be severely tainted despite his years of philanthropy and social justice work. He was so distraught that he wished he could just look up into the Sun, and burn out his own eyeballs. Even that wasn't possible, due to the clouds. And even Melony flicking his hand away in her usual aggressively sensual way did not cheer him up that night. Things were really serious. She needed to bring out the heavy artillery, to get Ronnie to push her own kind of emergency red button.

Ronnie certainly needed some intimate consoling from his dear Melony as his mood had not improved into the late evening. As she unbuttoned her massive brassiere and brought out her heavy-duty weapons of consolation - two giant silicone-filled shoulder-pads she had Velcroed to her collarbones, now to be slipped under Ronnie's teary cheeks - Melony, true to her name, was not to disappoint and pressed RECORD on her rooted Huawei phone.

Some of their sweet horizontal dancing that night, and Chump's near-suffocation beneath these pendulous orbs of love, will be described in more detail in my future publication, *Fifty Shades of Chump*, based on a revealing tape which was leaked to me much later that night in damp brown packaging, by a source who shall remain nameless, due to the fact she never revealed her name. For you see, dear reader: as thunder rang out and rain poured down upon me out on the sidewalk, after midnight - almost as though the elements had mimicked Chump's brooding mood - a mysterious long-haired informant approached me, hooded in a khaki jacket, with some white lettering painted on the back, and didn't seem to care that I should receive such a shocking video package, direct from Chump's private life: an explosive release, in a wet envelope.

Yes, all will be revealed in my steamy upcoming novella, *Fifty Shades of Chump.*

BUNYON AND CHUMP:
CLIMAX

Dr Jeb Goney woke up after a rough night's sleep, to the sound of jackhammering. Chump had directed the Fix-It Services Business crew to rip up the city's older water piping as he had a gut feeling it contained some lead or other impurities. Punkin, well and truly on the back foot since Hellsinky and now clearly seeking to make amends, had offered a cheap rate on fresh recycled pipes shipped in to the city from Pripyat, a small manufacturing town near Chernobyl.

With the water mains pipes being replaced, the Russians were working to divert the city's water supply to source from the swamp at the rear of Chump's property. Paula Moneyport had been called in to consult. True to her philanthropic nature, Paula had provided her sluice and drainage expertise at reduced rates, to match the piping. She also offered the services of her U-Crane business to help unload the new piping from the docks when it arrived. This would reduce the risk of any damage to piping which may occur during manual unloading. As a result, several U-Crane trucks had therefore been seen shuffling components around town.

Although Chump's swamp itself (which had filled significantly since his inauguration) had been shown to contain traces of Moscovium, Cad-mium and Arse-nic in its algal cocktail, both Moneyport and Chump felt that the levels were low enough to be undetectable by the drinking public. The installation of large enough pipes would flush any contaminants to the bottom. Chump agreed, knowing from experience that his own contaminants went straight to the bottom.

Russian voices could be heard outside in the street between the bursts of jackhammering which shook Goney's house and rattled the windows. It seemed the Russian workers were arguing over the high-pressure sewerage pipe they had just accidentally ruptured, which was now spraying untreated sewage over the houses of Washintown in a fine mist, with occasional chunks.

Only a few hundred feet away, another sinkhole had opened up in the middle of the road not far from City Hall, suspiciously close to an area where FSB had recently torn up the sidewalk and had dug deep pipe trenches. Had there been a leak? An FSB crew had been sent to the area to look into it, which is precisely what they were doing as they stood in a circle around the new hole with hands on their chins, mumbling in Russian.

Chump went down to the FSB's worksite on Main St, where renewal of the main sewer under the roadway was being carried out, but where there had been reports of a serious blockage in the new sewer main. Keen to get to the bottom of this, he was lowered down on a straining, creaking winch, and was followed down by a few members of the press who used the ladder, not fully trusting the winch having seen the tension it had just withstood.

When the press arrived down at the base of the sewer pit, Chump was already there. He looked right at home, chatting casually with the Russian tunnel-workers, before he proceeded to wander further up the new 12-foot diameter sewer line to inspect the works in the hope of finding the source of the blockage. The press corps followed up behind the mayor.

The delegation hadn't gone very far when one of the members of the press suddenly screamed out, "Look out! I see it! There's a giant fatberg, straight ahead!" They shone their torches, and indeed, it looked like a giant fatberg was indeed blocking the pipe. A large, corpulent blob seemed to be filling the entire sewer. Seeking more illumination, the media contingent stopped right there and turned on their brighter studio-grade camera lights.

"Hello, it's just me!" called a surprised Ronnie, squinting back in the dazzling light, having stopped ahead to pick his nose. "No, it's just me you're seeing. I'm not a fatberg, really I'm not."

With some relief that it had not in fact been a fatberg, only the Mayor's sizable form, the group continued on and it turned out, much further on, that a collapsed wall was the real source of the blockage. Chump, however, did not so easily brush off the incident, and remained unimpressed that he had been fatberg-shamed by the media.

* * *

Goney noticed a stench of smoke permeating his bedroom, accompanied by a fishy smell, mixed with the unmistakable odor of burning eucalyptus-scented diapers. Too tired and lazy to do anything about it, he rolled over and went back to sleep, having jammed the two lumps of used chewing tobacco on his bedside table into his ears to act as de facto earplugs.

Around the same time, Scummaratti, a Chupa Chup in his mouth, was putting in a call to Bunyon, and noticed that his cell phone was going straight to voicemail. Something wasn't right. He smelt a rat. It smelt burnt. He called Crohney. No answer. This was bad. He sucked hard on his own Chupa Chup.

Then the worst of the worst happened: Scummaratti's phone rang. It was Shirley Kissayak. Blurting through intense tears and sobbing, she finally managed to get it out that Chump's new house was indeed on fire. Her fellow FSB workers had seen flames gushing forth from the roof.

"Shirley, you can't be serious?" quizzed Scummaratti. She was.

"It must be true" she sobbed. "Moose News, zey has alreddy sent a vehicle, and you know zey only riport on ze real news. And zat famous journalist, Marta, what her name, Marta Skewermann, she is out ze front. She take notes. She vatching it all unfold, she iz write it all, for her book. She eating scone and write it down. Zis is really happening, Scummi. I need you, Scummi! Hold me, Scummi!" With that, the phone call cut out, possibly due to Shirley having fainted from the stress of the rapidly evolving crisis or, perish the thought, perhaps due to the phone line having melted.

* * *

But to fully understand the events of that momentous day, we will need to rewind a little to earlier that morning.

Two little refugee kids who had been playing in the street, Gretel Thunderberg and Hansel Jameson, first raised the alarm as they noticed the air becoming thick with soot as a thin wisp of smoke rising from Chump's house was gradually diffused across the neighborhood. The children, only recently resettled in Washintown from Kiribati, had never seen the air become so murky, and ran back to their families, pointing up at the sky in fear as the smoggy emissions began to spread out like a dark hand.

When these early signs of smoke had been reported by other concerned Washintown residents, well before Dr Goney had been woken, a cable news channel had put in a call to Chump's neighbor, farmer Dobbin Moonez, at his adjoining cattle ranch, to follow up the locals' concerns and about the weird weather conditions and the thin fog-like smoke which residents were seeing.

Dobbin noticed he had a mist call, and rang back. He immediately brushed off the reports as a false alarm, stating that it was probably just his neighbors' backyard barbecue letting off some smoke, or perhaps a pile of Fall leaves set on fire by Bobby Mauler's gang of degenerates. It could even be, he opined, just that one of his own dung-piles had spontaneously combusted, as dung-piles tend to do if stacked too densely; he knew that from experience.

Yes, he admitted that Chump had a dung-pile on his property too, and yes it was quite a big one, for he had donated cow dung to

Chump, who needed it for his vegetable garden. Collegial staffer Stevie Manurechin had again helped shovel it across from Dobbin's property, though once again somehow ended up with a large pat hanging from the bottom of his face.

Ever optimistic and jovial, Dobbin laughed heartily on the phone when the local news reporter suggested that it might be Mayor Chump's own house on fire, as a tall plume of smoke had now been seen rising from his neighborhood. Little did Dobbin know, that when the day was through, this would be no laughing matter for Greater Washintown. He would wish it was only flaming dung.

* * *

Earlier that morning, Chump realized that he had slept in for the day's planned team meeting, so resolved to call the team over to his own home to conduct the meeting there. It is only I, your dear Martha, who can now recount to you what truly transpired in the ensuing moments within the walls of Chump's new house.

Ronnie, more than a little overweight, was sauntering around the home in his embroidered "R.S." bathrobe, handstitched by Melony, looking like something between a proud Hugh Hefner and proud heifer. Having woken up late, he had first headed to the kitchen, thoughtfully, to prepare lunch for his team, setting some potatoes and a frozen goose garnished with rosemary in his slow cooker, with a drizzle of olive oil and a light marinade.

His radio played softly in the background. A news report came over the airwaves, stating that overnight a gang of youths, suspected of being linked to Bobby Mauler's gang, had carried out a break-in of Mickey Crohney's motor repair shop. The gang had made off with mny items of value, including Mickey's tools of trade, his old phones left in dusty drawers in the workshop, and even his copious supplies of tinned grease.

The live reporter at the scene was indicating that, for a gang of young punks, the thieves had been remarkably professional. They had stripped the workshop completely bare, even taking the fly-strips - those sticky tapes which had caught so many nasty critters - which Mickey had dangled all over his workshop. God knows why anyone would have wanted those.

"Poor Mickey" Chump mumbled to himself as he prepared a snack. "What a pity for him. I really care about him."

Then Mickey's voice crackled over the radio in the live interview: "This has been a real terrible bust-in for me. I'm so mad, this really makes me flip. This workshop is my life. These lousy rats have cleaned me out." As the interviewer pressed him for detail, Mickey went on to swear that he would stay faithful to his customers, and that he wouldn't let the robbery affect the servicing of their cars.

"Look, ok, it might force me to negotiate deals with some new customers, the income loss is gonna hit me hard. But I'll get through it. I know the Washintown P.D. needs their fleet maintained. I'll go for that contract. I'll get through this."

The reporter then passed the mike over to a witness of the robbery. It happened to be none other than Judy Ruelyini, who worked in an office close to Mickey's workshop.

"You should have seen it!" Judy exclaimed. "The gang stormed in like troopers! They were smashing down doors and taking whatever they could lay their hands on. It was frightening. I hope I never have to go through anything like that myself!"

"I wonder when I'm next due for a tune-up" Chump mused, before switching off the radio.

Chump had then poured himself a huge brandy before leisurely picking up the phone and summoning his underlings to his property. Heading to City Hall that day would have been inconvenient for him, as he had a book parcel delivery due around mid-morning.

* * *

You see, as was common practice, Chump had arranged for the staff meeting to take place at his own home that day. But today was special, not just an ordinary staff meeting, so Ronnie had poured out thirteen celebratory vodka shots, one per person, in preparation for his team's arrival. For in this case, it was to celebrate the team's exceptional performance.

In the parlance of Washintown's teenagers, the team had been developing legislation which was "fully sick". They had been winning almost every day, in fact winning so much that they were at risk of tiring of all the winning, so this was Chump's very personal way to instill more team spirits, allow for some 'release' and keep everyone's motivation on the boil. This would help regulate the large surge of positive energy the team was experiencing, particularly in terms of securing their future careers. Constant winning has been shown in detailed psychological studies, such as those referenced by Erran Morad, to result in elevated levels of cortisol, Corsitoll and Cardi-B neurotransmitters, so this was Chump's prudent attempt to bring these hormones down to safe and sustainable levels in the interests of maintaining a well-functioning team.

One by one, the team members arrived at Chump's house that morning, and I watched each one enter the house from the comfort of my folding chair at my rudimentary encampment on the sidewalk.

Chump addressed his Russian Amazon Echo: "Some soft music for my arriving guests please, Natasha."

Obligingly, the device started up with some pleasing ambient music, Kenny G I believe. The device's AI engine had learned that Chump's favorite album was Kenny G's Best (KGB), the most common request on his playlist other than Chump's beloved Genghis Khan with their unforgettable ode to the 1980 Olympics.

Out on the street I had managed to catch the attention of my rival journalist and author Mikey Bearr on his way in with some of the staffers, and I had offered him and the team a fresh batch of my traditional scones - topped with fresh whipped cream, blueberries and jam - to take into their special meeting with Chump that morning. Mikey, like some other biographers before him, was generally a little hard of hearing - in fact over the years had needed to remove his hearing aids during several live TV interviews due to them giving him a loud buzzing noise in his left ear, an irritation arising from his inflamed cochlea (as an aside, some of my fellow reporters had in fact taken to referring to Mikey himself as a 'giant inflamed cochlea'). In any case, that morning I had jumped, waved, hollered loudly enough, and showed just enough of my slightly hirsute foreleg, to garner Mikey's interest.

Pleasantly surprised, Bearr wandered over to me and happily accepted my generous gift on a doily-covered plate. Like an unwitting Trojan Horse, he then transported the scones in, across the lawn, and - after being greeted at the door by an early-arriving Bunyon - onto a small coffee table in the mayor's lounge room. Though we in the undercover reporting business rarely give away our methods, I will reveal to you now in this case, my dear readers, that in the true spirit of the skilled investigative reporter, and thanks to the wonders of modern miniaturization, I had implanted one of the scones with a tiny microphone and a blueberry with a tiny video camera in order to capture the goings-on at the meeting. As a result, I immediately had a clear picture on my Blackberry beamed directly from the blueberry in Mayor Chump's lounge room as the attendees arrived. Following State law this was quite legitimate, as audio provided by secret recording requires only the consent of one party, which I was happy to give myself after some spirited negotiation in my Kate Spade compact mirror.

From what I could gather, both from subsequent leaks and from my own direct recordings via the scone-cam, Chump had retired back into the bathroom to complete his "toilette" and to glue on his genuine, ethically-sourced, orangutan-fur headpiece. Meanwhile, the feeling as the team gathered for the meeting was cosy and intimate. Quite a deal of flattery was circulating in the room as the staff arrived, set up the room and waited for Chump to reappear.

Joy Hickey, eight-two, and Slobodan Milersevic, twenty-three, would chair the meeting, and began to arrange chairs in the living room which would act as today's meeting room, while they waited for Mayor Chump to get out of the water closet. My scone captured some remarkably crisp images of them setting up the table as I tested the calibration of its internal video camera.

Next door in Chump's dining room, Hickey and Milersevic, along with all the Kushywanker brigade, started to play with Punkin's home automation gift. They gave the device experimental voice commands, enjoying the discovery of its many features as it sat regally atop its raffia-work base in the middle of the table, which was set with a stunning nylon floral tablecloth from the Washintown two-dollar shop.

Nikita Sleety, ever something of a control freak, was "as curious as Lucifer" and couldn't help fiddling with the Russian Amazon Echo installed in the center of Chump's dining table. She began testing all its buttons and practicing multilingual phrases into it like "Chump, *voulez-vous coucher avec moi, ce soir?*" to which it correctly replied "*Oui, certainement!*". She tried again with "*Könnten Sie bitte das Fenster öffnen?*" meaning "Could you please open the window?". Immediately, an audible "Click" was heard as the machine promptly sent a signal to the window, which duly slid open, owing to the remarkable home automation Chump had installed in the new home, courtesy of Viktor Punkin.

"What does this button do?" she asked, pressing the 'Synk' button and seeing no immediate effect. The others were too keenly hurling questions at the device to even hear her. Over at City Hall, however, Boris, Natasha's sibling Echo, detected the Synk event and went on high alert for further remote signals.

At that point, Chump - together with his personal make-up artist, who had previously worked in the corrective surgery unit for bomb blast victims - emerged from the shower, still in his habitual bathrobe, to be met with a round of applause from his devoted staff. From the street, I could get a clear audio of the events inside, as my scone-cam was transmitting a strong signal, although the video was slightly blurry, owing to the decorative dusting of rice flour I had used atop the scones.

"I would like you to do us a favor though. Just wait for me there, I won't be long. I'll get dressed and be back with you all in a minute, fellas" said the very suave-looking Chump, his wet hair slicked back over his large bald spot, and his moist body glistening in the light like a hairy orca in a bathrobe, where the bathrobe was partly open over his manly, gorilla-like chest. For a moment I was at risk of experiencing another hot flash out at my encampment.

"But before I do that, just watch this" said Chump. "I'll get that thing to turn on the gas fireplace, in Italian. You just watch. You're gonna love it."

His eager aides could not wait to be involved in whatever he had planned. Their excitement was palpable, like a hyperplastic prostate.

Chump seemed to nonchalently sweet-talk the Russian Amazon Echo with his soft tones, saying "Per favore, accendere il fuoco", meaning "Could you please light the fire?". The staff watched and waited, like attendees at a congressional hearing, not stirring, as a gentle whirring was heard inside the device. The gas fireplace remained unchanged.

Unfortunately, at this point, the complexity of the foreign commands, and the lack of inherent understanding, appear to have placed an undue strain on the programming and rather cheap componentry of the Russian-built device, and the requested operation seems to have overwhelmed its puny 32-kilobyte Popov processors. Rather than remotely ignite the gas fireplace via the voice command as expected, the device itself, perhaps thinking it was doing the right thing, suddenly burst into flames in the middle of the meeting table, sending staff members recoiling in shock and scrambling backwards to gain some protection from the flames and sparks which, in a bright flash, sprayed out, like a madman's invective, from its plastic chassis, all over the table.

"Ooh, cripes! Stay calm folks, I've got this," urged the brave Chump, however it was hard to stay calm because the spray of fire and sparks which had burst forth from the home assistance device had immediately ignited Chump's nylon tablecloth. Chump grabbed the nearest implement he could find, a can of fly-spray on his sideboard which he had been using on his underarm gnats, and squirted it at the flames. Unfortunately, this only seemed to aggravate the situation as the flames drew a new vigor from the toxic propellant directed at them like the incitements of a nationalistic narcissist. The staffers coughed and wiped their arms and legs as the fly spray fired by Chump consumed them in a pungent cloud. Meanwhile, the now-melting nylon tablecloth began dripping hot flames onto Chump's faux Persian Ferahan carpet, woven in China from recycled polyurethane milk bottles.

Bunyon picked up a chowder jug and threw its contents onto the burning carpet, but this resulted in nothing but a sizzle of steam as the flames contemptuously consumed the broth with no sign of being quenched in any way, and continued to rage unabated. More disturbingly, after only a minute or two of sizzling and hissing, the high lard content of the chowder then seemed to have further fueled the ferocious flames in the Ferahan, flinging fiery flecks of fat over the floor.

Chump's extended family - including Melony, Dinah, Erika and Bruno - all ran for the doors, looking to save their hides. Several of the staffers looked on gormlessly, mumbling phrases like "Ooh, that doesn't look too good."

Chump looked on at Bunyon.

"You run, boy! Save yourself and whoever else you can! I'm going to stay and fight this, like the legend that I am known to be."

There, dear readers, stood a true hero. Yet nonetheless a flaming Chump.

* * *

Within a matter of seconds, the ceiling had caught on fire and as they all looked on in shock, a large rafter fell through the ceiling plaster, into the room, almost blocking the only exit.

A few of the staffers tried to scramble around the fallen rafter in a rush for the way out. "Get over it!" Mickey Mullvenality called out to his colleagues, for there was no time to lose. The fire was taking hold of the room. Thankfully that quick-thinking advice helped many of them scurry out the door, over the obstacle, without injury.

Pausing at the doorway as he stepped out of the burning house, Bunyon scowled and said "Jeez, it's going to be a wildfire in there!" And indeed, at that moment, another large piece of ceiling plaster collapsed, striking Chump's hand and injuring his index finger, plus his fourth and fifth digits. Bunyon started to depart quickly, seeing the imminent risk of further collapses.

Here, literally, was a threshold moment:

Bunyon, leaving, having served well, but with fire breathing down his neck.

Chump, staying, confronting the Inferno head-on like Dante's Malacoda, unflinching, with nothing but the welfare of others in his heart, nothing but a flammable cotton bathrobe to protect his tender and precious yet endearingly flabby hide. Flammable, and now, sadly, aflame.

Fire, raging, sizzling, crackling, all-consuming.

* * *

If, dear reader, this tale is one day made into a movie, as I strongly suspect it will be, then you can imagine that at this pivotal juncture in our storyline, the camera will pan slowly through the burning room towards the open doorway, in the style of the final shootout scene in the film *Mr and Mrs Smith*, as fiery beams crash down inside the burning house. Bunyon, reaching the doorstep, looks outwards, to blue sky, to freedom, momentarily weighing up loyalty to his great colleague and a BReak for the EXIT against near-certain death if he REMAINs.

Chump, well back in the room, surrounded by flames, almost a fried Chump, yells out (no audio), in slow-motion, for his dear friend to save himself and f*** off, gesturing to the open doorway before him with the only uninjured finger he had available (refer to hand injury just a few paragraphs back). The screen then fills with orange fire before we cut to a close shot of Bunyon's knobbly Right foot taking a step down to safety. Darkening smoke consumes the screen, leaving us with the bone-shuddering knowledge that our dearest Chump is still in mortal danger. A crackling is heard, like a pig's.

Fade to black.

* * *

It certainly looked like Chump was right in the thick of it, and that several of his loyal staff were similarly trapped. In fact, most of his resourceful staff, keen to preserve their own lives, had managed to prise open the rear kitchen window and one by one were scrambling out, along with other fleeing rodents. Elrond Resinstone, stony-faced, stood just outside Chump's house, handing out pamphlets on how to put out a fire, along with some handy survival biscuits.

Further out on the street, there had been endless dithering amongst the bystanders as to what, if anything to do. Finally, it was local paperboy Timmy Freeman who called it out. "This is code red!" he screamed through the streets. He instinctively knew that whatever the smoke was hiding was hurting all of them now. The dull and apathetic townsfolk finally seemed to show a little interest and emerged from the houses into the smoky streets like dozy drones from a smoked beehive.

Local boy Bobby Mauler, who as we have heard was normally engaged in all sorts of mischief and delinquency, was, being the most nimble onlooker, sent into the smoky house to see if he could find the source of the smoke and stench. By now the plume was covering several blocks and threatening to reach most of the city, and the wail of sirens could be heard throughout the municipality.

The Russian workers, sensing strife, had retreated into their dark tunnels and were laying low.

Back at the mini-golf course, Sylvie Clittafford's golf caddie, Michael Adenuffi, heard the sirens and rushed out onto the street to see what was causing the commotion. Seeing a number of emergency services vehicles racing past, he could tell that something serious was afoot and decided to pursue one of the ambulances on foot, in the direction of the mayor's new residence.

As the billowing smoke became thicker, Bobby darted into the obscurity and vanished from sight for what seemed like an interminable, nail-biting period. Time seemed to stand still as a growing crowd of people from the local community, press and emergency services looked on anxiously waiting to see what Bobby could uncover. Thankfully he emerged quite a while later, having first managed to flush out Paula Moneyport and Dicky Fences who had been making out in Chump's rear laundry, apparently close to the source of the fire, if there was in fact fire.

Bobby dragged them out by the ears, their clothes still giving off clouds of smoke, and passed them over to the waiting staff of the district's special counseling office, who led them off wrapped them in standard-issue foil blankets. He then turned on his heels and raced back into the smoke, calling back that he would try to save Roddy Pebble next. The officials promised that they would look after these two victims well.

* * *

By now the scene was indeed dire, not exactly looking peachy-dory. The house was well alight, with brilliant red and orange flames licking their way out of the dense fog of smoke and up into the sky above the rooftop. The radiant heat could be felt by all the bystanders, forcing its way through their clothes to be felt directly by their skin, reminiscent of a raging campfire before it dies down to coals cool enough to cook marshmallows.

The local fire department had sent a single fire truck, now parked up on the lawn at a slight angle which made it look ineffectual and precarious. Its giant tires sank into the mushy grass, sodden by leaking water mains cracked by the Russian team's overzealous jackhammering. When the captain attempted to move the truck, the wheels span, throwing up wet mud and splattering the onlookers with grass and mush, making them look blotchy and foolish. One wheel had squashed the base of a ceremonial tree which the mayor had planted with a visiting French diplomat, leaving the sapling tilted at a sharp angle. The scene was beginning to look utterly chaotic.

Adding to the complexity of the situation, the fire chief noticed that the vehicle had pulled up right alongside the largest of the sinkholes which, in the previous weeks, had opened up on the lawns of City Hall, presumably as a result of the underground flooding caused by the faulty FSB plumbing works which had pervaded the foundations of the building and the water table below it, an important aquifer feeding the town's fresh water supply. Would the fire truck be subsumed by the sinkhole? Would the ground hold out? These were all questions swirling in the minds of the onlookers as the fire truck - ostensibly there to help with this emergency - itself lurched perilously on the brink of near disaster.

At that point the firemen unrolled the large hose and turned on the massive faucets which controlled the water flow to the hose. What emerged was a puny stream of water, more of a dribble than a gush, which failed even to reach the side of the house, and which clearly had absolutely no chance of extinguishing any well-established fire. Unfortunately, Mayor Chump's earlier insistence that FSB rip up the city's old piping - despite detailed scientific tests to the contrary - had hampered the supply of water throughout the city. The decision had limited the amount of water which was available to fill the tanks of the vehicle back at the fire station, due to the pipes being clagged with algae and with the fat turtle who had blocked the flow of life-saving water. As a result, the truck had left the depot with only a meager amount of water, barely enough to wet a pussy cat.

Several bystanders began to wonder whether or not Bobby Mauler would manage to come out alive. Some argued loudly that he should have been sent in with more backup and protection, like one of the new asbestos jackets Chump had bought in bulk for the firefighters. Others insisted that he was a very capable young lad who could certainly not only find his own way out of trouble, but also had the skills to rescue others at the same time. While the house continued to burn, these groups quarreled on the lawn.

Adenuffi arrived on the scene, looking fit in his new Nike trainers, having just chased the ambulance from downtown as it screeched through the streets with lights and sirens blazing. He spent a moment to catch his breath, quickly assessed the situation then followed the same path as Bobby Mauler, running around to the back of the house and disappearing into the thick smoke.

When the firemen were finally able to enter the house, they encountered a scene of complete chaos and devastation. Chump's kitten, which by now had grown into a near full-sized animal the size of a small bobcat, had skittered to the library in a panic, running across the shelves knocking hundreds of books to the floor as fire began taking to the collection.

Snakes which had been housed in Chump's custom-built Animal Rescue Room and which, remarkably for cold-blooded reptilians, had grown very faithful to Chump, were now slithering for cover away from the fire and falling debris.

Johnny Notlob, standing in Chump's hallway as some of the ceiling plaster collapsed and fleeing animals raced past his feet, suddenly let out a squeal, exclaiming "Was it a rat I saw?!"

Sure enough, Chump's rescue rats too had escaped from their cages and had scattered towards the library where they had started maniacally tearing at books and papers with their teeth and claws. They had shredded many of the centuries-old texts, Chump's cherished law volumes and, in a frenzy of gnawing, had destroyed much of the oak shelving. Irreplaceable legal and ethical tomes were rendered mere torn scraps, defiled even further by rat urine and excrement. The great structure of the house itself and the artisan work of its original craftsmen was fiercely ablaze, severely damaged not only by fire by the scratching and gnawing rodents who had shown little concern for the fine carvings and marquetry which adorned the historic home.

Chump's once-pristine house now looked like a very dangerous and filthy place. The great library itself was now little more than a disgusting, rat- and rodent-infested mess. As for the rest of the abode, no human being would want to live there. Live electrical wires dangled through the collapsing ceiling. Smoke filled the corridors and a stench of rodent excrement mingled with an acrid smoke and the odor of burning plastic. With eerie echoes of the Vikings' nightmare at Hellsinky in 853 AD, parts of Chump's house were even breaking off, rolling down the embankment, bounding over a fence and ending up in his swampy lake. This was an equally historic event, at least in terms of Menda City.

As the rescue animals scampered hither and thither in desperate acts to save their own hides, through corridors now filling with an obscuring smoke, Notlob called out a timely warning to Chump's fleeing staffers: "Step on no pets!" Rats were so desperate to get out of the building that they had started fighting amongst themselves, attacking each other openly and issuing frightening, tormented squeaks.

In the music and tuition room, a huge timber support beam had fallen through the ceiling and completely crushed the grand piano, leaving little more than a heap of splintered wood and twanging piano wires in the middle of the floor. A discordant clang resonated eerily throughout the flame-engulfed residence, as one might expect in the score of a horror movie.

The kitchen, which had been the inspiration for the Chump Chowder Happy Hamper deliveries to thousands of folk all over the city, bringing Joy to each doorstep, was now belching thick black smoke, and broken containers of Chump Chowder oozed green, gooey, fetid liquid all over the floor.

Around the back of the house, Michael Adenuffi had been heroically attacking the rear laundry door with a garden hoe, seeking to break through for around 60 minutes. Part of him knew that Sylvie was still trapped there in the building.

As the fire took hold, Billy Barrb from Barrb's Barbed Wire Emporium on the seedy outskirts of Menda City, suddenly appeared in his beaten-up pickup truck, the rear tray loaded with rolls of barbed wire reclaimed from his recent salvaging trip in Eastern Germany. He swerved the vehicle around the City Hall sinkhole, then turned the corner and screeched to a halt outside. Poking his head out of the cabin while chewing on a stick of straw, he came to the determination that City Hall was not the main fire source, so he screeched off again around the corner to Chump's private residence.

Jumping out of the cab of his truck and glancing at his large load of industrial-scale barbed wire coils in the open rear of the vehicle, Barrb had the great idea to protect the emergency workers by creating a barrier around Chump's house with an improvised barbed wire fence. He would leave a gap just small enough to allow anyone trapped in the house to get out through the protective barbed-wire screen, but police and ambulance workers would not be tempted to get too close to the house. He was doing them a massive favor.

"Stand back, everyone! I've got this!" Barrb yelled as he unrolled a large reel of barbed wire all the way around Chump's house from the back of his pickup truck emblazoned with a peeling "Barrb's Emporium" decal featuring raised gold lettering. In typical tradesman style, his buttcrack was in vivid view all the while.

Just when it appeared that things could not get any worse, a call came through on the fire chief's walkie-talkie. A second fire had broken out, this time at City Hall, where in an incident of apparently unrelated origin, the cabling of the newly-installed wiring for the S.H. IT Project had only recently been covered up in the wall cavities and ceiling space at City Hall.

Yet as you will see, exclusively through your dear Martha's detailed reporting, this second fire was not at all unrelated.

For due to its 'Synk' setting having been activated, the Echo at City Hall had blown up in sympathy with the one at Chump's home, spraying fragments of burning plastic all over the council's conference table, ultimately setting fire to the great public edifice.

I will teleport you, dear reader, back to that exact moment.

* * *

Over at City Hall, as Chump's team played with his new toy back at his residence, the main council chamber was empty, and all that could be heard was the gentle chirping of sparrows outside. Most of the council staff had headed over to Chump's house for the team meeting. In the middle of the large oak conference table, alongside stacks of fresh legislative documents ready for signing into law, Boris, the second of the two Russian Amazon Echos, sat intently listening out for commands.

Unfortunately, the device's hearing was not the only way for it to receive Audible commands. For as I mentioned earlier, Nikita Sleety, in pressing the "Synk" button, had unwittingly yet inextricably, linked the actions of this device, dear Boris, to that of its counterpart which sat on the dining table at Ronnie Chump's private residence, being fingered by Ronnie's staffers.

And when the Echo on Chump's dining table - known lovingly to him as the ever-helpful Natasha - had been pushed past her tolerance limits and had self-immolated on his table, her final act was to send a matching set of signals to her twin Echo back at City Hall, obedient Boris. As a result, the quiet of the empty meeting-room was about to be shattered, like the peace of the English countryside before the arrival of a rambling, disheveled nut-job lugging a broken picnic-table.

Sparrows fluttered away in haste as a sudden, loud pop and crackle resonated out across the wide oak table, as the second Echo, Boris, exploded in the conference room.

* * *

Now this new, secondary fire based at City Hall, having made short work of the conference room including all its policy papers and furnishings, torched a path all the way along the synthetic carpet and down the main hall. The fire had waited for the lift as Muzak played, then traveled down to the next level on the lift's carpet, emerging and continuing along the hall in the carpeted basement.

Deep inside the once-majestic edifice of City Hall, a fearsome situation was developing. The fire had tracked its way along the basement hall until reaching the underground storage rooms. It was here, in the store room next door to the Asylum Seeker Gymnasium, that Dick Pickles, through his exclusive contract with Menda City Council, had stored the large drums of waste oil from Mickey Crohney's auto repair shop. The flames passed without impediment under the store-room door, then moved on the oil-drums like a bitch. They licked hungrily at the sides of the drums, as though taunting them to release their explosive contents prematurely, just as committees sometimes do with matters under active investigation.

As you can imagine, not many minutes later, a series of loud explosions suddenly rocked City Hall as the drums exploded one by one, like a string of firecrackers. Very big firecrackers. In fact, as each oil-drum exploded, the entire building shook with the force of the explosion, and plaster dust rained down even on the upper floors. A developing slick of unburned oil, feeding like a wick into a core of burning oil, made for a formidable energy source to fuel the massive inferno which would rage throughout the night.

As the fire took hold of City Hall, back at Chump's house, things were not going much better. Ronnie and Judy Ruelyini had been forced into the upstairs rooms. The intense heat downstairs had made them seek refuge in the upstairs wing containing Chump's law library, bedrooms and private studies. Disoriented, Judy Ruelyini lost the plot. She went into a mad panic, screaming and shrieking wildly as she ran from room to room, tipping over chairs and rifling through drawers looking for something - anything - which could be useful in this emergency. At one point her skirt caught on fire, a situation which would have almost certainly resulted in nasty burns were it not for the quick thinking of a fellow staffer sheltering in the upstairs bathroom who threw a glass of water on her (including Chump's spare dentures).

Judy found a loaded handgun in the top drawer of a bureau then continued running along corridors and into the upstairs bedrooms with no apparent direction, frantically waving the weapon in the air before finally sticking her head out an open first-floor window and screaming out incoherent gibberish in an attempt to attract any nearby media or emergency services. Flapping her arms wildly, she accidentally discharged the weapon into her own foot, with the bullet then ricocheting off the hardwood floor and grazing Ronnie Chump in the rump as he sought a hasty exit himself. Like the hero in a war movie, Ronnie initially didn't even notice that he'd been hit, so focused he was on helping others reach safety.

The fire's intensity was starting to heat the upper floor. Ronnie was getting desperate. He called out, wishing there was someone, anyone, even a U-Crane vehicle, which could winch him out of his house. He could see their trucks, way off in the distance, apparently still shifting property towards their depot. He called out to U-Crane, more than once, like a trapped man would do. No-one answered. Penny Social watched on from just a short way down the road, from the lawns of City Hall. Creepily.

"Judy, you've got a shrill voice. Quick, call out to them!" Ronnie implored. Judy happened to be great friends with two of the U-Crane drivers, whose tiny heads could be seen bobbing in the cabins of their trucks way off in the distance. But tragically, the trauma of the event appeared to have driven Judy into a kind of psychosis, for she could do little more than squawk incoherently and flap her elbows like a singed, maniacal pheasant on crack. In any case, it would turn out later that Judy's U-Crane truck-driving friends were themselves trying to escape the burning city, and at that time were heading out of town, having sought to flee the conflagration via Dullass airport.

* * *

The day care center at City Hall had been evacuated at the early signs of smoke, and the infants had been led out onto the grass where the staff conducted a headcount of the littlies. Luckily, only a few hundred of the children had been lost in the pandemonium, and staff were confident any misplaced infants would turn up, as Barbara Streisand so eloquently put it, "Somewhere". Anyway, there were still many to look after and keeping them entertained was proving to be a nightmare.

A loud "whoompf" noise was heard - not unlike the one heard in happier times during the staff photo - only this time onlookers to the disaster saw lights go out across the city. Only a moment later, the emergency services control center received a call from an onsite technician indicating that the main transformer at City Hall, recently fitted by the Fix-It Services Business down in the central cupboard, and which had been powering the firefighters' generator, had obviously succumbed to the exploding oil-drums, suffering a core meltdown which had frizzled the power supply network for the entire city of Washintown. The resulting shower of electrical sparks and hot oil were now creating a fearsome synergy.

Down in the Chumpy Care Day Care Center, which thankfully had been quickly emptied of children when the initial smoke reports came in, the fire had run along the freshly-painted skirting boards. Like an unwelcome orange visitor intent on ruining your life, it had entered the linen cupboards which of course were stacked to the ceiling with fresh cotton diapers and disposable liners.

As soon as the hungry licking flames came into contact with the cotton diapers and their fragrant eucalyptus oil infusion, the entire cupboard went up with a sudden "whoosh". The volatile mix of aromatic oils created a fireball which acted like the focus of an even greater inferno, a terrifying heat source powered by what was then, in essence (of eucalyptus), a storehouse of cotton and synthetic fuel.

In the children's play rooms themselves, the walls were quite literally on fire as the new paint frizzled and bubbled from the radiant heat even before igniting into flames with a pop. The weasel, rabbit and dinosaur decals which had once so pleased the mayor's youthful nature were now reduced to dripping shapes of burning hot plastic, creating ghoulish and horrifying new creatures on the blackening wall which would be the stuff of nightmares and terror for any child, almost as terrifying as being separated from one's parent.

It was tragic to watch. The tortoise went first. Then the rabbit. Pop went the weasel.

The burning plastic which dribbled from the melting decals onto the floor in flaming drips then set the entire synthetic carpet alight. This in turn spread along to the plastic slides, toys and children's furniture, each forming its own petrochemical bonfire. Before long the playrooms were transmogrified into an impenetrable and unsalvageable inferno of pure bright hot orange - reminiscent of a very bad hair day on a balding, demented geriatric - sucking oxygen through their windows cracked by the intense heat, which no firefighter could safely enter without being torched to a crisp.

It was only a matter of time before the ceiling above the playroom caved in completely, bringing the entire policy strategy room above, and all its furnishings, crashing down into this apocalyptic scene and providing fresh fuel in the form of thousands of policy document folders tumbling from shelves. Each of these was filled with years of council records, planning and legislative documents on thin policy paper. Smashed-up furniture then fell in layers on top of this, better than any scout would lay out kindling. In this case, however, rather than creating a cozy campfire, the result was the annihilation of the city's great historical records, its priceless legislative history and part of the city's own identity. All the incredible work of the Chump administration was set to fry. And fry it did. From the outside, the flames could be seen rising bigly from the roof space into the sky above. The building was certainly no longer in tippy-top shape.

Punkin's wiring, lacking surge protection, was sending sizzling sparks along the ceiling, showering the floor with hot embers and dripping plastic, igniting further spot-fires among the torn book pages.

Over in Stevie Bunyon's Star Wars-themed "space war" room, his plastic Death Star, Darth Vader and Super Star Destroyer models were similarly reduced to mere blobs of molten liquid dripping from the mantelpiece. Joy Hickey's pin-up pictures of younger men were peeling off the walls, one by one aflame, now rendered into genuine "hotties". Their faces seemed to wrinkle with disgust before being consumed by flames and being rendered into nothing more than floating ash and smoke.

Firefighters attempted to enter City Hall but found that the clutter of desks and stacked files in the hallways, due to the excessive staff hirings and high staff retention rate, prevented them from gaining easy access. In addition, several of the desks were surrounded by highly flammable documents which had erupted into new spot-fires, rendering the hallways dark and smoke-filled. Unfortunately these had included police reports of Bobby Mauler's delinquency, due to be passed on to higher authorities, and the lad's recent disturbing psychological reports.

For a few moments, Mayor Chump, nursing another bullet-grazed rump which had evoked a flood of traumatic war memories, was seen poking his head out another window, his hands white-knuckled to the safety rail. He was calling out urgently "You must tree clear to stop fire spreading!" and pointing frantically to the forest reserve, adding "... and quickly! Rake that forest!". Sadly, this critical information came too late, as the firemen were all fully engaged dealing with the building, with no resources left for clearing any surrounding trees, whose fronds were already starting to smolder from the enveloping heat.

In the mad panic he had grabbed a whistle from the second drawer of the bureau and began madly blowing into it to further raise the alarm, not realizing that it was one of his own leftover dog whistles from the election campaign, and was therefore out of the audible range of the human ear.

He then wasn't seen for several hours, with just a chilling, cryptic Tweet being received from the smoky building by way of the mayor's dwindling mobile phone as thick clouds of smoke and ash overtook the entire area: "My battery is low and it's getting dark." As more of the roof caved in and an ungodly, moaning wind was heard, like the sound of a terrible Martian dust storm, it seemed that Chump's Opportunity to escape the building must have passed.

The infants from the day care center were huddled on the lawn and watched in confusion as their play room and the adjacent city library sent brilliant flames high into the sky like the Kilauea volcano the orange glow flickering on their little faces as their cherished play spaces were reduced to ashes. Thankfully they were too young to understand the implications, but there, right in front of them, the future common wealth of the next generation was being reduced to cinders. Some of Chump's favorite toys from his visits to the center were now spewing hideous volcanoes of molten plastic into the roof space, providing further fuel for the ravaging fire.

From the lawn, the onlookers, adults and children, could clearly see a trail of embers sporadically sailing through the air and peppering the neighboring forest. While most of the adults were preoccupied with what was unfolding to the house before them, one of the children on the lawn stuck out a finger, pointing in the opposite direction, and called out to her carer "Look Miss Connie, there's a campfire too!" Sure enough, a new source of smoke was rising from the trees in the forest reserve adjacent to the house, only this time the smoke was not succeeding in shrouding the flames of a new fire which could clearly be seen building up among the undergrowth and occasionally bursting out through the smoke. Within minutes a full-fledged forest fire was alight, sweeping in a direction away from the city, and flushing out birds and other wildlife from their previous safety.

Someone attempted to put an emergency call through to the Chief Park Ranger and Environment Officer, Scotty Proveit, who had a tremendous conviction when it came to nature. He cherished every little bird, every rodent, every dung beetle which crawled on God's Earth. (In fact, Scotty's conviction was so enduring that it might take years for the conviction to wear off, in a special facility designed for working off convictions). Unfortunately, Scotty had flown out of town that day to a conference for an "all you can eat" banquet, and hadn't been able to take the call. The forest, meanwhile, continued to blaze away, and little birdies fell from the sky, cooked like chicken nuggets. Poor Scotty would have been horrified, had he only known!

To make matters worse, Scotty's private jet to the conference had accidentally sucked into its engines the last (previously) surviving individuals of a critically endangered duck species, the Northern shoveler, as it took off. Scotty, and the birds, were certainly having a bad day.

At City Hall, a member of the public had attempted to enter, via the front portico, what had once been the people's building, proudly hand-built by the early settlers. When she took hold of the main entry door, it promptly fell from its hinges with a loud clatter. A fireman ran up behind her and said "Sorry lady, this building's no longer safe. You can't go in there. It's a goddam mess."

Throughout the long dark night, chaos reigned, and fiery embers rained down across the City of Greater Washintown, which was in fact becoming Lesser Washintown by the minute as scattered fires then erupted in new districts and kept burning until the early morning. Occasional explosions could be heard as a car, petrol bowser or fireworks depository blew up in the Great Inferno. Dante and Virgil themselves would have felt quite at home in Washintown that night, having seen all this before, albeit with a traitorous, satanic demon in charge of the Hell they inhabited, rather than just a regular Chump.

Coincidentally, a young boy, about fifteen, sat at the edge of the grass outside City Hall - that same lawn where Kylie-Jo Connard had once Hatched some of the Chump administration's greatest ideas - wistfully singing an eerie rendition of *American Pie,* with the chilling lyric:

The day that Washintown fried.

He went on softly listing how the children screamed and how the poets dreamed, how lovers cried, how words were not spoken, and how the church-bells were all broken.

Indeed, the centuries-old bells at the Washintown Cathedral and other churches throughout the city had cracked under the intense, hateful heat of the Chump-induced inferno, which had set each church steeple ablaze during the course of that fearsome evening, and made Notre Dame look like a Scout's picnic fire. It seemed nothing of any sacred value could withstand the ruination wrought by the conflagration Chump had ignited.

* * *

Hours later, one of the little boys pointed to a figure running away from the ashes, stark naked, having found the small gap in Billy Barrb's helpful protective fence. "Look, the mayor has no clothes!" he called.

Sure enough, there, running off into the charred forest, was a naked Ronnie Chump, obviously delirious from shock. Having found a way out of the building, and having dropped his flaming bathrobe as it became ensnared in the barbed wire perimeter fence, Chump had finally fled the city he had incinerated, with his burnt, red-raw, bullet-grazed buttocks wobbling furiously as he ran to seek a mud-puddle in which to wallow for pain relief.

In my follow-up book entitled "**SINGE - Chump on Fire**" I plan to document these historical events in even more vivid detail.

A special padded vehicle from Washintown Psychiatric Services was dispatched to retrieve the mayor from the torched forest before he came to further harm.

* * *

When, after that interminable night, with every single asset of the Washintown Fire Department having been called into action, the fire had finally been extinguished and nothing but steam and dull smoke rose droopily over the ruined buildings, the townsfolk stood, huddled, in stunned silence. As dawn broke, the fire chief, looking at the ruins of City Hall, mumbled "This is extremely dangerous to our democracy".

Chump's house was no longer the brilliant white it had once been. The clapboards which had not been fully incinerated were severely blackened and smoke-damaged. I stood there, a solitary figure, still reporting, outside Chump's blackened house.

* * *

Washintown Psychiatric and General Hospital, known locally as "The Asylum" or just "The Can", had never been so busy. A fleet of wailing sirens had brought load after load of Chump's colleagues and staffers in from the cold, most sporting nasty burns and a few with squealing croup-like coughs due to having inhaled the thick, acrid, pollution-ridden smoke belching both from City Hall and from Chump's incinerated personal residence. Since the General wards were full thanks to Chump's wonderful Universal Health Care initiatives and the earlier bubonic plague outbreak, the victims had all been promptly ferried instead directly to the high-security Psychiatric unit.

There was Flout. There was Dicky Fences. There was Moneyport. There was Ganadobonus. There was Mickey Crohney. And of course, there was Chump, in the biggest bed of all (his, unfortunately soaked in urine due to his temporary loss of bladder control coinciding with an inattentive nurse being on duty). All were in plaster casts, some in traction, some unable to move due to their bandages, tubing, oxygen masks and restraints. For his own safety as much as for the safety of others, Chump, due to the shock he had experienced, had even been fitted with a straightjacket. Alvin McWeaselberger, who had miraculously escaped injury, was standing by his colleagues as a welcome hospital visitor, albeit one sporting a severely charred coat.

A couple of police officers stood on guard over the ward, near the door, to prevent any further injuries to these poor deplorably-injured council officebearers, and to prevent the patients leaving in their disoriented mental states. These guards had been advised not to let the patients leave the room, even if someone came to get them. That is, until someone came to get them, they were not to enter the room. They didn't need to do anything at all, except stop them leaving the room.

The scene was exactly like the hospital scene in the movie "It's a Mad, Mad, Mad, Mad World (1963)", minus the lady slipping on the banana. A somber air hung over the room, with occasional moans and groans as the patients, all bandaged in white, and looking quite the worse for wear, realized the extent of their physical and reputational injuries, and in particular, how badly they had been burned. The slightest movement caused many of them intense pain, and they seemed destined to be spending many long months trying to rehabilitate their sorry selves.

* * *

As the new day dawned and a thin plume of smoke dwindled skywards from the charred remains of City Hall (not to mention from the mayor's residence, the City Library, the Chump "Happy Tots" Day Care Center, the State Forest Reserve and the hundreds of other institutions and private residences torched by the prior day's inferno), the city elders gathered at a baseball park, one of the few parts of the city relatively untouched by damage.

A small ceremony was held, in which representatives of the city stood in silence with hands on their hearts to recognize the tremendous destruction and loss of amenity which had been caused by what, in time, I expect will come to be known as the Great Fire of Washintown, the Great Fire of MendaCity, or more colloquially, simply by the terrifying moniker: **Chumpferno**.

At this quiet gathering, they resolved to erect a plaque to remind future generations of this calamitous event, inscribed as follows:

"The   people   of   Washintown   SUFFERED CONSEQUENCES   THE   LIKES   OF   WHICH   FEW THROUGHOUT   HISTORY   HAVE   EVER   SUFFERED BEFORE."

The depth of the tragedy resonated with the entire community. No family was untouched. Even pets whimpered, and plants drooped. The moments of silence announced for the entire city's inhabitants allowed a full presence of all in the deep grief which overtook the community. Yet acknowledging this grief allowed the only path to a better future. Only in this way could the community then move forward to be able, one day, to issue a collective heartfelt chuckle when, at a future time, a figurative lady might slip on a figurative banana.

In that moment too, they were obliged to acknowledge their own role in having allowed this tragedy to unfold, through their own negligence, self-focus and blasé disregard for basic fire safety standards.

Mayor Chump, owing to his significant burns, had to retire from politics and - at the time of writing - looks likely to be spending many months in hospital, along with his great friends Mickey Flout, Paula Moneyport and his numerous colleagues caught up in the blaze. Thankfully his loyal and dear friends Dr Jeb Goney and Hildegard Glintin almost immediately began regular visits to his bedside, never leaving Ronnie unattended for long. Jeb announced that he would stick with Ronnie "forever and a day". Hildegard brought such beautiful wreaths of flowers for Ronnie that she hadn't even noticed that the blooms accidentally harbored numerous small but relatively vicious African bees. Jeb and Hildegard promised to visit Ronnie every day.

The city itself appears to have a long road to recovery, as so many of its once-fine institutions have been seriously damaged, if not entirely obliterated, including: the Washintown Sentinel newspaper (fried), the Court House (burned down), the City Library (incinerated), Washintown Psychiatric Hospital (roof shingles ignited, water damage to upper floors), the Chumpy Tots Day Care facility (frizzled, then melted to oblivion), City Hall chambers (charred), Washintown Grain & Meat Wholesalers (baked and barbecued) and of course Mayor Chump's new white house (blackened).

* * *

As the town elders stood in grim and somber silence, a young, free-spirited Hispanic girl, Alexandria, began playing catch with a baseball, tossing it up in the air, whirling around and laughing with delight each time she caught it, even on the times when she failed to catch it. Despite the devastation surrounding her, it seemed that she was fully present in the moment, totally centered in herself and at one with the graceful movements of the ball; as she twirled and weaved to catch, her play looked almost like a dance, uninhibited, free and full of grace. Her moves were so replete with unbounded joy that to watch her was utterly mesmerizing.

Nothing could dampen this girl's spirits. One by one her young peers joined in, until soon an impromptu baseball game had started up, and the sounds of youthful laughter and merriment washed over the groans and gloomy mumbles of the Washintown elders, keen to put the memories of the Menda City experiment behind them. One of the elder citizens of the community, Penny Social, encouraged Alexandria to gather some more of her friends together and to initiate a healthy, spirit-restoring game.

They still had each other, they still had their baseball ground, they still had their lives, their dignity, their values, their families and their loved ones. They still had their beautiful pets, and they still had hope and joy in their hearts.

These were young ones whom the older ones had let down, yet there was no sign of malice on their smiling faces, no resentment or any grudge being nurtured.

The elders stood and watched, enchanted, suddenly oblivious to the scene of utter destruction all around them, to the smoke, to the cinders still falling, to the burned-out infrastructure and to the ruined plastic signs touting the wonders of Menda City. They were transfixed by the present moment, by the aliveness and joy of the young people before them, and by the unquestionable, utterly certain hopefulness which was in full, living expression in front of their eyes.

Washintown will rebuild.

Washintown has a bright future.

* * *

THE END

Please consider penning your own review for *Dire and Puny.*
Much love, Martha

FINALE

Come senators and congressmen
Please heed the call

Don't stand in the doorway
Don't block up the hall

For he that does something bad,
Is he that is gone

There's a battle outside and its ragin'
It'll soon shake your windows and rattle the walls
For the times, they have to be a-changin'!

**- Michael Moore, Popcorn with Peter Travers
from 21m10s**

ACKNOWLEDGEMENTS

I am grateful to my family for tolerating my long hours of absence out on the streets of Washintown, then ensconced at my typewriter, to produce this Watergate-style exposé.

I owe much to my talented editor and devoted sister, Beth Skewermann, who has toiled selflessly to further enhance the already-high quality of my reportage.

Particular mention must also go to my devoted sister Thérèse Veronica (T.V.) Skewermann, who has unwaveringly supported my writing pursuits since childhood, even as my editors at the Washintown Sentinel gave me very little attention throughout my career in investigative journalism, relegating me to the back pages of the Sentinel and requiring me to ghost-write the Agony Aunt column under the embarrassing moniker "Molly Flowers".

I would also like to thank the dedicated family of Twitter #resist-ers and #GlobalResistance who have supported me through the writing of this book, and the public figures who maintained my spirits along the way. These include Glenn Kirschner, Rachel Maddow, Lawrence O'Donnell, Eric Idle, Stephen Colbert, Alyssa Milano, Seth Abramson, Bill Maher, Sarah Kendzior and many more. I am deeply grateful for the inspiring examples set by Rep. Katie Porter, Rep. Alexandria Ocasio-Cortez, and the late, great Senator Elijah Cummings.

To my children, I extend special gratitude for tolerating a professional working mother and trailblazing investigative journalist such as Martha Skewermann, whose undercover reporting activities border on those of the most intrepid secret agent.

Made in the USA
San Bernardino, CA
26 November 2019

ABOUT THE AUTHOR

MARTHA SKEWERMANN is a seasoned investigative journalist who has worked in relative obscurity until now.

Though a long-standing staff member at the Washintown Sentinel, she has never been a regular columnist for any magazines, nor has she appeared regularly in print before, largely due to the difficulties she experienced growing up as a fictional author.

She has received absolutely no awards for anything in her life, and seeks only the reward of truthfully chronicling these history-making events in the life of our city.

Dire and Puny - Outside Chump's Blackened House is Martha's ***opus primum*** as an independent fictional author, cementing Martha's reputation as the world's leading exponent of allegorical journalism.

We hope that Martha continues to pound her virtual keyboard for many years to come.

Martha lives in a constant state of curiosity and bewilderment.

She resides in rural Washintown East with her 2 cats and komodo dragon, Bruce. She has fed Bruce many draft pages of her book, which seems to have kept him happy.

Sadly her husband Bob passed away 2 years ago (not totally Bruce's fault). She has four children who love her to pieces but who wish she would take a long overseas vacation.

Martha will be happy to discuss screenplay rights to "***Dire and Puny***" with interested producers. Move over, *Fawlty Towers*!

* * *

You can visit Martha's website at:

www.marthaskewermann.com

or follow Martha on Twitter at:

https://twitter.com/skewermann

Martha's and Mayor Chump's favorite recipes can be found at:

www.marthaskewermann.com/recipes

Martha on Goodreads:

https://www.goodreads.com/user/show/83413269-martha-skewermann

Martha on Medium:

https://medium.com/@martha.skewermann

♥